ABYSS

Katherine Armstrong Walters

Book Three of the Arydian Chronicles

SCENE CO.™

ISBN 978-1-951411-06-0

www.thesceneco.com

To my family,

the heart and soul of everything I do.

PROLOGUE

THE PRESIDENT OF the United States sat at his desk in the oval office, sketching. He had been an art student at one time, before his father convinced him to give it up to study law. He had a name back then. Not Mr. President, just John Reed Thompson; an ordinary name for an ordinary person. That was a lifetime ago, but he could remember it so clearly. Much more clearly than the events of the past few weeks.

"What is he drawing now?" a man's irritated voice asked.

"Water or something," a woman's voice replied. The President tried to ignore them. It was difficult. He felt compelled to obey anything they said. He clenched his teeth and continued to sketch feverishly, as if it were the most important thing he could do. If he could just get it on paper, maybe he could make sense of everything happening to him. A picture took shape under his pencil; an ocean with the sun sparkling across its surface with a beach in the distance. A stout woman leaned over his drawing, her long, greying hair briefly obscuring his view.

"Looks like Hawaii," she said.

"Well, that makes sense, given what's just happened there," the man said, rising and moving over to the desk. He wore a neatly pressed white lab coat over his suit and kept a stethoscope around his neck like a name tag reminding everyone he was the personal physician of the President.

"Why did he have to start doing this now?" she complained.

The man folded his arms. "His dose is wearing off. He gets more anxious the closer he gets to his new dose." He watched the President for a few seconds, his breath making the corner of the paper flutter. "He really is pretty good. I wonder if this is some form of resistance he's trying to employ. Interesting, when you think about it. Too bad Hahn isn't with us anymore. I would have liked to hear his thoughts on this. He's the expert on this drug, after all."

The woman grunted in disinterest. "Can't you give him his next dose, then?"

The doctor shook his head. "No, not for another few minutes. Five minutes before he has to talk."

"He'd better be finished drawing this before the press gets here. I don't want him falling apart like he did last time you took away his picture before he was done." The woman leaned against the desk, cursing to herself. "We don't have time for this!"

The President continued to work. Below the watery horizon, a face appeared. He sketched feverishly now, wrestling with his mind even though it hurt him, made him want to forget, but he kept pushing himself, letting his pencil do the remembering for him. It was less painful that way. Maybe someone could see. Maybe they could help him.

The face was a girl, long hair flowing behind her, mouth open as if catching a breath of water, coming up from the depths of the sea. He kept his eyes on his pencil as he drew fish and bubbles around her. It reminded him of something, but he couldn't quite remember. His pencil moved to the beach where he drew a soldier, staring out at the waves. It looked like someone he knew. He sketched a hat on the man's head. Flat, military style. The sound of his pencil made a soothing scratching sound as he shaded around the man's eyes and chin. He looked a little like his friend. What was his name? Randall? Robert? No, Bob! Yes, it looked like General Bob Holt. He had seen him recently, hadn't he? And there was something about the island. It made him sad to see it somehow. He drew a palm tree and filled it in with black. It was dead. The island was dead. There! That was something important he could almost remember.

He tapped his bottom lip with the pencil forcing himself even further. Holt had been here, not long ago. Yes! He was talking… about… a girl! A girl from the sea! He smiled in triumph and gazed over his picture happily. It had worked! But slowly a frown returned to his face. There was something else he was supposed to remember. It was very important. He closed his eyes and let his pencil work by itself, half thinking about other things. He found if he didn't quite think of things directly, he could sometimes grasp hold of them, like catching a glimpse of a ghost by watching carefully out of the corner of his eye. He wished his chief of staff and his doctor weren't here. They always made it harder to think.

"He drew a girl! Do you think he knows about that underwater girl Zar was talking about?" the doctor asked in surprise. The President saw her shrug but tried to ignore her.

"It doesn't matter what he knows, as long as he keeps doing what he's told," the woman snapped, looking at her watch. "You'd better give him his dose now. They'll be here in just a few minutes."

The doctor reached into his lab coat pocket, pulled out a vial of medicine and loaded it into a syringe. The President's breathing increased. He was running out of time. His hand grew cramped as his pencil dug into the paper. He was pushing so hard the lead threatened to break.

"I thought you were giving him pills," the woman said in a worried tone. "We only have a couple injections left, and if Zar doesn't get Hahn back soon, even the pills will run out." Some part of the President's mind gave him a jolt of hope, but it was hard to understand why.

"Injection works faster," the doctor said. "It's getting difficult to make him take the pills, and I don't need him making a fuss in here. Besides, Zar has a lock on Hahn's location. He has to surface eventually, and Zar will ensure he makes more for us. Our assignment here is too important."

The woman rolled her eyes. "He's on a nuclear submarine, Sergio. They can stay underwater for months! We don't have enough to last until the end of next week."

The President tried to listen to them with part of his mind, while still letting his penciled hand roam free over the paper. He had to hurry, write words instead—the pictures were taking too long!

The doctor made an impatient sound directed at the woman and moved over behind the desk. He took the President's unused arm, rolled up the sleeve, rubbed an icy alcohol wipe on him, then jabbed him with the needle. The President didn't flinch. Time was up, but he didn't stop drawing and writing. He let whatever he was searching for bleed out onto the paper on its own volition as he closed his eyes, walling off his mind to everything going on around him. After several feverish minutes, the pencil stopped moving and he opened his eyes.

The President absently rubbed his arm where the needle had punctured him.

"I don't feel good, Sergio," he whispered.

The doctor threw away the syringe and sat down on the President's desk. "Don't be silly. You are fine, John," he said softly, hypnotically. "Don't you feel fine?"

The President looked up, slightly confused. "No. I feel…" he looked into the doctor's eyes. This man was his friend, wasn't he? The eyes were cold as steel. Something beat against the President's mind, but now he couldn't make it stick. He shook his head, trying to clear it, but as the drug took effect, the memory slipped out of his grasp. Finally, he dropped his eyes. "I…guess. I guess I do feel fine."

"Of course!" the doctor smiled. "You've had another one of your episodes, Mr. President. But you've taken your medicine and you're doing much better now, aren't you, Mr. President?" The President nodded and rubbed his temples with his index fingers.

"Yes, I'm feeling much better now. Thank you, doc."

"Let's go over your announcement. It will help you concentrate."

"Yes, yes of course. That will help." He stood up obediently.

The doctor glanced at the Chief of Staff. "Judy, get him looking presentable, will you?" She nodded as she rolled his sleeve back down and bustled him into his suit coat. The President reached out his hand and took a sheet of paper the doctor was handing to him. He cleared his throat.

"My fellow Americans, it is with deep concern for the safety and security of the people of this country that I make the following announcement. The turmoil and tragedy of the California earthquake has disrupted the lives of millions. And now it's with a heavy heart that I announce that once again our country has come under attack."

The President creased his brow and paused. "Attack?"

The doctor sighed impatiently. "Yes, attack. You know about this. Hawaii. Please continue reading, Mr. President, and this time without any pauses. The media will be here any minute to hear your statement and we don't have time to go over it again. You must show the country you are in control of your faculties, sir. Now, *read the paper!*"

The President blushed and looked back down at the paper. "Yes, yes, of course. I apologize. It won't happen again." He cleared his voice once again. "For the second time in U.S. history, our beautiful island state of Hawaii has been the target of a large-scale attack. A chemical or biological toxin of unknown origin was released yesterday, killing every living thing on the island of Lanai." The President frowned and glanced down at the dark palm tree on his paper, concern briefly flashing across his face, but he shook it off and continued reading before the doctor could say anything.

"This, in addition to the recent disaster off the California coast, has left my administration to believe the country is indeed under attack by terrorist forces. There are those who have reached out hands of compassion, helping strangers during this time of crisis, and to those people I say thank you. However, there are those who seek to take advantage of the confusion and chaos; looting, robbing, injuring and even sometimes killing those who are most in need of our help."

He adjusted his paper and cleared his throat. "It is for this reason that, effective immediately, I am declaring a state of Martial Law until this crisis has been averted. Local law enforcement will report directly to military officers that will be stationed throughout the nation to help keep the peace from within and protect our country from without. A nationwide curfew of ten p.m. will be strictly enforced effective immediately. I have the utmost confidence that the people of our great country will heal from these devastating wounds, and I promise you that I will work tirelessly to learn who is behind these abhorrent, malicious attacks and bring them to justice. Thank you for your cooperation, and may God bless the people of this great country."

The doctor let out a long, satisfied sigh. "Good. Very good. Do it just like that and we'll be fine. You'll be fine. I'm sure once this is over, you will feel much better."

"How am I supposed to remember all this, Sergio?" The President asked, looking over a long list of items he was supposed to address in the upcoming press conference.

"Don't worry; we have it all under control. Judy is fitting you with a tiny speaker that fits into your ear. All you have to do is pause a moment after each question and I'll provide the answer."

"You?" the President asked in surprise. "Shouldn't I answer the questions myself?"

The doctor glanced at Judy, who twisted the object into his right ear and then stuffed the wires down the neck of the President's collar. She shrugged. "He's just going to remind you of what we talked about earlier, aren't you, Sergio?"

The doctor smiled in agreement. "Yes, of course. These are your answers, not mine. I'll just be reminding you what to say."

"Ah, yes. That makes sense. Thank you."

The President nodded to himself and sank into the chair feeling slightly disoriented. Wasn't there something *else* he was supposed to remember? Another message he needed to deliver, even more important than the one he just read? He sighed as that nagging, urgent feeling faded.

A knock at the door startled him from his thoughts. "Judy, will you please see them in?" he asked. As the President rose from his chair, the doctor snatched the drawing off his desk, crumpling it in his hand and shoving it deep into his pocket before the President could catch a glimpse of the words he'd scrawled over his desperate note to himself and to the country.

Help Me!

The press swarmed in, quickly filling the room as the doctor quietly slipped out another door.

CHAPTER 1

MARIN

MARIN DIDN'T HAVE time to scream when Hahn wrapped his slimy arms tightly around her and tossed her from the bridge. She panicked, her old fear of drowning raging through her like a primal beast, but there was nothing she could do. There was a moment of flailing freefall before she hit the river hard, the last of her air forced through her nose, then a bone jarring slam as Hahn landed on top of her. She sank, pressed deep into the river by the weight of Hahn's body.

She fought to escape; kicking, biting, scratching at him, but he held her in an iron grip, pushing the side of her face into the muddy, reed-tangled bottom. Black mud oozed into her open mouth like thick tar, gagging her, smothering her. She bucked and twisted and one hand came free. She pulled her face out of the mud, spitting it out, desperate for a breath of clear water. Her hand was snatched back and she felt something hard wrapped around both her wrists, binding them tightly. Multiple hands grasped her legs and she realized Hahn had more of his henchmen down here with him. Her legs were forced together and fastened with the same material as around her wrists. Then she was flipped onto her back, suntil spitting goo and gasping to clear her lungs of mud, trussed and helpless as a pig ready for slaughter. She was dragged downstream, away from the bridge she had been standing on just moments ago. She could barely see Frank, her father, reaching desperately for her from the bridge, but choking on whatever poison it was that Hahn had just unleashed onto the island. Numb with shock, she watched his limp body tumble into the water.

The pressure squeezing her arms increased with their speed. Hahn and his people twisted through the river, dragging her rapidly through the winding canal until they broke out into the open sea. She finally cleared her mouth of the last bits of grit, but she still had gobs stuck in her throat. It was difficult to take in a full breath of water, and it hurt to exhale, but the deeper they went in the ocean, the easier it became.

After what seemed like an eternity of traveling, she hazarded a glance at her captors. Hahn swam ahead of her, his bulging eyes and wispy hair making him look much more like a frog than a man. On her right side, a wiry hand embedded in a wavelike fin gripped her. The fin spread outward like a blanket entombing the features of a man within a monstrous sting ray with a wickedly sharp tail trailing behind. As if feeling her eyes on him, the creature twisted its head towards her and met her gaze with glassy human eyes. Sharp teeth ringed a hinged mouth. A bump bulged where the nose might have been. Marin shuddered at the abomination Hahn created and looked away. She didn't dare look at whatever could be holding her on the other side.

Eventually they slowed and she could feel vibrations of a motor nearby. They swam upward and before long Hahn was opening the underside hatch of a massive submarine. She was pushed forward and shoved into the coldness of an air hatch. Hands grabbed her from above, pulling her into the sub and onto a metal bench inside the airlock, hands suntil tied behind her back, her hair hanging in streaks across her face. Hahn sat down across from her. As he closed the hatch below them, she could see the grotesque monsters disappear into the depths.

Hahn sat back and looked at her triumphantly. She tried to ignore him as she cleared her lungs of water, coughing it out on the grate below her feet. Hahn pushed the water out somehow, taking in a noisy breath of the pressurized air. As her coughing subsided and she choked in a couple breaths, he reached over and wiped the hair away from her face. She winced at his touch.

"You're afraid?" he wheezed, his voice still sounding heavy with water. She didn't respond, but her heart pounded in terror. Of course she was afraid. "Don't be concerned. I will take very good care of you."

The airlock opened with a hiss and a man stepped in. Hahn lifted his arm to him and the man injected him with a greenish substance. Hahn doubled over in pain, groaning. Marin pressed herself against the wall making the bands binding her arms dig painfully into her wrists, but she couldn't bear the thought of touching him, even accidentally. He struggled a few more moments before righting himself. He stepped out of the airlock as if nothing had happened and the man outside gave him a thick black towel to dry off with.

"Bring her," he said, nodding to Marin. Two burly men squeezed through the doorway and picked her up; one by her armpits, the other by her feet and carried her into the main body of the sub. The man at her head held her so tight she cried out in pain, twisting herself to get free of him. He lost his grip and she fell to the ground, hitting her head and crushing her wrist below her with a snap.

She screamed in agony, rolling to her side. Hahn was next to her in a heartbeat.

"What happened?" he demanded.

"She slipped out of my hands, sir." The man said, blanching. Marin writhed in pain on the floor. Hahn flipped open a pocket knife and stabbed the man deep in the thigh. He fell to the ground next to Marin, clutching his leg and howling with pain. Hahn jerked the knife free of the leg and cut the ties around her wrists, the man's warm blood dripping from the knife onto her palms. He rolled her on her back and inspected her arms carefully. Tears slid down her face, pooling in her ears. He carefully moved her left wrist back and forth. She jerked involuntarily. He barely touched her right arm and she screamed. He smiled happily.

"You've broken your right arm. Both bones. Have you ever had a broken bone before?" he asked. She shook her head, biting her lip. "Excellent! This will be most interesting. The other one is just a sprain, unfortunately." The man on the ground moaned. Blood pooled around his leg, but nobody moved to help him. Hahn looked at him for a moment, considering. He picked up her left hand, ignoring her cries and held it up over the man's leg, then nicked her palm with the knife. Blood oozed out and dripped onto the man's wound. Three, four, five, six drops. Hahn whisked her hand away.

"Get her a bandage and make her a splint. And take her to the infirmary." He looked around the room dangerously and added, "Carefully!" He crouched near the man on the ground, prodding his wound like a boy jabbing an ant pile with a stick, waiting for something to happen.

Marin was carried down a hallway and placed inside a large room on a bunk embedded in a niche in the wall. Medical equipment lined the perimeter and a smell of disinfectant permeated the air. Only once the door was shut between herself and Hahn did she dare glance at her wounded wrists. Her left arm seemed normal, but her right hand hung limp as if she had another joint between her elbow and hand. It looked *wrong*. She turned away feeling dizzy and nauseous. The thought of throwing up scared her because her feet were still tied and her arms hurt so bad she didn't even know if she could use them to roll over. She laid her head back, biting back the helpless tears leaking out of her eyes.

Another wave of dizziness hit her. Bile rose in her throat and she turned her head just in time to lose everything she'd had in her stomach onto the bed next to her pillow. Her body started shaking uncontrollably, cold seeping into her bones until they felt they were made of ice.

It felt like an eternity passed as she lay there shivering, but eventually the door slid open and Hahn entered, dried off and looking pleased. He took one look at her and his face soured. "Idiots!" he growled. "She is in shock! Why hasn't she been attended to?" Two men scurried past him carrying a canvas bag full of medical supplies and stepped up next to her. One attempted to put a blood pressure cuff around her arm while the other opened her eyes and shined a small flashlight into them, momentarily blinding her.

"Get out of my way, fools!" Hahn elbowed them aside. "Free her feet, get her a blanket and clean up this vomit!" he ordered, sending everyone scattering to obey his commands. He reached into the bag and brought out a strange apparatus that looked like a tangle of dollar store finger traps and started pressing her fingers into each of the thing's openings. Some part of Marin's mind wondered what was happening, but the excruciating pain blurred out all her curiosity. Once her fingers were all inside the device, he lifted it up and attached it to a small latch at the top of the bed. She moaned as her broken arm was raised, hanging limp from the contraption. Some part of her felt someone wiping the sick from around her head, a warm cloth rubbing around her face, cold scissors clipping loose the binding around her feet. Hands covered her with a blanket, but all she could concentrate on was the burning fire in her arm suspended above her.

"What are you doing?" she groaned.

"I'm setting your bones," Hahn said matter-of-factly. "Don't worry, Marin, I *am* a doctor," he said in a voice that somehow made her even more concerned. One of the men in the room cleared his throat. Marin couldn't see him, and frankly didn't care who was there at this point.

"I have pain medication ready for her, sir." Marin's heart melted with relief. All she wanted was to be knocked out, to not feel anything anymore.

"Absolutely not!" Hahn turned, fire in his eyes. "She will receive no medication, no fluids, nothing that will dilute or taint her blood!" The man looked surprised, but did nothing, leaving Marin's hope of relief to die.

"No!" she cried out, but he ignored her. Hahn pulled on her arm, making her scream with pain. She could feel the broken bones rubbing unnaturally, and the room began to spin. The pain was unbearable. She reached over with her other arm and tried to support it, but Hahn pushed it away.

"Hold her!" he demanded. Someone pushed her down, pinning her to the mattress. Hahn looked into her eyes. "Ready?" he said with an excited grin. "Here we go again!" She barely had time to draw in a breath before he pushed hard on her elbow, grating her bones together before they slipped back into place. Her screams echoed throughout the ship. A hand clamped over her mouth, almost suffocating her. She fought against everyone holding her, but there were too many.

Hahn's face came close to her ear. "This pain is nothing to what lies ahead if you defy me. Do you understand?" The agony in her arm faded slightly and she nodded. The hand was removed from her mouth and she sucked in air hungrily. Hahn stood straight and looked over her arm. He pressed on the break, causing her to cry out involuntarily, but a dangerous look from him silenced her to a quiet whimper.

"Good, the break is set. Now we wait." He glanced at an expensive looking dive watch on his arm and nodded. "I want someone in here with her constantly. Notify me immediately if there is any change in her at all, do I make myself clear?" he asked. "Take an x-ray of her arm now and again in thirty minutes and every thirty minutes after that. The men around him nodded and he left the room. Marin didn't pay attention to who stayed and who went. It didn't matter. She was helpless in a monster's lair.

CHAPTER 2

FRANK

FRANK CLAWED AT his throat, suddenly unable to breathe. Through the yellow haze, he watched his daughter being dragged away beneath the surface of the water by several of Hahn's mutants. He reached his arms out helplessly over the side of the bridge, as if by sheer will he could bring her back to his arms. He coughed, his vision blurring, gasping like a fish out of water as he suffocated. He tried to breathe, his chest heaving, but the air seemed insubstantial. His vision danced in front of him; pinpricks of light and dark bursting like bubbles, making it hard to see Marin disappearing further down the river. He leaned over the railing, straining in his delirium to reach her, then suddenly there was a moment of weightlessness and an impact. Cold water covered him. His body convulsed as he sank to the bottom, lack of oxygen starving his brain and shutting down his whole system. Stubbornly, he still strained for air, but instead he sucked in lungful after lungful of cloudy water as his consciousness left him. His heart stopped pounding and his body relaxed as he lay limp among the reeds.

***

Something brushed past his hand and Frank jerked awake in a confused panic. He was underwater, but he couldn't figure out where. His limbs were

13

so entangled in a mess of cattails and reeds that he felt like he was tied down. Memories of being held hostage by Hahn, tied down and tortured for information he refused to give flooded through his brain and he went crazy, thrashing and tearing at his arms and legs until he fought free and found himself sitting up at the muddy edge of a river. He rubbed the water from his face and tried to calm down; the realization of what brought him here finally coming back to him. Marin. The Mutagen. For the past fifteen years, the only focus in his life had been keeping his daughter safe from Hahn and Leviathan. He had distanced himself from her to stand in the shadows, watching another man raise his daughter while he silently built a wall around her that kept him out, but also his enemies. It was all worth it if she was safe. And now, the very moment he breached that wall, Hahn had struck like a viper and taken his little girl. It was almost too much to bear.

He bowed his head into his hands, wet, miserable and completely defeated, and cried until he had no more tears left in him. How could he let this happen? He should never have let her into the COAST program! It was his weakness, his need to be in her life, if only as an acquaintance, that had caused this. He cursed himself for his weakness. He had broken the last promise he had given his dying wife—to protect their daughter. He slammed his hands down into the water and threw his head back in a scream of helpless rage, all his grief, anger, and despair pouring out of his mouth like poison from a wound and echoing off the hills surrounding him. His voice faded and he sat numbly in the water, staring at the bodies of several ducks bobbing near the shore, more victims of Hahn's savage weapon. He almost envied them; their fight was over. But his…

"Why am I not dead?" he asked aloud to the deaf world around him. Everything that had been exposed to the mutagen was dead. Why wasn't he? He pondered for a few more minutes and then shook his head. With a heavy sigh, he struggled up the slippery bank until he stood on dry land, blinking in the early morning sun. He had drifted several blocks from the park, so he squelched his way along the river until he came to the bridge he'd fallen from. Chita's body lay sprawled on the ground, dried yellow mucus covered her once red lips, her eyes bulged and glassy, her hair filled with dust and twigs.

"Ah, Chita," he said, shaking his head. "You could have done so much more with your life. Look where all that hunger for power has left you."

He bent down and pried her cell phone from her stiff fingers and checked the battery, then pocketed it. His feet crunched on gravel as he made his way to Chita's car. He opened the passenger side and dragged out the sniper's body, but took the gun and put it back in the car. He dragged the driver out and laid him next to his buddy and searched both men, taking all the cash and credit cards out of their wallets and putting them on the dash of the car. He looked down at his own clothes, which were soggy, uncomfortable, and he was missing one shoe, and then glanced at the men at his feet. The driver looked about his size, but he couldn't help feeling uneasy about the thought of stealing the dead man's clothes. Still, it wasn't like the guy was going to need them.

Frank paused for a moment to consider his options and it occurred to him how utterly, eerily silent it was. No traffic, no bustle, no birds even singing in the trees. Only the wind, whispering spookily through the grass like the voices of spirits from the grave.

It was completely, suffocatingly silent. Hahn killed every living thing on the island. It was incomprehensible! Every man, woman and child, every cat, every dog, every little newborn baby and grandma and hummingbird dropped dead where they were when this mutagen was deployed. Cut off in their last act of living, frozen in time like the village of Pompeii, with no notice of their impending doom. The sheer magnitude of the horror Hahn released into the world hit Frank like a tidal wave. Hahn had to be stopped at all costs, not just so he could find Marin, but for the sake of every human alive. If he wanted any chance to do that, first he was going to have to find a way off this island. He bent down and took the clothes off the man and changed out there in the open air. There was no one to see him anyway.

Getting inside the car, he rifled through Chita's purse, adding several hundred more dollars and a few more credit cards to his growing stash. He turned on the car and checked the time. 7:38 a.m. He had no idea how long he had been out or even what day it was, but he refused to think about how much time could have passed since Marin had been kidnapped. Instead, he looked up the route to the closest airfield on Chita's phone and

15

pulled out to the main road, retracing the way they had driven him here. Only this time, the streets were silent; cars were scattered all over the road and off the road, the drivers slumped over their steering wheels. Bodies were strewn on sidewalks and parking lots. Mothers, babies, men, women, kids. Colorful clothing fluttering in a tropical breeze, now shrouds of death. His stomach churned and he pried his gaze away, keeping his eyes trained forward until he finally entered the airfield. The door to Chita's plane was open, and a man lay on the ground near the steps. Frank hauled him away from the wheels, then dragged the bodies of the pilot, co-pilot and stewards out onto the tarmac, wiping perspiration from his eyes before he closed the hatch and started the engines.

CHAPTER 3

MARCOS

EIGHT-YEAR-OLD MARCOS MINAS stood with his back to the ocean, daring the waves to hit him. He felt the sand under the soles of his bronze feet, hot and grainy. A cool wash of seawater doused him to his knees and his feet sank a few inches deeper into the gritty shore. He laughed with delight. Looking up, he saw his mother, her white dress billowing out behind her in the breeze, laughing as well. Her ebony hair rippled in a cascade behind her, lifted by the wind. She held a wide-brimmed hat on her head with one hand. Her other hand rested on the head of a little girl—an almost exact miniature of her with the same wavy black tresses, same golden skin, dressed in a similar white dress, but with a blue sash tied around her waist. The tiny spit of sand they called their private beach was half bathed in shadow from the rocky cliff face that enclosed it, the beach itself only appearing during the day and disappearing when the tide rose in the evening. A winding set of steps cut into the rock led back to their home far above them on the bluff.

Marcos soaked in the safe sounds and smells of his childhood home, clinging to the feel of the sun on his bare shoulders, the waves hitting the back of his calves again, almost toppling him. He righted himself and continued his game of chicken with the ocean until a large wave hit him hard from behind, sucking his feet painfully from the sand and sending him tumbling onto the shore, soaking wet. He got to his scuffed knees, spitting saltwater and brushing his unruly curls out of his eyes. A strong hand lifted him to his feet.

"You should never turn your back on the ocean, my little man. She is a woman not to be trusted!" His father let out a loud, rumbling laugh, tousling his wet curls and walking with him to the blanket his mother had spread further up on the dry sand. It was rare these days for his father to be home more than a few days at a time, so they had made it a small celebration.

"But soon we won't have to worry about the ocean, Father. Soon she will be tamed, and we can breathe it like air, no?"

Malcolm sat down on the blanket and took a fig from a bowl his mother had just placed on the linen. "Not yet, little one. And even then, we will still need to respect the ocean. Like a woman, she will never be truly tamed, only better understood." He winked at his wife with a sparkle in his eye. The little girl knelt down next to her father and tangled her fingers in his beard, a habit she'd had since she was a baby.

"Papa, will I be a mermaid one day?"

He beamed at his daughter. "Someday, Katerina. Someday soon, perhaps." He looked at his wife, noted the concern on her face and his expression clouded. "You must never speak of this outside our home, any of you. Not to your closest friends, not to anyone. Do you understand me?" Marcos and Katerina nodded, but Marcos swallowed a lump in his throat. Father had always told them not to speak of it, but he'd never mentioned friends. He'd always thought he meant grown-ups, not children. Marcos told his best friend, Christos, everything. How could he not tell him about his father's secret project to make people breathe underwater? It was better than T.V.! His father fixed a stern eye on his son and for a moment, Marcos wondered if he could read his mind.

"Marcos, you haven't told anyone about this, have you?"

Marcos tried to keep his face calm while his insides squirmed like a squid. "No, Papa!" he lied. The first lie he'd ever told. It stuck to the inside of his mouth, this lie, changing him, distancing him immediately from his parents. *Now, I am a liar,* he thought miserably. His mother, ever more perceptive, pushed further.

"Are you sure, my son?" she asked, giving him one more opportunity to confess and remove the lie from his mouth, but fear of his father's sharp temper made him a coward. "No, Mama, I haven't," he said earnestly, adding another lie to his mouth. His mother looked doubtful but nodded to her husband.

His father stared at him a moment more, the last of his chance at redemption slipping away. "Good, my son. See that you don't. It is very important you obey me in this."

"And you, Katerina? Do you obey me, too?" he asked brushing her hair away from her face. She looked up at him earnestly.

"Of course, Papa!" she said, looking almost offended that he would ask. He beamed at them both.

"Good, my children. One day, we may all be able to swim to the depths of the water to see the whales up close," he touched the nose of his little girl, "and hunt for treasure in sunken ships," he said to Marcos, who smiled back weakly.

The others ate their meal, laughing and talking, but Marcos merely played with his food, the weight of guilt filling his stomach like a stone. By the time they climbed the long staircase at sunset, Marcos's feet were leaden.

"Are you ill, Marcos?" his mother asked, touching his forehead.

"I don't feel well, Mama," he said, glad for once to be telling the truth. She sent him off to bed early, with the window open to let in the cool night air. He lay there, tormented, trying to justify his actions, telling himself it didn't matter, tossing and turning until his sister came to bed a little later. He turned his back to her, pretending to be asleep as she shuffled under the cool covers of her bed across from his. His mother came in soon after to tuck them up as she always did.

"Washed and brushed and all tucked up?" she whispered to Katerina. Katerina giggled. Quietly, his mother sang a lullaby, her voice melting him to silent tears. Normally her songs would fill him with peace and joy. Tonight, he just wanted her to stop, to go away and leave him to his misery.

She stopped her singing and kissed Katerina goodnight. He wiped the tears from his face, hoping she would finally leave, but she brushed his forehead lightly with her fingers, testing him for fever. She bent over and gave him a soft kiss on his hair and whispered, "I love you, Marcos," before she drifted out the door. He covered his head with his pillow and cried himself to sleep.

Hours later, something shifted in their room, bringing him to consciousness. The nightstand that stood between their beds and against the window grated against the floor as if it were being moved. He woke, but stayed still, waiting to hear the noise again. Something shuffled, like fabric moving. And there was breathing... heavy, not the light sound of his sister sleeping. His heart started pounding in his chest. He opened his eyes to the dark, hoping to see nothing but the familiar shapes of his room, but part of the blackness moved. There was a shadow standing directly over him, leaning over his bed with hands outstretched. Water dripped on his face from the shadow. Shiny black skin and strange protruding eyes flashed in the moonlight streaming in through the open window. Some part of his brain registered that whatever it was had come from the sea. A monster! He gasped and the thing lunged at him, but stopped short as a shrill scream came from Katerina.

Marcos saw her sitting up in bed, her mouth wide open, blankets clutched to her chest. The thing pivoted and clamped a hand across her mouth, cutting her cries off immediately. It swooped her up in its arms, her eyes wide in panic, and swept her out of the window before Marcos could fully comprehend what was happening. He jumped to his feet in time to see them disappear down the long stairway, Katerina's arms straining over the monster's shoulder toward him, her wide, white eyes shining in the moonlight. Her mouth was covered, but he could hear the scream going on and on and on, coming from everywhere, until he realized it was his own voice. His terror screamed into the night, never stopping even after the lights were thrown on and his father and mother raced into the room and saw his little sister was gone. A boat engine roared out in the little cove, buried now with water, taking Katerina away forever. Marcos couldn't see her, but his mind imagined her arms still reaching out to him, begging him to save her.

Marcos jolted out of his nightmare with the scraping sound of metal. Food. Someone had shoved food under his door. He lay there for a moment, calming his racing heart. He had dreamed about this part of his life many times since it happened, it was no stranger to him. In the years since, he'd realized the monster had to have been a man in a wetsuit, but that did little to change the terror and crushing guilt of the memory. It was a wound that refused to heal, an infection he covered during the day, but at night, the scab was ripped off. He was just grateful when Marin had entered his dreams several days ago that he'd been dreaming something else at the time. He hated that traitorous, cowardly part of him that had cost him his family. He rubbed the grit from his eyes and sat up. In the dim light of his cell, he could see the food near the slot in the bottom of the door.

"Thank you!" he yelled at whoever had thought to feed him. He couldn't be sure how long he'd been here, given that he'd been unconscious when they brought him in, but it felt like forever. In that time, he'd seen no one and been fed rarely. He threw the thin blanket off his bed and put his feet on the cold floor, tiptoeing over to visit the only piece of furniture in the room besides his bed—a chrome toilet bolted to the floor. Afterwards, he picked up the food and headed back to his bed with it. The room wasn't exactly cold, but it definitely wasn't warm, either.

"What's on the menu today?" he spoke to himself, peeling plastic wrap off a bowl of plain, tepid oatmeal. A few chunks of fruit were in a Styrofoam cup and two cartons of milk, one chocolate, finished out his meal. He ate as slowly as his hunger allowed, trying to savor the taste of the cantaloupe for as long as he could and drinking the milk in small sips. Still, it didn't take long before he was done and faced with another eternity of solitude. He didn't usually mind being alone but worry for Marin was driving him crazy.

He had no idea if she was alive or dead. The last time he'd seen her, they were trying to save a group of sailors from their wrecked fishing boat, not realizing that the monstrosity that tore their boat apart was still there, waiting for more victims. He barely had time to warn Marin before he was taken, wrapped in that things' slimy tentacles so tightly he could hardly breathe. He'd caught a glimpse of her being pulled underwater as well. Then there were vague flashes of being dragged through the sea for what seemed like an eternity before they were dumped in a boat where strangers had covered his head with a black sack and tied his wrists with zip ties.

The next thing he knew, he was locked in this room and Marin was gone. All that was left of her was a memory seared into his brain of a monster dragging her away, her eyes wide with panic and her hands reaching out to him to save her. And like his sister years before, he was powerless to do so. He tried to keep himself from worrying what was happening to Marin, but, with nothing but the four walls of his prison room to distract him, worry loomed like a specter in his mind. He shook his head wearily, deciding that nightmares of the past were slightly less horrible than the worries of the future. He curled up in a ball and went back to sleep.

CHAPTER 4

JAYCEN

JAYCEN CURLED UNCOMFORTABLY in the bunkroom at the back of the sub called The Minnow, wishing he were asleep. The healing cut on his cheek bothered him if he lay on one side, but the other side would get tired after a while. He twisted around and finally just ended up on his back staring in frustration at the springs of the bed above him.

The Minnow was big enough to house up to eight people; the cockpit, a kitchen galley and one bathroom were at the head, followed by the center of the sub filled with tubes, pipes and equipment. The back space was separated into two areas: the bunkroom where he currently was, and the lockbox, which was the pressurized room that could be filled with water or air to give them access to the ocean. Behind that was access to the engines. There were only a few bunks, and he was painfully aware that the beds were made for people much shorter than he was. Noburu, one of the original scientists in the AQUA program, was up front manning the helm with his son, Kazu, who was one of the youngest hostages recently rescued from Hahn. Paul sat on the floor of the bunkhouse near Jaycen, feverishly drawing a diagram on a dry erase board. Jaycen lay on a bottom bunk half watching him out of the corner of his eye. Paul paused, clearing his throat.

"Wanna talk about what's eating you, kid?" Paul asked.

"What do you mean?" Jaycen asked, pushing himself up on one elbow.

"You've been kidnapped, almost stabbed, thankfully rescued, and who knows what all else. You must be freaking out on some level. I just wondered if you felt like talking about it," he responded simply, keeping his eyes down and beginning to draw once more.

Jaycen felt awkward talking to him about his feelings, but he was touched by his concern and let out a long, drawn-out sigh as he lay back on his bunk. "This may sound weird, but none of that stuff is bothering me right now. It doesn't seem real yet, you know? Almost like I was living inside a movie or something." He draped an arm across his eyes. "I think it will bother me at some point, but it's like I can't think about it right now. Does that mean I'm crazy? I mean, the past few weeks have been insane! How come I'm not curled in a ball muttering to myself?"

Paul laughed and laid down the board, stretching his legs out as far as he could in the cramped space. "You're not crazy. It's something your brain does to help you keep in the moment and stay alive until an emergency has passed. And it hasn't. I experienced this whenever I was called into action in the Navy." He drew up his knees and twisted to see Jaycen better. "You see some messed up stuff when you get deployed. But you can't stop and process it because the next round of artillery is coming your way, and you have to keep moving to stay alive. But that stuff in your head isn't going anywhere. Your brain just puts it in a box until it's time to sort it out." He shrugged and gave Jaycen a half smile. "So you're not crazy. Yet."

"Well, that's comforting," Jaycen said sarcastically. They were quiet for a moment and Jaycen listened to the strangely comforting sound of Paul writing once again on the board. It kind of reminded him of simpler days of school, before he fell in love with a girl who could breathe water. Before he could, himself.

"Does it bug you to be an Arydian now, Paul?" He lifted his arm off his eyes and turned to see his reaction to his question. Paul grinned wide.

"Well, that depends on which part you're asking about. If you mean learning about the AQUA program developing a drug that makes it so I can breathe water? No, not in the least. I love the water! It's like suddenly learning you can fly! Sure, it's strange, and I really don't know if I have a handle on it yet, but being able to breathe underwater is probably one of the coolest things that have ever happened to me. And the change it's made in Marin…it's incredible." A sad look crossed his face at the mention of the girl he'd raised from a small child. "But if you mean the part about Leviathan doing everything they can to steal this drug from these people and Dr. Hahn kidnapping my little girl to experiment on her…" Paul stopped talking and grumbled, wiping his eyes. It struck Jaycen in the heart.

"I'm worried about her, too," Jaycen said quietly. "Honestly, that's more terrifying to me than anything I went through."

Paul nodded solemnly. "Yeah, that's what's keeping me up at night. I worry about Frank and Marcos as well. At least we know Marin was wanted by Leviathan for some reason, so chances are, they are keeping her alive. Frank and Marcos may not have been that lucky."

Jaycen ground his teeth at the mention of Marcos, jealousy burning a hole in his heart. Marcos had been with her when Jaycen had left. Stupid, pretty boy Marcos, with his fancy accent and his tan and his cool, wavy hair.

Paul glanced up at Jaycen's fuming face. "Hey, pal, I know you don't like him, but you should know he saved Marin's life. Aaron just about choked her to death and if he hadn't come along, he most likely would have succeeded." Jaycen's scowl darkened further and Paul prodded him with his marker. "Aren't you glad he saved her?"

Jaycen nodded reluctantly. He couldn't bring himself to say the awful things he was thinking, especially to Paul, but Paul could read it in his eyes.

"Ah, so one more thing he's got in his favor, huh?" Paul asked.

Jaycen grunted in agreement. "Right! Now he's saved her life. How do I compete with that?" he added sourly.

Paul coughed lightly, as if covering up a poorly timed laugh and Jaycen glowered at him. "Well, I'm not going to get involved, you three have to figure that one out. *If* the poor kid is even alive." Paul raised his eyebrow pointedly at him.

"You're right," Jaycen agreed quietly, feeling awful for letting a tiny piece of him hope Marcos might be out of the picture for good.

"You're absolutely sure this Shade lady that snatched you said they already had Marin?" Paul asked.

"Yes, I'm sure. She said, 'Hahn doesn't care about you anymore. The enemy's got your girlfriend now, and she's the one he wanted all along'." He felt an involuntary shiver at the memory of the Shade, the blade she'd sliced him with hovering over his heart. He shoved the memory back into the box. Paul was right; he would deal with it later.

"I have to assume she got picked up when Leviathan attacked the rig. We can hope the others were captured, not killed, but either way, I think the only choice we have is to get into Leviathan and find out."

"Are you working on a plan or something?" Jaycen asked hopefully, leaning up again in interest. Paul nodded thoughtfully as he rubbed the stubble on his chin.

"Tell me about this army guy that had you locked up. Sergeant Major Peter Bale. My guy said he's a tough cookie but didn't hate him. Do you think he's with Leviathan?"

Jaycen looked around uncomfortably. "He's actually married to my mom."

Paul brightened up. "He's your step-dad? Well, that's a relief. Why did he throw you in the brig, then?"

Jaycen pursed his lips. "He knew I was involved in the earthquake somehow. He seriously tracked me down from some dead guy's phone! They were watching my mom's house, waiting for me to try and call her, and when I did, they came for me!"

Paul frowned. "That sounds more like Leviathan than the military. I can't imagine why anyone would want to go to all that trouble to find you otherwise. I'm not sure the government would care about one kid when the whole area is one big disaster." Paul shook his head. "I hate to suggest this, Jaycen, but your step-dad may be working for our enemies. I'm sorry."

"Don't be. They just got married like a week ago. I barely know Pete. And I definitely don't like him. I'm pretty sure the feeling is mutual."

"Well, is your mom a good judge of character? Obviously she loves him, or she wouldn't have married him, but do you trust her judgement?" Paul prodded.

Jaycen's heart sank. "I really don't know. I wish I could ask her."

Paul gave his shoulder a squeeze. "I know, kid. I'm sorry."

"If I'd known I wouldn't find her, I would have never left Marin. Maybe none of this would have happened! I wouldn't have left her side, Aaron wouldn't have had the chance to try to hurt her, he wouldn't have run away..." he trailed off before the prickling in his eyes got worse.

"You can't play the 'what if' game, Jaycen. That's one thing that *will* drive you crazy."

"I didn't want to put anyone at risk, but I had a chance to cure my mom and I had to take it. I couldn't leave her alone in the middle of all that chaos in California without anyone to help her. I hope you can understand. I hope Marin understands."

"Yeah, I do. I'm sure she does as well. I know she doesn't blame you, and I don't either. I actually have a lot of respect for someone who is willing to sacrifice something that means a lot to them for the sake of others. It's very noble. And think of it this way; Leviathan would have hit us either way. They would have taken Marin no matter what. If we hadn't gone out looking for you, *we* would have been killed or captured and nobody would be out here to try to save her. So maybe it's all turned out how it's supposed to."

Jaycen flashed him a relieved half smile, a glimmer of hope briefly lifting his spirits. "Do you think we have a chance of finding her?"

"Want the truth? The chance is slim. But that doesn't mean we won't try." He picked up the dry erase board and showed him the diagram he'd been working on. "This might surprise you, but I've actually been in Leviathan headquarters."

"Really? I thought they were some international gangster organization or something."

"Well, yes, but up front they are an international shipping company near San Francisco with a fantastic research division. It was very much like COAST was before the earthquake messed up California. Only with a lot more money to burn."

"Huh. Interesting," Jaycen said.

"I don't have exact information, but I've got a rough draft, assuming they haven't changed anything. At least it's a start..."

"I don't know, Paul. I feel like I've gone from one dead end to another. Look how bad the last decision I made turned out. I left you guys and

Marin, spent all that time trying to find and save my mom, and instead I got kidnapped and almost killed. Several times, in fact. And I still don't know if my mom is alive or dead." His voice caught in his throat so he waited a moment until he could go on. "I'm starting to think I'm just bad luck, Paul."

Paul didn't answer immediately, but Jaycen heard him pick up the marker and start fidgeting with the lid. "Look, Jaycen. I know things didn't work out like you'd planned on land. But I think you've got the wrong outlook here. Was it bad luck you didn't find your mom? Sad, but given the massive disaster you were searching through, it's really not that unlikely. Thousands of people are looking for people they've lost. Was it bad luck that you got picked up by Leviathan? Again, not really. They put a big bounty on your head and everyone had a picture of your face and was looking for you, including the cops and military! I'd say that it was inevitable." He sat the marker down on top of the board and shifted positions.

"So far, I'm not seeing how my outlook should have been different, Paul."

"You got picked up by the Shade, but somehow your step-dad found you and rescued you before anything could happen. I'd say that was pretty lucky."

"Yeah, and later they shot me!"

"But they didn't kill you, just hit your leg. That's incredibly lucky!" Paul countered. Jaycen scowled, but Paul kept going. "And, when I came searching for you, I found an old friend who helped guide me to you. Tell me that's not lucky!"

"That sounds more like your luck than mine, Paul."

"And when that Leviathan woman snatched you out of your high security army prison and tried to kill you?"

"Yes, you saved me in the nick of time. Lucky me," Jaycen said flatly.

"Your leg got better..." Paul started, but Jaycen interrupted him.

Jaycen rolled over to face him. "About that. What's the deal? Is that something all these Arydians can do? I mean, within hours you couldn't even tell I'd been shot!" He raised an eyebrow. "And don't tell me *that* was luck!"

Paul dropped his eyes uncomfortably. "Uh, yeah. That's actually something kind of special only a few of us get." He lowered his voice, making sure Kazu and Noburu couldn't hear him. "Remember that accident at COAST when Marin got trapped underwater and we thought she had drowned?"

Jaycen nodded glumly. "Yeah, I remember. Because of my clumsiness, she almost died."

"No, again you're thinking about this the wrong way. Because of that accident, Marin overcame her crippling fear of water and discovered who she really is. But that's not where I'm going with this. She should have been killed, yet she came out of that accident like nothing ever happened. In my opinion, it's likely that she *had* been hurt, but because she heals so fast, it wasn't a problem."

Jaycen furrowed his brow, remembering something. "Actually, there was this one time she fell and scraped up her arm, but when we washed the blood off, you couldn't even see the wound."

"Her blood can heal other people, too. You were there when she healed the hostages, like Kazu and the rest," he said, tipping his head toward the front of the sub. Kazu, along with many other loved ones of the original AQUA team, had been hostages of Leviathan for years. They had been experimented on and tortured by Hahn, who changed them into water-breathing monstrosities brainwashed to find and kill the Arydians. Paul pulled his legs back under him while Jaycen waited for Paul to continue.

"Well, Frank developed what he thought was the formula for Arydia, but this one was derived from Marin's blood. He made four vials of it. That's what he used to change you and to change me, so that took care of two of them. You stole the third one and hid it in a tree somewhere back in California. Frank has the other."

"And this version he made is different than the version of Arydia that the Arydians originally used to change themselves so they could breathe underwater?"

"Yes."

"So you and I...we're different, too?"

"Possibly," Paul said, looking away.

"In what way?" Jaycen pressed, growing concerned.

Paul didn't meet his eyes. "Frank isn't entirely sure. But one of the effects is that we have the ability to regenerate quickly like Marin can. Marcos apparently got a blood transplant from her after Aaron stabbed him, and he exhibits some of the characteristics as well, but maybe not all of them."

Jaycen cringed at the mention of Marcos's name, but asked his question anyway. "Characteristics? Like what?"

Paul shifted uneasily and Jaycen had the feeling he knew much more than he was letting on. "I don't have all the facts. You'll have to talk to Frank when we find him. But you can heal extremely quickly like Marin now. And," he smiled, "you can breathe underwater, which I, personally, think is a big bonus. So that's lucky that you and I got the magic serum and everyone else got the garden variety, right?"

Jaycen rolled his eyes. "Ugh, seriously? You've circled back to luck again?"

Paul nodded. "You know, Jaycen, most of luck is in the belief that you are lucky."

"Sounds to me like luck is just choosing to have a good attitude about the crappy hand you're dealt."

Paul grinned. "Now you're catching on!" Jaycen suddenly sat up, hitting his head on the bunk above him. He winced and rubbed his head but continued to talk excitedly.

"Paul! Do you know what's really lucky?" Paul shrugged and shook his head, baffled.

"I know someone who might have an exact idea of where Marin is... someone who's actually been a prisoner of Leviathan!"

Paul's eyes widened and they both smiled, speaking at the exact same time.

"Kazu!"

CHAPTER 5

MARCOS

THE CELL DOOR suddenly slid open, startling Marcos awake. The lights went on, momentarily blinding him. He rolled over and sat up, stifling a yawn. A large man, with skin as dark as midnight, leaned against the door frame, studying him. He wore an expensive looking suit and very nice shoes. His father had always said, "You can tell a lot about a man by the shoes he wears." By the look of them, this man seemed like he was used to the best of everything. For a moment, Marcos was keenly aware of the unwashed smell of his own body and rubbed the stubble on his chin that was quickly becoming a beard, but with a dash of defiance, decided he didn't really care what this guy thought of him.

"Can I help you?" he asked the man. The man sauntered in with his hands clasped behind his back. A moment later a nervous looking woman in her mid-thirties scurried in and stood beside him, wearing a lab coat and carrying a clipboard.

"This is the one Chita brought?" The man asked, his voice a deep rumble.

"Y…Yes sir. Mr. Zar. Sir." The man turned and slapped her face with the speed of a rattlesnake, sending the woman's clipboard and papers clattering to the ground. Marcos was on his feet in an instant, catching the woman as she stumbled sideways in shock.

"Never use my name here, idiot!" the man hissed at her, shoving Marcos back onto the bed with surprising strength.

"I'm…sorry…sir. It will never happen again," she said, scrambling to pick up the papers she had dropped. Marcos bent over to help her.

"See that it doesn't. Stand up, boy," the man said, pointing a thick finger at Marcos. Marcos stood, stepping closer to the man. He made a slow circuit around Marcos and stopped once again in front of him. Marcos watched the man's dark eyes, but his gaze was drawn to a prominent scar along the man's neck, as if he'd been knifed in a gang fight.

Marcos pointed to the scar and asked the man, "Did you have trouble shaving?"

The man's black eyes narrowed and he shot a fist into Marcos's jaw, making him see a burst of light as he staggered back several steps. Zar straightened his suit coat, dusting the edges as if nothing had happened.

"I see nothing unusual about him, other than his obvious death wish. Why did she want him?"

The woman sniffed quietly and cleared her throat. "He's…he's one of *them*. An Arydian. He was with the girl. That's all I know." Marcos struggled to hold his tongue, fury chewing him up, his breath shallow. He couldn't remain silent.

"Do you have Marin? Where is she!" he demanded.

"How do you know he's one of them?" Zar asked disdainfully, as if Marcos hadn't spoken. The woman walked over to Marcos and lifted the hair from off his neck, exposing thin lines behind his ear. Zar moved in and ran a finger down the lines, then looked on the other side of his neck for the matching set.

"And these are what? Gills?" Zar demanded of Marcos. Marcos shrugged. Zar punched him hard in the gut, doubling Marcos over. The woman flinched and almost dropped her clipboard again. "Answer me when I speak to you," the man growled. The woman cleared her throat and answered for him.

"Chita said they act like gills. The ones given the drug, Arydia, all have these like his. They weren't like the girls, though. Hers were lower, more prominent. They branch off into the lungs and close off when not in use."

"You are the one Chita left in charge of this facility, correct?" The woman bobbed her head up and down. "And have you put him in water to observe what his would do?" he demanded.

"Well, no," she said uneasily.

"What have you done with him, then?" he said, circling Marcos again.

"Nothing, I'm afraid. We'd had no instructions…" Zar rolled his eyes and shook his head, as if thinking he was surrounded by idiots.

"Where. Is. Marin!" Marcos interrupted through clenched teeth.

"So, the only reason you have him is because he came with the girl?" Zar asked, ignoring Marcos.

"Well," the woman began, choosing her words carefully, "she was different from him, so we thought we could use him for a comparison. For study."

"So he is a lab rat. A control for your experiments. Have you learned anything in all this time?"

"He…he was going to be. But then Chita took the girl to Hahn to make the exchange for the mutagen, and…never came back," she said cautiously, glancing at Zar. Marcos's heart dropped into his feet.

"Never came back?" Marcos repeated quietly. He sank to the bed in shock. Both the woman and Zar kept talking as though he were invisible.

"We weren't sure what to do with him, so we just kept him locked up, in case the conflict with Hahn was resolved and he…" she glanced up at Zar and she quickly amended her comment, "or you returned and wanted him for something," the woman said. Zar spun on her, his eyes flashing and she winced, stepping back as if in anticipation of another violent outburst. Zar stepped forward menacingly.

"This 'conflict' with Hahn will *never* be resolved. He is a traitor to our cause and will pay for his betrayal with his life. I never approved of this overpriced science experiment he claimed was so critical to the Plan, and now he has tipped our hand to the world and stolen the key to our triumph. I will see him writhe in agony for making fools of us, along with any of his followers." He stared at her and Marcos felt the threat he was sending her. It appeared Zar wasn't sure about the loyalties of his people here. This visit was an assertion of power over them. Maybe an attempt to regain control. Interesting.

Zar stepped back in front of Marcos, once he seemed satisfied that his veiled threat had been understood. "What did Chita have planned for him once the girl was gone?"

"She thought we might be able to use his DNA to replicate the Arydia formula and come up with our own version since Hahn took all the Mizu with him."

The man's face twitched in annoyance. "Hahn's ridiculous imitation never worked. All he succeeded in doing is making monsters, not the water-breathing army he promised. And Chita was foolish to ever try to exchange the girl for the mutagen without consulting the rest of us. Now Hahn has the mutagen, the warheads, and even the stupid girl, though I don't know why he wanted her so badly."

Marcos breathed a sigh of relief that at least Marin sounded like she was still alive, even if Hahn had her.

"Rumor has it she can heal him."

The man looked truly surprised. "Heal him? Of what?"

"Hahn took a dose of Mizu and changed himself, but he couldn't survive on land without the antidote for it. The antidote only lasts for a few hours and the transformation was incredibly painful. He wanted to be rid of the Mizu in his cells and be normal again."

Zar threw back his head with a deep mocking laugh. "So, even Hahn had to admit it was a failure and yearns to start over. Serves him right, the pompous little freak. He always did think he was more important than anyone else." The man rubbed his chin, making a dry, scratching sound. "Wait a moment. Can the girl heal anyone? Of anything?" he asked.

"That is the rumor. We have surveillance video of her blood healing a cut on someone else. And Hahn said she transformed one of his operatives completely with her blood."

His eyes moved around Marcos again, looking him over, like a piece of meat in a butcher shop. "What about this fellow? Can he heal people too?"

The woman shrugged. "I don't know. . ." Zar shot her a threatening look and she hurried on, "yet, but we will find out."

"Where is Hahn now?" he asked her.

"On his sub, we assume. We are tracking him with this receiver," she said pulling a black device out of her pocket. She glanced at it, pushing a few buttons while Zar waited impatiently. "His last heading was near the Bering Strait, but we have no way of getting to him. He's too far down for anything we have left to reach him. Plus he disabled the engines on The Pursuer, which is our biggest ship."

Zar sniffed and glared at Marcos distastefully, as if just now realizing he smelled bad. He turned to leave the room, talking over his shoulder to her.

"Send everything and everyone we have left to maintain a perimeter around Hahn's position. Notify me at once if he starts to resurface, or if his heading changes. We have got to get the mutagen out of his hands immediately." He stepped through the door and cast a final glance at Marcos. "And figure out if this boy has anything worthwhile in his blood. If not, kill him."

The door closed behind them and the light went off, leaving Marcos alone in a darkness that for some reason felt even deeper than it had before.

CHAPTER 6

JAYCEN

NOBURU LEANED HIS head into the galley. "I detected another group of vessels leaving the Leviathan facility. It looks like they are sending out every boat they have."

"What's their heading?" Paul asked.

"Due west," he replied.

"As long as it takes them away from us, the news just keeps getting better. Wonder what's got them so worked up?" Jaycen asked, rummaging through the kitchen cupboards, his stomach growling.

"Who knows? I am just glad it isn't us! How is your plan coming along?" Noburu asked, taking a seat around the small table. Paul slid his dry erase board over to him. Jaycen sat down next to Kazu with a bowl of cereal and ate while Paul explained.

"When I was on active duty, they let us do simulated rescues on Leviathan's compound. My commanding officer knew a guy there. Anyway, I've drawn out what I can remember from our stay." He shifted closer to the table to show everyone the drawing. "See, they have a bunch of outbuildings and a huge main circular building that goes down several floors and branches out underground, like the roots of a tree."

Paul made some marks on the board. "And they have this gorgeous aquarium that goes all the way down through the center of the building. When we did our diving sims there, they told us not to go any deeper than the mark they set up for us, but some idiot greenie lost his tank and when I went down to grab it, I got a glimpse of the bottom two floors. The lowest one was full of all this super high-tech security stuff. I would bet Marin would be kept down there." He twisted the corner of his mouth slightly and added, "But that was a long time ago, so I don't know if anything has changed." He glanced at Kazu, obviously hoping the boy would volunteer some information, but he stayed silent, his eyes haunted. Noburu prodded him encouragingly and Kazu swallowed hard, picking up the marker with a slight tremble to his hand.

"Hahn has a bunch of cages under the warehouse where he keeps people he'd changed with Mizu," Kazu said, his voice lowered. He glanced around, as if afraid Hahn would walk in at any moment and overhear him. "She may be held there, below water…" he said hopefully. Kazu cleared his throat and all eyes snapped over to him expectantly. "But unfortunately I think Paul is right. She will be where they can keep a close eye on her. Bottom floor, right hallway is where the prison cells are. That's where the highest security is…" he trailed off as if not wanting to go there, even in his memory.

Noburu nodded solemnly. "Do you have any idea how we can get to the main building? It looks like it's a long way from the road."

Paul chimed in. "I do. The complex is far from the road, but fairly close to the sea. And they have three open-air aquariums, plus the facility is built right on top of the cliff face. All we need to do is climb up and jump into the nearest one. The tanks themselves all likely share the same water system, and I'll bet the ranch the one inside the main building does as well. If we can get inside the water lines, we have a straight shot up through the drainage system to the main building. Once inside, we break out of the pipes and we're in!"

Jaycen swallowed his cereal, his mouth suddenly dry. While he didn't relish the idea of running into Leviathan unarmed, he liked the idea of trying to swim up the tailpipe of their water system even less. Just the thought of getting trapped in a couple hundred yards of pipe buried at least twenty five feet below ground was enough to send his pulse pounding. He hated closed-in spaces, let alone dark, slimy ones filled with animal waste.

"*And* it's possible the drainage will come out the bottom of the cliff, most likely underwater, somewhere in this vicinity." Paul circled an area in red. "If it does, it eliminates our most exposed portion. We don't even need to get out of the water. Easy peasy."

"I wouldn't describe it like that," Jaycen muttered and Kazu chuckled.

Noburu scratched his arm absently, thinking. "Possibly," he said as he took the marker from Paul. "But," he continued, "there are several obstacles I can think of. One is that we don't know how wide the pipes are, and if we can't fit in them, there's no way to proceed."

Paul raised a finger and continued. "Yes, but Leviathan has a gravity waste system. The water leaving the facility basically pours out through a barrel filter with sand and mesh barriers and then drains into the ocean. If it serves all of their aquariums, the pipes should be fairly large, and the water isn't pressurized, so, theoretically, the water flow should be manageable with our smallest waterjet scooters."

Noburu stared at the diagram carefully. "Okay, I've read about these systems," he said, "but that brings up a second problem. We don't know where the barrel filter is. It could be on the bottom floor of the facility, the top or somewhere in between. Plus, once we breach the barrel, whatever building we are in will flood, and while I agree the chaos that would cause could help us, it's not ideal conditions for searching for someone. It would slow us down almost as much as the enemy."

Noburu glanced up at his son and said his name quietly. "Kazu. Do you have any more information that could help us?" The three sat waiting while Kazu played with a stray piece of cereal that had fallen from Jaycen's bowl. "Do you know where the filter is?" he pressed, but Kazu just dropped his head.

"No, sir. I don't know anything about that."

Jaycen shook his head. "No offense, Paul, and maybe I'm just nervous about pulling this off, but so far it all just feels like guesswork."

Paul raised an eyebrow. "It is. That's why we are brainstorming this, to work out the kinks."

Noboru spoke again. "This might be more than kinks. We also don't know what kind of obstacles we may come across. If we hit a ninety degree bend in a pipe, again, we can't proceed. Even if you cut a hole in the pipe, it could just lead you to solid rock or dirt."

Paul set the board down and rubbed his eyes wearily. "Well, that's the best I've got. All the information I have is in front of you. I'm open for ideas."

Jaycen dragged his spoon through the dregs of his cereal, despair creeping into his heart, as his hopes of rescuing Marin diminished the longer they spoke.

Noburu ran a hand through his graying hair. "Paul, I think we need to consider another line of attack. There are too many variables in this one."

"I'm all ears, pal," Paul said, his face clouding over with frustration.

Everyone stared at Paul's map of the compound as if wishing for ideas to surface, but nobody said anything. Eventually, Kazu's fingers closed around the marker and he started drawing and talking at the same time.

"Well, there *is* a different way inside. There's a ladder that runs up the side of the main building for roof access. I didn't want to mention it because you would be totally exposed from the top of the cliff and across the yard, as well as the whole way up the wall, though I guess there are a few things that could offer some cover. The roof has a glass dome over the middle that covers the aquarium. Stairs from the roof go to a stairwell that leads down to the ground floor and below. The doors to the lower levels would definitely be locked, but with some small explosives you could take care of that." Jacen sat up and leaned forward. Paul and Noburu worked on the diagram for a few minutes excitedly.

"I am not crazy about a relatively direct assault, but with all the craft they dispatched from the facility, there may not be many people left there to care. Maybe our best chance of getting into the main building would be the roof access, rather than trying to navigate blindly through the pipe works," Noburu said.

"I agree," Jaycen said, though, truthfully, he was terrified about the whole thing. But he would do it if it meant saving Marin. And if it kept him from having to go through the sewer pipes.

"And it *would* be easier to locate the drains with a quick look at the aquarium. If something goes wrong and we need to get out of there fast, we can always use the pipes as our escape route. At that point, we won't care if we flood the place," Paul stated.

"As a last resort," Noburu added. "The other factors are too great to ignore. If we get caught in a bend, we would be finished."

"Noburu, what do we have in the way of supplies?" Paul asked. Noburu unlocked a case built into the wall with a variety of tools, tanks, wires and packages.

Jaycen frowned. "Is this all we have to work with?"

Noburu raised his eyebrows in surprise. "This sub is designed to help with the construction and maintenance of Arydia and the oil rig. Did you expect us to carry missiles?"

Jaycen shrugged. "I'm not gonna lie, it would have made things a lot easier." Kazu laughed, but Paul and Noburu ignored them, instead looking over the supplies with interest.

"You have a couple of portable O2 acetylene tanks here. Those will come in handy. Do you happen to have any explosives?"

Noburu looked through the case and then dug out a couple of packages of what looked like grey clay bricks from an insulated container.

"Plastique. That's great."

"Think we'd need rope or anything like that?" Jaycen asked Kazu.

Kazu shook his head. "No, the ladder is built into the wall."

"If that's the case, a rope would just slow us down," Paul said. "I think we have what we need."

"Now the next order of business…who's going in?" Noburu asked quietly, looking at Paul and Jaycen.

"I'm not going back there," Kazu suddenly whispered.

Noburu reached a hand over to his son's shoulder and squeezed. "No one is asking you to. Others will go when the time comes." Noburu smiled at him encouragingly.

"I'll go." Jaycen and Paul both said. Kazu looked up, relieved. Noburu made a slight grimace.

"What?" Paul demanded.

"It is just that… if we *do* end up having to use the pipes for an emergency escape, it will be a tight fit. And you are…" Noburu let the end of his sentence dangle in the air, gesturing to Paul's thick waist with his hands.

Paul's face turned red. "I'm what? Fat? Are you saying I'm too fat to rescue my daughter?"

"No, Paul. But if you are honest with yourself, I would be much better at fitting in a tight spot, as would Jaycen and Kazu."

"Father!" Kazu protested, his face blanching, and Noburu put a hand on his son's shoulder.

"I won't ask you to come along, Kazu. I won't risk sending you in there, but I will go. I must do what is right for this mission and give Marin back the freedom she deserves. I owe her that much for bringing you back to me."

Kazu's face clouded over, clearly unhappy that his father was going, but he didn't object further. Jaycen watched him for a moment, wondering if he was okay emotionally or mentally for that matter. The imprisonment and torture he'd endured surely had to have left its mark somewhere one the young man's psyche, but Kazu took a deep breath and nodded his agreement. Jaycen was impressed. *Tough kid*, he thought. Paul was still sitting with his arms crossed, red faced and fuming.

"Out of the four of us, I'm the only one with rescue training. I should go. Besides, the pipes are only a last resort!" Paul muttered, still trying to win the fight.

"It is still a contingency we need to take into consideration. Is there anything you have not told us about the layout of the place that would make a difference?" Noburu asked Kazu.

"Not that I can think of," Kazu admitted. "I didn't have access to much of the compound."

"I wish I'd paid more attention to the water system and layout while I was there," Paul lamented.

"I bet you didn't think you'd be planning an assault on the place at the time," Jaycen joked.

"Be logical, Paul." Noburu cut in. "It doesn't make sense to risk one more member of our group than necessary. We should send the fewest number that can accomplish the job and only those with the highest chance for success."

41

Everyone was quiet, watching Paul, until he reluctantly agreed. Jaycen couldn't help but pity Paul being left behind in the attempt to save Marin's life. But then again, Paul and Kazu might be the only ones alive this time tomorrow. Maybe it was he and Noburu that needed the pity.

"Ok then," Jaycen said, rubbing his hands together with fake enthusiasm, "looks like you and me, Noburu. Let's get ready to infiltrate Leviathan!"

CHAPTER 7

MALCOLM

THE RAGGED, DEFEATED group of Arydians huddled underwater at the foot of a steep slope as Malcolm herded the remaining few stragglers along. They'd had no time or materials to help many of the injured and were forced to leave their dead behind them in the crushed sub. It had been a long trek with wounded and children in tow, but at last they'd made it to the safe house, the last point of retreat they had left on earth. The sense of relief they all felt was palpable.

Malcolm flashed them all an encouraging smile before he left the rest of the Arydians below, swimming up the slope and venturing out of the water and onto the shore. Water dripped from his greying curly hair and he brushed it back from his face impatiently. Though in his fifties, he was strong and intimidating, despite the bandage around his injured arm. The wound still wept pink around the bandage. He crouched behind a rock, waiting, cautious, listening for anything that would signal that their safe house had been compromised.

Campo Este was an abandoned lobster camp on Guadalupe Island, off the coast of Baja, Mexico. This island was sparsely inhabited, mostly by a few villages of fishermen on the northern tip. Trespassing on the island was forbidden by Mexican law. This was nowhere near an ideal safe house, but they had stocked it with provisions as a last option emergency retreat. The abandoned lobster camp was close to the water, isolated and nestled in a cove that afforded protection. Buildings hidden beneath a grove of tall palms provided shelter.

He glanced around one last time and stood up, water still pooling around his bare feet, and crossed the gritty sand until he reached the main building. Carefully, he pushed open the door. The only thing he could hear were the waves and a warm wind shushing through the trees. A layer of fine sand covered everything and Malcolm let out a small sigh of relief. Quickly he searched the remaining buildings, but they all seemed empty and forgotten, the way he and Marcos had seen them last time they had visited. He crossed the bare expanse of the water and dove back under, taking in a deep breath of water and feeling himself sink. The remaining Arydians were huddled in the shallows, fearful.

"*Two great whites are out there*," Emily said, nodding her head towards the open water. Her golden tail glinted in the sun slanting through from the surface. Malcolm still had a hard time reconciling the memory of his old friend and colleague from the AQUA project, Emily, with this transformed and eerily beautiful version in front of him. "*I think they can smell the blood of the wounded.*"

Malcolm frowned. "*I'll get them out and come back for you. We have a small supply of Arydia in the safe house. We can see if it will help you. Be careful while I'm away.*"

She nodded and swam to the back of the group, her long tail swirling up sand around them. He motioned for the others to follow him and they left the danger of the ocean for the danger of the land. They emerged, coughing out water and stumbling across the beach, carrying the wounded, or helping them walk. Malcolm pointed them toward the abandoned village and waited until every one of them were on their way before following them, kicking sand over the footprints they left behind. Once they were safely inside the main building, Malcolm went into a closet and lifted a trapdoor. An older man with a slight limp joined him as Malcolm led the way down a flight of creaking stairs until they emerged in a large, dirt-packed basement. Throwing off a dusty tarp, they searched for the first aid kits, water, and cases of food, and hauled them up the stairs to the others.

"I want the wounded in the back room," Malcolm directed. "Any of you with medical training, please accompany them. The rest of you, we need to get the water supply running. There is a pump behind the main house that should provide enough water for us, but it needs to be primed. As I explained on the way here, we need to be very careful not to be seen from the sea or the air. Most of the fishermen stay well to the north of this area, but you cannot guarantee that. There is a landing strip not far inland from us, so we must be cautious when we are outside also. The trees should cover our activities fairly well, but always listen. And as you might have noticed, this area is very popular with great whites, so do not go to the sea alone. Ever." He cleared his throat, which was scratchy from unuse. It was so much easier to communicate underwater by just directing your thoughts to whomever you were addressing.

"There are several smaller huts behind us, feel free to pick up blankets from the storeroom below us and go choose a place to call home for the time being." He looked around at the room full of miserable people, getting to their feet and shuffling past him to their various areas, his heart aching for them. It was hard for him not to curse the day that his son, Marcos, lured Marin from land to their first home, Portus, showing her their secrets and reuniting her with her family she'd never known. Since that day, everything had gone wrong. She had unwittingly led their enemies down to Portus, their base, where Leviathan's army of monsters created from their loved ones fought the Arydians and destroyed their home. True, they had stopped them and she had healed many. But not his beloved daughter, Katerina. Now Portus was destroyed, and the home he and Marcos and the rest had worked on all these years, was in ruins. He had no idea where Marcos or Marin were now. If they had been on the oil rig when it was attacked, they were surely dead or captured. Knowing the horrific experiments Leviathan inflicted on prisoners, he hoped for their sake they were dead.

He pocketed a syringe and a small glass vial of Arydia from a cabinet, an old shirt and jeans from a weathered duffel bag, then dug around for weapons in a trunk near the wall. Leaning in a corner were some long harpoons. He grabbed one and went back to the water, hoping the sharks hadn't given Emily any trouble.

CHAPTER 8

FRANK

L EVELING OFF IN Chita's luxury jet, Frank nosed closer to the Northern
California coast, hoping he had enough fuel to get him to the mainland. He put on the headphones and waited. Far below him a huge amount
of ships littered the seas, many military, but also several cruise ships, yachts
and even fishing boats that he assumed had been enlisted in the rescue
and cleanup effort taking place down the coast where the earthquake and
tsunami had destroyed Los Angeles and the surrounding areas. The skies
buzzed at lower altitudes with helicopters and single-engine planes and at
higher altitudes with military aircraft and fighter jets defending the coast-
line. Two peeled off from formation and took position on either side of him.
The intercom crackled to life.

"Unidentified aircraft, please identify and state your flight plan
immediately."

Frank leaned forward and cleared his throat. "This is Doctor Douglas
Franklin Gilbert, sole survivor of the terrorist attack on Lanai, requesting
permission to land and to speak with General Robert Holt." He waited
impatiently as the line went quiet, his stress level rising as his fuel level
lowered by a tick. He clicked the comm link again.

"This is Douglas Franklin Gilbert. I am the director of the California

Oceanic Alliance for Science and Technology. Please contact General Robert Holt, he will recognize my name. I have information vital to the military and I am running low on fuel and will need priority landing. Please respond." Silence and static was all he heard. The two fighters stayed tight by his side and a third came up on radar directly behind him. He had no doubt they were awaiting orders whether or not to shoot him down. He swallowed past his dry mouth. Maybe running out of fuel was the least of his worries.

"Unidentified craft, you are cleared to land at Half Moon Bay Airport, California, at the following coordinates. Do not deviate from your course or you will be fired upon."

"I understand. Thank you." He let out a small sigh of relief as he took down the coordinates and tapped them into his navigation system. Now all he had to worry about was running out of gas.

***

Frank let out a deep breath as his wheels touched down in the furthest landing strip in Half Moon Bay airport. The engine sputtered out and died as he coasted and came to a stop in a hangar that was surrounded with a small army of military and emergency vehicles. The radio crackled to life just as he was about to unlock the doors and depressurize the plane.

"Unidentified aircraft, stand by. Do not open doors or you will be fired upon. Please acknowledge."

"Copy," he said into the intercom. He sat back and waited…and waited. It felt like a standoff between the military and a plane full of hostages, not one man with important information sitting alone on a small craft.

"I am going to go use the bathroom. Please don't take my movements as hostile," he said, half- jokingly.

"Understood. Do not open doors and deplane," was the response. He carefully got up and walked to the center of the plane to use the bathroom, then rummaged in the galley for a drink and a sandwich before returning to the cockpit. He'd turned off the A/C and it was getting hot and stuffy, and the wait was getting ridiculous. Still, nobody outside the plane moved and a sea of intimidating weapons were trained on him. He didn't blame them for being cautious. They couldn't know if he had the mutagen on board,

47

or if he was responsible in some way for what had happened in Lanai. But that didn't change the fact that time was ticking and the longer it did, the further out of reach his daughter and Hahn would be.

Finally, his impatience growing, he clicked on the intercom again. "Look, I know you want to be careful, but I have information critical to the safety of the United States and time is of the essence. Plus, it's getting hot in here. Have you made contact with General Holt yet?"

"Please stand by," the voice responded. He waited another twenty minutes before something moved outside his window. He leaned forward, watching apprehensively as a team of heavily armed personnel in hazmat suits moved in close to the plane.

"Have you reached General Holt yet?" he snapped into the radio. Sweat was beading on his forehead. He held the last of his soda can to his face, enjoying its fading coolness, then drank down the final swallow.

"Unidentified craft, open the doors and come down with your hands high above your head. If you make any sudden moves, you will be shot."

Frank depressurized the door with relief and released the steps. A cool burst of air filled the plane and he took a moment to enjoy the relief before putting his hands up and walking carefully down the steps, keenly aware of the amount of firepower aimed at him. The guards surrounded him, guiding him to an armored van waiting with doors wide open. He stepped in and found a seat, surrounded by a dozen armed guards, all glaring at him menacingly through their thick masks. One of them leaned forward and put his hands in handcuffs.

"Is that really necessary? I'm on your side!" he protested. Nobody responded. The doors were closed and the van started moving quickly away from the airplane. Frank tried to lean back and make himself comfortable in the swaying vehicle, but the bumps and turns made it difficult. It was all he could do to not end up in the lap of the person next to him. Finally they came to a stop and the doors opened again. He was ushered into a building and down two flights of stairs and into a room with only a table and a chair that looked exactly like a holding cell. He stopped in his tracks.

"Look, I know why you are doing this, but please, please listen to me. What I have to say is URGENT! I am innocent, and I have information that can save millions of lives. I saw who instigated the attacks on Lanai, and I know who caused the earthquake in California, and if you don't get me to General Holt IMMEDIATELY, he will get away!"

"Step inside, sir," the man closest to him said, his voice muffled by his suit. He lowered his weapon and aimed it at Frank's chest.

"You are making a terrible mistake! Please let me speak to someone. If you can't get in touch with General Holt, find someone else, but I have to speak to someone in charge!" The man poked him with the point of the gun and Frank stepped backwards into the room.

"Please," he begged, tears stinging his eyes, his voice catching. "Please, they have my daughter!" The man paused for a moment and their eyes met. Frank could see compassion in the other's face, but the man shook his head as he backed out of the room, locking him in. He sat down on the chair, crossing his arms as well as he could in handcuffs, put his head down and closed his eyes to wait, glad that at least it was cool in here.

CHAPTER 9

MARCOS

MARCOS WAS SURPRISED to be woken up the next morning by the same woman who had been in his cell the day before with Zar—still wearing a lab coat—but this time without the clipboard and accompanied by two black-clad guards.

"Get up, please," she said, handing him a banana, a plastic wrapped sandwich and a bottle of water. "My name is Dr. Shanna Curtis. I'll be running some experiments over the next few days."

"Before you kill me, you mean?" Marcos added sardonically. The woman pursed her lips but didn't answer. Marcos sighed. "Well, it is preferable to dying of boredom in here. Can I use the um…" he said, nodding to the toilet. He set the food and water on his bunk and Dr. Curtis handed him a cup with a lid.

"Yes, but I need a sample first."

Marcos shrugged and turned his back to them to take care of her request, handing her the filled cup when he was done. "Grab your food and follow me," she said, heading out the door with her sample and her bodyguards.

He followed her out into a long hallway, ripping off the cellophane as he walked and devouring the sandwich within seconds. He handed the cellophane to one of the guards and kept walking, eating the banana and downing the water, handing the peel and empty bottle to the other guard with a smug grin.

"Hey, I have no pockets," Marcos said. The guard grumbled but took the garbage as they made their way into a circular room built around a tall, cylindrical aquarium that looked like it was about ten feet across. A desk ran around the perimeter of the aquarium and served as a workstation for several people. On the outside rim of the room were banks of computer monitors, radar equipment, more workstations, several rows of what looked like built in file cabinets, and about twelve busy looking people.

Marcos whistled appreciatively. "This is quite a beautiful workplace."

Dr. Curtis looked back over her shoulder at him and flashed him a half smile. She stopped in front of a chair where an unshaven overweight man was unwrapping some wires.

"This the guy you've had locked up back there?" he said in an Australian accent, without looking up.

"Yes. This is your subject, Marcos Minas."

"How do you know my name?" Marcos wondered.

"Marin kept asking about you, of course. Take off your shirt please," the woman said curtly.

"Oh." He pulled off his shirt and the man stood and placed several small white buttons, which Marcos assumed were electrodes, on his chest and arms. He covered them with a jellylike substance and a plastic film that clung to his skin.

"This is fun. Are you going to give me my yearly physical?"

The man laughed at him. "Hahn's prisoners don't usually have a sense of humor."

"You have taken everything else from me. Why should I allow you to take that as well?" Marcos asked with a serious face.

"You got a point, kid," the man said. He turned to the woman. "The sensors should give us a good idea of when he changes from air to water." She nodded and handed him the urine sample, which he took reluctantly, wrinkling his nose.

"Get this to someone to analyze it, will you?" he said, passing it off to someone else as soon as they walked past. He picked up his laptop and kept typing on it as they followed Dr. Curtis to a door that led to a stairwell, which they all ascended. After three floors, the man stopped and clapped his laptop shut, wiping his forehead with his free hand.

"I'm not as young as you two," he huffed, though Marcos thought he looked like he was only in his early thirties.

"That spare tire probably doesn't help either, Gary," Dr. Curtis commented.

"Thanks for that," he shot back at her. He grasped the railing and they walked the last few floors in silence. At the top there was another door, this one locked with a keypad. Gary flipped open his computer and typed something. The door opened and a grating within the walls startled Marcos.

"What's that sound?" he asked. They didn't answer. Instead they led him out onto the roof of the building where a large glass dome was sliding away on tracks from the top of what Marcos decided must have been was the aquarium he'd seen from below. It stopped with a bump and the sound ceased.

Two guards came through the doorway and stood on both sides of it, sunglasses reflecting the light of the sun glinting off the sea.

Gary continued typing while Dr. Curtis watched over his shoulder, so Marcos took a moment to look out from this vantage point. He had an amazing view of the ocean from here. Two plastic chairs and an ashtray sat by the wall surrounding the roof. Marcos wondered if this is where people took their cigarette breaks.

He moved slightly to face the water, his back to his captors and whatever they were doing with the aquarium. He took a deep breath, surprised to smell a hint of fall in the air. He couldn't recognize exactly where he was, but it seemed like he was still on the west coast somewhere. Maybe northern California. The feel of the wind on his bare skin and the ocean air made his eyes prickle with longing. He moved quietly to the edge of the building. If he could just make a break for it, maybe he could get to the water before they shot him dead. Even so, he'd rather be shot free than die in that hole they'd been keeping him in down below, punctured and tested like a lab rat.

He made it to the edge and looked down at the sheer drop. There were several balconies below him, facing out to the sea, but the roofs over them were glass and angled towards the ground. They would do nothing but help him on his way down to his death. He took a deep breath, contemplating it anyway, but there was too much at stake. He had to find Marin and save her from Hahn, no matter what the cost. Looking down once again, he knew the answer. This wasn't going to help anyone.

"Going somewhere?" a guard placed his hand on his shoulder and physically moved Marcos away from the edge.

"Just enjoying the view. I do not get out much," he quipped.

"Okay, Marcos, we are ready to begin," Dr. Curtis said expectantly.

He looked at her and shrugged. "Begin what?"

"Get in the water," she said, pointing to the surface of the aquarium, rippling in the breeze.

"Wow, how big is this thing?" Marcos asked, glancing down at the massive tube of water.

"Dr. Hahn was passionate about the ocean and spent much of his time in the aquarium when he was here," the woman said.

"Was?" Marcos asked.

"As you heard, he is no longer part of our organization, unfortunately," she said tersely.

"You sound unhappy about that," Marcos pressed. "Did you have a thing for him?"

Gary chuckled and Dr. Curtis shot him a nasty look. He busied himself with his laptop, so she turned her anger on Marcos.

"Dr. Hahn is a brilliant scientist. Without him, none of this you see would be possible!"

"He is also a murderer and a psychopath. Or did you not read that on his dating profile?"

"Get in the water, smart mouth!"

"Gross. Do you know how many fish have pooped in there?"

She grabbed his arm, a dangerous look in her eye. "Either jump in or they'll throw you in," she said, inclining her head to the guards. "You choose."

Marcos sighed and stepped over to the rim of the aquarium. He was barefoot, so the cool water felt good on his feet as he put them in, twisting his torso and slid the rest of the way in. He tread water, watching them.

"Go under! Breathe!" she said impatiently. He eyed her, rebelliously wondering how on earth they could force him, but he really didn't see the point in protesting and the water was inviting so he sank deep below the surface. He picked the sensors one by one from his chest and arms before letting out his air and breathing in the acidic water around him, relishing the look he imagined would be on Gary's face about now as all his precious sensors went blank. It felt good to be able to swim again. He dove deeper, going through floors of the building, enjoying the illusion of freedom and the odd looks he was getting from people passing by. He kept going till he arrived at the bottom, recognizing the control room where he'd had the sensors placed on him.

He rested on the gravel, alarmed tropical fish fleeing to hide in the rocks and coral, and looked straight up the tube to the blue sky far above him. Eventually, the fish cautiously emerged and flitted around him, sometimes stopping to nibble gently on his skin. Dr. Curtis's head leaned over the edge, beckoning him to come back. Marcos grinned back at her and waved. The look on her face showed she'd finally realized they hadn't thought of a way to remove him from the aquarium. He laughed to himself and circled the bottom slowly, examining the control room to get a better idea of the layout of the building. It looked like there were only two hallways branching off down here, plus the stairway they had come up that led to the roof. Some movement near one area caught his attention and he pressed closer for a better look. An older man was holding the device that Dr. Curtis had said they used to monitor where Hahn was. That would tell him where to find Marin!

The man pointed with the device to a computer display on the wall, discussing it with another man. Marcos tried to get a look at the map they were talking about, but a third person came up and blocked his view, but in that quick glimpse, he saw a dot in the middle of the Pacific Ocean. His heart sank. Finding Marin would be like finding a needle in a haystack. Worse, even, because it was a million times bigger. The older man put the device in a drawer and the screen went blank. Marcos sat in the sand and leaned against the glass, resting his head on his knees. He had no idea how to escape this place, let alone with that device which seemed the only feasible way to find Marin. A rock fell down beside him. He looked up and saw they were dropping gravel from the roof on him, trying to get him to come back up. He laughed to himself, imagining the arguments going on as they tried to figure out how to get him out. If they were dropping rocks, they must be extremely low on ideas.

"*Come get me if you want me so bad!*" he muttered to himself. He waited at the bottom for several minutes and then slowly circled to the other floors, making mental notes as he went. An eel slithered past him and he moved out of its way, eyeing its needle-sharp teeth. The sky above him was beginning to turn dark when divers finally dropped into the water. Marcos sighed to himself. Looked like his field trip was coming to an end. Still, he didn't need to make it easy for them. As they moved closer, he dodged around, much more agile than they were in their cumbersome tanks and gear. They tried to box him in, but he maneuvered around them easily until one of them brought out a device that looked like a wide barreled gun and shot him. Marcos raised his arms defensively, but instead of the bullet he was expecting, he was hit by a net that wrapped around his torso, smashing his arms to his face. The two divers grabbed the net, fastening it so he could barely breathe and started upwards. He felt a prick in his shoulder and realized as his vision began to blur that they had drugged him. Before his eyes closed, he looked up at the darkening sky one more time, wondering if this was the last time he'd ever see it.

CHAPTER 10

MALCOLM

MALCOLM WALKED OUT into the sand, grateful that the sun had passed behind the cliffs and the sand had cooled in anticipation of the night. He waded cautiously out into the waves, then dived under the surf, breathing in the water and calling Emily's name. She responded, swimming to his side. He dug out the syringe and held it out in front of her.

"There is no guarantee this will help you, Emily. It could make things worse, or even kill you!"

"Malcolm, when did you get to be such a pessimist?" She teased.

"I have always been a realist, Emily. You know that."

"Yes, I do. However, you should know I have a theory that if you give me a dose of Arydia, it will act as a sort of jump start to my system, allowing me to go back to the way I was before Hahn experimented on me and turned me into this," she said, gesturing to her tail.

"There's no proof of that. It could just as easily do nothing!"

She laid a hand on his arm. *"Malcolm, this is my area of expertise. Trust my instincts on this one, please?"*

Malcolm scowled, but handed her the dose. *"What am I supposed to tell your daughter if this kills you?"* he muttered. Emily paused and shrugged, then plunged the needle into her bicep.

"Did you grab me some clothes in case this works?" She said, gritting her teeth. He pushed a wet wad of clothing toward her and she slipped on the long shirt just as a spasm of pain curled her into a ball. She let out an inhuman moan, throwing her head back; her hair fanning out around her. Malcolm reached out a hand to steady her, but she jerked out in agony, hitting him in the face. The metallic taste of blood filled his mouth and he shrank back from her, nursing the cut on his lip. *"I'm sorry!"* she gasped, shaking with pain.

"It is nothing. I will just keep watch," he said, as he moved out to the open water where a shark had caught his eye earlier. That made three that he could see. There were probably more on their way. He hoped the blood seeping from his lip wouldn't be enough to embolden them to come in for an attack as he placed himself between the deep water where the cold, black eyes of the sharks were watching them hungrily, and Emily's body, thrashing in the shallows. One came too close for comfort and he thrust his harpoon out, slapping it in warning. It snapped at the weapon, but turned away.

If only Marcos were here. He had such a way with those creatures, he thought wistfully. For a moment, an aching worry filled his heart, but he pushed it back. It did no good to worry about his son, just as it did no good to grieve about his wife and daughter. Pain only served to distract him, and he could not afford to be distracted.

Finally Emily's cries of pain subsided, and he hazarded a glance in her direction. She was floating in the surf, limp and unconscious, her body rolling with the waves. Malcolm raced to her side, cursing himself for letting her try this foolhardy experiment on herself.

"Emily! Emily, can you hear me?" He scooped her up and struggled through the shallows to carry her onto the shore, where he laid her down gently in the damp sand. He felt for a pulse and was relieved to feel its steady thrum beneath his fingertips. He leaned down to hear if she was breathing but didn't hear anything. Had her lungs changed? What if she couldn't breathe air now? He wrestled with indecision and had just started to gather her up to take her back to the sea when she started coughing, spewing water into the sand. He laid her back down and knelt by her side.

"Are you all right, Emily?" After a tense moment of waiting, her eyes fluttered open. She coughed some more and sat up.

"That was....painful. I would really like to never do that again!" They both looked down at where her tail had been and instead saw two legs, still covered in golden scales, sticking out of her overlong shirt with pronounced webbed feet. The spaces between her fingers were slightly webbed as well. She hit the sand in frustration. "Ugh! It didn't work!"

Malcolm raised his eyebrows. "You have your legs. You can breathe. From a practical standpoint, it seems to have worked. Mostly."

Emily rolled her eyes at him. "Would you like to be *mostly* human?"

Malcolm shrugged. "I am sorry. That was very insensitive of me. I simply meant it could have been much worse. You survived; you improved your situation."

Emily shook her head. "No, I don't mean to snap. I just...want to be myself again. The drug I stole from Hahn changed me much more drastically. I thought Arydia would do the same. It was stupid of me to try, given all the things Hahn has done to my DNA. Maybe this is as good as it ever gets. I don't know." She wiped sand off her face. "Help me up. I need to see if these legs even work."

Malcolm lifted her, draping her arm around his shoulders. She put weight on her legs, but struggled as she limped up the beach, as if getting used to walking for the first time.

"Perhaps the blood of your daughter could help. She was able to change the monsters Hahn had created into humans. It seemed to revert things back to their original form. They were human again."

"What?" she said, incredulous, stopping fast in her tracks.

Malcolm glanced up cautiously at the sound of an approaching plane. "We should get under cover. We can talk as we go." Emily nodded and they continued up the beach to the tree line and the huts. He spoke quickly, huffing as they went.

"The hostages that were taken by Leviathan, to ensure we would continue our work, Hahn used his incomplete version of Arydia to change them into monsters, twisting their minds, making them do his bidding." They made it to the cover of the porch stairs and he sat her down and ran in to grab a jacket for her. When he returned, he wrapped it around her wet shoulders, sitting down beside her.

"I was afraid Hahn was doing something like that. When I was his prisoner…" she started, tightening the jacket around her, though it was humid and warm outside.

"You don't have to speak of it, Emily," he said gently. She nodded, putting her head in her hands. Malcolm sat for a while before he continued.

"Hahn used them to attack Portus. They were monsters out of nightmares, human heads, faces, hands…that's when we noticed left pinky fingers missing and realized they were our friends and family that had been taken as hostages all those years ago, transformed and turned against us. Marin was mortally wounded by one of them, but as soon as that creature came in contact with her blood, he became human once more. Your husband understood immediately what had happened and we all retreated to the bay. The monsters followed. Her blood in the water was all it took to change them back to humans. We regained almost all of them."

Emily looked up at him when she heard the catch in his voice. "Almost?"

He swallowed, pursing his lips, waiting a moment before answering. "My Katerina did not survive the transformation."

"I'm so sorry, Malcolm. I can't imagine how awful that must be for you."

Her kind words pricked his heart. Malcolm didn't dare speak, and thankfully, she didn't press him further. After a few moments she cleared her throat and asked another question he dreaded answering.

"Malcolm, what happened to my sister? To Aggie?"

He rubbed his beard, searching for the right words to tell her. She knew Aggie was dead, but not the details. He could barely stomach the details himself, but there was no reason to torture her with the images that haunted him almost as much as the death of his daughter.

"One of the creatures killed her." She waited, expecting more of an explanation. He took a deep breath and went on. "It was Thomas. She recognized his face and let down her guard. The monster that he had become got to her and killed her." Emily's hand went to her mouth, eyes wide with horror. "He was changed by your daughter, but the guilt of what he had done was beyond his ability to cope. He died before we ever left Portus."

"Oh, how horrible!" Emily's eyes overflowed with tears and she hung her head, letting them fall to her lap. Malcolm reached an arm out and put it on her shoulder and she leaned into him, crying, until the sun dimmed and her tears were spent.

"Thank you for telling me the truth, Malcolm. And poor Thomas! He was always such a quiet, gentle man." She looked in his direction, her eyelashes wet with tears. "And I am so, so sorry about Katerina. Sometimes I wonder... if we'd only known the price we would pay... we would have never become involved with the AQUA project!"

"I have often cursed the day, myself. The cost was much too high." They sat in silence for a few minutes, watching the gulls soar over the breakers, dipping down quickly and rising again.

"The only thing that gives me hope is my belief that Leviathan would have found others to do their work," he said. "Maybe others without the courage to withstand them or fight against them as we did." He met her eyes and continued. "Perhaps we were *meant* to work the AQUA project because we were the ones brave enough to fight against them."

Emily nodded thoughtfully, as if pondering his words. He hoped she could draw some measure of comfort and courage from them.

Eventually she stood, dusting the sand from her feet. "I'm going to go wash off and find a place to sleep for the night. See you in the morning, old friend."

Malcolm nodded and let her go, thinking, remembering and wondering, staring at the waves crashing up against the sand until the light was long gone.

CHAPTER 11

JAYCEN

KAZU POINTED OUT the front windows of the sub as they approached the cliffs near Leviathan. "There's the waste pipe. Right there, by that pile of rocks." He brought the sub to a stop with just enough engine power to maintain his position several feet above the ocean floor and a few yards away from the slope that led up to the shore.

Jaycen squinted to see what Kazu was pointing at. "Do you have x-ray vision or something? It all looks the same to me."

"Here, let me put it through thermal imaging." He pushed a couple of buttons and the view on the window changed to varying degrees of red. Billowing clouds of orange seemed to be coming from a now completely visible pipe jutting from the slope.

"Oh, man! Yeah, that's much better. Why does it look like its spewing lava?"

"It's not. It's just showing the temperature difference. I figured the water coming from the facility would be warmer, so I augmented it so it shows up better. It's probably just a few degrees warmer than sea water, but that's enough of a difference."

Jaycen shrugged. "Yeah, good idea. That's...totally what I would have done." He shook his head in disbelief. "Can I ask you a question that may sound seriously dumb?"

Kazu shrugged, so Jaycen went on. "How did you learn all this stuff? I mean, you've spent your life a prisoner of Leviathan, so are you just super smart, or did they teach you?"

Kazu pulled the throttle to a stop and the sub hovered within view of the drainage pipe, but he stayed silent for a few moments. Jaycen regretted asking him the question and was about to apologize but Kazu interrupted him.

"I wasn't held with most of the prisoners. There were a few of us younger ones that were separated from the rest and kept on land, unlike the others that were kept in the submerged cages for large periods of time." His eyes clouded over. "I haven't talked to anyone about this, not even my father. It hurts to even think about it. I just want to move forward and forget, but it's hard, dragging along a past like mine."

Jaycen nodded sympathetically but stayed quiet in case Kazu wanted to talk more, in case he was able to reveal anything else that might help them in their upcoming invasion of Leviathan. Kazu looked out into the water and began again.

"There were a few of us that Hahn took special interest in. There was a redheaded kid named Peter, me, and a girl named Katerina. They taught us, but they also tested us, experimented on us, hurt us. They tested my I.Q. Probably the others as well. Tested my blood, my vision, my hearing. We slept in metal bunks, Peter and I in one room, Katerina in another. It was terrible at first, but after a while, it was all we knew. They made us compete against each other all the time. Games of skill, physical ability, mental ability, bravery. Peter always beat me physically. I always beat him intellectually. And Katerina never beat either one of us at anything."

"Then one day they took Peter away and I never saw him again. But they left Katerina. I wondered why they let her stay. I was terrified that they would take her, too, and leave me alone." Pain shot through Kazu's eyes as he talked about Katerina. "But they didn't. And then, suddenly, things changed and it wasn't so bad. Hahn got interested in some other projects so we were mostly forgotten. We couldn't leave, but we had whatever we needed. And we had each other," he said wistfully.

"Wait, then how did you end up back with the Arydians?" Jaycen asked, confused.

The pain in Kazu's eyes hardened into anger. "Hahn said he was going to end the war and he wanted everyone on the front lines. He took us and some other people I'd never seen before down to the warehouse. He injected us with some chemical and pushed us into the water. It was terrifying! I couldn't breathe or see and every cell in my body was screaming with pain! Something underwater caught me and shoved me into a line of cages built under the docks. I couldn't see Katerina. When the pain stopped, I… wasn't…"

"Human anymore?" Jaycen finished, fascinated.

Kazu nodded and dropped his head as if he were ashamed. "We were kept down there for a long time. Weeks. Then Hahn showed up. He was different, but I could tell it was him. He could breathe underwater like us, but he didn't look like a monster. He told us we had to fight to be free and he had others herd us out into the ocean. I couldn't find Katerina. I doubt she would have recognized me, though."

Kazu shuddered at the memory and Jaycen grimaced. How awful to have your whole face, body, and identity forcibly changed. "So then you were sent to attack Portus?" Jaycen asked, but before Kazu could respond, Jaycen heard footsteps coming toward the cockpit.

Paul swung around the doorframe and asked, "You ready, kid?"

Jaycen nodded and followed him out the door, giving Kazu a sad smile as he left.

CHAPTER 12

MALCOLM

IN THE MORNING Emily seemed to be walking better. She had a determined look in her eye when she brushed past Malcolm and caught his arm.

"Malcolm, we need to talk." He followed her out onto the wide front porch where two rickety rocking chairs sat by a dilapidated table and sat down.

"You're leaving, aren't you?" he guessed.

"I have to. I'm sure Hahn is already moving on his plan."

"You should rest a while first. You've had a lot of changes going on." She nodded. He could see fatigue written all over her face and wondered if she'd slept much or at all. She leaned her head against the back of the chair and closed her eyes.

"Ok, I'll rest for a few minutes, you talk. Tell me more about them, will you, Malcolm?" she asked. Malcolm cleared his throat uncomfortably, recalling the bitter feelings he'd been having against Marin lately. "My daughter. What is she like?" she asked without opening her eyes.

"She is beautiful, just like her mother," he said and caught a hint of a smile on her face. "She has light brown hair, long. My son, Marcos, is completely in love with her."

"And she can heal people. That's about all I know about her," she finished for him. He was glad her eyes were still closed and couldn't see the expression clouding his face. She could heal. Just not everybody. Just not Katerina. He swallowed back the lump in his throat and forced his voice into a calm tone.

"Yes, that, and other abilities we hadn't quite figured out yet," he said. Emily opened her eyes and leaned forward, resting her elbows on the table.

"Other abilities?" she asked. Malcolm nodded.

"Like I told you, she was near the brink of death, torn almost in half by one of Hahn's monsters, but yet she healed herself within a few hours. She is also able to communicate underwater on a different level. She can actually perceive others' thoughts as if she is in their mind and communicate her thoughts and feelings by touch as well."

"Telepathy?" Emily asked, astounded.

"Not quite. I'm not sure what to call it and I am unsure if it only happens underwater. I suppose if she is able to do it out of the water, then telepathy would be an accurate name for it. Frank was doing several tests on her to try to learn more about her condition, but there hadn't been time for much."

Emily looked thoughtful, leaning back into her chair and rocking back and forth. "There is a theory that certain animals and insects can communicate on frequencies unknown to mankind, sensing the feelings and instincts of others, and acting on them as if one mind. Like when a flock of birds all rise into the air at the same time, as if one sensed danger and they all could feel it," she said, her eyes sparking with interest. "And if it *is* a frequency, touch would definitely amplify it."

"Fascinating," Malcolm agreed.

"What was the last you heard from them?" she asked, though she thought she knew the answer.

"Right before we left to search for Aaron," he said. "We split up when Aaron left and discovered Jaycen had taken a vial of the drug with him, presumably to find his mother and change her into an Arydian. Most of us went after Aaron, and you saw what happened. Paul, Noboru and his son, Kazu, went after Jaycen in the smaller sub."

"Why did Aaron leave in the first place?"

Malcolm stroked his beard and leaned back in the creaky chair, wondering why he was the lucky guy to break all the bad news to Emily.

"He seemed to have gone crazy after Aggie died. He stabbed my Marcos before we left Portus, then tried to choke Marin to death later on. We had no way to lock him up, and he left, presumably to go to Leviathan. He told your daughter he'd been hearing voices calling to him all his life."

Emily looked uncomfortable. "The man that rescued me from Hahn, he saw them working on Aaron. He said they had a network of wires embedded in his head and Hahn repaired it. It sounds to me like this poor boy was a trap set by Hahn, using the child as some kind of transmitter/receiver to find all of you, only the transmitter somehow was broken or removed."

Malcolm frowned deeply. "I wonder if Aggie knew about this and if she did, why did she keep it from us? She took the boy as her own the moment we found him."

"I'm not surprised. I know she and Thomas wanted children desperately. I'd like to say I can't believe Hahn would stoop so low, but I know well how absolutely evil he is. And whether my sister knew or not, I doubt we'll ever know." She shook her head. "The man I mentioned also thought Hahn turned Aaron into the creature that attacked your sub," she whispered. "I think he's correct."

"Poor boy," Malcolm murmured.

"Wait just a second," she said, walking into the building. She returned with the backpack she had been carrying with her since she'd left Nathan Greer.

"We…" she said, stopping herself, a shadow crossing her face, but she shook it off and continued, "We found this on the beach at Isla Cedros. I also saw a photo a local girl took of Marin. The girl said there was a boy-friend with her as well. I wish I had the picture to show you. You could have told me if it was them or not." She unzipped it and dumped out all the contents on the table between them. "I believe Marcos and Marin left this there before they were picked up by the monster, Aaron." Malcolm picked up the objects and inspected them carefully while Emily rummaged through all the pockets of the backpack, adding to the pile.

"Yes, this is Marco's knife!" he exclaimed.

"So, we know they survived the attack on the oil rig," Emily said.

"But why would they have been on that island? If they'd had any warning, Frank would have certainly sent them away," Malcolm agreed. "Why wouldn't he have sent them here? To the safe house?"

"Maybe they were looking for you?" Emily guessed, and Malcolm nodded. "Wouldn't they have contacted you, though?"

Malcolm shrugged, puzzled. "We never heard from them. Even if Frank gave them directions to find my group and they somehow weren't able to make contact...why would they end up on Isla Cedros?" Malcolm stated uncertainly.

"They could have been chased there by the creature. Aaron," she suggested.

Malcolm nodded. "That makes sense. After we left, the only contact we had from anybody was with Paul, saying they had arrived in California and were going on land to search for Jaycen."

"Paul? Who is he?" Emily asked.

Malcolm smiled. "He is the Landy who raised your daughter." She frowned and he reached out a hand and placed it over hers. "I'm sorry if that pains you. I do not know him well, but he seems a very good man." He squeezed her hand reassuringly and she gave him a weak smile. "He is one of us now."

"And who is this Jaycen that ran off to save his mother?"

"He is Marcos and Marin's age, and is very much in love with your daughter as well."

Emily rolled her eyes. "Teenagers!" Malcolm laughed heartily. "Do you have the last coordinates of Paul's sub?" she asked. "I may be able to find them and enlist their help."

"Where do you think you're headed?" Malcolm asked.

"It seems like the best option would be to try to find them and head up to Oregon, to Leviathan. I would bet that is where they were taken."

"First of all, they moved their facility to San Francisco ages ago," he said.

"Well, that's good. Much closer."

"Second of all, what do you plan to do once you get there? Storm the castle?"

Emily stuffed the items back into the backpack, minus the packets of Marcos and Marin's clothes. "I'm not sure, but I can do more there than I could here. I have to at least try. Surely you understand that."

"I do. I will help you gather supplies for our trip." Malcolm rose and stretched.

Emily glanced at him with a look of relief. "Our trip? You'll come too?"

"Of course. You knew I would. My son was taken by the monster as well."

CHAPTER 13

FRANK

OVER THE LAST few hours, Frank had been subjected to a full body x-ray, urinalysis, skin and throat swab, plus had been passed over not once, but twice, with some version of a Geiger counter and had what felt like several pints of blood samples taken. They had finally left him alone, exhausted and impatient.

He had no idea how long he had been sitting there with his head resting on his crossed arms, but now his left hand was completely numb. He shook it as two men walked into the room flanked by armed guards. Everyone wore hazmat suits. A chair was brought in and placed on the opposite side of the table and one man sat down on it. He had an air of authority about him. Probably the local commander of whatever base they had taken him to.

"It's not contagious. The suits are unnecessary," Frank said dryly.

"How can you be sure of that?" the man behind the desk asked.

"For the fortieth time, I saw the formula. I know its source. It's an airborne mutagen with about a three hour half-life."

"And how do you know this? Did you develop it?"

"No, but I know who did. I need to speak directly with General Holt."

"Why him? If your information is so important, it seems like you would want to get the word out to anyone who would listen."

"I don't trust anyone but him."

"Why him?" the man pressed. "Do you know him personally? Have you ever even met him?"

"No, all I know is that he is on our side."

"What side is that?" he asked, folding his gloved hands in front of him.

"The side that wants to protect the lives of everyone on this continent! The side that will sacrifice everything to keep terrorists and murderers from taking over our world!" Frank slapped his hands on the desk in frustration. "My daughter was kidnapped by the man who did this to the country. Every moment I waste here with you is a mile farther he is taking her away from me." He put his hands out on the table in front of him. "I beg you; please let me talk to General Holt immediately."

"How did you survive the attack? If you give us some straight answers, then we'll see about contacting the General."

Frank hung his head and let out a long sigh. "I don't know if I can trust anyone with this information. People will kill for what I know. People *have* killed for what I know."

"How about we start with the results from your blood test and x-ray?" the man said, sliding a paper over the desk to him. "Tell me, Dr. Gilbert, how did you survive the attack on Lanai?"

Frank looked up and met his eyes, not knowing how much he could or should tell this man. The man signaled to the rest of the people in the room and they filed out, one by one, locking the door behind them. It was just the two of them now. Frank relented and began to speak in a low voice.

"My daughter and I were prisoners of Leviathan. Chita Vasquez brought us along to an exchange between herself and Dr. Hahn because she wanted me to verify if the chemical formula of the mutagen Hahn had created was real. Hahn gave Chita Vasquez a copy of the formula, which she showed to me. It seemed legit. Then Chita's phone rang with a message that really shook her up. She accused Hahn of moving too early, but Hahn double crossed her. He had planted containers of the mutagen all around the island and had a vial of it with him. He broke the vial and detonated the mutagen, infecting everyone and everything on the island, including me and my daughter. I was choking and dying, just like Chita Vasquez, and I assume everyone else. That's when Hahn grabbed my daughter and jumped in the water, I was already starting to black out. I fell in the river after them and that's all I remember."

"Jumped in the water." The man looked hard at him, unbelief in his eyes. "Why would he do that?"

Frank bit his lip. Not only would the story he told sound absolutely crazy, but it would put everyone he loved at risk. He had guarded this secret for so long, it felt wrong to tell anyone about it, especially this stranger in front of him. He glanced down at the information in front of him. They knew he wasn't...quite human. The die was already cast. And besides, at this point, there was much more at stake than risking the peaceful lives of the Arydians. Leviathan had found them anyway. Frank took in a deep breath and leaned back against the chair.

"Fifteen years ago, I was recruited to be part of a program to find a way to change people's DNA so they could breathe underwater. It was called AQUA and was funded by Leviathan; a wealthy global organization that we thought was interested in science and humanity. Dr. Hahn was part of this program, as was the woman that became my wife.

As we made progress on this program, it became clear to some members of our group that the goal of Leviathan wasn't the betterment of the world, but the domination of it. Leviathan was a front for an international group of warmongers and terrorists that have been meddling in politics and business for years, and Dr. Hahn was one of the ringleaders behind it. We had come far enough in our research that, for the safety of everyone, we stole our research from the AQUA program and destroyed the facility in Oregon. We transformed ourselves using the drug, Arydia, which we had developed, and took our knowledge with us to the bottom of the ocean."

Frank looked at the man, wondering how long it would be until he called the rest back in and locked him up in the psych ward, but his expression was unreadable.

"So, you're telling me you are some kind of fish-guy and you live in the ocean," the man said flatly.

"No, I'm an Arydian, a product of genetic manipulation. My body has developed the ability to breathe underwater. My lungs are totally different from yours."

The man frowned, looking over Frank with a furrowed brow. "Right. So you have, what? Gills?"

Frank leaned forward and pointed awkwardly with his chained hands to a place behind his ear, partially hidden by his overgrown hair. The man leaned forward and inspected the lines on Frank's neck with a gloved hand. Frank turned his head to the other side to expose the twin lines behind his other ear and then sat back. "If you don't believe me, try to drown me. I'll take the test." The man didn't react so Frank kept talking.

"Hahn created his own version of Arydia which he called Mizu, but it didn't work as well. It relied too heavily on the DNA varieties he used and the subjects became unstable, taking on the characteristics of whatever samples he'd used. For instance, if he'd used shark DNA, the result would be a shark-like hybrid."

The man blinked slowly in disbelief. "And now you're talking about turning people into monsters?"

"Essentially, yes. Arydians can come and go on land or sea, but the unfortunate creatures Hahn experimented on are trapped in their forms and kept underwater. Still, he got part of what they were looking for. They really only wanted to have access to the ocean for the control it would give them on land." He took a deep breath and continued.

"Hahn devised ways to make these monsters comply with his wishes and they found our base near Point Mugu Naval Base. Hahn destroyed it with a missile, which is what triggered the San Andreas Fault."

"That's quite a fairy tale. And what does it have to do with how you survived the attack on Lanai?"

Frank shrugged. "I'm not sure how I survived. I woke up this morning floating in the river alive, while everything else was dead."

"Convenient that you don't remember the one piece of information we need."

Frank's eyes hardened. "I'm not going to make up details I have no knowledge of."

"You're a smart man. Speculate about it."

"Fine. Obviously it poisons or suffocates the victim. Maybe my lungs are different enough that it didn't affect me as badly. That's the best I can figure out."

They stared at each other for a moment, the man seeming to be evaluating Frank and whether or not he believed him.

"What time did all this happen? The meeting on the bridge, the text this woman, Chita, received…"

Frank tried to remember. "It had to be around noon." He folded his arms, his temper rising. "I've told you enough. I'm not speaking another word until I see General Holt."

The man reached down next to his feet and pulled out a paper folder which contained several photographs and pointed to one that appeared to be a set of rungs embedded in solid rock, and another one containing a large screen TV and a refrigerator sitting in a pile of rocks under the ocean.

"Do any of these things look familiar to you, Dr. Gilbert?"

Frank looked the photographs over and then pushed them back towards the man. "What you are looking at is the remains of our base by Point Mugu. We called it Portus. I can give you the coordinates this was taken, or at least an approximate, if that will help verify my story. 34° north 119° west."

The man looked down at one of the papers in his hand and raised his eyebrows in surprise, then set down his folder on the table and removed his mask and gloves. He had greying hair and a square jaw. He reached into a pocket, retrieving a key which he used to remove the handcuffs from Frank's wrists. He then put out his hand. Frank dubiously shook it.

"I am Sergeant Major Peter Bale. I've been assigned to work with General Holt, whom you will meet shortly. Doctor, I have been investigating you and your people and their connection to the California earthquake since it happened and you disappeared off a ship in the vicinity of the explosion." The man paused, and lowered his voice to barely a whisper.

"Do you happen to know the whereabouts of Jaycen Webb? Is he…one of you?"

Frank blinked in surprise. "Yes. He is 'one of us.' I gave him the Arydia to save him from drowning. No, I have no idea where he is now. I'm afraid he took off shortly after the earthquake to try to find his mother. Why?"

"We can discuss that later." The man unzipped the rest of his hazmat suit and peeled it off awkwardly. Frank waited patiently until the man emerged in full uniform and produced his identification which Frank examined before handing it back to him.

"You're in luck, so to speak," Bale stated. "We have learned that so far there were seven other survivors of the attack at Lanai-all of them were in the water when the attack hit and survived as you did. They reported passing out while swimming and waking up washed up on the beach." Frank nodded in relief; glad at least a few had made it. Bale continued speaking.

"I have a million questions about all this, but I'm going to stick with the pressing ones right now. We picked up a transmission shortly before noon yesterday. I'm assuming this was the notification Chita also received on her phone and adds credence to your story. It was sent to all the major governments of the world as far as we know. It claimed that the world would soon be unified under one banner and that the countries that did not comply and submit to the rule of this new entity would be destroyed by a new weapon that was about to be deployed in America to show the unquestionable power the new regime possessed. We at the pentagon had barely enough time to read this ultimatum before reports started coming in that something happened in Hawaii. We put the country on high alert. Five minutes later we learned that Lanai had gone dark." The Sergeant Major shifted in his seat and sighed. "It is signed by our new 'overlord', Emperor Hahn."

"Wow, ambitious little jerk," Frank said, barely containing his disgust.

"Apparently. But given the massive wipeout of Lanai, there is serious talk about listening to his demands."

Frank rubbed his wrists where the cuffs had been and weighed the ramifications of what Hahn was claiming.

"It's obvious from Lanai that he's got the means of delivery for the mutagen," Frank said. "Warheads or ICBMs of some kind."

"And if he has access to the deep water off any of our coasts, he could plant devices right under our noses and we couldn't do anything to locate, let alone disarm them," the Sergeant Major finished for him.

"I need to get in contact with my people. Can I have access to a radio?"

"That depends. Are your people loyal to the United States of America?"

Frank sighed, knowing the answer he was about to give wasn't the one this man wanted to hear. "We were recruited from various countries, so we are not all citizens of America, no. We have all voluntarily left our homelands and, for all intents and purposes, we are our own nation. The Arydian Nation."

"Well then, that may be a problem."

"I figured it would. But take this into consideration. The Arydians have lived peacefully and quietly for fifteen years inside the borders of one of your military bases. We are only interested in our colony peacefully surviving in this new, under-discovered frontier we live in."

"Forgive my skepticism, but that is your word on it. From the government's point of view, it seems odd you would decide to live inside a military base when there is the entire ocean to choose from. Unless, of course, you were using that close proximity to spy on us."

Frank blinked in surprise. "Spy on you? Why would we need or want to do that?"

"If you were in league with Hahn. Or any of the many radical groups that would like to see America brought to its knees. And you seem to have been successful, given the attack on California and now Hawaii."

Frank grew heated. "You think we are terrorists?" he shouted in disbelief. "Look, the reason we chose to build Portus so close to Point Mugu had nothing to do with what was *on land*, but rather what was *under the ocean*. The geological formations there were perfect living conditions for shielding us from detection as well as providing geothermal energy. And it was always thought of as a temporary home while we built a permanent one, much farther away. That's why it's called Portus, even. It means a temporary harbor. A safe place to stay for *a while*."

The Sergeant Major was silent, apparently weighing what Frank was saying, his expression stern. Finally, he spoke. "Believe me; I want to trust you, for more reasons than you know. But give me a reason why *our government* should."

"As a leader of these people, and an American Citizen myself, I can promise you that we have the same interest in stopping Hahn that you do."

"Would your people be willing to prove this claim?"

"How?" Frank said skeptically.

"Cooperate with us in finding Hahn and destroying any warheads he may have planted."

"That's not just cooperating...you are asking us to do all the heavy lifting for this! We are scientists and civilians, not trained combatants."

"Understood, but if Hahn *has* moved ahead with his plan, I'm sure he's deeper in the ocean than we can go. You might be our only hope with this."

Frank was silent for a few minutes as he considered, then slowly nodded. "Okay. If we agree to do everything we can to help you, I have two conditions."

"I'm listening,"

"You have to help me rescue my daughter from Hahn *first*. I'll need help locating him and extracting her. Then I don't care at all what you do to him, as long as she is safe with me."

"I'll do my best. What's the second condition?"

"You leave my people alone when this is done. You destroy the tests you ran on me and swear to keep us a secret. No experimenting, no blood tests, no pressing for the formula, nobody knows who we are and we keep it that way."

"The people helping you will have to know, Doctor, as well as my line of command."

"I understand, but seeing how this is the government, I'm sure you can figure out something."

"Agreed. Follow me," the man replied, scooping the pictures into his folder and leading Frank from the room.

CHAPTER 14

MARIN

THE NEXT SEVERAL hours were a blur to Marin. It was impossible to be comfortable with her arm dangling over her, swaying with every move of the submarine. She desperately wanted to sleep, to get away from the pain and fear of her new reality, but the moment she drifted off, they would wake her again, unhook her arm, and slide it into a portable x-ray machine. The first two times they did this, she would feel throbbing pain with every movement, but after a while the pain became numbness, and then she couldn't feel much at all, other than annoyance for being disturbed. Hahn didn't return for several cycles of this, and she fell into a half sleep daze, ignoring every hiss of the opening door until even the touch of the people incessantly messing with her arm stopped rousing her. Then she heard *his* voice.

"Well, my dear, you certainly do live up to your reputation!" Hahn said loudly, snapping her fully awake. She shrank back from him into the alcove, part of her mind registering numbly that the contraption had been removed from her hand at some point.

"Now, now, don't be shy," he chided, reaching into the bunk to take her hand. He looked over her wrist, then bent it forward and backward. Marin drew in her breath, expecting to feel a jab of pain, but, surprisingly, it didn't hurt. He poked the area where the break was, but she felt nothing but the pressure of his finger. He took it in both hands and squeezed the area, feeling the bones through her flesh. Still, it only felt uncomfortable because of the pressure, but didn't hurt. Not like it had. She rotated her wrist in awe.

"Give me your other arm."

She did, too awestruck to even hesitate. He moved her hand back and forth, testing her extension.

"How does it feel?" he asked.

"It feels…fine!" she said. "How long have I been out?"

"Just a few hours. The break knit together within a half hour and was completely healed within two. At that point, there was no point for further tests on your arm. The results were conclusive. If I hadn't set the bones myself, I would quite honestly not have believed it. You, my dear, are even more astounding than your mother!"

"My mother?"

"It took her over twice as long to mend bones, depending on the size. Her small finger bones took longer than this did. It was almost eight hours for her to heal her femur."

At first, Marin couldn't wrap her head around what Hahn was saying. When she figured it out, her heart froze in her chest. Was this the life she had ahead of her? To have her bones broken one by one so Hahn could time her rate of healing? She withdrew her hand from his grasp, horror in her eyes. He ignored her and picked up his tablet, scrolling through her x-rays, occasionally pausing to magnify an image. "Astounding," he repeated to himself. "At this rate I could almost watch you heal!" He turned his eyes to her hungrily. "You are the most valuable person on this planet, Marin. Your body holds the cure to almost everything!" He moved closer to her and brushed a hand over her head, holding onto a few strands of her hair. She cringed away from his touch and he tightened his fingers around the hairs and pulled.

"Ow!" she cried out involuntarily.

"I need samples. Blood, saliva, urine," he said almost to himself. He wound the hairs into a small, clear dish and set them on a counter.

"You have become the one thing that I most desire," he said, talking to her in a quiet murmur. "Your mother could only heal herself. You can cure others!" He whispered the last bit, so she could barely hear him, as if it was a secret that only he knew. He scooted his chair closer to her alcove as if he wanted to confide in her, though no one else was in the small room.

"Do you recall the man that dropped you?" he asked. Marin nodded slowly. "The wound I gave him, remember that? And your blood...I dropped some of your precious blood onto his wound?" Again, she nodded her head. Hahn grinned, his pointy teeth making her withdraw further away. "He was better within mere minutes!" Marin let out a small sigh of relief that the man was okay.

"It is true! You were worth everything I went through to acquire you!" He looked giddy with joy. She stared at him, not knowing where he was going with this information. Hahn caught the look in her eye and scowled. "Don't you see, girl? You are going to heal me!" He held up his hand in front of her face, his fingers splayed to show a thin, greenish membrane, like the webbing on a frog's feet stretching between them. She tried to hide her disgust.

"The boy said you healed my creations. You changed them back to human. Is this true?" he asked, leaning into the alcove eagerly.

"Yes. They said I did," she said shakily.

"What do you mean? Don't you know?" he demanded.

"I was hurt. Your guy Dave had almost chewed me in half!" she shot back at him. Hahn sat back and considered.

"What happened to Dave? That idiot I sent to capture you," he asked impatiently.

Dave. He'd been a friend of Paul's. She'd known him for years, never knowing he was a tool of Leviathan, until he brought her and Jaycen down in the mini sub to deliver her to his masters. Jaycen almost died that day. The sub took on water and he'd drowned, and if her father hadn't come and given him his special dose of Arydia, he would have died down there. Dave had voluntarily taken Leviathan's imitation form of Arydia, which allowed him to breathe underwater, but made him take on the traits of the animal it was derived from, in this case a tiger shark.

"Well, like I said, he...he bit me. I guess he got some of my blood in him, and it healed him back to what he was. And when he changed back, he drowned."

Hahn smiled. "What a suitable ending for the fool. And what about the rest of them?"

"The rest of them?"

Hahn slammed his hand down on the nearest counter, making her jump. "The others! The army I sent to destroy your group of traitors?"

"I don't remember. Dave hurt me really bad and I was out of it."

Hahn's eyes glittered dangerously as he lowered his voice to a sinister whisper. "Surely someone told you what happened to them."

Marin nodded. "I...I was bleeding and they let my blood go into the water where they were trapped. They all changed. "

"So, they breathed in your blood? Drank it? How? Mixed with water?" he asked, picking up a notebook and scribbling words feverishly. She shrugged, but he didn't pay attention, instead talking to himself as he wrote.

"So exposure of some sort to your blood healed these people back to their normal, human shape?" he asked. She nodded. "Could they still breathe water?" She shook her head.

"No, they had to be given a dose of Arydia again. Some didn't want to take it. So they are just human, I guess.

"Have you ever healed anyone else this way?"

She thought of Marcos, bleeding to death after Aaron had stabbed him. She had cut her arm and bled directly into his wound, and he had survived. But she didn't want to tell him anything about Marcos. And she definitely didn't want him cutting her.

"Well?" he shouted impatiently.

"I healed Dave before." She remembered suddenly. "Dave pricked my finger on the ship and it healed his cracked hands."

"The boy said some didn't survive. I need to know about them."

"What boy?" she asked.

"Your cousin, the leviathan, Aaron!" he said impatiently. "Tell me about those that died."

She tried to remember. Things had happened so fast and they left so quickly, and she was wounded and not really paying attention to who had died or not. All she knew was Marcos's sister was one of those that didn't. "It's true. Some didn't survive the change."

"How many?" he demanded.

"Two or three?" she guessed. "I don't know for sure. I don't really know anything. I'm not sure why it didn't work with them."

Hahn held his hand up in front of him, his fingers spread wide.

"Would your blood heal me?" he asked almost to himself. "Or would it kill me, like those others?" Marin didn't answer, her heart beating hard in her chest. Hahn frowned and for a minute she was afraid he would lash out at her, but his expression resolved and he leaned back and crossed his arms.

"Very well, I have the subject; I will just experiment until I'm sure it is safe."

He thought for a few moments, then brought out a syringe and several vials and started taking blood samples. Marin looked away. Then he offered her a drink, the first she'd had in as long as she could remember. She took the straw in her hands and drank it down gratefully.

"You are too dehydrated." She handed him back the cup and he set it down distastefully before he stood up, walking to the door. "I will send you more." He turned his back on her and walked out the door as another man walked in.

Marin stared at the roof of her bunk cubicle while the new man x-rayed her arm yet again. The pain may have been gone, but her despair settled like a poison in her soul. Her father, Frank, was most likely dead. Marcos was gone, probably dead. Who knew where Jaycen was, and Paul was off looking for him. She swallowed back the aching feeling of hopelessness. Anyone who knew what happened to her was dead and nobody else would know where to begin to look. She felt like she'd been swallowed by a whale, carried off into the depths, never to see the light of day again.

CHAPTER 15

MARCOS

NOBODY CAME TO check on or feed Marcos for two days. During the first day, he didn't care much. Whatever they had knocked him out with had left him feeling sick and groggy, so he'd stayed huddled in bed feeling miserable. By the morning of the second day, though, the effects had worn off and his hunger was back with a vengeance. His stomach growled incessantly, like an angry animal. To take his mind off it, he did pushups and sit ups until he got so thirsty, he almost dunked his head in the corner toilet for relief. Instead, he lay back on his bed and let his mind wander to Marin. He tried to imagine every line of her face, even the little freckle below her left ear that he bet she didn't know about. Worry gnawed at his insides almost as badly as hunger did, but he forced himself to believe she was still alive. She had to be alive! And somehow, he would find her. When he did, he would never let her go again.

At the end of the second day, he was feeling incredibly weak. It was hard to keep a rational line of thought. Had he pushed Dr. Curtis too far that his punishment was going to be death by dehydration? No, he thought. He figured he was getting to the point where the toilet water was looking pretty good, but lack of food…that was going to be the killer. As he contemplated the grim aspects of starving to death, the door opened again. Three guards entered and flanked the doorway. Marcos noticed it was always the same guards that came to his room and wondered if they were short staffed or if they just never let the guards go home. A moment later, Greg walked in.

"If it isn't my good friend, Greg. Did you bring me a pizza?"

Greg chuckled. "You still have your humor. That's good. As a matter of fact, I did bring something for you." He turned to the guards. "Hold him down." Marcos backed away from them on his bunk crouching like a panther. As they surrounded the bed and reached for him, Marcos kicked against the wall shooting towards them, knocking the closest one over and rolling between the feet of the other two. Greg let out a gurgled yelp.

"Grab him!"

Surprised that it actually worked, Marcos scrambled for the open door-way. He was out the door and halfway to his feet when he was tackled outside by a fourth guard he hadn't seen before. He fell hard to the ground as the guard smashed his face into the rough carpet in the hallway. He could feel his feet and hands being grabbed by the guards in the room. Greg walked into the hall.

"Hold him down, we'll do it out here," he said, squatting down in front of Marcos. "Keep his head still." Two hands pushed down on his head pain-fully. He could barely breathe, let alone move. Greg took a syringe out and brandished it in front of Marcos's face, grinning maliciously, then injected something behind Marco's ear.

"What are you doing to me?" Marcos demanded.

"It's a fabulous invention of Hahn's. A tiny little electrode inserted at just the right place that will activate all the pain receptors in your brain at the same time. I'm just making it easier to control you. Don't worry, this will be fun. You'll see." Greg laughed. "Let him up."

The guards let go and Marcos got cautiously to his feet, rubbing the injection site with a worried look on his face.

"Ok, let's give this a shot," Greg said. "Let me see...um...Marcos, I want you to...kiss my shoe." He lifted up his tattered, untied sneaker and waved it under his nose.

Marcos looked at him in disgust. "You can kiss my..."

"Now, now. I mean it," he interrupted. "Kiss my shoe." This time he pulled out a small remote control device and pushed a button. Instantly, the room started to spin and a lightning bolt of pain shot through Marcos's head, dropping him to his knees screaming. He grabbed his head, hoping to hold the pieces of it together. There was no way there could be that much pain without something exploding in his brain. Then, abruptly, the pain ceased. Marcos still held his head as if afraid it would fall apart again, but slowly let go and looked up at Greg, who was smiling with satisfaction.

"I said, kiss my shoe. The left one. Right there in front of you." Greg wiggled his filthy shoe again beneath Marcos's face.

Fury built in Marcos's soul and he rose to his feet, balling his fist. "You creepy little…"

Greg pushed the button again, sending Marcos to the floor writhing in agony. He let go of the button, then pushed it again and again, each time a little longer until Marcos thought for sure he would die, he wanted to die, anything to stop the pain, anything!

"Kiss. My. Foot." Greg said, accentuating each word with a sting from his device. Marcos couldn't stand it anymore. He had to die; it couldn't go on!

"I said, kiss my foot. That's all you have to do and the pain will stop."

"NO!" Marcos screamed, the pain engulfing him. Nothing would stop it! He thrashed in the hallway, trying to escape the torture, but it did nothing. Finally, Greg took his finger off the button. Marcos lay in the hallway panting, sweat streaming from his face. He didn't dare move for fear the pain would come again.

"Kiss my foot," Greg said softly. "It's not a big deal. Just do it and I'll leave you alone."

Marcos opened his eyes, looking up at the hardened faces surrounding him, searching for any sign of sympathy or mercy and finding none. How could they all be so sick and cruel?

"What's wrong with you people?" Marcos whispered. Greg raised his finger to the button again, waiting. Marcos looked at Greg's shoe in disgust, then spat on it. The pain started again, smashing him against the wall. His screams echoed through the hallway, drawing spectators to watch the show. This time, Greg held the button while Marcos rolled around on his back, clawing at his head in animalistic instinct to stop the agony. His whole world was the pain, throbbing through every cell in his brain, burning like fire through his body.

"Stop it! Kill me, just kill me!" he sobbed. The pain stopped, but Greg held his finger close as he leaned over Marcos sneering.

"Kiss. My. Foot!" he yelled.

Marcos rolled over, tears of pain and shame coursing down his face. He touched his lips to Greg's shoe and fell back to the ground sobbing. Greg smiled in satisfaction.

"Throw him back inside. I think he understands me now, don't you, Marcos?"

The guards heaved him onto the bunk, but Greg hit the button one last time as he walked out.

"Don't forget who won," Greg said just before the door slid closed and the lock clicked. Marcos held his head, rocking back and forth until exhaustion took over and he fell into blissful oblivion.

CHAPTER 16

PRESIDENT THOMPSON

GENERAL HOLT SHUFFLED his papers after the security briefing as the rest of the Security Council left the room in small groups. He watched President Thompson out of the corner of his eye, hoping if he waited long enough, he could catch him alone before he got up to leave. A group of self-important people crowded around him, asking his advice or offering their own to the current crisis they were facing as a nation. The group started moving towards the door and he could see his opportunity was disappearing. He stood, taking the room in three big strides to intercept them.

"Mr. President, could I speak to you alone for a moment?" he said. His voice was deep and he didn't need to speak loudly to be heard over everyone else's conversations. President Thompson nodded and smiled apologetically to the people around him as they left him alone, except for the Chief of Staff who stood stubbornly by his side, and Zarobi, an imposing man that seemed to watch everything the President did with intense interest.

"Alone, please, Judy, Zarobi," General Holt said angrily. Lately that woman never left his side, or that doctor, for that matter. It might have been his imagination, but for just a moment Judy and Zarobi shared a meaningful look, as if communicating silently, but he quickly turned his back to her and walked out.

The President gestured the Chief of Staff towards the door. She shot General Holt a poisonous glare before turning on her sickly-sweet smile.

"Remember we have a meeting in a moment, Mr. President. I don't want you to be late," she said as the door closed behind her.

"What is it General?" the President asked.

General Holt frowned slightly. He and John Thompson had been friends for over thirty years. He almost always called him by his first name when they were alone. "I'm sorry, John, but you don't seem yourself lately. Is everything all right?"

"Sure, sure it is, General. Why do you ask?"

"Martial law? I didn't think you would be in favor of something that drastic."

There was a slight pause before the President answered. He'd been doing that fairly often during the meeting, as if he needed extra time to process answers. General Holt's concern deepened. "It's an unwanted but necessary step to keep the people safe."

"Are you sure you are feeling alright?" The General asked again, touching his friend's arm. He leaned in close, lowering his voice. "Are you in some sort of trouble? Do you need help?"

The President looked up quickly. "Help," he whispered breathlessly, staring into his eyes with an intensity that chilled the General to the core. Then, suddenly he twitched as if stung by something and the look was gone. "Help?" he asked with a casual laugh. "Who wouldn't need help in times like these, huh?" he started walking them both to the door. "I'm just glad our country has the likes of you to depend on. I've got to make a phone call, but thank you for your concern, General Holt."

CHAPTER 17

MARIN

MARIN CLENCHED HER teeth, refusing to scream as Hahn drew a scalpel slowly across her forearm. Out of the corner of her eye she could see a line of red welling up and oozing out of her skin. She closed her eyes tightly and tried to think of being anywhere but where she was. She could hear as Hahn dropped the blade and started his stopwatch.

She felt warm blood trickling down the side of her arm, and a washcloth swiped below her wound as Hahn wiped it quickly so he could better view her arm as the blood began to congeal. Never in her life had she imagined anyone could be so cold and evil. In her worst nightmares she couldn't believe people like this could exist on the same planet she lived on. Her arm ached where he'd sliced her. Tick, tick tick…Hahn's stopwatch echoed off the walls of the medical area which had become her room and torture chamber, tapping off the seconds until she healed.

Paul always told her never to panic; people who survived were the ones who kept their head. But how was she not supposed to panic? There was nothing she could do to stop this!

She tried to think of something else, anything to not be here in this room with this monster, but all she could think of was Marcos and wondering if he was alive was almost as painful to bear. She cried a silent prayer that Hahn would stop, that someone would find her, and that Marcos was okay, wherever he was. Her thoughts turned to Jaycen, hoping to find better thoughts to distract her. At least he was free and hopefully safe. She hoped he'd found his mother, that he'd healed her with the vial of Arydia he'd stolen. She tried to concentrate on details so her brain couldn't dwell on the cut in her arm. She remembered the blue of his eyes, the way his hair would fly in the wind. His tan skin and his sideways smile. How was it possible to feel so strongly about two different people? Marcos was so mysterious and sad, Jaycen so confident, yet so vulnerable. Away from them both it was a little easier to look at them in her memory…to try to diffuse the feelings she felt for them. She noticed delving into her conflicted feelings distracted her from the pain of the present fairly well.

"Forty-nine seconds! Impressive. Let's try again, only a little deeper," Hahn said hungrily. Marin grit her teeth and pushed her mind deeper into her memories. Kissing Marcos for the first time underwater and feeling the rush of emotions that connected them as if—she gasped as the fire in her arm grew, but she forced her mind away from it—connected them as if they had known each other all their lives. Memories would flood together when she touched him, creating closeness that was unbelievable and surprising to both of them. The closeness was intoxicating. She could feel his thoughts underwater. Most of them, anyway. It created a bond between them that she missed, like an amputated limb when they were separated. It was something she loved, she craved, but also feared. What if she never saw Marcos again? Would she ever be able to recreate that closeness with someone else?

And what about Jaycen? She thought of his false bravado that had turned her off when she first met him months ago at the beginning of their summer internship at COAST. He was so full of himself; with all the girls in the program falling all over themselves to get his attention, yet all he seemed interested in was her, the moody girl trying to overcome her overwhelming fear of drowning. He was the reason she discovered what she was. He was there the day she was trapped underwater and drowned but didn't die—when she learned she could breathe underwater. There was a steadiness to him that drew her like a moth to a flame. And even though Jaycen could breathe water like Marcos now, for her Marcos still represented the dark, beautiful, moving depths of the sea, and Jaycen was like the sand and the sun, constant and stable. Sea and land: two different elements, two parts of the earth, two sides to her own personality. No wonder it was so hard to choose between them.

"Sixty-three seconds! I'm going to do several now at varying depths and compare." The pain in her arm was gone. Just a tingle remained. But that wouldn't last long. It never did.

He came towards her.

She shrieked in agony as he drew the scalpel across her forearm again and again. She needed to think of something painful to take her away from all this.

"Jaycen!" she screamed, tears coursing down her cheeks as the blade bit deeply into her flesh. Jaycen. She went to the most painful memories. Jaycen kissing her goodbye, leaving her to go back to California to try to save his mother from the earthquake and the devastation. It broke her heart, but she loved him even more because of it. She thought of Aaron, her cousin, as he struck at her with a knife, wanting to kill her for exposing his people to Leviathan. Marcos had taken that knife wound for her and almost died because of it. She cut her arm herself and bled into his wound, trying to save him with whatever magic was inside her blood. She could feel that knife wound on her arm now. She told herself she was back in the sub, trying to save Marcos. The slices came relentlessly over and over again until the memories weren't enough to protect her. Fear and rage combined, building until she couldn't contain it anymore.

"STOP IT!" she shrieked, jerking away from the scalpel. Hahn stepped back, the sadistic look on his face replaced with surprise. He put down the blade and left the room, not even bothering to watch her wounds heal. She stared at the door, shocked that he had left so abruptly, holding her breath for him to come back, but the door remained closed. She cradled her lacerated arm against her chest, curling into a protective ball in the corner of her bed and screamed until her voice cracked and the walls of the room rang.

CHAPTER 18

MARCOS

FOOD WAS FORCED through the slot in the bottom of the door, waking Marcos. He rolled off the bed and crawled over, not even bothering to pick up the tray. He ate every scrap without even tasting it, his hungry stomach cramping around the food like it was a foreign substance. Two bottles of warm water went down his parched throat next, tasting like heaven. He lay back on the cold cement floor listening to his stomach working uncomfortably, eyes closed, dreading the next time anyone would open the door to his cell. He didn't have to wait long.

A half an hour later, Greg came in, smiling at Marcos, followed by three guards and Dr. Curtis.

"Take off your shirt, kid," Greg demanded. "You know the drill."

Once his shirt was tossed on the bed, the guards grabbed Marcos's arms and pinned them behind his back. Marcos felt panic clutching his heart, not daring to imagine what horrible pain they intended to inflict on him now. Dr. Curtis took out a syringe and drew a blood sample from his left arm without a word and the guards relaxed their grip. Greg took white buttons out of his pocket and started placing them once again on Marcos's arms and torso.

"Let me guess, another field trip?" Marcos asked through clenched teeth.

Greg glared at him. "This time the sensors stay on. And you come up the second we signal you, got it?" Greg brandished the device that had caused Marcos such agony. Marcos tried to shoot back something flippant, but the thought of Greg pushing that button again stopped him.

"Good boy. Let's go. Don't try anything stupid or you'll be on the floor crying again." Greg sneered.

Marcos followed in silence as they made their way up the flights of stairs leading back to the roof. Despite the apprehension he had about Greg using his pain button again, he couldn't help but feel a small dose of relief at the simple joy of being able to be outside again. The sky was overcast this time and rain was in the air; the wind blew in from the mountains, heavy with the scent of desert grasses and sage. He breathed in the heady aroma, closing his eyes and imagining himself anywhere but here with these heartless people bent on experimenting on him until the game got old and they killed him. Dr. Curtis grabbed his arm and pointed to the open aquarium, jerking him out of his brief fantasy of freedom. He nodded, and got up on the rim with both feet. He stood for a moment, then jumped, flipping himself into a cannonball and landing on his back, sending a splashing wave over his captors. He didn't bother to wait around for their reaction, swimming towards the bottom as fast as he could, hoping if he got enough distance between himself and the transmitter that it wouldn't work.

He was wrong. A blaze of pain stopped him in his tracks and he curled into a ball, arms wrapped around his head, all thoughts of rebellion gone, replaced by the white hot poker melting his brain. Abruptly the pain stopped and he slid down the glass wall until he landed with a puff of sand. He drew in ragged breaths of water, not daring to unclench his hands from around his head, waiting for the pain to return. He didn't swim anywhere this time, instead, he just lay in a heap at the bottom, feeling utterly miserable and helpless. Several minutes passed before he finally ventured to look up above him. Dr. Curtis was motioning for him to return. His first inclination was to ignore her, but the thought of the pain brought him reluctantly to the top. He was happy to note that both Greg and Dr. Curtis seemed at least damp from his cannonball stunt, but Greg was nodding in satisfaction anyway. "You see, Shanna, I told you my way would work."

Dr. Curtis shrugged reluctantly as Marcos climbed out of the water, shivering in the cold wind that had begun to blow. He wrapped his arms around himself for warmth. Greg looked at Marcos and snarled, "This is for getting the back of my laptop wet!" Marcos put his hands out in front of him as if he could ward off the next moment, but Greg pushed the button sending Marcos to the ground, writhing on the gravel covered rooftop. The pain seemed to go on forever, and Marcos hurt so badly he couldn't even draw a breath to scream. Then it ended. He lay there panting until one of the guards hauled him shakily to his feet. Greg put the device in his pocket and went on talking to Dr. Curtis like nothing happened.

"I got all the readings you wanted. And nobody had to go in after him."

"I still think that method is awful," she said with a shiver as they closed the glass dome and headed down the stairs. "I hated how they used it on that teenager."

"But necessary when you have to break someone. And even though we have no way of registering this guy's level of compliance like Hahn could with the boy, the effect is still the same. Think of how effective implants like these could be in other areas?" Gary gestured with one hand, clearly pleased with the torture device he possessed. "Like politics! Or in business! Or relationships, even," he said with a creepy smile. "You could bend the will of anyone to do what you wanted."

Dr. Curtis glared at him, obviously uncomfortable with his thoughts. "Yes, until the charge on the implant wears out. Then what?"

Gary rolled his eyes as if dealing with an idiot, gesturing at Marcos as he answered her. "Really? You want to discuss this in front of a prisoner?" He shook his head in disbelief. "All we have to do is inject them again. Easy."

Marcos tried to stay quiet as they descended, his head still echoing with a ghost of the pain he'd endured and his stomach turning at the thought of the power sick people like this possessed. They stopped at Gary's workstation long enough for him to wipe down his computer with a paper towel and pick up his can of soda. Water pooled around Marcos's feet into the carpet. It was cold in here with the air conditioner on. His head was clearing, but he didn't dare make eye contact for fear of provoking another episode with Greg.

"Take him back to his room," Dr. Curtis commanded the guards. "I'm going to go get something dry on."

The guards led him down the hall and pushed him inside, locking the door behind them. Marcos took off his wet pants and put on his shirt before he crawled under his thin blanket, praying for some miracle to save him from the purgatory of his existence.

CHAPTER 19

JAYCEN

JAYCEN AND NOBURU sat with their feet dangling into the water in the sub's aft port. Kazu looked in and gave his father a thumbs up and then left. Paul handed an acetylene welder and tank to Noburu and gave each of them a small pack of explosives, wires, and a detonator.

"I'm still ticked that you think I'm too fat to help out!" he said, glaring at them both.

"You're not fat, Paul." Noburu chuckled. "Think of yourself as sturdy."

"Yeah, you're just a little fluffy!" Jaycen added, laughing out loud. Paul growled at them both. "Besides, you *will* be helping. You are our getaway driver."

Paul twitched his mouth sideways. "Whatever. You two be careful now. Keep in contact and…" he paused, suddenly serious. "Please save my daughter. Godspeed to you both."

Noburu strapped on the welding tank and they slid into the water, both of them grabbing a portable water jet from the ledge before sinking into the darkness of the ocean. It was late at night, a time when they had all agreed most people would be gone from the facility, so the water was black as ink. Still, Jaycen was surprised at how well he could see. He shrugged it off as another bonus of being part fish now. He filled his lungs with water, feeling himself sink below the sub, following the light of Noburu's head-lamp towards the rocky shore.

"How are you doing?" Noburu's voice sounded in his head. Jaycen shrugged. Then a thought hit him.

"When we talk like this, underwater, how far does it travel? Can anyone hear me?" He said, his hope surging that maybe he could shout and Marin would somehow hear him wherever she was. If she was being held in the sea, that is.

"Not terribly far. But well enough for us to communicate for this mission. Think of it like your voice. You can speak at different volumes, even yell and everyone in your vicinity will hear you. But, unlike your voice, you can talk to just one person and only they can hear you."

"Oh." He said, disappointed. *"That makes sense."*

They left the water jets near the drainage pipe from Leviathan's aquariums and swam up into the dark night, stroking silently along the surface until the shore became too shallow and they had to emerge into the cool night.

Thunder rolled in the distance and a cool breeze lifted goosebumps along Jaycen's arms and legs. Jaycen easily pulled himself onto a wooden walkway over the water, but when Noburu tried to follow, the oxygen tank and the acetylene welder slid off his shoulder and hit the wood with a resounding clang. They froze, Noburu half hanging off the pier, their hearts stuck in their throats, waiting for lights or gunshots or shouts, but nothing happened. With a quiet sigh of relief, Noburu finished pulling himself onto the rough deck and stood.

A large building extended from the cliff into the bay, presumably housing boats and other equipment, similar to COAST. Except COAST was now a pile of rubble, thanks to these people, Jaycen thought angrily.

A huge cutter, prickly with antennas and radar equipment, was tethered to the dock, bobbing with the lapping waves. Jaycen wondered why it had been left behind when it seemed almost all the other vehicles Leviathan owned were gone. He didn't have time to worry about it now, though. They walked quickly down the dock towards the shore, their wet dive shoes squelching too noisily on the wooden planks. Two piers straddled the boathouse and a boardwalk led from them up to a set of steep and rickety wooden steps built into the cliff wall.

Noburu nodded to the building and whispered, "Doesn't look like many people use that stairway. There's probably an elevator up to the top inside that building."

"Let me guess, we're not going to take it."

"Correct." They moved to the steps and started up, twisting back and forth on the switchbacks until they came to a latched wooden gate at the top of the stairs. Noburu knelt down and inspected it for any sort of sensors, but not finding any, he shrugged and they both hopped over it. In the darkness they could barely see the wide, round shapes of the open-air aquariums. They looked more like waist high horse arenas until they got closer and Jaycen peeked over the edge. They were filled with water.

Ahead, Jaycen could see the main offices that Paul had sketched for them. It was a beautiful round building, five stories high with a wide, covered patio on the bottom floor dotted with chairs and tables with closed umbrellas sticking out of them. Each floor had a balcony surrounding it, overlooking the aquariums and courtyard and probably sporting a fabulous view of the sea from every level. It seemed Paul had given them a fairly accurate description of the place, which made him feel a little more confident. Beyond the main building were many smaller buildings and several warehouses. He could just make out the main gate close to the passing lights of the coastal highway.

"Man, this place is big. I hope we don't have to search every one of these buildings," Jaycen whispered. Noburu didn't answer. They paused at every noise they heard, pressing themselves against the cold Plexiglas of the aquariums, but so far it looked like they hadn't been noticed.

"We need to head to the right of the building. The ladder to the roof access should be there," Noburu whispered. They veered to the right and were almost to the building when suddenly floodlights snapped on, blinding them in pure white light. Sirens sounded from everywhere, blaring loudly into their brains.

"Run!" Noburu commanded as they both took off as fast as they could. They reached a covered patio of the building and dove behind a row of decorative hedges just as footsteps rounded the corner on the left side and spread out to search for them. They kept low, hugging the building, looking frantically for the access point.

"There!" Jaycen hissed, grabbing Noburu's arm. A closet sized enclosure twenty feet ahead of them had caged ladder rungs coming out of the top, rising straight up the side of the building. They stood up and ran for it, grabbing the door, but it was padlocked shut. Noburu spun Jaycen around and frantically dug in his backpack, finally producing a chunk of clay and some wires. He jabbed a small blob into the lock and shoved a wire connection into it.

"Wait, won't they hear this?" Jaycen asked in a panic.

"Definitely. How fast can you climb?"

"With people shooting at me? I guess pretty fast."

"Good. Plug your ears and get ready." They ducked around the side of the closet and Noburu pushed a button. A sharp crack, loud as a gunshot, echoed between the buildings. Jaycen turned in time to see the door spin drunkenly off its hinges and clatter to the ground.

"Go, go, go!" Noburu shouted into his ringing ear. He leapt into the dark, smoke-filled room and grabbed hold of the bottom rung, pulling himself rapidly upwards. He could hear Noburu's breath and knew he was close behind him. He rose above the little closet and out into the exposed open air, expecting to be shot at any moment, adrenalin propelling him forward as fast as he could. He reached the third level before his forearms started burning from the vertical climb. He hazarded a glance at the courtyard below and saw a dozen armed guards swarming around the building. This side of the building wasn't as brightly lit as the other one, but it couldn't be long before someone thought to look up and they would be done for. He reached the fourth level, sweat dripping into his eyes, when he heard Noburu slip, hitting the ladder hard. Jaycen glanced back, afraid to see Noburu falling into space, but he had caught himself and was hanging tightly to the rungs with one hand. A wave of vertigo hit Jaycen as he looked down the sheer height of the building they were scaling. He swallowed it back, concentrating on Noburu.

"You ok?" he called down.

"Yes, go, keep going!"

Movement caught his attention farther below where a group was gathering around the broken door. Almost in slow motion, one of them looked up, following the ladder until he met Jaycen's eyes. Jaycen turned to face the wall and raced up the ladder with a surge of adrenalin, straining to get to the top floor before his hands gave out or the shots started coming.

"They're headed to the roof! Send a team up there!" voices shouted from below. His heart was pounding in his ears so hard he could barely hear them. Sweat was making his hands slick and his next grab slipped. For one terrifying moment, he swung out to one side, held only by one hand, but he caught himself and Noburu grabbed one of his feet and guided it back onto the steps. He didn't even slow down, but continued upwards just as a piece of concrete exploded where he had just been hanging. Another shot hit above him, sending a spray of grit into his eyes. He closed them and kept going, concentrating on putting one hand above the next as fast as humanly possible. A shot rang off the rung he was holding, sending vibrations jolting through his hand. He shook it off and kept climbing as fast as he could to the top of the rungs. More gunshots echoed around him and he heard a sickening wet *thunk* below him. Noburu shouted in pain.

"Noburu!" Jaycen called, not daring to look, in case the older man fell.

"I'm fine, keep going! We're almost there!"

CHAPTER 20

MARIN

Hours later, Hahn returned. Marin watched him move around the equipment, picking things up and setting them back down distractedly. She tried to steel herself for whatever was coming next, but Hahn didn't come near her. As he left, he glanced over to her and their eyes met. A jolt of hatred and disgust for him shot through her eyes and for a moment she caught a strange look on his face, one she had never seen before. It almost looked like he was…afraid.

She lay awake on her bunk, puzzled by what she saw. Why on earth would a man with no conscience, or even a soul for all she could tell, be afraid of her? She had nothing she could hurt him with. She rolled over, her now healed arm tucked under her cheek, and tried to find a peaceful memory to hold onto so that maybe she could go to sleep. In her mind she found the perfect memory. She was on the beach at Isla Cedros the night before she and Marcos were captured by Leviathan. The steady thrum of the submarine engine became in her mind the rhythmic pulse of the ocean surf. Darkness surrounded them, except for little lights bobbing from fishing boats out in the bay and the moon glowing high overhead. The air was warm and humid, the sand soft beneath her feet. She found the more details she could remember, the more vivid she could build up her memories, the greater power those memories had to take her away from the horror of the here and now. She imagined the water reaching out to cover their footsteps behind them. Marcos held her hand as they talked.

They discussed their ability to connect underwater, and she told him about research she had done on animals communicating telepathically and empathically, even to the point of changing emotions around them. She had tried to make him angry at her to see if she could do it, too, but she was feeling too calm and peaceful at the time and only succeeded in drawing him closer to her. The memory made her smile, but in the back of her mind, something important kept nagging at her, but she couldn't put her finger on it.

She tried to remember the rest of their conversation. She was worried that maybe he didn't love her as much as he thought he did, that maybe she had some power that was making him care more about her than he would on his own. He'd laughed at her, but it really bothered her. She had been afraid she had the power to affect his emotions.

She sat up in the bunk and swung her legs off the edge. Though she was chained to the wall by one wrist, she stood up and paced back and forth beside her bed. She thought empathetic power was negative—like changing how people felt so you couldn't trust what was real. That's what had disturbed her when thinking about using it on Marco, that maybe he loved her because she was putting those feelings in his heart.

But if this power *was* real, could she use it to change the feelings of people around her, to use it as a weapon? She paced faster. What if her outburst earlier today to stop Hahn was a push from that power within her? For the first time in days, she felt a surge of hope. Maybe it was insane, improbable, desperate, but maybe not! There was a lot about herself she didn't know! If someone would have told her last year that she wouldn't be afraid of water ever again, she would have called them crazy. Nature didn't leave anything unprotected. Even snails had ways to escape enemies. Maybe this new species, the Arydians, came with its own brand of defense. And she even more so, since she was the first and only one born to Arydian parents. She nodded to herself, feeling the black pit of despair in her stomach morph into a hard rock of determination.

It was time to do some experimenting of her own.

***

It was impossible to tell time in the submarine, except for a clock above the door that was hidden in the dark. Still, it felt like it should be morning. Not that it mattered, she hadn't slept much anyway. Sounds outside Marin's cell-like room showed increased activity. She waited in her bunk alcove impatiently. Finally, a short, thick man entered Marin's room carrying a tray with food on it. She kept her eyes closed, following his movements in her mind by the sound of his footsteps.

When he got closer to her, she pressed outward with her feelings, willing him to feel what she wanted him to feel. Pity. He set down the tray and moved next to the bed, checking the heart rate monitor and oxygen sensor attached to her. She cracked her eyes just a fraction of an inch to see if it was having any effect. He watched her and she creased her forehead with exertion. *Pity. Me.* If he could have enough pity, maybe he would help her escape. He walked to the wall and unlocked the length of chain holding her there. Hope surged in her heart, but she tried to keep up the waves of pity she was throwing at him.

"Get up," the man growled. She rolled to her side and climbed out of the bunk, looking up at the man expectantly. "Time to clean up. Go to the bathroom and stuff." Her hopes fell and she trudged after the man, leading her down the hall by her chain like a dog. He stopped outside the bathroom door and let her go inside while he waited with the door partially closed awkwardly around the clunky chain. She rinsed her mouth out with water to get the stale feeling out of it. She used the bathroom, trying not to think of the creepy guy just two feet away, then washed her face and arms with a washcloth hanging by the sink. The man tugged at her chain.

"Come on," he said impatiently. She dropped the washcloth and left the small bathroom behind to follow the man. He chained her back up in her room without a single comment. She sat back down on the bunk and tried not to fall back down into the well of hopelessness. Experiment one: failure.

She spent the rest of her day dreading every time the door opened, fearing it would signal another torture session, but so far it had only been for two meals and three bathroom breaks. When Hahn finally did come in later in the evening, she backed into the alcove as if hiding from a monster. He pulled a chair next to her bed and sat down.

"Be at ease, Marin. I'm not here to hurt you. This time." She turned to her side to face him. He seemed relaxed, wearing a white button front shirt with the top two buttons undone and pressed gray slacks. He leaned back in his chair and rolled a vial of blood between his fingers. "Tell me, how does this blood thing of yours work?"

"I…I don't know what you are asking."

Hahn sighed in exasperation and set the vial down on a metal tray, then leaned forward, rubbing his hands on his slacks. "I have an idea for another experiment." Marin shied away from him, fear squeezing her heart like a fist, her eyes glued to him in mounting terror. He pushed up the sleeve up on his own left arm and picked up a clean scalpel. She wrapped her arms close to her, willing him away, but he didn't come any nearer. Instead, he cut a small line in his *own* forearm.

"My, that does hurt, doesn't it?" he said, giving her a mocking grimace. She glared at him in answer. He pulled the stopper off the top of the vial of blood and poured a drop onto his cut, letting it drip down the length of his incision, blending with his own blood. He tipped the vial back up and pushed the stopper back into it. Then he leaned back into the chair watching with interest.

"You see, Marin, it finally occurred to me that I could gauge whether your blood would kill me or heal me by this one simple experiment. I had been looking beyond the mark, trying to match up blood type factors or genes or DNA that could predict whether your blood would be effective on me, when all I needed to do was perform this simple exercise." He waited another couple of moments, then took a cotton ball and started dabbing at his cut. He winced. The cut wasn't healed. At least not yet. Marin smiled in satisfaction. At least hers wasn't the only failed experiment of the day. Hahn frowned, glancing up at Marin for an explanation. She shrugged, giving him a sweet, sarcastic smile and he stood up, kicking the tray over and shattering the vial of blood on the floor, storming out the door.

CHAPTER 21

JAYCEN

JAYCEN REACHED UP for the next rung but grasped only air. He opened his eyes and to his immense relief, he'd reached the top. He hauled himself over the side onto the roof, bullets pinging around him. Noburu reached up a hand and Jaycen grabbed it, dragging the man onto the roof with him. Blood was splattered over Noburu's chest; he was panting and sweat beaded across his forehead.

"Oh, no. No, no, no. Are you ok?"

Noburu held his shoulder, grimacing. "We aren't going to be able to make it down the stairs like we planned," he said through gritted teeth.

"What do we do?" Jaycen asked.

"Get out the Plastique. Quickly!"

Jaycen swung his backpack off his shoulders and grabbed out another blob of the clay while Noburu searched with his one good hand in his pack for more wires. He pulled them out and gave them to Jaycen, fingers slick with dark blood.

"Over there. On the dome," Noburu gasped, shoving his backpack back together and putting it over his good shoulder. Jaycen ran to the huge glass dome that looked down into the central aquarium that Paul had told them about. He spread the clay out and inserted the wire, stringing it out as he dashed back to Noburu. Noburu attached it to a detonator just as a door flew open, spilling guards onto the roof, guns trained on both Jaycen and Noburu.

"Drop it! Hands in the air!" One man shouted. Noburu paused a moment, meeting Jaycen's eye, and with an imperceptible nod, he pushed the button. Immediately, the glass dome exploded into a cloud of shards, flying into the guards and sending them stumbling backwards to the doorway. Jaycen's back was turned, but shrapnel hit his legs and back like a thousand bee stings. Noburu, mostly sheltered from the blast by Jaycen, pushed Jaycen forwards, towards the smoking gap in the dome just as the guards started to regroup. Jaycen and Noburu dove in, blindly falling until they hit the water hard and sank, scattering startled fish in every direction. Jaycen took in a breath of salty water, noticing a trail of red fanning out from Noburu's shoulder where he'd been shot.

"You're losing a lot of blood." he said. *"We need to put some pressure on it to stop the bleeding."*

Noburu nodded and shifted the backpack onto his wounded shoulder, tightening the strap with a grimace. *"This will have to do for now. It's not as bad as it looks. I think the bullet went straight through. It hurts, but it won't kill me."*

A bullet flew down between them in a streak of silvery blue. The guards were firing at them from above. They dove as fast as they could, keeping to the edges of the tank. Jaycen tried to count the floors they passed, but he lost track dodging bullets. Suddenly the gunfire stopped and he wondered if someone in charge had finally realized what a bad idea it would be to shoot a hole in the tank. They continued to swim downward past dark hallways, occasionally seeing people outside looking in at them in surprise as they passed out of sight. Finally, they hit the sandy floor and looked out into the heart of Leviathan headquarters. It was a circular control room surrounded by computer consoles and monitors of every kind, with two hallways branching out from it. The rooms outside were dim, but still there were several people working, all of them pointing at them and gesturing in alarm. They could hear the muffled sound of the intruder alert blaring through the compound.

"Look!" Noburu said as he pointed to a filter vent in the bottom of the aquarium wall. *"I would imagine the drainage equipment is down this hallway. That is where we may need to go if this gets worse. Last resort. Remember which hallway it is."*

"Okay great, but where would Marin be?"

"Down the other hallway?" Noburu guessed. Guards crowded into the room outside the glass with guns pointed at them, although they didn't look like they had any good ideas about how to catch them. One woman came close to the glass as if examining them. She pointed to them and spoke to one of the guards.

The man's eyes narrowed and Jaycen read the word Arydians on his lips as he said it out loud. Jaycen scowled at him.

"Got any more explosives on you?" Jaycen asked.

"Working on it," Noburu answered. He plugged the wires into the clay and slapped it onto the glass wall in front of them. It took a millisecond for the people outside to realize what was going to happen. When they did, their eyes opened wide in disbelief and panic and they scrambled for the exit. Noburu gave them a moment to clear the room before he pushed the button. Water belched out a cloud, knocking them backwards before the thick glass wall exploded outward, spilling tons of water, countless fish, and two Arydians into the control room.

CHAPTER 22

MARCOS

MARCOS WAS STARVING. He had hardly moved from his cot since his last swim in the aquarium and his muscles were stiff from unuse. Plus, he felt like he would never be warm again. The sound of a tray of food scraping through the door seemed like a dream. He wasn't sure if it was day or night anymore. He lay there, staring at the food tray, his mind so fatigued from hunger that it took several minutes for his muddy thoughts to accept that the food was indeed real and waiting for him. He crawled over to the door and ripped open the packaging containing some kind of meat, soup, a roll and soggy steamed carrots. He crammed the food in his mouth so fast he barely had time to taste any of it. He drank the hot soup, not even caring that it burned his mouth. The meat was tough and chewy, but he wolfed it down, licking the plate clean. He picked up the tray, making sure to find every crumb or drop and eat it, then he held the tray to his chest and closed his eyes, relishing the exquisite feeling of being full.

The dim light that filtered in through a grate in the wall gave little to see by, but he turned the tray around and looked at his reflection mirrored in the silver metal. His beard was getting full, his hair long. With a shock, he realized he looked like a younger, much thinner version of his father. Hollows around his eyes made him think he'd lost a lot of weight since he'd been here, but how much he had no idea. The one pair of pants he'd been captured in were fitting him loosely. His shirt was getting ratty and was thin to begin with. He ran his fingers through his hair and tried to take out the worst of the tangles in it, wondering if Marin would even recognize him if she were to see him like this.

As the food started to digest, his mind slowly began working again. He felt like he was awakening from a long nightmare, though truthfully, he still didn't know how to escape from it. Something Dr. Curtis said nagged at the back of his mind. He closed his eyes, trying to remember why anything she said would matter. She was as complicit in his captivity and torture as the rest of them, even if she wasn't the one pushing the button.

It was something about the implant they injected him with. He felt around the injection site, hoping if there was a lump there that maybe he could get it out, but he couldn't feel anything out of the ordinary. Implant batteries wearing out, that was what she had mentioned! And Gary said they could just inject him again. But how long did he have to survive the torture before it went out?

Suddenly, a sound pierced the quiet of his cell. A faint popping sound, like fireworks coming from somewhere above him. He got to his feet, straining to hear, but the sound stopped. His hopes soared for a moment that maybe, somehow, someone was coming to rescue him, but he didn't dare hope for long. Nobody knew he was here. It was probably some maintenance being done, like someone hammering. He sat back down in his stupor of misery when he heard a shout outside. He stood, pressing his ear to the door. He could hear muffled yelling coming from the control room down the hall. His heart pounded in his throat. Something was happening! Anything that made those unhuman beasts that worked here unhappy was great in his book.

A deafening crack shook the building and the air pressure around him suddenly changed, like a wind from nowhere blasted down the hallway and through the rooms. He felt something wet at his feet and reached down to feel water gushing under the door. The flap where they slid in food was being pushed wide open by a torrent of water. He backed up, completely confused. He heard screaming out in the hallway, things bumping his door and hitting the wall, probably pushed by the flood. It was already rising to his knees. He took the tray and hit it repeatedly against the door.

"Help! Hey, I'm in here! Let me out!" He shouted at the top of his lungs. He doubted anyone would hear him. The door was thick and felt like it almost absorbed sound, but he beat it anyway. Suddenly the door opened a crack and he shouted out in elation, but with a loud snapping sound, the door froze and all light was gone. He'd thought his cell was dark before, but now it was absolute pitch blackness, as if his eyes had just shorted out. It took him a second to realize the power was out. The water was rising higher, pouring now through the cracked door as well. He dunked his head under and took a deep breath of water. The taste of it was salty and acidic. It was the aquarium. He didn't dare believe someone was coming to rescue him, but he couldn't stop himself from hoping. He pushed against the door as hard as he could.

CHAPTER 23

JAYCEN

THE WATER PUSHED them down the hall in a maelstrom of papers, office chairs and displaced tropical fish. Noburu caught himself on a doorway, but Jaycen tumbled to the end of the hall and slammed into the wall before he was able to find his feet. The water was quickly rising. A few of the doors swung open, pushed by the pressure of the water, and he sloshed his way past, checking each one, and finding mostly more offices.

One room he passed held several tanks with strange things floating in them, their tops just barely above the rising water level, but he gave them no more than a curious glance before he moved quickly on, opening every unopened door until he hit one that looked different than the rest and was locked. Marin! He thought he could hear banging on the other side of it and so he struggled to open it, kicking at it, but to no avail. Noburu swam up to him, his wet hair plastered to his forehead, carrying a key card on a black lanyard.

"Think this will come in handy?" he asked with a grin. Jaycen took a deep breath and went underwater, swiping it over a keypad next to the door. The keypad blinked green and the door started to slide open, but suddenly the power went out and the door stopped. He stood back up in the sheer blackness, the water nearing his neck.

"What happened?"

"Maybe the water has done something to the power," Noburu guessed. They both flipped on the lights of their headlamps.

"Can you help me pry this open?" Jaycen cried, grabbing the door once again. He felt the brush of fingertips from the other side and drew back in shock.

Someone *was* locked in there. It *had* to be Marin! The water was too high to bother standing in, so he ducked under and worked his fingers into the crack, braced his feet against the doorframe and pushed with all his might. He felt the hands from the other side grab onto the door and try to slide it open as well. Noburu joined him with his one good arm and, straining together, the door slid open enough for someone to get through. They held it, grunting with effort, and Jaycen yelled in his mind, hoping she could hear him, "*Get out, I can't hold it much longer!*"

Golden brown hair drifted out of the gap illuminated by his headlamp. Jaycen's heart leapt with triumphant joy until he saw the ragged, bearded face attached to it.

Marcos squeezed out and pushed himself into the hallway. Jaycen let go of the door and it slid shut with a muffled thump, barely missing Marcos's foot.

"*You!*" He shouted accusingly. The disappointment was more than he could bear. How could the person he wanted to see most be replaced with the last person he wanted to see? He couldn't even wrap his mind around it. "*What are YOU doing here? Where is Marin?*" Jaycen repeated angrily, "*Where's Marin!*"

"*She's not here. Hahn has her.*"

Jaycen grasped the wall, completely dumbstruck, defeat and disappointment overwhelming his mind and heart. How could she not be here? "*You mean I risked my life getting in here, getting freaking shot at…all for nothing?*"

Marcos narrowed his eyes at Jaycen. "*Yes, thank you for saving my worthless life, you idiot.*"

Jaycen knew he was being cruel, and part of him cringed at being so petty but the feelings of frustration and failure were almost too much to bear. How could she not be here? And worse, he'd rescued his competitor and rival, Mr. Movie Star himself! His mouth twisted into a bitter knot.

Noburu swam between them and grabbed Marcos in a huge embrace as if they were old friends, which, he realized, they probably were. Then Marcos turned on Jaycen, yanking the light off Jaycen's head.

"Give me this and get out of my way, I need to find something." Marcos shoved past him and swam into the control room. Jaycen followed behind, his temper boiling, his thoughts on fire. He turned the corner to the control room to see Marcos searching everywhere in the dark, flooded room, opening drawers and digging through filing cabinets. He swallowed down molten anger at the trick fate had played on him.

"What are you looking for?" Noburu asked. *"Perhaps we can help you find it".*

"It's a black box about the size of a cell phone with an antenna sticking out of it." Marcos said distractedly, ducking under desks, searching frantically. *" "* Marcos explained. *"Hahn left Leviathan and is working on his own and he has Marin on his submarine. But they were tracking him…"* His hand closed around a small handheld device which he held up triumphantly, *"with this!"*

"Look, are you absolutely certain she's not here I mean, how do you know they weren't lying to you?"

Marcos gave Jaycen a withering glare and turned to Noburu. *"Do you have a plan to get us out of here?"*

"We have a plan b, still working on plan a. I'm open for suggestions," he replied.

CHAPTER 24

MARIN

HAHN WAS WAITING for Marin when she and her guard came back from her morning bathroom break. Instantly her mouth went dry and her feet refused to move her forward. The guard jerked her chain until she shuffled close enough for him to lock her back up. She stood next to her bed with her arms wrapped around her, trying to contain the shuddering of fear that shook her to her bones.

Hahn dismissed the guard with a jerk of his head and walked over to her. His hands were cold and calloused as he pried one of her arms from around her body. She winced at his touch, every molecule in her shrinking from him, but he held her arm firmly, running a finger up and down the arm that he had sliced up, as if looking for any sign of the damage he had done. He paused at the crook of her arm and felt for a vein with a practiced finger.

"What...what are you doing?" Marin asked, dreading any answer he might give her.

"The blood I used yesterday was old. It worked, but not as quickly. I need fresh," he said quietly, almost to himself. He took a rubber band out of his pocket and wrapped it around her arm, still feeling her pulse with a cold finger on her arm. For the first time she noticed the cut on his forearm was still there. Less pronounced, but not completely healed. He took a scalpel from a tray and she squeezed her eyes shut, pulling away from him as much as she could, but nothing happened. She heard him take a quick intake of breath and opened her eyes in apprehension. To her surprise, he'd run the blade across his own arm again; making a slightly smaller cut than the one he'd made yesterday. He dropped the scalpel with a clatter and moved her arm straight, forcing a needle into her vein. A tube ran from the needle and she watched as her blood filled the tube and started dripping out the end and onto the floor. He waited a moment, cleaning his wound with a cotton ball. When he had staunched the bleeding of his own arm, he took the end of the tube and let her blood drip directly onto his new cut, as well as the old one until his arm was completely covered and her blood ran down his elbow, splashing dark red stains onto the white floor. He then pulled the needle out of her arm and handed her a cotton ball to stop the bleeding. She sat down on her bunk wordlessly. Hahn pulled up a chair and stared at his arm as if willing it to heal.

"What if it doesn't work on you?" Marin tried her experiment again, lacing her words with feeling, trying to sound braver and more concerned than she was, hoping she could somehow affect him, maybe gain some advantage over him.

"It has to. I will make it work," he replied without looking at her.

"Why did you do this to yourself?" she asked, coating her voice with curiosity. *Trust me,* she pushed out to him.

Hahn looked at her in surprise. "Why? To ensure my objectives were carried out. My experiments were the key to all my organization's plans! The others wouldn't believe it could be accomplished unless they could see proof. I *was* that proof, but I realized once they had their hands on my research, they would kill me and use it for their gain. I have seen them do it to others. The only way for me to win was to be the only one with the ability to control my subjects."

"What plans?" she asked, crossing her legs on the bed. She tried to project the feeling of trust. Maybe if he talked to her, she could somehow get him to release her.

"We want to create one government to rule them all. Every country answering only to us. Access to the resources of the entire globe."

"How were you going to do that?"

"I...I don't know why I should tell you this," he said, a frown creasing his brow.

"I'm just curious. It's not like I can tell anyone." *Trust me.*

He paused, as if uncertain whether or not to continue, but then he spoke again. "I have created an airborne mutagen that coats the lungs and changes them, but only for a short time. The mutagen is installed in three warheads which, when detonated, can spread over an entire continent. One is in the Arabian sea where it will drift across India and China, one in the Celtic sea that will drift over most of Europe and one in the Hudson Canyon off the coast of New Jersey that will take out most of the east coast. All I was lacking was a means to install the warheads deep enough that they couldn't be disarmed, but your cousin, Aaron, was my solution to that problem. He is now my hands under the sea, my own, personal leviathan."

"I thought he was working with Chita. My father said..." Hahn held up a hand and silenced her.

"Surely you don't think I wouldn't have other ways to control him? He has a device planted behind his ear that allows me to track him, talk to him, to give him direction, and, when necessary for motivation, cause him excruciating pain. It didn't take long to locate him and explain the new order of things. Pain is an incredible motivator." He chuckled to himself, making Marin's stomach churn. Poor Aaron. "Currently he is with my team installing the warhead in the Celtic. China was completed a few days ago. Soon he will be near New York finishing up his work."

"Then what will happen to him?" she spat at him, disgusted at his callous use of humans.

Hahn looked surprised at the question. "Keep him, of course. He is very useful. I don't even need to monitor him anymore. If he disobeys my direct orders, he automatically is given a jolt of incomprehensible pain. With him, I will never have to go under water again. I can live my life as a normal human, and he will be my watchdog for the subaquatic world. He could take down an entire aircraft carrier in a matter of minutes! After this, I suppose his next assignment will be to find each and every one of your

Arydian people and kill them. I don't want to have anyone underwater that I don't control completely."

"You would force him to kill his own people? His own family?" she asked, in shock.

"But of course. Who else is better equipped? He has already destroyed most of them. Your base was simple to take down, and the sub with the escaping Arydians was crumpled like a toy by him."

"Which sub?" Marin asked, suddenly terrified for everyone, but especially Paul's small group that had gone in search of Jaycen.

Hahn raised his eyes in surprise. "Which? There is more than one, then?" She cursed herself for giving him more information. Hahn leaned back, contemplating. "I will have to keep my eye out for it then." He knit his hands together and placed them behind his neck, relaxing back into the chair. "But, if you must know, it was the one I saw when my army attacked your first base in California." He smirked at her, as if hoping this news would be devastating.

Marin swallowed past a lump in her throat. So Paul was safe, for now. Still, Marcos's father was on the other sub, and all the rest of the Arydians, including Tania and the other families, including children. She felt sick.

"Why are you doing this to everyone?" Marin asked, dumbstruck.

"Power, my dear. Nobody has ever appreciated my genius. And now, everyone will know my name and see me for what I am. A visionary. A pioneer in the world of medicine and exploration. The creator of life and death!"

"A monster!" Marin growled at him.

"Perhaps," he said thoughtfully. "What is a monster but intelligence without a conscience? I beyond qualify with intelligence and am thankfully unburdened by conscience. If I am a monster, I am one that will soon have the world at his feet. Shortly before I captured you, I sent an ultimatum to the major governments of the world informing them of my demands and notifying them that a sample of the destructive power of my weapon was about to be deployed. The remaining members of the Leviathan council are no longer a threat to me, except perhaps Zarobi, but he has no way to reach me down here. Once the governments comply, I will install myself as the leader of the new world order and have Zar hunted down and killed. I will keep the warheads alive and active in case anyone wants to challenge me. They are capable of killing millions in just a few short hours and should prove a powerful deterrent now that I have proven how lethal my mutagen is."

"Is it poison?" she prodded, remembering the object of this experiment was to learn his plans. It was hard to concentrate on keeping the trust vibes going strong, especially hearing how many people he had so casually slaughtered.

"No, not at all!" he scoffed. "How primitive you make it out to be. This is a brilliant compound that makes them unable to breathe air. It was actually inspired by the AQUA project your mother and I worked on together."

"Wait, is this what you threw down when we were in Hawaii? It was, wasn't it?" she said, thinking of her father choking on the yellow dust on the bridge and falling into the water. She felt the first glimmers of hope since Hahn captured her. He continued animatedly.

"Yes, yes, it is!" he said, strangely delighted. She wondered for a moment if he was feeling some of the hope she couldn't help but radiate. "It is a mutagen because it physically changes the victim. Basically, it turns them into one of us, for a short time."

"So, they could breathe water, not air?" she asked, excitement lacing her words. She had to be sure.

"It changes the lungs much like your Arydia except the victims can no longer breathe regular air, but yes, they can breathe water. That is why you and I were unharmed when we jumped into the river." Hahn beamed as if he was very proud of his ingenious murder weapon.

Marin leaned forward eagerly. There it was! Her father had fallen into the water; he *could* have survived. And if he did, she realized, a smile touching her lips, he would know what happened to her! Maybe, somehow, he'd be able to save her.

Hahn also sat forward, his eyes sparkling. He dabbed his cut with a towel and let out a satisfied sigh. The cuts were gone.

"At last I will be whole again!" he whispered.

CHAPTER 25

JAYCEN

NOBURU AND MARCOS swam quickly with Jaycen trailing behind. Jaycen banged into something hard and cursed Marcos for taking away his light. The two of them were so far ahead of him that the light from both headlamps barely reached back to him. He pushed forward and caught up just as they reached a door partially ripped from its hinges. The flooded stairwell was behind it, and Jaycen let out a breath of relief. This must be the way up to the roof! They headed upwards in unison. Light filtered in from above and Noburu and Marcos switched off their headlamps simultaneously, leaving Jaycen to wonder if they were talking to each other and planning the next move without him, making him feel even angrier at Marcos and now somehow betrayed by Noburu.

When they reached the second landing, the water was too low to swim so they stepped cautiously out into the cold, black air. A metallic ping ricocheted off the railing and splashed into the water, followed by shouts and another shot that whizzed past Jaycen's head. Suddenly something punched him in the side and threw him backwards with a splash. Marcos and Noburu dove in next to him as a hail of bullets started pelting down around them.

Noburu tackled Jaycen around the chest and dragged him downwards shouting, *"Move! Move! Get down!"* They raced back to the control room and down a hallway before Jaycen begged them to stop. His hands were shaking, his heart was pumping too fast and he felt…wrong. He clung to the wall, struggling to keep upright in the drifting water.

He looked up to see Marcos and Noburu staring at him with faces that made his blood turn to ice. He followed their gaze to his chest and gasped. Blood was pouring out of a bullet wound in his side. He faltered, grabbing Marcos's shoulder, tears springing to his eyes. He was going to die! Noburu pulled out a knife and cut away one of the straps on his backpack, while Marcos dug a chunk of soggy Styrofoam padding from a worn office chair. Some detached part of Jaycen's mind realized they were talking to each other again without him, but this time he didn't care. Marcos held the Styrofoam against Jaycen's wound while Noburu clumsily fastened the strap around him to stop the bleeding. Then the pain came.

He moaned as they tightened it as much as they could. Marcos took over and pulled it tighter, tying it in a knot. Jaycen's breath was coming in short, trembling bursts, his body shaking with shock.

"Come this way," Noburu nodded, heading into a room marked maintenance. The room was filled with pipes and wires and a huge cylindrical tank lying on its side with several pipes coming into it and one larger one going out of it. Noburu seemed relieved.

"This is the gravity filter Paul was talking about. Once we get inside, we should be able to follow the flow downstream with the waste water and come out in the ocean near the sub."

Jaycen was shaking so much he didn't care. *"I'm going to die, aren't I?"* he asked numbly. Nobody answered. Instead, Noburu pulled out the welder and fitted a straw to the nozzle.

"Don't look, this will burn your eyes," he said, sliding dark goggles over his own eyes before igniting it.

"Does it matter?" Jaycen wondered to himself. Still he closed his eyes. Even behind Jaycen's eyelids, the light was brilliant. The acrid taste of burned metal filled their lungs as they breathed in the water surrounding them. Soon the light was gone and Noburu told them it was safe to look. He had sliced down the side of the tank and it had peeled down like wet

paper against itself. They followed him into the cavity of the filter. A thick metal mesh grate blocked the path to a narrow drainage pipe. Jaycen closed his eyes again as Noburu melted the grate for them to pass. Everything went black and suddenly Marcos was shaking his leg, yelling in his mind.

"Jaycen, wake up. Come on, you can do this." He shook himself, feeling disoriented, as he realized he was jammed in a pipe, head first with one arm in front of him, the other at his side. Noburu was in front and he was being pushed from behind by Marcos who was holding onto his foot. His shoulders barely fit and if he tried to move any part of his body, he hit the sides of the slick tube. His side hurt like it was on fire, but he didn't feel as shaky as he had before.

"I'm awake, I'm awake. How long have I been out?"

Marcos let go. *"I don't know. I haven't been counting. I was more concerned with making sure you weren't dead."*

Jaycen grunted. *"Not yet. You're not that lucky."*

"How would it be lucky to have to push your limp corpse through this disgusting sewer line in order for me to escape?"

Jaycen had to agree with that. The water coming from the pipe tasted nasty and heavy, like chemicals mixed with urine and poop, which he supposed it probably was, along with other disgusting biological waste.

"So, this is basically the toilet drain for anything they hold in all those aquariums, isn't it? Dolphins, whales, hippos, whatever?" Nobody responded to him, which he took as an agreement.

They followed the pipes for quite a while when Noburu finally broke the silence. *"How are you feeling, Jaycen? Are you still with us?"*

Jaycen did a quick self-assessment. *"I'll be okay. It hurts, but I think it's okay."* He suddenly remembered Noburu's injury with a stab of guilt. *"How is your shoulder doing?"*

"It's going to need to be looked at. I'm betting swimming in the sewer isn't going to do either of our wounds any good. The sooner we get out of here the better for all of us, I think." Unease laced his voice and Jaycen wondered if it was because of the injuries they'd sustained, or the oppressive environment they were in.

Jaycen tried not to think of how much he truly hated tight spaces, but it was almost impossible. He tried to relax, letting the water pressure pull him downwards. He redirected his mind to something else, focusing on the injustice of rescuing his rival instead of the girl he loved. All his dreams of Marin running into his arms, of him being her true hero and putting a nail in the coffin of any thoughts she may have had about Marcos were now a joke. His anger kept the pain at bay, but the darkness and the closeness of the tube around him made it hard to concentrate. His shoulders and hips rubbed the slimy sides of the tube as a constant reminder of where he was.

The pipe kept going on and on until he thought surely they were never coming to the end of it. Noburu abruptly stopped ahead, and Jaycen caught himself to keep from crashing into him. His heart started pounding as he suddenly remembered what Noburu said earlier. What if they hit a right angle and couldn't go any further? There was no way they could get back up the pipe, and no way to get out! They would be trapped down here buried alive, until they starved to death. Noburu moved forward a bit and Jaycen let out his breath.

"Tight spot here…my shoulder…" he groaned. Noburu twisted, wiggling slowly through the junction, then started on again. Jaycen hit the spot and his shoulders, wider than Noburu's, stuck. He sucked in his breath, over-whelmed with fear. He was wounded, bleeding and now trapped in some sick drainage pipe, breathing wastewater from a freaking whale enclosure or something. There was no way to turn around; they were stuck in this tube with no way out! His fingers scrabbled against the slick tunnel, his knuckles white, trying to find traction. He slapped the sides with all his might, trying not to think of the tons of earth around him, but his confidence was losing ground fast. He twisted his shoulders, pushing with his bare toes against the slippery tube, straining to find something to brace against, but the pipe was so tight he could barely bend his elbow.

Water pressure built up behind him, and the level of water dropped in front so far that his head was half in and half out of the smelly waste. Panic pulsed through him like poison adrenalin. He reached, willing him-self thinner, almost dislocating his shoulder in desperation. The wound in his side protested with white hot, searing pain, but he didn't care. In a flurry of utter insanity, he lost control, screaming out incoherent gurgles, twisting around, banging his hips, his knees, his elbows and head, clawing with his hands and feet. With a sudden lurch, he slipped through to the wider end of the pipe and was pulled along again by the flood of water that built up behind him. He felt the water pressure drop as Marcos struggled through the opening behind him, and then the water pulsed out, pushing him along again as Marcos made it through.

He closed his eyes, sucking in the sour water in ragged gasps, shaking from head to foot, his courage utterly gone. The light from Noburu's head-lamp ahead of him stopped, but Jaycen let himself be dragged closer to him. It was all he could do to hold on and keep breathing. Noburu's calm, measured voice came into his head, soft and reassuring.

"Jaycen, it's okay. Calm down."

Jaycen closed his eyes again, trying to keep his mind off the narrow tunnel. *"I...I was stuck. How can we get out of here if something like that happens again?"*

Noburu laughed in his mind. *"The water will propel us. All we need to do is let it push us out, no problem."* It took a minute for the terror to recede enough for Jaycen to listen to him.

"What if we hit a right angle or some bend we can't take?" he said, his panic rising again.

"Why would they suddenly put a bend out here? If we were going to hit something like that, it would have been closer to the building," Marcos said impatiently.

"Oh," Jaycen said sheepishly, embarrassed that they had both witnessed his freak out, but still glad for the knowledge. They began to move forward again at a faster pace. *"Do you think we're close?"* he asked, trying to keep the conversation flowing. Somehow the talking focused his thoughts and kept his mind from dwelling on all the horrible what ifs. Even Marcos's voice was better than nothing in this awful situation.

"It's hard to tell. I think the pipes will be our best gauge. We should have one more grate to pass and then we will be free." Noburu said.

Jaycen closed his eyes again, trying to imagine he was anywhere but here. He caught hold of his favorite memory of Marin, the one where she was standing on the end of the pier at COAST, with the wind whipping her hair. Or the night she first talked to him about her fear of the ocean and how it was keeping her from taking the assignment in DeepWater. Man, that girl did things to his heart. Marcos bumped into his feet and brought him back to reality. Jaycen hoped the other two couldn't hear the thoughts he was having about Marin, or the mean ones he was sporting toward Marcos right now.

It wasn't long before the pipe opened up to the last grate. Noburu stopped and Jaycen bumped into his feet with Marcos right behind him. Jaycen could taste the hint of fresher saltwater mingling with the wastewater and sighed with relief. They'd made it!

"What's the problem?" Marcos asked.

"I can't reach the tank to start the welder!"

"You're kidding, right?" Jaycen asked. It took a minute for the impact of Noburu's words to sink in. When they did, Jaycen's hope of escape vanished. *"You mean we're stuck in here?"* he asked, his voice rising with alarm. After all they had been through they would die within a yard of freedom. Noburu beat against the grate, looking for a weakness in the metal, but nothing budged. He reached his arm through the holes, waving it around frantically and trying to feel for any sort of latch or weakness on the outside, but it seemed he couldn't find anything.

Jaycen felt numb and weak and hopeless. All of this pain was for nothing. Marin was still a prisoner, and now there was no one who could save her. They waited, Noburu occasionally squirming despite his wounded shoulder to reach around to his back to release the welder, but it was too tight and eventually he gave up, panting with exhaustion and pain. They waited, all bound together in their miserable fate, but each alone in their dismal thoughts.

CHAPTER 26

MARIN

A NEW GUARD CAME into Marin's room the next day. He was taller than the last one and he treated her differently, even greeting her with a hastily mumbled, "Good morning." She yawned and stretched, stepping out of her alcove onto the cold floor, curling her toes away from its icy touch. The man seemed to notice and dug around in a drawer for a moment until he produced a pair of clean white gym socks, which she gratefully slid onto her feet.

"Thank you!" she said. "I can't remember the last time my feet were warm."

The man sternly put a finger to his lips and she hastily whispered an apology, suddenly wondering why the man seemed familiar. Her breath caught in her throat as it occurred to her that maybe this guy was one of the Arydians, come to rescue her, but when she studied his face as they walked down the hall to the bathroom, she couldn't place him with the people she had seen back on the oil rig or in Arydia before it was destroyed. Still, he did seem kind of familiar somehow. Plus, he was nicer than her regular guard.

The moment they got back into her room, she tried to press her feelings toward him. It seemed the trust experiment had sort of worked on Hahn, but she wasn't sure how much she could accomplish by making people trust her. She needed to work on a more helpful emotion, like compassion or empathy, or maybe just a willingness to help.

Help me! She thought, pushing outwards as hard as she could. Immediately the man moved closer.

"Is there anything else you need?" he asked in a quiet voice with a strong German accent.

She couldn't believe her ears. "You...you want to help me?" she asked.

The man stepped back. "No, I mean, I cannot help you escape or anything. But I can get you something to eat or drink. Or more blankets if you are still cold." He leaned in closer, as if afraid someone would hear him. "Dr. Hahn is gone for a little while. I can bring you more food if you'd like."

Help me more! She thought, concentrating.

"I wish I could do more. I just don't know what. And Dr. Hahn...you know he is ruthless." The man looked down at the white floor, his voice barely audible. "You know he is. I've heard your screams. He does terrible things to those who disobey. And sometimes even to those who do obey." The man sighed.

"Then why do you want to be kind to me?" she asked.

"You are the one who healed me, do you remember?" he said, almost reverently. "My leg. Dr. Hahn would have let me bleed to death, but your blood...it healed me! You are like an angel."

"Oh," she said, disappointed. "I thought I recognized you." Unsure of how to proceed and now uncertain if it was really her that was manipulating his feelings, or if he was feeling kind towards her anyway because she healed him, she walked over and sat on the bunk.

"Gonna chain me up, then?" she asked dully. Maybe this whole idea of changing people's feelings was just fantasy.

"Oh. Yes. If you want me to, I will." He walked over to the wall and started to attach the other end of her leash to it.

"No, I don't want you to. I want you to help me get out of here. I want you to save me from this man that is hurting me every day and help me stop what he is going to do to the world." Tears of frustration slid down her cheeks. She kicked her food tray, scattering its contents across the room.

"I hate this place and everyone in it! This torture chamber I live in, this submarine where there is no sunlight, no air, and these chains, stealing my freedom, my life! I want you to listen to me and do what I'm telling you to do! I want you to get me out of here!"

The man blinked a few times, still holding the other end of the chain in his hand. "I...want to help you. I just don't know what I can do."

"Let me out! Take the chains off me. Take me to the portal and let me go out into the water." The man chewed his lip, fidgeting with the chain uncertainly.

"What will happen to me when you are gone?" he asked quietly. Marin knew the answer. The man did, as well. She swallowed down a lump in her throat, realizing she was expecting this man to sacrifice his life for hers; to die for her. She stopped pushing her feelings towards him and slunk back to the bunk. The man looked sadly down at the chain. He moved towards her and pulled a key out of the pocket of his jumpsuit, bending down as if he were going to unlock the band around her ankle, but the door swooshed open. Dr. Hahn stood in the doorway dripping wet, triumph burning in his eyes. The man stood and locked her chain swiftly to the wall and moved past Hahn who barely even acknowledged him as he slid behind him into the hall. Hahn strode into the room, his eyes never leaving Marin's and thrust his wet hand into her face, spreading his fingers out as far as he could. All traces of the webbing were gone.

"It worked. I am human once again!"

CHAPTER 27

JAYCEN

SUDDENLY, A BRIGHT light shone around Noboru. Jaycen closed his eyes, half wondering if he was hallucinating, since there was no way Noboru could have gotten to the welder, but a few minutes later, Noboru slipped out of the tube and into the open ocean with Jaycen and Marcos tumbling out behind him. Paul waited for them, beaming.

"And that is how you save the day, my young friends!"

Noboru grasped his shoulder, smiling. *"How did you know we were stuck?"*

Paul shrugged. *"It's not like there's a lot to do, waiting for you. I was watching the end of the pipe and saw your arm waggling all over and figured you were in trouble. I grabbed the other portable welder and here we are. Where's Marin?"*

Jaycen glanced at Marcos, leaving it for him to answer, as if he was responsible for Marin not being there. Marcos took the handheld unit and gave it to Paul.

"She is with Hahn. We can track them with this. We should hurry in case they figure out where we have gone."

Paul, Marcos, Noboru and Jaycen swam into the shadow of the sub, completely exhausted from their long night and utterly discouraged. Jaycen still stung from the disappointment of rescuing Marcos, not Marin, but he was getting so tired nothing seemed to matter anymore. The water was getting bright now that the sun was coming up. It felt weird for him to be this tired at the start of the day. He hoped someone else could drive and let him sleep and recuperate. Paul stopped abruptly at the hatch, suddenly tense.

"What's up?" Jaycen asked.

"I left the hatch closed."

"Maybe Kazu opened it in preparation for us coming," Noburu suggested.

"Then where is he?" Paul responded, looking up into the sub. He cautiously pulled himself inside, trying to be as quiet as possible. Marcos and Jaycen helped push Noburu in, his wound making it hard for him to manage it himself. Then Marcos and Jaycen slipped inside.

"Wait here, let me check it out," Paul said as he ducked through the portal, grabbing a wrench off the wall as a weapon before moving quietly towards the galley. Jaycen realized he could hear voices coming from the direction Paul was walking. They didn't sound upset, just conversational, so Jaycen followed him with Marcos and Noburu close behind.

They walked into the galley to find a burly older man and an extremely beautiful woman sitting around the galley table drinking hot chocolate. Jaycen was dumbfounded. Paul broke into a huge grin and laughed out loud.

"Malcolm! What on earth are you doing here?"

Malcolm stood, his bearded, leathery face breaking into a rare smile, his eyes crinkling at the edges. He shook hands with Paul, then Jaycen, as they tried to shuffle one by one into the tiny kitchen. When he got to Marcos, Malcom let out a deep breath that ended in a laugh and pulled his only son into his arms, squeezing him tightly.

"Oh, Marcos, my boy. You are safe at last!" He held Marcos a moment longer and then let him go as if to inspect him for damage.

"Father! How are you here? Why?" Marcos seemed completely taken aback at the sight of his father here in the middle of the ocean as if he was just dropping by for tea.

"Sit down, sit down, we will talk!" he said, shooing people into the room to sit on anything sturdy enough to hold them. Noburu came in last, but as Malcolm threw his arms around his old friend, Noburu jerked back in pain. "You are injured!" Malcom cried, as Noburu released the strap from the welder that had been holding pressure onto his wound.

The woman immediately jumped into action. "Kazu, get the first aid kid, right away!" She gave Noburu her seat and started inspecting the wound. Marcos turned and looked at Jaycen.

"I thought you were shot, too! Were you not dying just a little while ago? Or are you just a major wimp?" Marcos scoffed.

Jaycen looked down at the strap and packing job Noburu and Marcos had done around his waist and began untying himself. When it fell to the floor, he pulled up his shirt, expecting to see a bloody, bleeding mess, but all he could see was a slight indentation marked by a ragged, pink circle on his skin.

Marcos jabbed him in the spot he'd been shot.

"Ow! What was that for?"

"That is all you are hurt? Where is the blood and the big wound killing you?"

Jaycen shrugged, rubbing the spot Marcos had jabbed. "I...I don't know. It was there. You saw it!" He looked up and met eyes with Paul. "Is this that bonus you were talking about? The magic dose?"

Paul looked away, like he wished Jaycen hadn't said anything. The woman glanced away from her work on Noburu to check out the mostly healed wound in Jaycen's side. Somehow she didn't seem surprised.

"Seriously, what's going on? And who is this?" Jaycen said, gesturing to the woman who had gone back to thoroughly cleaning Noburu's shoulder with antiseptic.

"I am Doctor Emily Gilbert. I am the wife of Douglas Franklin Gilbert, and the mother of Amanda Gilbert, whom you know as Marin Donnegan."

Jaycen's jaw dropped open and Paul stammered in disbelief, "You're Frank's wife? I thought she was dead!"

"No, I'm afraid that was a grossly mistaken rumor. I've figured out who Marcos is, now who are you two?" she said, nodding with her head at Jaycen and Paul as she pushed gauze down on Noburu's shoulder. He winced, clenching his jaw muscles.

"I'm Paul Donnegan." He stared at her, face clouded. "Wait one minute. You seriously expect me to believe you are Marin's birth mother? You're hardly old enough to have an eighteen-year-old!"

She smiled, and her whole face lit up like a sunrise. Jaycen could see where Marin's looks came from. "Why thank you, Paul! I can tell we'll get along splendidly! And trust me; though I may not look like it, I'm definitely her mother." She finished packing Noburu's wound and taping the gauze around the edges. "You should go lie down, Noburu. You look like you've lost a lot of blood."

Noburu agreed and Kazu helped him out of the room. Emily washed her hands off in the sink and sat down with them, wiping her hands on a small towel. It was only then that Jaycen noticed the woman was walking strangely. He glanced under the table and was shocked to see her legs were covered with scales. He nudged Marcos and pointed subtly to the woman's legs, looking up at Marcos expectantly for a reaction. Marcos's eyes widened and he gave Jaycen a non-committal shrug.

"So, Paul. You are the one who raised my little girl." Paul nodded, still obviously trying to wrap his head around the situation. She grasped his hand in both of hers warmly. "You have my eternal gratitude for providing her a good life. I'm sure we will have much to talk about as time goes on, but for now, Malcolm and I have travelled almost six hundred miles. He's found his son, now where is my daughter?"

Paul placed the tracking device on the table. "Hahn has Marin. He is on a submarine and the only way we can locate him is using this tracker Marcos stole." Emily's smile dissolved into anguish.

Malcolm picked it up and turned it over in his hands. "We may not have a way to interface with this. Did you see how it was used?"

Marcos nodded. "They had a monitor with a map, they would turn this on and it would pinpoint Hahn's location. I couldn't get a good look at where it was, but we need to start heading west as soon as possible if we want to intercept him."

Paul looked over to Jaycen. "That's the direction all those ships from Leviathan headed yesterday. Bet that's where they were going."

"I'd bet you're right."

"Jaycen, chart a course to follow their heading and get us moving that direction while we figure this out, will you?" Paul asked.

Jaycen left the table and went to the control room, turning the craft west at full throttle. He watched the ocean pass by without caring about what he was seeing. All his dreams of rescuing Marin, even seeing her again, were now tainted by the arrival of Marcos. Sure, she had told Jaycen she loved him, but that was just as he was leaving her life forever. She wouldn't lose anything by saying it. And she had spent all the time between then and now in the company of Marcos, with his movie star hair and his stupid, sexy accent. Who knows what had happened between them while Jaycen was gone? He kicked the bulkhead in frustration, trying not to imagine Marin wrapped in Marcos's sculpted arms. What did Jaycen have that could compete with him? Marcos was an Arydian, he knew her family, plus he looked like he belonged on the cover of a fashion magazine. And Jaycen had nothing. Nothing but an aching love for a girl he couldn't live without, lost in a vast ocean of blue.

CHAPTER 28

MARIN

MARIN STARED AT the wall of her cubicle, concentrating; attempting to recreate the feelings on the night she had reached out a finger and shocked Marcos. It could have been coincidence, but it was possible it wasn't. And if manipulating feelings couldn't get her out of this, shocking someone definitely could.

She strained, trying to find some way to generate electricity in her fingertip like the one time she managed it before. They had been walking along the beach and talking about how some marine animals have the ability to shock their prey and she had just…shocked him. It had been easy to do at the time, maybe too easy-like it was just a weird coincidence—normal static in the air that presented itself at a very convenient time.

And maybe she was grasping at straws, imagining she had special powers because she was desperate to escape this horrid place. She rolled onto her back, mentally clawing herself back from the depression she felt herself sinking into. How long had she been here, a week or two? And Marcos-had he survived? And what about Paul and her father, Frank? If Frank was alive and knew what happened to her, what good was that information? There was no way he could find them on this death ship, wherever it was located. They could be beneath a polar ice cap for all she knew.

She hit the wall hard with her fist, hating this feeling of waiting for the next torture session with nothing to break up the time but sleep, worry, and more waiting. She couldn't fathom how her mother survived this, if this had been her fate so long ago. The door hissed open and Hahn entered. She didn't even bother to roll over; she knew it was him by the sound of his footsteps and the overly sweet smell of his cologne.

"It's time for some more experiments, Marin," he said. She could see his sick smile in her mind. She ignored him, hoping he would go away. He didn't. He took her by the shoulders and rolled her over. She tried not to tremble beneath his hands but couldn't stop herself.

"Marin, I'm surprised that this even hurts you at the rate you heal. Besides, it's not just you who will suffer today. I plan on running a comparison study, so you will have company."

The door opened again and the nicer guard, the one who gave her socks, was shoved through the door. Both his hands and legs were in shackles, and he stumbled and fell to the floor at Hahn's feet. Two guards hoisted him to a standing position and ran a chain through both sets of shackles, forcing him into a crouch, then fastened it to the wall in the same loop Marin's chains were locked to. One guard, the surly one Marin usually saw, kicked a chair under the man and he sat down. They pulled Marin out of her bunk and placed her on a chair in front of Hahn, strapping her down with her arm extended.

"Tell her your name," Hahn demanded of the man once the guards left.

"Kirk," he mumbled.

"There now, Marin. Kirk here will keep you company. Whatever pain you will experience, he will experience as well, only for much longer." Hahn flipped open his notebook with the precision of a robot and started jotting down notes. He then rolled his chair to Kirk and pushed up the man's sleeve. The man stared down at his own arm dully.

"Don't do this, Hahn," she pleaded, strengthening her voice with pity and remorse. "He is innocent. I am innocent. Don't hurt us."

"He is *not* innocent. I know he wants to help you. He has been talking to others, conspiring against me. He knows the rules."

"Don't!" she said, pressing as hard as she could towards him. Hahn stared at her, tilting his head sideways as he did, like a dog trying to pick up on an unusual sound.

"I always feel something when I'm with you, Marin. A peculiar sense of grief, tinged with pain and fear. It's stimulating, really. I wonder if you have a more advanced version of the empathic qualities your mother exhibited."

She sucked in a surprised breath. So he *could* feel it!

He pulled out a scalpel and wiped it with a sterile alcohol pad. "Believe me, the feelings you send me are a distraction at best. When you tried it on me the other day, I'll admit, I was shaken by your outburst, and I'll also admit, you captured me for a while by the trust you engendered, but once I realized what you were doing, it took away any effect you may have on me other than to make my experience more enjoyable. I look forward to feeling your pain."

He held down her arm and started to cut at her elbow. If he wanted to feel her pain, then he would! She screamed, taking all the agony she was feeling and shooting outwards in one powerful wave. Hahn's voice joined in her own; his cries mingled with Kirk's as well. Hahn gasped, the bloody scalpel clattering to the ground. Her cries turned to sobs. Hahn's hands were shaking, and Kirk held his right arm cradled to him as if he had been wounded. The door slid open and the guards came in, alarmed.

"Leave us!" Hahn shrieked. They backed out without comment. Hahn sat back in his chair and took a deep, shaking breath, holding his arm tight to his body. He gingerly rolled up his sleeve, staring at his arm in disbelief. Nothing was there. He touched his arm and winced as if he were poking at a fresh wound, but still there was nothing visible. He turned to Kirk and snatched his arm to reveal a perfectly healthy arm, yet Kirk flinched as if the movement was excruciating. Once Hahn let his arm go, Kirk jerked it back and held it against himself with a groan. Marin watched them, tears running down her cheeks.

"What did you do?" Hahn roared. He struck her across the face and she gasped in pain and surprise. He backed away and stared at his arm, completely astounded, as if in shock, and not expecting an answer. "I can feel the wound as if it were my own! I can even feel the blood dripping off my fingers, yet nothing is there!" He held up his hand and touched the imaginary wound in awe. Finally, he lifted Marin's arm and let the blood drip onto his arm as if he wanted to heal it, just in case, then set her arm down gently. Kirk moaned in the corner, terrified.

"Well, it looks like you've found a way to defend yourself after all." Hahn said, standing up and leaving the room. Her wound slowly knit itself together and the pain subsided. Kirk stopped moaning and sat in silence until the guards returned and removed him, leaving Marin alone to contemplate what happened.

She had done this! She *did* have power--real power! She wanted to shout with relief and joy.

"Try to hurt me now you slimy piece of trash!" she yelled at the closed door. She wiped the drying blood from her newly healed arm, feeling fierce and defiant. She wasn't helpless. And Hahn would have a price to pay if he ever tried to hurt her again. She had power, wait, pow*ers*! Healing herself was definitely a superpower. And now this new whatever it was that hurt Hahn and Kirk. Still...

She frowned for a moment. Maybe those kinds of superpowers were helpful, but they seemed more reactive. She needed something she could seriously use as a weapon.

She took a deep breath, pointed her finger at the metal wall and concentrated. Nothing happened. She tried again, and again, but nothing happened. She tried to think about what was different about now and when it happened before. She'd been with Marcos, walking along the sand, barefoot, feeling safe and secure with him by her side. But when she had projected pain to Hahn and Kirk, she was afraid and angry. They seemed so different, yet they both had resulted in something happening.

She lay back on the bed, frustrated and exhausted, racking her brain, trying to unlock the secrets hidden inside. Maybe it wasn't the *kind* of emotion, maybe it was the intensity. She sat up and thought of Hahn's placid face as he cut into her arm, seeing her as nothing more than a piece of meat to be experimented on.

Hate and loathing filled her, and she nursed it like a fire, laying image after image of the past weeks of torture onto the burn pile until her anger raced up and down her spine like electricity. Then she reached out to the lock on the cuff around her ankle and touched it. A blue spark sizzled from her finger into the lock, acidic smoke rising from the metal.

She clenched her teeth, muscles working in her jaw, and tried again, this time holding the arc for as long as she could, feeling the heat singeing her skin painfully. She tried to ignore it until, finally, the lock melted and the cuff fell off her leg. She rubbed the burn on her ankle, confident it would be gone soon. *Now this is more like it!*

CHAPTER 29

JAYCEN

A FTER A FEW unsuccessful tries, Jaycen eventually found the cable he and Paul used to patch the tracking device into their computer system. It was working, but they were having trouble getting a consistent signal. Paul sat in the pilot's seat while Jaycen lay contorted on his back next to the copilot's seat with his head under the console.

"Don't fry anything while you're down there, hotshot," Paul said, half seriously. "Remember what happened last time you wired a sub?"

"Been there, done that, not interested in doing it again," Jaycen shot back distractedly. "If I could just get this electrical tape around this spot back here, I think we'd be good. But it's so tight back here, it keeps sticking to everything except what I need it to stick to. Ugh!"

"How is it going boys?" Emily said from somewhere near the door. Her voice was so similar to Marin's it startled him.

"I think...I almost..." Jaycen said, pressing himself harder into the side of the console to reach the connection. "Got it!" he said triumphantly. He scooted out from below and flipped a switch on the dashboard. A light appeared on their navigation map.

"Good job, kid!" Paul said, slapping him on the shoulder. "And you didn't fry us!"

Emily beamed at him and he smiled back, pleased with himself. Suddenly the radio crackled to life, surprising all of them.

"Minnow, can you read me?"

Emily's face went white and she dropped to her knees between the seats and snatched the microphone before either Jaycen or Paul could touch it.

"Douglas?" she almost whispered into the radio. She closed her eyes and waited, not breathing.

"Emily!" Frank's voice shouted back in disbelief. Emily caught her breath in a half sob, nodding as if he could see her. Tears coursed down her cheeks.

"Douglas! Oh, my love Douglas! I can hardly believe it's you!" Jaycen noticed her voice suddenly had a stronger accent, as if she was letting her guard down and speaking in her true voice.

"Emily, how? I thought you were…" His voice caught and went silent, as if he were trying to compose himself. When he began to speak once more his voice had risen to a frantic pitch, as if he were afraid of being cut off and losing her once more. "Where are you? Are you all right?"

Emily nodded again, as if he could see her, not even bothering to wipe the tears pouring freely down her face.

"I'm here. I'm fine," she choked out, laughing and crying at once. "I'm with Paul, Malcolm, Noburu, Kazu, Marcos and Jaycen. We are looking for Marin."

"Where? How?" Frank stammered. He seemed like he couldn't wrap his head around the idea that he was actually talking to his wife again. Jaycen didn't blame him. If anything, he just felt awkward sharing this precious moment with them as an unwanted bystander.

"Oh, my love, there's too much to tell! Where are *you*? I have to see you! Can you join us?"

"I'm in California, but headed to Washington DC in a few minutes to meet with a few people about Hahn. Did you hear about Lanai?"

Paul and Jaycen looked at each other and shrugged. Emily sniffed and shook her head.

"No, what happened?" she asked.

"Hahn released a gas that killed every living thing on the island. He's got an even bigger plan in the works now and I'm trying to recruit help. We've got to find and stop him before he strikes again."

"Marcos!" she shouted into the mic excitedly. "Marcos has a tracker pinpointing Hahn's location. Jaycen just wired it into our computers and we are following him now. If you can send help, we can get our daughter back and stop Hahn!" Jaycen watched the relief and hope cross her tear-stained face. He had to be honest, the thought of having the military back them up made rescuing Marin seem almost possible.

"Darling, my plane is about to leave. Let me write down your heading. Keep going, but don't do anything until you hear back from me, understand?"

"I understand, Douglas. Please, come quickly!"

"I'll be with you as soon as I can. The very second I can, my love."

"I'll be waiting." The radio went silent. Emily stayed there, holding the microphone like a precious treasure, then stood and silently excused herself without meeting anyone's eyes.

Paul finally broke the silence. "That has got to be the saddest and happiest thing I've ever heard in my life." Jaycen nodded in agreement. "Can you imagine thinking your wife's been dead all these years and learning after all that time that she's alive?" He shook his head slowly.

"That's awful about Lanai. I wonder how many people lived there? That's in Hawaii, right?" Jaycen asked

Paul raised an eyebrow at him. "Aren't you supposed to be super smart? Didn't you take geography in school?"

Jaycen blushed. "That wasn't my best subject, if you want to know the truth."

Paul shrugged with a half-smile. "Well, mine either. But yes, that's Hawaii. It's one of the smaller islands. I'd guess a few thousand people. Probably more than we lost in the Twin Towers attack or Pearl Harbor, though." He let out a heavy sigh. "How can one person have so much power and knowledge and only use it to make people suffer? This Hahn guy sounds like the devil himself."

"I agree. I hope we never get the chance to meet him."

CHAPTER 30

FRANK

FRANK WIPED HIS eyes and cleared his throat. His hands shook slightly as he put down the microphone. Sergeant Major Bale leaned forward, offering him a tissue.

"Are you all right, Doctor?"

Frank waited a moment for his emotions to calm down before he answered. "That...was my wife."

"So I gathered."

"I thought..." he couldn't go on. The Sergeant Major patted him on the back. An ensign entered the radio room.

"Plane's waiting, sir." The Sergeant Major nodded.

"If you're ready, Doctor?" he asked. Frank gave a curt nod.

Frank took in deep breaths of the damp air to calm himself as he was led onto a windy tarmac to the steps of an airplane, flanked by the Sergeant Major and an array of guards in military fatigues. It felt strangely similar to his entrance into California several hours ago, only played in reverse and minus the hazmat suits and handcuffs.

A stocky man in a uniform bristling with medals met them as they walked on board. He carried himself with the air of someone used to giving commands and having people obey them.

"General Holt?" Frank guessed, extending his hand. The Gfeneral nodded and shook it firmly.

"Good to meet you, Doctor. I'm quite pleased to find you are alive and well. Please, take your seat," he said, ushering him to sit down. Sergeant Major Bale scooted in next to Frank and fastened his buckle. General Holt shrugged and took a seat across the aisle. Bale looked like he wanted to talk, but Frank quickly excused himself and went to the restroom for a few minutes before the plane was ready for takeoff.

He put down the toilet seat and sat down, holding his head in his hands. He still couldn't believe he'd just heard Emily's voice. He'd known it was her the moment she'd said his name. She always insisted on calling him by his first name, Douglas, even though everyone he knew, including his parents, always called him Frank. And even without that, her voice was unmistakable.

He used to swear he could hear her crying out for him whenever he went in the ocean, but no matter how hard he tried, for some reason she could never hear him. Then, suddenly, he couldn't hear her anymore, as if her voice had been silenced. He felt that was the day she'd been killed and mourned her from that day forward. Now that he'd spoken to some of the prisoners of Hahn's, he understood why she never seemed to hear him. Hahn would torture them, experimenting with sound frequencies, trying to break their will and control their minds. And now to find out she'd been alive all these years!

He kicked himself for giving up on her, for not finding a way to save her. He hated himself for staying at COAST, pretending to live a normal life, but with Hahn one breath away from him at all times he had never dared make a move. And he never wanted to be far from Marin, guarding her from the shadows of her life. Emily would have wanted that more than her own life, as he would have if their roles had been reversed. Still, the guilt was almost too hard to bear.

A knock at the door startled him from his thoughts. "Sir, we are ready for takeoff. Please take your seat." He blew his nose and splashed some water on his face, rubbing it off with a rough paper towel before moving out to the main cabin and sitting down. Moments later the plane pulled out and they were airborne. Frank looked out at the moonlight glistening on the Pacific Ocean, wishing with all his heart he was flying out to see the one woman he'd ever loved. Instead, the plane banked east, blocking his view of the water, taking him thousands of miles away from where his soul ached to be.

"I'd mentioned earlier that I have a personal question for you, Doctor," Bale said, once they were airborne.

"Yes?"

"About a young man who worked with you, Jaycen Webb? Do you know him?"

Frank was surprised. "Yes, of course I do. What about him?"

The Sergeant Major looked uncomfortable and lowered his voice until it was hard to hear him over the thrum of the engine. "What do you know about him?"

"He's a great kid. Smart, hard worker. He's been with me at COAST for two summers and has a bright future. Why?"

"He's...one of you?"

Frank sat back and exhaled slowly. "Well, yes. Now he is. It's not our practice to give this drug to just anyone, but he and my daughter were captured and Jaycen was left to drown. The only way I could save him was to change him. And thank heavens it worked," Frank said. "Why are you so interested in the boy?"

"I...I'm a friend of his family. And when the attack on California happened, there were reports that the sub that went down triggered the fault. My information led me to believe he might have been responsible, or at least been involved with the people who were."

"Well, before that day, the only involvement he had with us was a crush on my daughter. I'm fairly sure he had no idea what he was getting into. For that matter, neither did she," Frank chuckled.

"You are absolutely certain he is not wrapped up with Hahn or any of the people involved with this terror attack?" Bale pressed.

Frank laughed out loud at the idea. "No, Jaycen is one of the kindest and brightest young men I know. He worked hard to get into COAST and do a good job for me. He has a mother with disabilities that he thinks the world of, and the last I heard of him he was headed back to try to find her, no matter the cost. Now, he's on a sub with my wife," he shrugged, "and I have no idea how he got there. I only hope the poor kid found his mom alive and well."

He noticed a dark look crossed over Bale's face, so he patted Bale's knee and said, "If anything, the disaster in California made his life much worse, and I guarantee he had nothing to do with causing it. I may not always agree with his methods, but I respect his integrity and his loyalty."

The Sergeant Major relaxed into his seat. "Thank you for the information, Doctor. It gives me a lot to think about."

***

At four a.m. Frank's flight landed in Arlington, Virginia, in the middle of a heavy thunderstorm with a bitterly cold wind. Their airplane was escorted to a private hangar. He felt rumpled and unshaven as he was walked into a black vehicle that felt more like a limo than a Suburban. Most of the guards got in with them, as well as the Sergeant Major. General Holt placed his hat on his head and got in the front seat next to the driver. Frank leaned forward and tapped his shoulder.

"Where are we going?" A deafening clap of thunder answered him, making everyone in the car jump and several of the guards grab their guns. The General waited until the thunder rolled away before answering him.

"White House. I'm going to need you to tell your story to someone. We should be there in about twenty minutes." He glanced at Frank and added, "Try to spruce yourself up. You're a mess."

Frank scowled at him. "Yeah, I bet." Still, he tucked in his shirt and tried to smooth his disheveled hair. He couldn't do much about his unbrushed teeth and the general unwashed, swampy smell he was sporting, but after the past few days he'd been through, he thought he looked pretty good, considering.

He leaned his head back and closed his eyes, letting exhaustion lull him to sleep. A short drive later the vehicle stopped, and he was awoken by a cold breeze mixed with a splattering of rain coming through the driver's open window. He yawned, rubbing his eyes as they passed a guardhouse and Frank registered where he was. The rain was going strong, but through the darkened windows, he caught the full sight of the White House, brightly lit, despite the rain and the late hour. The sight made him pause.

"Wow, the White House. I've never been this close. Pretty impressive," he said to the guard next to him. The guard didn't respond, but Frank thought he saw a shadow of a smile in his eyes. "Well, you guys probably come here all the time. But take it from the new guy, it's pretty cool."

They drove to the side and down a steep driveway that took them under the building. Another guardhouse stood outside and the driver rolled down the window, showing his I.D. This guard had a plastic cover on his hat that splashed the rain into the driver's face and lap. He shone a flashlight into the back of the vehicle, momentarily blinding all of them before he finally stepped back and opened the gates. The driver pulled in and drove past a legion of cars to a wide set of double doors that looked equal parts elegant and menacing. General Holt got out, brushed down his coat, and motioned for Frank and the Sergeant Major to join him. They stumbled out and the SUV drove away.

"You still look like a sack of crap," the General said matter-of-factly.

"Yeah, well, I've had a rough couple of days," he retorted. "Why are you so concerned about how I look? Are we meeting the President or something?" He laughed.

The General glowered at him as he scanned his way through a heavy door. The door swung open and he steered the other two men through. "Yes."

Frank tried not to look surprised.

"Oh. Really? Right now? It's the middle of the night! Will he even be here?" Frank squeaked, all pretense of calm disintegrating. General Holt rolled his eyes and chuckled.

"Of course he's here. He lives here, Dr. Gilbert. And yes, right now." The General's brows drew together. "I'm hoping a surprise visit might lend some answers to some questions I've been having. This is a dangerous time for our country," he added quietly, almost to himself.

"Dangerous, how?" Frank pressed. General Holt didn't answer but walked to a set of metal doors and pressed the up arrow. A moment later, they were standing in a gilded elevator with a white-gloved operator whose only job seemed to be pressing the buttons for people. Frank was impressed that the guy looked so fresh and awake for the unheavenly time it was, as if it was perfectly normal for people to come and go at all hours around here. When the doors pinged open, they found themselves in a lush hall, decorated with live flowers and exquisite paintings. The carpet was thick with flowers and other decorative shapes carved into it. Beautiful statues rested in alcoves along the walls, lit with subtle lighting. Even at this early hour, there were a few people walking here and there with purposeful strides.

They made their way to a large wooden door flanked by two guards who rose as they approached. General Holt gave them his identification.

"I'm sorry, sir, but he's asleep," the one on the left said, handing him back his wallet.

"I'm sure he is. It's four thirty in the morning. Nevertheless, I have to speak with him immediately." The guards glanced at each other uneasily.

"We were given orders that he was not to be disturbed."

"Who gave those orders?" General Holt pressed. "Was it the President himself?"

"Well, no," the guard on the right said. "It was the Chief of Staff. The President hasn't been feeling well."

"And the Chief of Staff is in charge of his health?" General Holt raised his eyebrows. "Look, I don't have time for this. I have clearance, and I need to talk to him immediately as a matter of national security. If you get in trouble, blame me," he said, reaching for the doorknob.

"Hold it right there!" A voice shouted, stopping everyone in their tracks. Dr. Boscolo stomped down the hall and inserted himself between General Holt and the door.

"What is the meaning of this?" General Holt demanded. "I need to talk to the President. This is urgent!"

"You have no right to barge in like this in the middle of the night! The President has been feeling off and is under my care!" The doctor's voice rose in pitch. He glanced down the hall and relief seemed to wash over his face as he saw the Chief of Staff almost running in her haste to get to him.

General Holt paused for a moment, but twisted the doorknob anyway, shouldering past the doctor. "As I said, this is urgent. President Thompson will want to hear this."

As he walked into the room, automatic lights lit the ceiling. He dragged Frank in with him, past the desperately protesting doctor. The President sat up in his bed, startled.

"What on earth is going on here?"

The doctor shouldered his way into the room and gasped in alarm when he saw papers littering the bed, sketches done in pencil and on any scrap of paper, from tissue paper to white house stationary.

CHAPTER 31

MARIN

MARIN PLACED THE cuff back around her ankle and melted it back a bit so it would stay on, at least temporarily, just seconds before the short, burly guard came in to take her to the bathroom. The guard grunted at her. She'd started calling him Spud because he seemed like something dug up out of the ground with his knobbly head and big muscles. Spud didn't talk to her, he just unlocked her chain and rattled it expectantly. She wasn't sure if she was imagining it, but he left a lot of distance between them as they walked.

She went to the bathroom, washed her face, then stepped out into the hallway, trying to orient herself to the layout of the ship. It didn't seem like she was on a level that had anything important going on, but she couldn't tell which direction the control room was, or more importantly, the passageway to the airlock. She started walking away from her room, knowing Spud would surely do something to stop her and give her the fuel she was looking for.

Sure enough, he grabbed her arm and spun her around, shaking the chain in her face.

"Where do you think you're going, missy?" he snarled. Anger arced up and down her back and she could feel the hair along her scalp start to rise.

She grabbed hold of the chain with both hands and pushed electricity down the links, blue sparks crackling, racing along the surface, speeding towards Spud. He tried to drop the chain, but instead his hand clenched around it. He began shaking uncontrollably, hitting his knobby head against the wall repeatedly until his eyes rolled back in his head and he slid to the floor. Marin let go of the rage inside her and the blue light disappeared. Spud's hands went slack, so she jerked the chain from his grasp and searched his pockets for the key quickly until it hit her…she didn't need the key. She touched a finger to the cuff, feeling the power well up inside her, and melted it off her leg. She stood, free for the first time in ages, picked a direction and started moving.

Moments later, red lights started flashing and a siren began to shriek overhead. They must've found Spud. She moved more quickly down the metal stairway. She had been in such pain right after she was brought on board that she hadn't paid attention to where they were taking her, but she assumed any sort of port entry would be on the bottom level of the sub so she headed down. As she reached the bottom of the steps, several crew members appeared, surrounding her. She held up her hands in what she hoped was a menacing attack stance. Running electricity down a chain was one thing-- shooting at a moving person was something completely different. She tried to look confident.

"I just killed your buddy, Spud. Don't make me hurt you, too!" The men looked amused. One stepped forward. She took a step backwards up the stairs. Then another.

"I wouldn't want you to hurt me either, but I'm willing to take that chance, pretty lady," he said, reaching a hand towards her, placing the other on the railing. The moment his hand touched the metal, she grabbed the railing with both hands and let energy flow from her like a jolt of lightning, knocking the man onto his back. The others drew back in shock. One pulled a knife from his belt and slashed it into the air in front of her. She tried to send her energy to the knife, but for some reason it wasn't working. Maybe she had to touch it, or she needed to recharge or something, she wondered as she cursed this unpredictable gift she possessed.

The man with the knife lunged toward her. She didn't react fast enough and he sliced her hand. She shouted in surprise, jerking her hand back and taking two steps up the stairs. The men drew closer, but with a snarl, she pushed the pain in her wounded hand out to everyone around her and they all fell back in surprise, as if they had each been cut.

"Don't hurt her!" she heard from behind. Hahn was slowly descending towards her. She pressed herself against the wall as more people flooded into the room behind him. She was surrounded.

"Don't come any further!" she shouted, her voice cracking. Hahn stopped.

"Where do you think you are going, my dear?" Hahn asked, his voice dripping with amusement.

"I'm not your dear," she spat, "and I'm leaving."

Hahn laughed. "Well you are going the wrong way. You are headed to engineering. There is no escape back there."

Marin didn't know what to believe, but she doubted anything Hahn would say to her. She tried to get her bearings, to find some way out, frustration eroding her earlier confidence. It did look like she was headed the wrong way. She hesitated, not knowing how to proceed. A pop sounded and something struck her neck with a sharp jab. She reflexively swatted her hand up, pushing the projectile in further. She curled her fingers around a small object and barely had time to register that it was a dart before her vision blurred and she was sliding down to the metal floor, unconscious.

***

When Marin awoke, she was back in her bed. The only difference in her room was that now there was a porta potty sitting next to her cubicle.

Great! She thought. She briefly felt herself slipping into despair, but she stopped herself angrily. *Survivors don't panic,* she heard Paul's voice in her head once again. If only he were here! She tried to think about her situation logically, to work the problem like Paul would. Experiments three and four hadn't exactly been successes, though she felt much less helpless than she had before. Hahn did not visit her the rest of that day, and neither did the guards, even to bring her food or water, which she had to admit wasn't a great improvement in her situation. Still, knowing she had some weapons in her arsenal gave her courage to plan. Obviously, Hahn did not feel safe around her, and that brought her great joy, if only for the thought that his sadistic torture sessions were at an end. But it didn't get her any closer to escaping, and if they didn't feed her or give her something to drink soon, it wouldn't matter. She fell back to her thin mattress in exasperation, stomach growling. She tried to make a spark, but couldn't seem to find the energy, so she curled in a ball to sleep.

She awoke to a prick in her arm. She tried to pull it back, but it was tied down. Tight. They were putting an IV in her!

"Are you drugging me?" she shouted, feeling her energy rise. If she could just get enough to zap these guys, but her face started going numb and her eyes went out of focus. "No!" she cried but the room went black and she was asleep.

***

When she started to come to, she heard Hahn's voice nearby.

"Good morning, my pet. You've had a busy day, haven't you?"

She turned her head toward him, feeling dizzy. Her mouth felt like cotton. Another man moved forward. He seemed like a doctor of some sort, but definitely not as high up the food chain as Hahn. She decided to call him Toady because he had bulgy, frog-like eyes.

"I gave her enough to keep her out for hours," he marveled. "It's been less than thirty minutes."

"She recovers to her normal state exceptionally fast," Hahn said, leaning forward to observe her. "She will be fully conscious in moments."

"Shall I give her more?" he asked.

"Not yet," he replied. She could picture him as he sat next to her, his legs casually crossed, waiting for her to open her eyes. She refused, but he wasn't fooled.

"Marin, I hope you realize there is no out for you. Anything you think of, we will develop a countermeasure for you. I know you are just figuring out what you can do, and perhaps you cannot even control these…powers. You will be tempted to continue to try me and attempt escape. Let me make your situation easier for you to understand." He moved closer to her and she gagged on the sweet stench of his cologne. She finally opened her eyes to glare at him, but he seemed perfectly calm, almost amused.

He smiled smugly. "While you were asleep, I implanted a capsule under your skin. With this device I hold, I can push a button to break that capsule, which will deliver a narcotic straight to your bloodstream and knock you out faster than you can blink if you disobey me. Don't bother looking for it, you have already healed over it, there is no way to tell where it is. I can keep you sedated indefinitely and you will live in a medicated stupor, your muscles atrophying day by day until you lack the strength to lift your head." He picked up a pen and twirled it absently. "And I can promise you, if I need to use it, even once, you have resigned yourself to lying there helpless as an invalid, so I can drain your blood whenever I get a paper cut."

Marin quailed at the thought.

"I want your stay with me to be pleasant, Marin," he said, rubbing a lock of her long hair between his fingers. "There's no need to make things worse for yourself."

"Sounds like I lose either way," she said, still trying to get her mouth working correctly. She sat up on one elbow, jerking her hair out of his grasp. Hahn withdrew a few feet away on his rolling chair, just out of her reach.

"Marin, other than the occasional blood draw I need for my experiments, there will likely be no more torture sessions. You get to eat food with your mouth, not shoved down your stomach by a tube in your nose. You get to sit up, read, and interact with me and the others that attend to you. Believe me; it's immensely preferable to the life you will experience if you rebel." He turned his attention to Toady.

"Knock her out again," he said, "but keep the sedation minimal. Time her on how long it takes to wake from this next dose and adjust it accordingly." He stood, then reached out a hand to stop Toady. "Wait, there's one more thing she needs to hear." He leaned over her, his eyes glittering with malice.

"Just in case you decide to try anything with your newfound electrical powers, I want you to think about this. Remember the warheads placed off the coast of major continents? They are tied to this submarine. If something should happen to the electrical system of this craft, or if for some reason it is destroyed, it will start a thirty-six hour countdown to detonate all three warheads, and I am the only one with the password access to shut them down."

"Thirty-six hours? That seems weak for you Hahn. Why give me three whole days to destroy your warheads once I escape?" Marin mocked. "Or are you worried something else might happen to trigger them and you'd need time to fix it? Maybe you're not so excited about being left with a dead world to rule." Hahn's eyes sparked and Marin knew she'd hit a nerve. He raised his hand as if to hit her, but she didn't flinch, so he dropped his hand to his side and lowered his voice to a sinister whisper.

"Millions of lives are at stake, Marin, not just yours. I would be careful if I were you." He gestured and Toady nodded, adjusting the IV. She struggled to stay awake, but blackness claimed her.

***

When she next awoke, she stayed completely still, trying her best to keep her breathing evenly spaced. She couldn't tell if she was alone in the room, but didn't dare open her eyes in case she was monitored. She reached out with her feelings, trying to see if she could tell by anything other than her ears if anyone was there. She waited for an eternity, and almost took a deep breath and opened her eyes when she heard movement in the corner of the room. Footsteps approached her.

"Respiration is altered," she heard Toady muttering to himself, and a pencil scratching as if he were making notes. "Patient was out twenty four minutes, pulse began rising two minutes ago. Astounding. This should have kept her out for hours. Patient's metabolism is unlike anything I've ever seen."

Marin concentrated on building electricity deep inside her bones. Her hands were tied in front of her with some fabric and her bare feet were trussed together with similar material. Apparently they figured out how Spud died. But did she need metal to deliver the energy she needed, or would it work with just a touch, like it had with Marcos?

Toady leaned over her. She could feel the fabric of his shirt brush against her face. She delved deeper. These men were monsters, torturers, gangsters. They would kill or maim her with one word from Hahn.

"Heart rate is rising dramatically," he said as if talking into a recorder. "Hopefully that doesn't mean she is going into arrest." The man leaned closer and touched her face with one antiseptic hand, opening her eyelid to look at her eyeball. She jerked her eye closed and pushed her energy out as hard as she could, releasing her pent up power. She felt the charge race across her face and into the man's hand and heard him shout out in alarm before falling, clattering to the ground. She opened her eyes and rolled over to look at him. He lay in a heap on the floor. She had no idea if he was alive or dead, nor did she really care as long as he didn't wake up anytime soon. She swung her legs over the edge of the bed, pulling at the fabric around her wrists to no avail. Lying on the floor next to Toady's head was Hahn's horrible scalpel. She grabbed it with both hands and awkwardly sawed at the bands at her wrists. She nicked her arm, but barely noticed in her haste to be free. The fabric sliced fairly easily and in a moment she was working on freeing her feet. She searched Toady's pockets until she found his key card. He moaned, but didn't rise. So he wasn't dead. Pity.

She held onto the scalpel, her only physical weapon so far and ran to the door. Just as she touched it, it slid open to reveal a surprised-looking Hahn about to walk in. She barely hesitated, rushing through the opening and shoving the scalpel into his abdomen as hard as she could. He stumbled against the wall, doubled over, eyes wide with shock, blood gushing down his white shirt.

"Doesn't feel so good on the cutting edge, does it, Hahn!" she hissed at him as she turned her back and ran to the front of the sub. She moved cautiously down a stairway and through several portals until she abruptly burst into the control room. Men looked up from their stations in surprise. She spun around until she found what she was searching for--a passageway to the left that led to the diving chamber. Her way out! She had taken one step when she saw Hahn stumble into the control room, holding his stomach and scrambling in his pocket until he produced a device in his blood soaked hand. Her heart stuck in her throat.

"Stop her!" he croaked. "I need her blood!" He pushed the button on it and she felt something on her inner arm burst.

"No!" she shrieked, racing toward the chamber door, but within two steps she stumbled to her knees and collapsed.

CHAPTER 32

FRANK

FRANK WAS IMPRESSED with the sheer volume of the pictures covering the President's massive bed, but before he could get a good look at them, the doctor scrambled over, sweeping them into a trash can. One small slip of sketched paper with the white house insignia on it drifted unnoticed to the floor and Frank discreetly picked it up, slipping it into his pocket as a souvenir of his unusual visit.

"The President is in no condition to be receiving visitors this time of night," the doctor was saying, as he took the trash can into the bathroom out of sight.

"Nonsense!" President Thompson said, waving off the doctor. "I feel fine, just a little tired. Come in, Bob! What's got you so worked up at this time of night?"

"It's time for your medicine, Mr. President," the doctor said, pushing to the head of the bed and reaching for his arm.

"A shot? In the middle of the night? What's wrong with you, man? First you throw a fit for waking him up, and now you want me to believe he's due for medicine right now?" General Holt asked skeptically.

"I keep telling you, Sergio, I don't like how that stuff makes me feel." The President pushed the doctor's hands away. "Let me talk to Bob, and leave me alone, would you?" The doctor's mouth hung open, but nothing came out. The Chief of Staff appeared at the foot of the bed.

"I'm so sorry to have let these people intrude and wake you, sir," she said, looking at the doctor like she expected something of him. Frank got an uneasy feeling about both of them.

The President slid his feet out of the bed and rose, almost shouting. "Sergio, Judy, General Holt has clearance to see me as both a high-ranking commander and my personal friend. Now would you please leave us alone and let me talk to him! And close the door on your way out!"

They looked at each other, their faces tight and worried, but after a quick glance at the guards standing at the door, they shuffled out the doorway.

The President sat back down on his bed as if all his strength was gone. Frank couldn't help but notice he looked a lot more tired and weak in person that he did on TV.

"Are you all right, John?" The General asked, putting a hand on the President's shoulder. The President nodded slowly. "I'm so sorry to bother you. They said you weren't feeling well, but time is of the essence."

"It's all right. I'm fine. What's the emergency?"

The General turned and gestured to Pete. "John, I'd like you to meet Sergeant Major Bale. He's the man I've had investigating the suspicious activities near Point Mugu and was also the one who provided the photographs I showed you several weeks ago. And may I present Doctor Douglas Franklin Gilbert, head of the COAST program. He is the leader of the water people I was telling you about." Frank put out his hand, but the President didn't seem to notice, so he dropped it to his side.

"Water people again? Are you serious, Bob? I really thought that was a bunch of hooey."

"You sent me out to find proof of these people. Someone who knew what was going on. Here he is."

"Well, you're tenacious when you get a lead, I'll give you that, Bob." He turned his attention to Frank, ignoring Bale. "You're a merman?" the President said tiredly, rubbing his temples.

Frank blushed. "Well, I wouldn't want to put it that way, Sir," Frank stammered. "But I *can* breathe underwater."

The President locked eyes with him, as if judging his truthfulness. "Prove it."

"Excuse me?" Frank asked.

"Prove it. Breathe water and then we'll talk."

Frank looked at the General, who shrugged, looking around the room. Then he gestured to the oversized jetted bathtub in the adjoining bathroom.

"I would like to see this as well," the General added.

"I'm curious, too," Bale chimed in.

Frank rolled his eyes at them, muttering "You've got to be kidding," under his breath. He went to the tub and started filling it. Then stripped down to his boxers, shivering a little under the scrutiny of the three men.

"I really didn't think I would be half naked in the bathroom of the President of the United States when I woke up this morning," he said to ease the awkwardness of the situation. The President laughed.

"I wouldn't call what we got last night sleep, so technically, you haven't had a chance to wake up this morning yet, anyway," General Holt pointed out. Frank had to agree. When the water was high enough, he got in and sank down into the tub. He'd been too nervous to pay attention to the temperature and it was uncomfortably cool. The men came in and stood over him expectantly. General Holt took out his phone.

"I'll time him," he said.

The water continued to rise up over Frank's face. When it was well over his head, the President reached over and turned it off. Frank waited until the water was as still as glass, then let the air out of his lungs. The bubbles rumbled to the top and popped and the men looked down at him in surprise.

"You've never seen him do this?" He could hear the President ask, his voice distorted by the water. Bale shook his head.

"Nope. First time," Holt answered as well.

"And you dragged him in here and woke me up without knowing for sure?" The President sounded irritated. Frank wondered if they knew he could hear them or if they even cared if he did. Frank sucked in a mouthful of water, over exaggerating the act of breathing the water in and out. They leaned forward and stared down at him incredulously. He turned his head to the side so they could see the gills behind his ear flutter lightly as water passed over them. The men watched him for several minutes, engrossed in his ability, but he was getting cold and this was wasting precious time, so he sat up and pushed the water through his gills before taking a deep breath of air.

"Satisfied?" he asked, snatching an extremely fluffy towel off the side of the tub and rubbing his face and hair dry with it.

"Unbelievable. Simply unbelievable," the President said, poking at the gills behind Frank's ear.

"Hey! Stop that!" Frank said irritably. "Sir," he added.

"I'm so sorry. I just can't believe my own eyes!"

Frank stood up and toweled off while they stared at him like he was an alien. "Look, I don't mean to be rude, but I'm cold and wet and now that I've shown my little trick to you both, could we please make arrangements to stop the man that has destroyed two states and kidnapped my daughter?" He held up three fingers one by one. "I want to get to my wife, I want to find my daughter, and I want to stop Hahn, in that order. Time is of the essence so can we get moving on this?" His voice rose in frustration. The other two men stood as if shaken from a trance.

"Yes, of course! I apologize," the President said, though he still appeared to be struggling to accept the fact that he now lived in a world where humans could breathe water. General Holt stepped in.

"Sir, perhaps you can arrange an emergency meeting with the secretaries of Defense, Homeland Security, CIA and the Director of National Intelligence," the General suggested. Turning to Frank, he added, "Then we can locate an asset in your wife's vicinity and give them instructions to stand ready to receive you and transport you to your people." The General glanced over and the President agreed. Relief flooded Frank's heart and soul. He sank to the rim of the bathtub and nodded his thanks.

"You look exhausted," the President noticed, putting a hand on Frank's shoulder. "This will take some time to arrange, despite our haste. Might I suggest you take this opportunity to shower and change and perhaps eat before our meeting?"

"That would be…wonderful. Thank you, sir."

The President pulled an extremely well pressed set of clothing out from his own wardrobe and an expensive looking disposable razor and gave them to Frank, leaving him alone in the bathroom to take a quick warm shower and clean up in privacy. Frank was slightly taller than the President, but for the most part, everything fit exceptionally well. He folded his dirty clothes and left them in a pile next to the tub. When he came out, he was pleased to see a fire had been stoked in the fireplace and a round table had been set up near it with silverware, plates and fluted glasses.

"You clean up remarkably well," Bale noticed. "You don't look at all like the half-crazed lunatic that came off the plane from Lanai." Frank scowled at him, but the other two laughed heartily.

"Don't take that too hard, Gilbert. We are all just glad you are able to look like yourself before the meeting. It will help your credibility," General Holt added.

"As opposed to meeting the United States President looking like I'd just escaped from prison?" Frank asked sarcastically.

"Point taken!" he said, prompting another round of laughter.

"I took the liberty of ordering breakfast for us all. It should be here shortly," the President said, motioning for him to sit down nearest the fire.

"I appreciate that, Sir," he said, taking the welcome seat by the flames. "Have you located a ship near the submarine my wife is on?"

The President had a pen in his hand and was doodling on a napkin absently. "We are working on it. I've sent a message to the Security Council and the Department of Homeland Security. We are meeting with them in a little over an hour, so in the meantime, please sit and recover from your long adventure."

Within minutes, the food was delivered on heavily laden rolling trays. Frank noticed the doctor was still hovering around the open door.

"Mr. President?" he said, stepping into the room.

"Later!" the President roared as the food was laid out on the table and the servers took the carts back out with them.

A dark look passed over the doctor's face as the door closed, and Frank couldn't decide if he looked angry or scared. But the food smelled delicious and he couldn't remember the last time he'd eaten, so for the next several minutes he busied himself with trying the wide variety of fruit, fresh breads and egg dishes placed before him. A beautiful ceramic bowl filled with some sort of creamy spinach and egg dish quickly became his favorite, topped off with a drink of a tart pink liquid in a crystal carafe, which he assumed was pink grapefruit juice. The President, General Holt, and Sergeant Major Bale finished their smaller meals quickly, but kindly waited until Frank had staved off most of his hunger before asking him questions. Frank was just reaching for another helping of the egg dish when the President spoke. He pulled his hand back, embarrassed.

"Please, go ahead. It's one of my favorites. Oeufs en Cocotte." Frank smiled and took a bit more for his plate and refilled his glass again.

"Ah, I haven't felt this good in months! Perhaps I should wake at four every morning," the President said with a satisfied smile, pushing his chair slightly away from the table. "So…this…ability you have. How exactly did you acquire it? Bob has explained most of your story while we were waiting for you, but I have many questions, as you might imagine."

Frank wiped his mouth with a monogrammed napkin and cleared his throat. "It's a medicine, a drug, which my wife invented. It basically adds marine DNA to your own and gives you the ability to breathe underwater, as you just observed." The President nodded.

"I have a question for you, Doctor," General Holt said, leaning forward. "I was told you were asking for me specifically. How did you know who I was?"

Frank smiled sadly. "We had a common friend, Ahsan Ahmed. Do you remember him?"

Holt thought for a moment, then his face lit up. "Yes! He was my translator many years ago. A brilliant man! He spoke impeccable English, Persian, Arabian, Chinese and Thai! How do you know him?" he asked, genuinely pleased.

"He was recruited to work on the AQUA project shortly after he worked for you."

Holt's eyes grew wide. "You mean he became an…a…whatever you are?"

"Arydian. Yes. He was one of the seven original members. He spoke very highly of you and was impressed with your integrity, following your career with interest. So when the time came, yours was the first name that came to mind."

The President cleared his throat. "Bob here mentioned a girl that was picked up by the Navy several weeks ago. Do you know her?"

Frank nodded past the lump in his throat. "Yes, Mr. President. That is my daughter, Marin. She has been taken captive by Hahn and they are believed to be in a special submarine designed to go extremely deep, deeper than anything the military owns. My wife and a group of my people are in a smaller submarine in pursuit, using a tracker they acquired. Sergeant Major Bale has assured me that if my people assist you in locating Hahn that they will help me rescue her."

"What do you know about this mutagen Hahn unleashed on Lanai?" he asked, taking a sip of his drink, neatly avoiding Frank's comment about rescuing Marin. Frank frowned but answered his question.

"All I know is it seems to have killed every living thing, even animals. It was killing me as well, but I fell in the water and when I awoke, its effects seemed to have worn off. I had no trouble breathing hours after."

"Apparently," the President agreed, taking a roll and putting jam on it, before dipping it in his coffee and taking a bite.

"When we brought you in for questioning in California, you'd said this Chita Vasquez woman took you to this rendezvous with her so you could verify the chemical makeup of the toxin," Holt said. "Did you get a good enough look at it to copy it?"

"Mutagen," Frank corrected, rubbing his hand through his hair and messing it up. "I'm sorry, Sir. Not from memory. The strange thing is that it resembles the compound in Arydia, but with several differences." Holt and the President looked at each other, but Frank put up his hand in protest. "Before you ask, no, I don't have the compound for Arydia memorized, either. And even if I did, I wouldn't just hand that information over. I had two conditions going into this, the first one was that you help me get Marin back, the second is that you leave us completely alone after this. No tests, no imprisonment and experiments. We want to be left alone to live our lives in peace."

"That might be a hard sell, Doctor." The President said. "This is a global threat. If we use your people to help neutralize it, other countries, other governments will *have to* know about you. I can only speak for the United States, and on that note, you have my word that we will do our best to keep your existence quiet. I'm afraid I can't offer more than that."

Frank considered his offer and agreed, but a disturbing thought hit him. He looked the President in the eye. "And if we get you to Hahn's sub, do I have your word you will help us extract my daughter *before* you do anything to Hahn?"

General Holt cleared his throat. "We will do our best to help you in any way we can. We must rely on you to get her out, though. If he can go as deep as you say, you might be our only way to get to them, and then it is in your hands. We have an aircraft carrier and three submarines en route to rendezvous with your wife's team."

"How soon can you get me there?" he asked hopefully.

"We can leave as soon as the transport is ready," the President said, checking his watch. "If you are not against flying in a fighter jet, we can send you as soon as our meeting with the Security Council is finished." There was a knock at the door, and the doctor looked in.

"Are you ready for your medicine now?" he asked gently.

"In a moment. We are wrapping up," he said, dismissing him with a wave of his hand. The doctor scowled and closed the door.

General Holt frowned. "What is this medicine this guy is pushing down your throat?" he asked gruffly.

The President put his hands behind his head and stretched out his legs in front of him. "I started having heart palpitations and they are trying to keep my heart steady. I can't really fault him; he's just doing his job." His brow creased for a moment. "But something about this medicine makes me feel odd. There are often times I can't remember long stretches of time, and that, frankly, scares me to death. I really feel so much better without the medicine."

The General leaned forward, talking just above a whisper. "Do you think this medicine is doing something to you? I mean, do you trust they are not using this to harm you, or control you?"

The President blinked his eyes in surprise, but then the lines on his forehead drew together even more. "Sergio has been my personal physician for years. How on earth could you even suggest such a thing?"

Frank leaned forward himself, joining the low conversation. "Sir, if he is affiliated with Hahn, they are capable of worse actions than these. I *know* Hahn has worked tirelessly on drugs that manipulate thought, devices implanted that control people through pain, not to mention bribery and threats that can be used to…motivate people to act against their natures."

"Are you saying my people have been bribed?" the President said, appalled.

"Not necessarily, and perhaps not all, but your physician may have been. Why was he insisting you have your 'medicine' before we even spoke to you?" Frank asked. "And those drawings all over your bed. What were they? He seemed anxious that nobody see them."

The President seemed thoughtful. "I…I don't really know. They help me to relax, but Sergio almost always takes them away."

"Where are they?" Sergeant Major Bale asked. "He tossed them in the garbage, let's take a look." He pushed his chair back and walked into the bathroom, returning with an empty wastebasket.

"It's been taken out!" he said.

"Probably when breakfast was brought in," the President said, growing concerned.

"Wait! I may have picked one up when we first walked in," Frank said sheepishly. He went into the bathroom and came back with his dirty clothes, digging in the pocket. He pulled out the slightly damp stationary, pressing it down on the table to smooth it out. It was a picture of a hand reaching up out of a lake, fingers curled like they were straining to grasp something just out of reach.

The President looked it over, his brow heavy. "This is what I mean, I really don't even remember drawing this, but I feel like I did. It feels familiar."

"This image is truly disturbing, Mr. President. No offense intended, but if this is something pouring out of your subconscious mind…"

"What are you suggesting?" The President demanded.

General Holt folded his arms across his chest. "John, I know you don't want to believe ill of people, but surely you must see the need to be cautious. There are plenty of physicians in the world. Put your man under observation and get a second opinion on your condition. If it turns out we are wrong, at least you will know you are taking the right steps. But if we are right, the safety of you and millions around the world is at stake."

The President took a deep breath and puffed it out through his lips slowly. He stood and went to the phone on his nightstand. "Send up a security detail immediately."

CHAPTER 33

MARIN

MARIN TOOK A deep breath and coughed. Her back was stiff and she couldn't move her feet or her left arm. There was an IV in her right hand running to a clear bag of something dangling above her head on a hook. Probably a sedative. Rolling her head to the side, she saw her arm was strapped down to the side of the bed and a silver tube protruded from a deep cut in her upper arm with plastic tubing running into Hahn's elbow, who was asleep on a cot right next to her. His clammy fingers were near enough to touch. They were using her to heal him! She snarled and reached for the tubes, but her hand was caught by the Toady.

"Don't make me sedate you again," he said calmly, pushing her arm back down and fastening straps over her wrist and elbow. "Such high doses are bad for Doctor Hahn. He's already going to be out for hours."

"Like I care," she spat at him. She twisted, but her legs were strapped too tightly to do more than wiggle. "Sedate me all you want! I hope it stops his creepy little heart. If he has one!"

Toady shook his head and moved over to inspect Hahn, pulling up one eyelid and then the other. Hahn's shirt had been removed and his wound dressed. Toady peeked under the bandages to see if the bleeding had stopped.

"You are truly remarkable. Your blood…it's like nothing I've ever seen.

He is healing unbelievably fast. Hahn has guarded you well and for good reason. You are literally the fountain of youth!"

"Yeah, well, we all have our skills. Yours seems to be kissing up to this piece of trash and torturing innocent girls," she retorted.

Toady glared at her. He was an average-sized man with a wide mouth and a round nose, which emphasized his frog-like attributes. His protruding eyes hid behind dirty glasses.

"I would think a girl in your situation would guard her tongue more carefully," he said, stepping closer to her and caressing her hair. "With Hahn incapacitated, I am the authority on this ship."

Marin shrugged. "You can't kill me; Hahn would have your head."

Toady smiled at her. "Oh, you have no imagination. I don't need to kill you to make you wish for death." He breathed in, leaning over her.

Marin swallowed hard, her anger melting into fear. Toady stared her down and finally she looked away, shrinking from the naked evil in the man's eyes. Of course the people working for Hahn would be monsters. Who could bear him otherwise? Toady smirked and left the room.

Marin tried to gather her anger and find some way to zap Hahn, but she was so weak, she literally felt drained. She closed her eyes, wishing her blood would poison Hahn, but after a while opened them again with a sigh. Hahn was breathing deeply, as if he had no cares in the world. She turned her head to get a better look at him. He seemed to be in his late forties or early fifties, thin and wiry. If he wasn't so horrible and old, he might even be considered to be slightly handsome. He had a little grey peppering the black hair around his temples.

He looked peaceful, lying there. He had no business looking peaceful, even in his dreams. She had a cure for that. Marin couldn't move her arm much, so she stretched out her fingers as far as she could until she brushed his hand. Inching closer, she reached into his mind, tapping into his subconscious dreams, just as she had done on accident to Marcos on Isla Cedros a lifetime ago. Only this time she was going in with a purpose. She curled her fingers around Hahn's and pushed herself into his mind.

Suddenly she was sucked into a jungle outside a small village. She was standing several feet behind a line of ragged people making their way through thick underbrush, chatting and laughing animatedly, all carrying containers and headed toward a wide, slow river. The mood was light and friendly, the sun warm and the breeze cool. She stepped forward, pushing aside the tall grass and instantly the mood changed as if the jungle and everyone in it was suddenly aware of her presence. A group of helicopters flew low overhead and everyone paused when they got close, crouching down in the underbrush and watching the canopy of trees overhead like scared animals. All except one boy. He stood still, his back to her, then slowly rotated to look at her, his eyes widening in fear.

"You!" he said in a croaking voice, decades older than he looked.

Hahn.

"Me!" she retorted, her soul raging with power. The helicopters descended, the trees whipping around as if in a hurricane, birds screeching into the air from the branches. She stood tall against the wind, gathering power from the maelstrom she was creating. The villagers scattered, screaming, the noise of the birds and the helicopters and the leaves so loud it was almost unbearable. She sucked in the energy like a deep breath and pushed it out through her hands towards him. All the pain he'd caused to her and her family came flying out of her fingers like a swarm of black crows and dived toward him.

He screamed in terror, turning to run, but the birds surrounded him and flew into his body, lifting him a few feet off the ground, his mouth wide as he aged in front of her, his bare feet now in high priced shoes, his ragged tunic turning into a blood-stained button-down shirt. She forced all her fear and pain and sorrow into his unprotected soul, slamming him down to the ground, pinning him there while the birds flew into his chest, each one hitting him like a hammer and vanishing inside him with a puff of black smoke. His screaming never stopped as she stood over him, willing him to feel the pain he inflicted on others, meeting his horror-filled eyes with her own grim determination.

"You can't chain me down here, Hahn. My mind is free. I can do anything I want to you!" She reached to the ground and picked up a heavy stick which sharpened into a spear in her hands. Lifting it high above her head, she laughed as Hahn's hands flew out protectively in front of his body as if

166

it would help him. She longed to kill him, to see the light of his evil eyes doused forever, but there was something she needed from him first.

"Tell me about the warheads, Hahn. Where are they?" He looked at her, confused, terrified, and shook his head. "This is all a dream, Hahn," she said in a soft voice. "It doesn't matter what you say in a dream." She silenced all the sounds around them. Hahn lay flat on his back, chest heaving.

"You can't find them, you can't reach them!" he said fighting back a little.

"Then what does it matter if you tell me about them?" she said in hiss. "All you have to do is think it. I'll do the rest."

Instantly in her mind she saw a map focusing in on the Hudson Canal, the English Channel and a canyon near Pakistan. She smiled triumphantly, and he looked at her in horror.

"You can't disarm them! They are tied together. If you destroy one, the other two will detonate."

"You know there is a way to disarm them. A weasel like you always leaves a back door," she said. "Tell me how to access them and shut them down." Hahn remained silent, sweat making his thinning hair slick. She walked over to him and placed her foot on his chest, pressing down heavily.

"You can't just shut it down! It's a password. You have to enter the password manually."

"Good. Just say the password and you can come out of this, Hahn. Just say it." She tried to control her voice, to make it sound sweet, comforting, tasting the words like thick honey. She calmed the wind slightly, lifted the weight of her foot just a fraction of an inch. "It's just a dream; you can say anything in a dream. You won't remember this anyway. You'll forget everything but the feeling you have now, once you wake up." She wasn't sure if she could make him forget this, but while she was in here, she was certainly going to try. It wouldn't do her any good if he changed the passwords.

"Tell, me, Hahn!" He shook his head again and she lost control, her voice joining once again with all the cacophony around her, the jungle wind, the helicopters, the people shrieking, the earth itself, shaking him to the core from below and around him, making the air a living, angry thing.

"SAY IT!" She screamed with the voice of everything.

"I CAN'T" he cried, pushing back, resisting.

"SAY. IT." The entire world shook, colors bending together, the ground below him bucking and twisting as if creation itself was coming undone.

"WATASHI WA KAMI!" he screamed, the words taking form in the air in front of him. "I AM GOD!"

She took a deep breath, burning the phrase into her mind, then turned to him, making the javelin in her hand sharp as a razor. This was it; she was going to kill this monster once and for all. With a victorious scream, she grabbed the spear in both hands and suddenly it was gone. The jungle, Hahn, everything vanished. Her hand had been jerked away and the contact was broken. She opened her eyes to see Toady and several other men in the room. One was holding her hands down painfully while Toady tried to calm the unconscious but still screaming Hahn.

"What did you do to him?" He shouted over Hahn's shrieks, trying vainly to control Hahn's flailing arms.

Marin watched without speaking.

"Hold him!" he ordered. It took three people to keep him still enough for Toady to get a good look under Hahn's bandage. "I'm going to disconnect the line. His wound appears to be improving. We must move him away from the girl before she does him more harm." He took the tube from Hahn's thrashing arm with much difficulty and wrapped it. The tube fell to the ground, Marin's blood spilling out the end in a small, red river. Her heart started pounding in response to the rapid blood loss on top of her already weakened state and her lips started to feel numb, her fingers turning to ice.

"Get him out of here!" he ordered. They rolled him out the door.

"What about the girl?" one man ventured to ask over his shoulder. "She's bleeding to death!" Toady snarled at him, looking at the puddle spreading across the floor. He hesitated for a moment, as if he'd like nothing more than to let Marin bleed out then and there, but he grabbed a wad of gauze and started to remove the drainage system he'd placed in her vein. She cringed against the pain, and he smiled whenever she flinched, as if enjoying every moment as he clamped it off and stitched the incision shut.

"No matter how fast you heal, I hope you'll still have a nice scar there to remember me by," Toady said as he cut the last thread. He walked to the other side of her bed and opened a valve on the tube leading to her other arm, releasing a sedative into her bloodstream. "And don't even think about escaping. I've implanted another sedative under your skin. Just one little click of a button and you'd be right back here. Now be a good girl, and go to sleep!"

***

An intense aching in Marin's wrists pulled her out of the depths of the drug induced sleep she'd been in. It was quiet, an empty quiet. Cracking her eyes, she hazarded a glance around her, but, thankfully, the room appeared to be deserted. She was back in her cubicle, her hands and feet tied tightly together, this time with rope. Now that she was awake, the intensity of the ache in her hands and wrists increased. Closing her eyes, she tried to assess her situation. She knew the codes. She knew where the warheads were. She had been so close to killing Hahn, it almost seemed impossible that she hadn't been able to finish the job. Yet, with all that knowledge, here she was, back where she started: trapped, tied down, helpless and no closer to escaping.

She wriggled her swollen fingers, wincing. What was the use of all she'd learned if she never got the chance to stop anything? She could feel the black pit of despair reaching out to her, trying to pull her in, making her want to give up. There was no escape from this, it whispered to her. No matter what she tried, they would find a countermeasure to prevent it. Nobody would find her and she would spend her life here in this submerged prison. The negative voices in her head never stopped tearing her down and suddenly she lost the will to find arguments against them. She was scared. Hunger gnawed at her insides, pain dug at her outsides. She teetered on the pit and then dropped in, falling into the depths of despair and hopelessness.

Even with superpowers, she was useless. How much good did her pathetic powers do, anyway? All she had done was shock Spud and Toady, and escaped twice only to get captured again within moments. She curled herself into a protective ball, nursing the hurt as miserable, hopeless feelings raged freely inside her. Some small part of her brain kept repeating to her the chant Paul had always taught her. "Survivors don't panic, they keep their heads," but she couldn't use her head anymore! It hurt, like every other part of her. And every time she tried, she just ended up right back in the same situation. It was hopeless. She cried until the tears wouldn't come anymore.

CHAPTER 34

FRANK

FRANK WALKED INTO the wood-paneled room with a sense of awe. He'd only seen this kind of room on television and some part of him felt like he was having a dream, standing with General Holt and the President of the United States like he was in some kind of international spy movie. If only it were.

The men and women stood around the large conference table until Frank and General Holt were shown seats and the President sat down, then they all took their chairs. Glancing around the room, Frank saw many people he didn't recognize, but there were several that he'd seen on news channels over the years, giving updates and briefings on various topics. These were some of the most important people on the planet. It was impossible to not feel a little insecure.

"Ladies and gentlemen," the President began, "I'd like to introduce Dr. Franklin Douglas Gilbert, head of the California Oceanic Alliance of Science and Technology, which we will refer to from this point forward as COAST. He will be briefing us on the situation. Dr. Gilbert?"

Frank worked his tongue around his suddenly dry mouth and cleared his throat. "My apologies, I thought I was just attending this meeting, not running it," he said with an uncomfortable laugh. Stares greeted him. He cleared his throat again, digging up his courage for the sake of Marin and Emily.

"The man who has threatened our nation and our world is a man I worked with many years ago by the name of Doctor Tadashi Hahn, an exceptionally gifted geneticist, perhaps bordering on genius. He was overseeing a research project I was on, known as AQUA, that was tasked with developing a way for humans to breathe water and colonize the oceans. We succeeded." He paused, expecting looks of scorn and disbelief. He got them. General Hahn stepped in and rescued him.

"I understand your disbelief, but if you will each look at your monitors, I will show you a small sample of proof that what this man says is true." The general connected his phone to his monitor and suddenly Frank was watching a video of himself in the President's bathroom breathing water. He cringed inside, his face flaming red as he realized that now everyone in the room had seen him in his underwear. Great. He had thought the General had just been timing him, not recording him.

The video continued until he sat up and pushed the water out of his gills and stood up, shivering, unshaven and wet in his boxers.

"Seriously, General! Do you mind!" Frank asked in astonishment.

"Oh… sorry," he mumbled, turning off the video.

Frank looked around the room, his face still aflame. Every eye was upon him. Frank turned his head and pointed to his gills. "Yes, it is true. No, we are not kidding. The President himself witnessed this. And no, I don't have time to try to prove it to each of you. You are going to have to come to terms with this as a reality if we are to protect the citizens of this planet from Hahn." All eyes turned to the President who dipped his head in agreement.

"It is true. Listen to him."

"We developed a drug we named Arydia that changes human DNA to imitate that of sea creatures and allows us to breathe underwater, as you have seen. We have hidden that technology from Hahn and for years have been living peacefully in the ocean. Those who have taken the drug are called Arydians. I am one of the leaders of these people."

"What does this have to do with Lanai?" a woman at the end of the table interrupted.

"Hahn is the head of a massive criminal organization and has almost limitless resources. He has used these resources to create a mutagen that he has weaponized. This is what he released in his attack on Lanai. As far as I know, I was one of the few survivors of that attack."

General Holt interrupted. "We have now heard from twelve more survivors. All were in the water, swimming either in the ocean or pools when the attack happened." Frank nodded, considering the odd circumstances of the survivors.

"This weapon," a younger man, perhaps in his early thirties, asked "it makes people become…like…like you?"

Frank turned to the President, slapping the table and making everyone startle. "Sir! That's it! That's why I survived! I've been wracking my brains to figure out why this didn't affect me like it did everyone else. It DID affect me. I was suffocating until I fell off the bridge, but once I was underwater, I could breathe. If this drug is fundamentally similar to Arydia, it could be that it enacts a temporary change in the lungs of whoever breathes it in! They can ONLY breathe water for a certain amount of time!"

"So…you're saying that people become like you, but only temporarily?" the President mused.

Frank nodded, feeling in his gut he was right. "It isn't exactly like Arydia. There were some stark differences. This has to be one aspect of those differences."

The younger man spoke again. "So if he does deploy these warheads, all we have to do is tell everyone to jump in the water for several hours and they'll be fine?" he asked, arching one eyebrow skeptically.

"Well, in theory, it might work. But even if we could convince the leaders of the world, which is doubtful, getting that information to every man, woman and child, and getting them to not only believe it, but to act upon it, seems unlikely," the President said. "The best course of action will be to locate and destroy the warheads Hahn mentioned in his threat."

"And how are we supposed to do this?" demanded an extremely strong looking man with dark skin and a bald head. Frank tried not to stare at the jagged scar on the side of the man's neck. "We've turned up nothing in our search to find this Hahn guy, not even a picture, and now you want us to believe he can breathe water and has unlimited resources? This Hahn seems to be a figment of your imagination."

The President turned to Frank and gestured for him to continue. "Not only can I testify to the reality of Hahn, my people have access to a tracker that can pinpoint Hahn's exact location," Frank said firmly. "He is on a sub somewhere in the Bering sea." The man with the scar twisted his mouth as if tasting something sour.

"And where did you get this tracker?" the man asked, his voice strangely ominous.

"Mr. Akuna, that is a story longer than we have time to go over," President Thompson said. "Suffice it to say I trust his source." The man looked like he wanted to say more, but he nodded and sat back in his chair.

A woman with extremely short grey hair, also in military uniform chimed in. "If we have Hahn's location, then let's target him! If we kill him before he can detonate these weapons, the threat is gone."

Frank blanched, his blood running cold. "No!" he cried, standing up. "No, we can't kill him. Not yet."

"What?"

"Why?"

"What are you talking about?" Voices erupted around the table. The President held up a hand.

"Dr. Gilbert has reason to believe his daughter is a prisoner on board this submarine. We have given him our word we will try to rescue her before moving on the target."

The room boiled with objections. The President let the chatter ebb and flow for a few minutes before putting an end to it. "Enough. We need to take this one step at a time. Dr. Gilbert will rendezvous with some of his people who are already in pursuit of Hahn. I've ordered the U.S.S. Carl Vinson to the coordinates. Doctor, what else do you need for this mission in your opinion?"

Frank rubbed his chin, anxious about almost every aspect of this. "Hahn's sub can go deep, really deep. Three or four subs that could cut off any escape would be wonderful. Deep sea divers if it comes to hand to hand combat. Air cover in case he surfaces. And I need transportation to my sub, the Minnow."

"*Your* sub! Seems like you have some serious resources yourself! I'm starting to side with Zarobi Akuna over here," he gestured to the gruff man with the neck scar, "in thinking maybe you are part of this somehow. How many people are like you, Doctor?" the younger man questioned skeptically.

The President cleared his throat. "You should all know that the existence of Dr. Gilbert and his people are strictly top secret. They are officially under the protection of the U.S. Military as of now. The two assurances we have given to him in order to secure his assistance and he, ours, is that the existence of the Arydians stays unknown, and that we attempt to rescue his daughter before moving against Hahn."

"Surely this 'rescue' will alert Hahn to us. How on earth are we supposed to rescue someone from a submerged craft without Hahn detonating the warheads? Even to attempt it is foolish!" another man shouted a few seats down from Frank.

"I agree!" said the man with the scar, Mr. Akuna. "There is no way to even try this without risking the lives of millions!"

"My people can get to the sub and get on board. I just want you ready to take care of Hahn once that is accomplished."

"I'm sorry, Doctor, but I have no faith in your ability or in the soundness of any of these decisions. Surely you can see our point," the woman with short hair said.

General Holt held up a hand. "Gilbert, if it comes down to making a choice between saving your daughter and stopping this attack, I would hope you would be willing to make the choice that saves the most lives." Frank bit the sides of his cheeks and frowned, but slowly nodded. "Then we will have to trust you to follow through with that," Holt said firmly.

The General looked at his phone as a message rang through. "Doctor, your transportation has arrived." He stood, motioning for Frank to follow him. Frank got to his feet but leaned forward on his arms on the table.

"I understand your concern; I know your responsibility is to the people of this country and those other countries that will be affected by this. We have all lost people we love during this time. I lost my sister-in-law during the disaster in California. You may be thinking 'what's one life compared to many,' but I want you to think, Hahn is one man and look at how he has changed the landscape of the world. I am one man, yet I stand before you with the information you would have never found on your own, tools to help you fight against Hahn. My daughter, Marin, is the only one of her kind in the world. She was born an Arydian and has powers and gifts I have yet to know the limit of. Who knows what her life might mean for this world? Do not be so quick to judge the value of one life against others when you do not know what their destiny holds."

CHAPTER 35

MARIN

THE ACHING IN Marin's arms had become the defining feature of her life. Having her hands tied together for so long was starting to mess with her head. Even simple things, like scratching an itch, were almost impossible. She had lost all track of time. It could have been days or hours since she'd attacked Hahn. Maybe a day or two, because she hadn't seen him since they removed him from the room, and she assumed he would have come in if he were better. She let herself halfway daydream that maybe she wounded him beyond repair, or maybe even killed him, but she doubted she was that lucky. Besides, Toady wasn't much better.

The door slid open and someone walked in. Slow, measured steps, not the shuffle of Toady. Curious, she rolled her head to the side and was surprised to see Hahn. He moved carefully into the room, each step intentional. He sat down far from her reach, watching her silently.

She turned her face back to the roof of her cubby, all her dreams of Hahn's death dashed. She could hear him breathing in and out, in and out, silent and staring. She could feel his eyes on her. She cringed inside, hating him with every molecule of her being, hating him looking at her, hating him breathing her same air.

"What do you want, Hahn," she finally snapped, turning to meet his gaze.

Hahn didn't answer immediately. Then he stood, walking closer to her, but staying well out of reach. He picked up a scalpel and she winced, pulling herself as far away from him as she could, but he didn't come any nearer to her. Instead, he drew it lightly across his own arm, making a red line appear. He started his timer, watching the numbers click off one by one until one minute had passed. He took a clean pad of gauze and wiped away the blood that had pooled on his arm. The wound underneath had gone. A crazed smile crossed his face, and he raised his eyes to meet Marin's.

"That was nearly as fast as you heal. I may not need your services anymore, my dear. I do believe you have made me immortal!" He stood up straight and walked to her side, running a finger down the side of her face. She shivered at his touch. "I wonder what other gifts I've inherited from you," he said with an evil smile. "I look forward to finding out. Don't get too comfortable with your situation, my pet. Your value has decreased exponentially." He turned and walked towards the door, but paused, looking over his shoulder. "I shall look forward to watching you suffer for the pain you've inflicted on me," he said, his eyes narrowed to a slit. "I don't forgive easily." He left the room, leaving her shaking in his wake.

How could he have healed so quickly himself? She was amazed and horrified that her blood had given him the power to heal like she could. And if he could always heal, did that really mean immortality? Was *she* immortal? She wrinkled her brow, contemplating the thought. Aging really meant your cells stopped regenerating. And if your cells were always regenerating, then, technically, you would never age. But could you die? She rolled over on her side, trying to puzzle out the answers. Frank said he'd learned something about her before the attack on Arydia. Something about her blood. She'd thought it was something bad, but what if it was good? Wasn't that, in essence, what he told her, word for word, when he said *I promise you are not going to die?*

She traced a pattern absently on the walls with her fingertip, weighing the implications. Suppose Frank *did* mean she is immortal…she'd given her blood to Marcos…did that mean he had the same powers as she did? And what about the vials derived from her blood that had been given to Jaycen and who knows who else? Were they immortal, too? And would they have the same powers she had been learning she possessed? Reaching into people's minds, generating electricity? What about the Arydians that were changed back by exposure to her blood? She shook her head, trying to clear her thoughts. Dave had been exposed to her blood, and it had changed him, but he died. So maybe it was just certain concentrations of it.

Her heart froze in her chest as a new, horrible implication now occurred to her. The situation she was in was almost unbearable, but there was always the knowledge that, at some point, at least there could be the freedom of death. If she couldn't die....Hahn could torture her forever.

The thought of living *one* lifetime like this was horrendous, but the possibility of a thousand lifetimes as Hahn's prisoner was too horrible to contemplate. As bad as things were before, it looked like her situation was going to take a terrible turn now that Hahn felt he didn't need her. She sat up, fear pushing her forward. There had to be a way to escape. She'd been so close before! But now, with drugs embedded in her skin they could activate at any moment with the push of a button...

She caught her breath. A push of a button meant an electric impulse! Inside her body! What if she could trigger it first, without them knowing? Her heart skipped a beat as she realized if it really *could* work, there was some slim hope of escaping this nightmare. But she would have to time it right...

She lay back down, waiting, planning. An eternity later, Toady came in and checked on her.

"What time is it?" she asked, trying to sound tired and bored. Toady looked up in surprise.

"What do you care?" he growled.

"I'd just like to know if it's day or night. I've lost all track of time."

"It's 9 pm," he grunted, logging something down in a notebook.

"Can I have something to eat?" she asked, realizing her stomach was aching more than her wrists for once.

"No," he said without looking up. "You get nutrients through your I.V."

She sighed, twisting her arms to try to take the pressure off. Her left pinky finger was tingling with numbness.

"Could you loosen these bands on my wrists at least?" she asked, frustrated.

"Look, girl, I'm not coming near you again unless you're out cold. Don't blame me for the situation you're in. So just shut up and go to sleep." He finished what he was doing and left the room, flicking out the light as he left.

Laying there in the darkness until she felt he was long gone, Marin started to power up her energy, fueled by anger. She let images of Hahn and Toady run wild in her mind until she could feel the electricity sparking around her. For a moment, she almost chickened out. What if this didn't do what she wanted it to do and instead fried her brain or stopped her heart? It's not like she had any control of how much energy she put out. Everything she had done so far was done out of desperation and knee-jerk reactions; nothing was planned out.

The energy crackled along her fingers in blue-white iridescence, making the hair on her arms rise. Now that she was getting more used to it, she liked the feeling of powering up her energy. It made her feel strong, invincible. The lightning playing across her skin felt good, like a physical manifestation of anticipation. It wanted to go somewhere and so did she. She could feel it tingle and crackle across her skin without hurting, and for a moment she worried it wouldn't even affect her, since the electricity was just going back to its source. She watched the strands of lightning dance between her fingers for a moment longer, then, taking a deep breath, she spread out her hands on her abdomen and pushed the power through them.

A quick flash of light illuminated her body and then dissipated. She let out her breath in a long sigh of frustration, angry at herself and strangely exhausted from the effort. Of course if she was generating the electricity, it wouldn't affect her. She closed her eyes and tried to summon everything she knew about electricity, electric eels, anything that might give her some ideas, but she kept coming up empty. But...what if...what if she pulled electricity from somewhere else? Would that up the amps or whatever she needed to short-out the capsules under her skin? Could she even do that? She laughed grimly as she realized she really didn't know *what* she could do, so *everything* she did was an experiment of one kind or another.

Taking another deep, calm breath, she tried another tactic. Gathering her strength, she started a spark in her hands and scooted to the back of her cubicle, reaching her fingers out to the metal wall. The electricity in her hands seemed eager to meet with the wall, but before she let it go, she thought of Hahn's warning to her. If anything interfered with the ship, it would start the countdown to the warheads. She hesitated, considering her options, not wanting to be responsible for unleashing death upon the world, but also desperate to escape the tortured life or impending death Hahn planned for her. Besides, if she died here, who's to say Hahn wouldn't release the warheads anyway?

She teetered in a moment of indecision before dialing back her power just a little and touched one finger to the sub wall. The electricity left her hand and raced happily into the steel, seeking out its own. She kept the connection: feeding it, feeling it like an extension of herself, crackling almost instantly to the nearest power source, surging into an outlet in the adjoining wall. She felt her power connect suddenly with the wiring of the sub; an instantaneous wave of power pushed back to her so fast that it jerked her up hard against the wall and broke the connection. The lights above her surged on, shot out a shower of sparks, and went out. Her eyes rolled up into her head as she fell back to her bed, completely unconscious.

***

It was still dark when Marin opened her eyes and looked around the room. Her head throbbed with an unearthly headache and she had a metallic taste in her mouth. Her hands felt stiff and chapped. She instinctively reached up her hand and wiped her lips, then realized happily that her hands were free. She could feel charred tendrils of rope clinging to her wrists. It appeared like her bands had been scorched off! She bit her lip, worried that she might have short circuited the entire ship with her experiment and caused the warheads to start their countdown. Worse, she really didn't know how long she had been out, minutes or hours? If she'd started the countdown on the warheads, how far into it were they? *Survivors don't panic!* She tried to calm down and quickly assess her situation. She was alive, though she wasn't sure if she short circuited the capsules in her body, or if it was the electric shock that knocked her out. Doubts crept in about her plans, but she pushed them back, deciding to believe her experiment worked. She had to believe it worked. So, what next?

Work the problem, she thought to herself. More than anything else right now, she needed her freedom and information. She reached down to her ankles, and untied the remaining fabric binding her legs together, then stood, enjoying the simple freedom of moving without restraints. It was pitch black in the room, except for a red light over the entrance. She flexed her hands, wishing they didn't bother her so much, and walked over to the door, pressing her face against it to listen, but she couldn't hear anything. Surely if she'd done anything to the sub, Hahn would have had someone come and check on her right away. Unless it was so bad they were all busy trying to fix it.

She tried the light, clicking it on and off several times, but nothing happened. She did a quick search of the cupboards for tools or weapons of any kind, but it seemed that the place had been emptied. No matter, she thought. She wasn't looking for a fight tonight. Stealth was the only weapon she really wanted. She put her hands on the door and tried to open it, but it wouldn't budge.

Closing her eyes, she reached inside herself and caught hold of whatever it was that generated electricity and tried to send just a little jolt into the door mechanism. The door made a popping sound inside and she tried again. This time it slid open with minor difficulty. She poked her head out, relieved the lights seemed unaffected out here. She looked both ways, but didn't see anyone coming, so she slipped out the door, silent on her bare feet. She headed up a flight of steps towards the control room, fighting the fear that she was walking into a den of lions. All Hahn's guys would be there. But she only knew of one way out, so that was the way she was headed. She padded up the rungs of several staircases, ducking through rounded doorways, always half-expecting someone to come around a corner, but she didn't run into anyone until she stepped into the busy control room.

All eyes were instantly on her, including Hahn's, as he stood near the wall speaking intensely with someone. She only paused for a second, then forced her mind to remember the last time Hahn had cut her, capturing the feeling of a knife in her flesh until she could almost feel it herself, then she pushed it as hard as she could into the minds of everyone in the room. They reacted as one; all of them crying out in unison, shouting, and looking down to see the cause of the pain they were experiencing. She immediately dashed down the hall to the opening.

"Catch her!" she heard Hahn screaming behind her. "She's headed toward the lockbox!"

She raced inside the room, slamming the hatch shut behind her and spinning the heavy latch. She pulled a red lever across the wheel, hoping it was a locking mechanism, and water started pouring through the grate at her feet. A red light appeared overhead. She grabbed the wheel on the hatch in the floor, desperately trying to turn it, but it seemed locked in place. Hahn hit the door, beating on the thick window with his bare hand and screaming at her to open it. Veins in his neck and forehead stood out and his eyes were wide with fury. He looked like he would rip her apart with his bare hands if he could only get through the door to do it. Toady appeared next to him and handed him something. She watched Hahn's face relax into a smug smile as he held up the controller to the window for her to see. She backed away from the door, stumbling and splashing through knee deep water, until she was pressed against the rounded back wall. He met her eyes and she could see him hungrily enjoying the terror reflected in her face. He mouthed the words, "You are mine!" then pushed the button.

She winced, waiting for the pop that would knock her out and end her brief taste of freedom forever, but it didn't come. She cautiously opened her eyes, half expecting to feel it any moment, but still nothing happened. Hahn pushed the button again and again, holding it close to the window, pointing the small antenna directly at her. The water was moving up to her chest now and the room was close to being flooded. She sank down until only her head was above the water and watched the window in fascinated horror. Hahn pushed the button, smashing it up against the window until it crumbled into pieces, screaming obscenities like a maniac. He beat the door, shrieking, shouting commands at anyone unlucky enough to be near him, tearing things off the wall to smash against the glass, but it was no use. The rage of Hahn was terrifying, and she knew if he got hold of her, she was going to pay dearly, probably with her life. It quaked her to the core, but she tried to block it from her mind and concentrate on the task ahead.

CHAPTER 36

ZAR

ZAROBI AKUNA SLIPPED out of the cabinet meeting before Dr. Gilbert and General Holt walked out. Once he got to the hall, he trotted quickly through the maze of passageways beneath the White House and up two flights of stairs to the Chief of Staff's office. Without knocking, he walked in, closing the door behind him. She looked up from her phone call and her face blanched.

"I'm sorry, I'll have to call you back." She hung up the phone and stood up, crossing quickly to Zar and speaking in a hushed, but urgent tone. "Sir, someone might see you here!"

"Have you lost control of him?" Zar demanded, grasping her shoulders.

"Of… of President Thompson?" Judy stammered.

"Of course, President Thompson! I don't have time for your idiot questions. Have you lost control of him?"

Judy's eyebrows constricted together and suddenly her confession came out in one long, panicked rush. "We couldn't help it! General Holt caught the President early this morning. We haven't been dosing him at night so the drug supply would last longer. General Holt has been with him constantly since this morning, so we didn't have a chance…"

"Where is Sergio?" he said, shaking her hard, once.

"He's been taken into custody! Holt got suspicious and Thompson had him taken away."

Zar let go of her shoulders, grinding his teeth in frustration, the muscles on his jaw flexing dangerously. He glared at her as if he was strangling her in his mind. She shrank away from him reflexively, retreating behind her desk.

"You should have contacted me immediately!" he hissed menacingly. "Do they suspect you?" he asked in a voice barely above a whisper. She shook her head.

"No, no I don't think so."

Zar moved to the window and closed the blinds. Judy backed away from him as if fearing he would lash out. *Good*, he thought. *Let her fear me.* She stepped into a corner and Zar shook his head at her stupidity. In two quick strides he had her trapped. He stood in front of her, blocking any exit she might have. He watched her struggle to remain composed, despite the fact that there were people all moving outside in the hallway constantly and all she had to do was scream and security would be here in a moment. He would never risk blowing his cover to kill her, no matter how much pleasure it would give him.

Besides, he still needed her. But she didn't know that.

He took another step towards her, his body towering over her, intimidating her. "The President has a way to track Hahn," he growled. "The Arydians had to have taken it during their attack on our base. We *have* to get him first. He has already installed the warheads, and he is the only one with the codes to disarm or activate them."

He looked down into her frightened face, fighting the urge to strangle the fool. She shrank further into the corner like a mouse. He clenched his fists, hating the fact that he had to deal with these stupid politicians to get anything done. Not for long, though.

"It is imperative that you get Thompson back under control immediately and get me access to that tracker!" he said in a menacing voice. "If Hahn decides to detonate, this world will never look the same. All of my empire will be destroyed—my connections, my supply chain." Judy nodded mutely. "But," he added, lifting a finger in front of her face, "you have to be careful. If Hahn thinks he is backed into a corner," he stepped closer to Judy, pressing her physically against the corner with his bulk to emphasize his words, "he will detonate just to spit in the face of us all. We have got to get access to that tracker and either take Hahn alive or make sure he's dead. If we can't get the tracker, destroy him immediately. How many assets do we have in the area?"

"Before the attack at Headquarters, you...I mean...they... sent everything we had out to look for him," she stammered. Zar snarled at the mention of his recent mistake.

"Do they still have his heading?"

"Yes, they have a tracker on board. They are near his location awaiting orders."

Zar rubbed his chin in thought. It wouldn't do for a bunch of random ships to be circling the target when the might of the U.S. military was called in.

"Have them move back to the nearest shipping lane and blend in but stay close. We will need them when we either extract Hahn or destroy him."

Judy nodded.

"Good. Here's a list of two of my men in the system. Make sure they are on the front lines of this, understand?" He held out a scrap of paper.

Judy took the slip of paper from his hand, trying hard not to touch him. Zar glared at her in disgust.

"And get rid of Sergio before all this is over. He's nothing but a liability to us now." He turned and slipped out the door, melting into the knots of people striding through the hallways.

CHAPTER 37

JAYCEN

IT WAS JUST past three a.m. when Jaycen tiptoed to the galley for a quick drink of water before going back to bed. Most of the sub's occupants were already asleep, but worry about Marin had been making sleep hard for him to find. He quickly rinsed his glass and put it back in the cupboard when he felt the Minnow slow down and tilt as it moved against the current in a sharp right turn. Paul was at the helm when Jaycen popped his head through the door.

"Did we just turn around?" he asked, almost accusingly.

Paul scowled. "The coordinates just came in for the rendezvous with Frank. We're gonna have to go off our heading and backtrack by several kilometers to meet up with the aircraft carrier." Paul stretched in his seat. "Hey, kid, I know you were headed back to bed, but would you mind taking my place for a few? I gotta go to the bathroom."

"No problem."

Paul squeezed past him into the hallway. Jaycen slipped into the captain's chair and took a look at the coordinates himself. It was going to lose them almost a full day's travel to get to the rendezvous and back to this exact point. He hated the thought of breaking off their pursuit of Marin for so long, even if it meant Frank and a couple others would be there to help. It just felt wrong to be travelling in the exact opposite direction from where he wanted to be going. He couldn't bear to think about what Marin must be enduring at the hands of her captors. He shook his head to keep his brain from going there again. A few minutes later, Marcos came in and sat down in the copilot's seat.

"Did you just change our heading?" he demanded.

Jaycen's lips tightened and he stared straight ahead. "No, Paul did. New heading. We are meeting up with Frank and getting some help," he said curtly. Marcos took a deep breath and looked at him thoughtfully.

"Do you think this will work, rescuing Marin from Hahn?" Marcos asked, making Jaycen uncomfortable with his odd way of getting straight to the point.

"Why wouldn't it?"

"Well, I can think of a million ways it could not work. We are basically unarmed. All we have are the portable welders, and even those are low on acetylene. I just checked. And I am sure Hahn's sub will be guarded outside by more creatures like we saw when he attacked Portus, and we have no way to defend against them. He may have Aaron with him, who destroyed the big sub, not to mention the oil rig and all of Arydia pretty easily. He could crush this sub in a second. And once we get in, assuming we get past all that, I am sure he has plenty of firepower and men on the sub itself. It seems like we have little to no chance of success for this mission."

Jaycen glared at him. "So, what are you suggesting? Give up on her? I thought you were all in love with her!" he spat.

Marcos met his eyes, making Jaycen shift uncomfortably in his chair. "I am in love with her. I would do anything for her. But I'm not sure what we are doing is going to help, and maybe it will hurt her."

"Hurt her? What are you talking about?" Jaycen asked, getting heated. "Honestly, Marcos, this is bad enough without your negativity right now."

Marcos took a deep breath as if trying to keep from lashing out at Jaycen. "I am not being negative. I am trying to look at this situation from an objective point of view. Think about this from the government's angle," Marcos snapped impatiently. "They probably want Hahn dead at all costs. All costs, Jaycen. They are sending people to 'help' us, right? What is their priority going to be? Marin?" Marcos held out his hands and shook his head. "Of course not! They want Hahn. They are using us to get them there and Marin is going to be caught in the crossfire. A tragic casualty worked carefully into their equation."

Jaycen opened his mouth to shut him down, but the truth of the accusation left him stunned. Worry dropped like a stone in his stomach. The government would have nothing to lose, but everything to gain by ignoring Marin and going after Hahn. The thought made him queasy because it seemed so obvious that he was stunned he hadn't thought of it before. Why would they risk a rescue with so much at stake? "What are you suggesting?" he asked quietly.

"I am suggesting we go in alone, before we give the coordinates to anybody. You and me."

"How?" Jaycen demanded. "You said it yourself that we have no weapons, no way to get past any guards they might have."

"We take skimmers and the tracker and take off before we rendezvous with Frank and the Navy. That way the government will be forced to let us try to get her first. And we have to hurry. I did not plan on a course change. Every mile we go away from her is a mile we have to make up with time we do not have."

The idea of taking action felt good to Jaycen but facing Hahn and his mutants and infiltrating a sub alone with no weapons sounded suicidal. He didn't want to admit to himself how much he was subconsciously relying on the older adults to take care of all the details of rescuing Marin.

"Marcos...if something happens to us, then there is no way for them to find Hahn. Millions might die because of us. Would Marin want that?" He hoped his thoughts behind that were noble, not some cowardly part of him showing its ugly face, but he couldn't be sure.

Marcos frowned. "No, but I couldn't live with myself if we led them to her and they betrayed us, could you?"

Jaycen shook his head. He had a point. "Why do you want to involve *me* in this? Why not Noburu or Kazu or Paul? Or even your dad?"

Marcos folded his arms and looked at Jaycen with a raised eyebrow.

"Seriously, do you think they would let us go?" Jaycen inclined his head and agreed with him. "Besides, Noburu is injured, I don't know Kazu and he seems a little unpredictable. My father is not as invested in this. Paul would insist on either going himself or trusting the government to do what is right. Either way, neither you nor I would be involved in the operation, if there even *was* one." He looked out the view screen and sighed. "You're not my first choice, but other than Paul and Emily, you and I are the ones who want her back the most. I know how you feel about her. And I feel the same. You know we have to do this."

Jaycen looked at the heading, his heart thumping. Not only would they be going alone, but their only backup support would be a long way behind them. He squeezed all his worry into a knot of resolution. "I'm in. But we have to give them some kind of way to track Hahn if something happens to us."

"I know," he said, concern darkening his features. "I was hoping you'd have some ideas."

Jaycen glared at him. "I thought you had it all planned out."

Marcos gave him a sarcastic smile. "You want me to do all the legwork, your highness? Fine. They already have his last location heading. He's been stationary for the last twenty two hours; we can just hope he'll stay at that location until they get there."

"And if he moves?"

"We take a pair of communicators. They can track us with them if we let them. We leave within the hour and get as far away as we can before morning. Once we're sure they are at the rendezvous point, we can let them track our movements and our heading. If Hahn goes on the move again, we can notify them of the change. But no access to his exact location until we have Marin."

"That…is actually a good plan," Jaycen admitted grudgingly. "But aren't you worried the sub will catch up with us?"

"If we keep a skimmer at full speed the entire time, we'll beat them. Not by much, but enough."

"How much time will that give us?" Jaycen asked.

Marcos looked uncomfortable. "An hour if we're lucky." He stood up.

"I got my knife back from Marin's mom. I'll pack some supplies and meet you in the lockbox as soon as you can. Try to find some kind of weapon. I'll leave a note somewhere my father will find it when he wakes."

They heard a flush in the head and the door opened down the hall. Marcos vanished down the hall and Paul appeared a minute later.

"Sorry that took so long, kid. Thanks for covering for me." Jaycen squeezed past him into the hallway.

"Don't mention it." Jaycen stood up and stretched, giving Paul an exaggerated yawn. "Man, I'm beat!" he moved into the doorway.

"Get some sleep, will you?" Paul called out as Jaycen walked down the hallway into the galley.

"As soon as I can," he replied to himself, grabbing a couple of steak knives and a mean looking meat fork out of the galley drawers before heading to the back of the sub.

CHAPTER 38

DOCTOR BOSCOLO

DR. SERGIO BOSCOLO sat in a windowless room, with a bed, a chair and a table for furnishings, biting his nail nervously, his heart hammering in his chest. If Thompson got another doctor's opinion, he and Judy would be discovered. And that meant being tried and possibly executed for treason. He had to think of some cover story. He tapped his forehead with his knuckles, willing his brain to kick into gear. Finally, a flash of thought hit him. He could claim the drugs were being tampered with! He sat up straight, his face brightening. Of course! He was only administering the doses he thought were necessary, but the drugs themselves were suspect. If that buffoon, Judy, had been taken into custody, perhaps he could blame her. He walked in circles, fabricating different versions of his story for each scenario he could foresee. He was so engrossed in his thoughts, he almost didn't notice when the door opened and closed.

"Judy!" he exclaimed, surprised. He tried to regain his composure, this room was surely being monitored. "What are you doing here?" he asked, his voice laced with unspoken meaning.

She smiled and handed him a steaming mug of coffee and a Danish. "I'm just checking up on you to see how you are holding up." Sergio took the plate and mug and sat it down on a small table. "Please, go ahead and eat, I already had some in the breakroom."

"I'm too worked up to eat, but the coffee is a welcome treat," he said, taking a sip. "What is the story outside? Surely they don't think I'm guilty!"

"I'm confident they will get to the bottom of this. I plan on talking to the President about it shortly."

Sergio relaxed and sat down on the bed, taking another sip of his coffee. So, she wasn't suspected and still had access to the President. All was not lost. If he could just convey to her his ideas! They still had plenty of the pills they'd used before they switched to injections. She could grind them up and slip them into his food, or a drink, as they did when they first started this project together.

"I'm concerned that in my absence, he may fall ill. You know where his pills are located…"

Judy's look hardened. "I don't intend to poison the President for you, if that's what you mean. They have already found your stash of what appears to be Ricin in your office. It's being analyzed as we speak. I've come here to urge you to confess."

Sergio's face went pale. She wasn't here to rescue him, but to frame him! He stood up, outraged. If he was going to burn, he wouldn't be alone! He opened his mouth to speak, but his words came out slurred and distorted. The room shifted slightly and he sat back down, confused.

"Judy?' he asked, trying to gauge her expression, but he found he had trouble focusing on her. She moved to his side.

"I never thought you would betray your county, Sergio. You had us all fooled."

No! His brain screamed inside, but his words couldn't make it past a whimper on his lips. What was happening to him? He shook his head and tried to stand, but instead he bumped into the table, knocking it over. The coffee spilled onto the rug from the broken mug. *The coffee!* His eyes widened in terror. *No!*

"The only thing you can do is confess. You wanted to slowly poison the President, didn't you, Sergio?"

His mind struggled to free itself from the grip seizing down upon it, but with every heartbeat it grew more difficult.

"You were working with foreign nationals in this plot, weren't you?"

NO! he screamed in his mind. *This can't be happening!* He grasped his head in his hands. "But...you..." he managed to press out of his mouth between waves of confusion.

"Me?" she asked, as if flabbergasted. "I had nothing to do with this, you know that." Her eyes bored into his with an intensity he shrank from. Then she smiled at him sadly. "You must confess your desire to kill the President to gain the power and money they promised you. It's the only way." Her voice sounded so reasonable, so engendering of trust. It felt wrong, but it made sense. If he was guilty, he would have to confess. It would be easier for everyone if he did. She leaned forward and pressed a shard of the broken mug into his hand, then closed his fingers around it, whispering in his ear so only he could hear. "And when they leave you alone, you will find a way to kill yourself. It's the only way to make this right." She stood up and smiled down at him. His heart beat against his rib cage, his eyes wide with horror.

"It's the right thing to do. It's your only chance, really. For once in your life, do the right thing," she said, standing to leave. The screaming part of his brain pushed through the complacent fog for just a moment.

"Judy!" he groaned. "Please! Help me!"

She looked down at him, loathing in her eyes. He shrank from the look. He wanted to please her, to do what she asked. He dropped his eyes from hers and nodded, giving in to the feeling. The relief felt wonderful. Of course Judy knew what she was talking about. Hadn't he always trusted her?

The door opened and three armed men entered. "I think he's ready to talk. I'll leave you to the questioning," she said, walking briskly out of the room to meet with the President.

***

Twenty minutes later Judy arrived in the oval office with two cups of coffee, one with the handle facing her, the other with the handle facing away. She smiled as she sat down across the desk from the President, setting one cup near him, the other near her.

"How are you holding up, John?" she asked, concern wrapped around her voice like a soft blanket. The President laced his fingers together and met her gaze, saying nothing. She sat back casually and took a tiny sip of her coffee, trying to hide the tremble in her grip. She set the cup down quickly.

"I will admit, I'm rattled by the day's events. Doubtless you've heard about Sergio."

Her brow creased with worry. "Yes, and I'm still in shock. I've known Sergio for years! I can't believe he is capable of what they are saying."

The President sighed and shook his head sadly. "I can't believe it either. I don't want to believe it, because if it is true, he likely had accomplices, which means I don't know who I can trust anymore."

Judy twisted her hands together nervously, doing her best to keep her face frozen in an acceptable expression. *Just drink the coffee, you idiot!* She screamed inside her brain. "I know what you mean, John. The implications are terrifying. We could all be in danger. I've been worried sick about this." She took another small sip of her coffee, hoping he'd follow suit. He didn't.

"You worked closely with Sergio, didn't you, Judy?" he said, leaning back away from his desk. Away from the sip that would make all her problems disappear.

"Well, yes, only in the fact that as your Chief of Staff, I needed to know the extent of your condition and how it would affect your ability to run the country."

"And did Sergio ever discuss the medications he was giving me with you?"

She blinked hard, taking another sip of her coffee to hide the panic raging through her. A direct lie might be easy to detect, she needed a diversion with bits of the truth embedded. "Of course he did!" she said, smiling.

"And...what was it he was giving me?"

She laughed, setting the coffee back down on the desk. "Oh, John, I'm good at a lot of things, but I have no memory for those long difficult names they give drugs nowadays. I'm afraid I had to defer to someone with medical knowledge and trust he had your best interest at heart. I trusted Sergio, much like you did. Like we all did." She cast her eyes down mournfully and straightened a wrinkle from her skirt with an absent brush of her hand.

"Yes, like we all did." The President leaned forward and rubbed his eyes with one hand.

"You look exhausted, John. You can't have gotten much sleep last night," she said.

"I am exhausted. I've got the country on lockdown, I'm getting pressure from every branch to ease up on the Martial Law I imposed, and honestly, I agree with them. Now they want me to postpone the election? It makes me look like a power hungry monster. I've had protests from almost every allied country we deal with."

"You are under a lot of stress right now. Surely the world knows you are doing what is necessary for the safety of our people."

"One would think. But I guarantee when this is all over, I'll be out of a job." He laughed mirthlessly. He reached out and took the cup. She tried not to lean forward in anticipation. He took a sip and set it down again, and she relaxed visibly.

"And what was that commotion this morning all about?" she asked sweetly. "I can't believe you let those men crash into your room at that awful hour. What did they want?"

The President took another sip of the coffee and set it down with a scowl. "This tastes bitter. It…reminds me of something…"

"Oh, I must have forgotten creamer in your coffee. I should know you don't take it black like I do." The President's brow wrinkled as he looked at the coffee, like he was trying to see something hidden inside.

"So what were you saying? About General Holt and the strange men this morning?"

The President shook himself and looked up at her. "Oh, I'm so sorry, Judy. They had information about Hahn. They have a way to locate him. I'm sending support out as we speak."

"To capture, or to kill him?" she asked, leaning forward.

"I…" he rubbed his temples. "I feel odd."

"Yes, of course you do. Take another sip and you will feel better. It even tastes better now, doesn't it?" she smiled. "That's a good lad. Now what are your plans for Hahn?" she asked impatiently.

"They want us to extract the girl."

"Good, good!" she said, excitedly. "Then what?"

"We will extract Hahn, find the location of his warheads and persuade him to disarm them. Then we will destroy them."

She slid a piece of typed paper towards him. "I want these two men on the front lines of the extraction, Mr. President. They are loyal to our cause and can be trusted with any decision. When you find Hahn, they will be the ones to either extract him or kill him. Do you agree?"

The President looked at the paper carefully, then slowly nodded. "But what about Gilbert's daughter?" he asked sadly.

"She is not part of the equation. We must capture or kill Hahn. Millions of lives are at stake."

"But...I gave my word..." he said, clearly struggling. Judy sighed in frustration.

"You will trust these men. They will make the best decision," she said forcefully.

"I..." he said, struggling, but then his face relaxed. "I will trust them to capture Hahn. It's for the best."

"Yes. Or kill him. Whichever makes the most sense. Make sure they are on the mission, Mr. President. This is urgent. We need to make sure we have the most capable people for a mission like this. People you can trust."

"Of course. People we can trust. I will make sure they are assigned to the detail. Thank you for your help, Judy."

Judy smiled sweetly. "That's what I'm here for, John. May I take your cup? It looks like it has grown cold while we've been talking."

"How thoughtful of you, Judy. Yes, please."

She looked at her watch and did some quick calculations. "I'll bring you another cup this evening at eight o'clock sharp. Please send for me then."

"Yes, I will. Thank you for your concern."

"Don't mention it," she said, grinning smugly as she left the room.

CHAPTER 39

PAUL

THE DAWN WAS just barely lighting the surface of the choppy waves when Minnow broke the surface of the sea. Through his periscope, about half a nautical mile away was the massive aircraft carrier. U.S.S. Carl Vinson looking like a skyscraper turned on its side. Paul retracted his viewer impatiently. They had been waiting submerged for over an hour for word that the helicopter meant to deliver Frank to them was ready to take off, and Paul had finally decided to bring the Minnow up to periscope depth to see what was going on. Emily was sitting next to him in the copilot's seat, waiting even more impatiently.

"Still nothing?" she asked.

"Nope." He noticed the worry in her face and smiled reassuringly. "This is the government we're talking about. I'm sure there's no problem. They always take forever."

Though he still had a hard time reconciling that this woman who looked to be in her twenties was Marin's mother, when he looked at her, eye to eye, he could tell she was older. Something in her look spoke of hardship beyond her years. The radio crackled to life.

"Minnow, this is Dr. Gilbert," a voice said. Emily startled a little bit and leaned closer to the radio, as if she could touch her husband if she could just get close enough. "I'm sorry for the delay. We've had a last-minute replacement to our group. Do you have room for two more?"

Paul flipped on his speaker. "We'll be at our eight man capacity when you get here, and above it, if you bring two more. Are they really necessary?"

"Special order of the President, so, yeah. We're waiting on them. They should be here shortly and then we'll be over," he said.

Paul thought for a moment. "Noburu is wounded and is getting worse. He seems to be fighting an infection and could use medical help. How about we make room with an exchange? We can send him over along with his son. That should give us room for the two extras."

"Roger that," he said.

"By the way, the wind is picking up. It's going to get dicey if they don't get here soon. Have you ever done a helicopter pickup from a sub?" Frank asked.

Paul glanced over at Emily, trying to keep his face from turning red like it did every time he was put on the spot. "Well, no. But I saw it done once when I was on active duty."

They heard Frank sigh. "Well, I haven't done this before, either. The men here are making me more nervous every time they explain it."

"Well at least you don't have to worry about drowning if ye are dropped!" Emily piped in, her musical accent coming out. Paul and Frank both laughed.

"The men are landing. I'll see you soon!" Frank said, his voice happier than Paul had ever heard it.

Paul clicked off the radio as Malcolm leaned in.

"Paul, we've got a problem. My son and Jaycen are gone."

Emily sucked in an alarmed breath. Paul jumped to his feet, hitting his head on the low roof. "Ow!" He rubbed his head irritated. "You're kidding me, right?"

Malcolm shook his head somberly, handing Paul a handwritten note. "This was on Marcos's bunk when I went to wake him. I have no idea how long ago they left."

"Just what we need!" Paul grumbled, his stomach constricting into a tighter knot. He snatched the note and read it over quickly, his face growing angrier by the minute. Then he passed it to Emily to read.

"What are we going to do?" she whispered. "They took the tracker!"

Paul sat back down at the helm and shook his head slowly. "I just don't know. What on earth got into those stupid boys' heads? They know how important this is! Why would they risk Marin's life on such a foolish, hair-brained, idiotic…" His temper rose with each insult he lobbed until he ran out of words. Malcolm shifted in the doorway, silent. "What are we supposed to tell the government guys on their way over here? Not to mention the armada that's supposedly going to follow us to intercept Hahn!"

"If we tell them, I fear they may abort the mission," Emily stated plainly.

"I worry about that as well," Malcolm added. "At best it will delay things and put Marin at greater risk."

"Why would they do this?" Paul exclaimed, slamming his fist into the palm of his hand. "I could just wring their necks!"

Emily put a hand on his arm. "You said they both care about my daughter, did you not?" She glanced at both men as they nodded. "And they are intelligent boys, are they not?" Reluctantly, the two others agreed. "Then, I will assume they had a good reason for taking this action."

Malcolm rubbed his eyes tiredly. "I would suspect they do not trust the government will have Marin's best interest at heart. Truthfully, I have worried about the same thing."

Paul didn't want to believe it was possible. He wanted, no, *needed* to believe they were all united with the same goal. But if he stepped back from his frantic desire to save his little girl, he could see this was one of those problems he hated dealing with whenever he was deployed. Innocent people that got in the way of the more dangerous target usually didn't survive. Collateral damage. Civilian casualties, lost to the cause. Unwilling sacrifices. He swallowed hard, finally understanding the motivation behind Jaycen's and Marcos's actions, and suddenly very grateful for their insight and bravery.

"So what now?" he asked in a quiet voice.

"We don't tell them until we have to," Emily said firmly. "We go on the last projected course until we run out of options. And we hope we get there before them so they don't have to rescue her alone."

"Yes," Malcolm said, his heavy brows lifting. "They did leave us a heading. They promised to contact us if Hahn moves. We still have access to the tracker. In a manner of speaking."

Paul nodded his head slowly. "Agreed. We tell no one until we have to." He turned back to the controls. "And we pray those boys succeed if we don't make it in time."

CHAPTER 40

FRANK

FRANK DANGLED LIKE a fly from a spider's web, rotating around below the belly of the helicopter. Paul held tight to the safety rope fastened to the sloping top of Minnow, shielding his face from the fierce wind the helicopter was kicking up. A wave sloshed over the top of the sub, knocking Paul painfully to his knees. He waited for the rocking to subside before trying to regain his feet.

Frank swung lower, reaching out a hand to grasp Paul's but he missed and went wide over the open sea. Paul muttered under his breath, and stretched out, waiting for Frank's return swing. He came past and Paul touched him, but their hands didn't catch. Paul signaled the helicopter to lower him a few inches more, not enough that he could hit the sub, but hopefully closer for him to grab. This time, as Frank swung past, Paul caught hold of his jacket, wet with the spray flying through the air all around them. He held on with all his strength, straining against the momentum of his pendulum swing. The men in the helicopter lowered the rope further and Frank's feet finally touched the wet metal decking, scrambling for purchase as he grasped Paul with both hands. Paul attached a tether to him, pulling him to safety while Frank disconnected his harness, allowing the helicopter to reel it up to its open door.

"Permission to come aboard, Captain?" Frank shouted with a smile over the deafening sound of the rotors above him.

"Hey there, buddy!" Paul said, grasping him by the elbows. "I'd love to catch up with you, but I know someone inside is looking forward to seeing you!" He inclined his head towards the open hatch.

"And I can't wait to see her!" He grinned like a teenager, making Paul chuckle. "But I'll help you get the other two over and get Noburu loaded up for transport first," he said. Paul accepted his help gratefully, looking up as a marine, heavy with equipment, began his descent. After the first man was reeled in, a large, lumpy bag was lowered. The three men caught it and hefted it down the hatch to waiting hands. The remaining man came in easier with Paul, Frank and the other marine there to catch him.

Before long, they were climbing down the ladder into the sub and helping boost a sickly and weak looking Noburu up the ladder with his one good arm, Kazu close behind. Frank helped him through the top hatch, while Paul lassoed the rescue sled that was being lowered from the chopper.

"I should be here to help you," Noburu protested weakly over the roar of the chopper. His face was flushed and sweat beaded on his brow.

"I know, old friend," Frank said, squeezing his good shoulder. "But you'll do us all a favor by healing up under the care of a team of doctors back in the States, not jammed in the back of this crowded boat."

Noburu smiled sadly and let himself be lowered and fastened into the sled before rising into the spraying mist. Both Frank and Paul watched until he was safely on board, then helped Kazu get ready.

"Take good care of your dad, okay?" Paul said, cinching the harness tightly around his body. Kazu nodded, looking excitedly at the helicopter above him.

"Tell Marcos and Jaycen goodbye for me when you see them again. I wish I could have talked to them before they left," Kazu shouted. Frank looked at him quizzically and Paul glanced nervously at the marine nearby, hoping he didn't notice anything odd about the exchange and that Frank didn't ask any questions.

"Sure, kid. Have a safe trip!" He gave the chopper a thumbs up and they rose, angling Kazu away from the tower and out into the misty air. The marines led the way down the ladder with Frank and Paul behind them, locking the hatch as they ducked into the sub. Paul wiped his face with his hand to get the water out of his eyes. Frank looked soaked to the bone and was shivering, but smiling.

"Douglas?" Emily pushed past the first Marine, an older balding man and took hold of her husband's hand.

Frank turned with a cry and stumbled into his wife's arms, holding her as if he would never let her go. "Em! Oh, Emily!" His voice choked with tears, his face buried in her hair. Paul and the marine looked away awkwardly, not wanting to intrude on the tender moment, but having no room to go elsewhere.

Frank pulled slightly away and looked his wife in the face. "Emily, I… just…never…" he broke up and pulled her close again, both of them crying tears of joy. The couple put their foreheads together, talking quietly for a moment.

"You…you look younger than ever, Em!" Frank whispered. "I'm not just saying that! You do!"

Emily laughed quietly. "As do you, my love. We have so much to talk about." The bald marine cleared his throat uncomfortably and the two looked up as if just now realizing they weren't alone.

"Sorry, you two," Paul said gently. "How about you both go catch up and we'll all get some dry clothes on. We can meet in the galley in an hour or so if that's okay with you."

Frank nodded gratefully and walked down the hall with his arm around his beaming wife. Paul turned to the bald man and held out his hand. "I'm Paul Donnegan."

"Ed Dawes," the man replied, briefly shaking his hand.

"Great. Let me show you where you can put your stuff."

Paul held back an impressive yawn. Though Malcolm had driven yesterday and part of the night before, Paul had been up since before midnight to relieve him, and the nap he'd hoped to get after picking up Frank hadn't happened yet. Worry about Marin, Marcos and Jaycen was not helping. They were four hours into the return journey toward Hahn and so far they hadn't heard a word from the boys. He hoped that meant they were all right and still in pursuit. So far, the new men on board didn't know anything yet, but he worried about the repercussions that were coming as soon as they found out. And he was sure they would find out soon. As if on cue, Dawes came in and sat down in the vacant copilot's seat.

"What's our heading?" he asked, looking over the instrument panel. Paul was instantly irritated by his impersonal demand but tried to remain calm.

"Almost directly northwest."

"Has the target moved position?"

Paul hesitated for a moment, but shook his head no. The bald man picked up on his hesitation. "Is there a problem?" he asked.

"No, no problem."

The other marine stepped in. He sported a close-cropped beard and arms as thick as tree trunks.

"You said you were at capacity. There are two extra bunks back there." He folded his massive arms and glared at him.

"We sent two men back in the exchange," Malcolm said from the hallway. Paul was relieved to hear him.

"Right, but you said you were at capacity already," the bearded man pointed out. "I count six people on board."

"Are you saying we don't know how to count?" Paul said with a nervous laugh.

"Perhaps you lied, so we wouldn't come aboard. Seems like you're hiding something," Dawes said.

Malcolm put his head in through the doorway and met eyes with Paul. "Now is probably a good time to have a talk," he said. "I'll go grab the others." He returned shortly with Frank and Emily.

Paul stood, stretching his lower back. "Malcolm, do you want to be part of this, or would you rather drive?" Malcolm moved past him to the captain's chair.

"Given a choice like that? I'll drive."

The rest filed into the galley. Once they were all seated, Paul spoke. "Everyone, this is Ed Dawes." He pointed to the bald man who held up a hand and interrupted him before he could go on.

"I'm Master Chief Petty Officer Ed Dawes. This is Second Class Petty

Officer Clint Riggs," he said pointing to the muscled bearded man sitting next to him. "We are the eyes and ears of this operation for the President." Paul scowled at them. If they wanted to try to pull rank on this ship, they had another thing coming.

"I'm Retired Naval Commander Paul Donnegan, SEAL unit 1180. This is Dr. Gilbert, and his wife, Dr. Emily Gilbert. They are the biological parents, and I am the adopted father of Marin, the girl we are going to rescue. The man driving is Malcolm Minas."

"*Doctor* Malcolm Minas, if you do not mind," Malcolm said loudly from the other room. Emily, Frank and Paul smiled. The two marines waited, obviously unimpressed. Paul let his smile fade and began to reluctantly relay the news.

"Two of our young men, Jaycen and Marcos, took off some time during the night and went after Marin alone," Paul said hesitantly. Frank's jaw dropped. Riggs' muscles bunched around his thick neck.

"Marcos left a note on his bunk. Malcolm found it when he went to wake them before we surfaced this morning." He tossed the piece of paper onto the table for all to see. Frank looked at Paul, his face stern.

Paul grimaced as he returned Frank's stare. "I'm sorry; I thought Emily would have told you. I saw Jaycen around midnight. If the boys left shortly after that, they would be halfway to Hahn's last known position. That means that no matter what we do, they will likely beat us to him."

"You should have told us immediately!" Riggs shouted. "They are jeopardizing the entire mission!"

"And what would you have done differently?" Paul snapped. He'd served with this kind of men in the military and never did like their self-important attitude. "We were already at the rendezvous point when we discovered they had gone. Should we have left you on the deck of the carrier and turned around?"

Dawes snarled at him. "I would have notified command."

Paul rolled his eyes at the man. "And we would be where we are now anyway—headed after them as fast as we can."

Riggs made a disgusted sound. Frank took the note from the table and read over it. "They took the tracker?"

Paul nodded. "Yeah, they did," he said somberly. Dawes leapt to his feet.

"Are you kidding me?" he demanded. "You're saying," he said, pointing an accusing finger at Paul, "that not only do they have a day's gain on us, but we're flying blind as well?"

Paul glared at the man. "We have their heading and Hahn's last position. They said they would check in with us if Hahn moved. Besides, in the skimmer they can't travel nearly as fast as we can. Based on Hahn's last location and my best estimate, they will beat us there by about forty-five minutes to an hour. If they have any problems, we may catch up to them."

Dawes looked ready to spit venom. "Unacceptable! Have you even considered the implications if something happened and these two *boys* were killed or captured? We'd have lost our only chance to neutralize this threat!"

"These kids have recklessly put millions at risk," Riggs agreed in a resounding bass voice. "If we lose this chance to take out Hahn, you and everyone involved in this outrage will have a lot to answer for!"

"Take out Hahn?" Frank shouted, his temper rising. He took a deep breath, but when he spoke, his voice was low and threatening. "May I remind you *both* that this mission has three consecutive objectives? FIRST is to rescue my daughter. SECOND is to capture Hahn. THIRD is only to come into play if the SECOND objective fails. Not the first, that is non-negotiable. This is a rescue mission until I decide otherwise. I own this ship, it is mine to command and the decisions about Marin's rescue will be mine and mine alone. Do you understand?" The two men looked at each other and something passed between them, but finally Dawes thrust out his chin in a distasteful consent.

"Fine. Make your plans for this 'rescue'. We're going to radio in our situation to the President."

The men pushed past everyone and went out the door. Frank let out his breath in a huge sigh. "I thought they were sending me with real help, not a couple of heavy-handed enforcers. I don't get it, I had two good men that were going to come with me and at the last minute, these guys took their place." Emily put a hand on his arm and he took it with a halfhearted smile.

The group was quiet, lost in their thoughts for a few minutes. Malcolm came in briefly, his brow heavy in concern. He spoke quickly, leaning forward and speaking low.

"I do not trust these men, or their objectives," he said barely above a whisper. "We need to keep both eyes on them."

"Let us know what they say on the radio," Frank whispered. Malcolm nodded and went back to the control room.

"We need to come up with a feasible plan, taking two, maybe three scenarios into account," Paul said. "Scenario one, the best and unfortunately the most unlikely one, is that Jaycen and Marcos locate Hahn, get past whatever Hahn has guarding his sub, get on board without being noticed, get past Hahn and his men and get Marin off." Paul looked around the table at the bleak faces surrounding him as they each ran through the dismal prospects of the first plan succeeding. Paul ran his fingers across his forehead, thinking, then plowed forward.

"Scenario two, and the one I'm hoping for, is we somehow catch up with Marcos and Jaycen and we help them with the assault. Those men brought weapons, so that should help us even the odds of fighting past Hahn's defenses and extracting Marin. Then we give the coordinates to the government, and hopefully they blast that stinking piece of garbage into oblivion. Or they extract Hahn and let him answer to justice. I'd rather they blew him up, though," he said, with a small, grim chuckle.

"Scenario three, unfortunately the most likely, is that Jaycen and Marcos attempt at a rescue and fail, alerting Hahn and he captures or kills the boys. Then he takes off, and all we can hope for is that the military subs tailing us are able to track him."

Emily thought for a moment before responding. "Nothing can be done by us in either scenario one or three, so I suggest we pray for number one to succeed, but make our plans for number two and hope for the best."

Frank nodded. "Those boys are smart and resourceful. They may have a much greater chance of getting in there unseen than we would have coming in with a sub. We'll definitely be showing up on their radar. I choose to believe they have a good chance."

"Do they even have any weapons?" Emily asked.

"Marcos has his knife," Malcom said. "At least I didn't find it in his locker."

"I'll bet Jaycen grabbed something as well," Paul said.

Paul scratched his stubble and frowned. "As far as option two, I'm not sure what we can plan since we have no idea what we are up against. All we know is that we have weapons, and we plan to fight through Hahn's defenses and get Marin."

The room fell silent again. Paul suppressed an enormous yawn prompting Frank to look at his watch. "If they truly left close to midnight, they would be pretty near to Hahn in a few hours. Paul, why don't you get some sleep so you'll be ready to help us when we get there. The rest of us will try to brainstorm."

Paul almost protested, but Frank was right. He needed to be alert when the action started. He stood, stifling another yawn. "You let me know if anything changes. Anything. Got it?" he said, meeting the gaze of each of them.

"Of course," Frank insisted. "The second anything changes. You have my word."

"Good," Paul said, and headed out the door. He walked to the back of the sub and found an empty bunk, jumping in fully dressed, shoes and all.

CHAPTER 41

JAYCEN

THE NIGHT HAD been one long blur of speeding through the dark ocean and avoiding predators, and now Jaycen could barely keep his eyes open. Skimmers were an efficient way for one, two, or three people to move through the water quickly, but holding on to the bowed handles and being dragged through the water for hours on end, even with the clear shield protecting them, was wearing on Jaycen. He had to keep adjusting his grip and changing his position. Marcos, however, seemed at ease on the skimmer, holding himself loosely and letting his legs undulate through the water in a way that Jaycen found impossible to mimic. It was easier to hold on for dear life and let himself be dragged. Jaycen grumbled to himself, mad that Marcos could make something so difficult look so graceful and easy.

They pulled to a stop, hovering twenty feet above the ocean floor, and Jaycen rubbed his shoulders while Marcos checked the tracker. Hahn's sub had moved, but he hadn't gone too far, so they decided not to touch base with the Minnow just yet. For the most part, neither of them spoke, but as the darkness turned into morning, and morning stretched into afternoon, even Marcos began to look exhausted, and the silence and apprehension were driving Jaycen nuts.

"*Maybe this is a bad idea, Marcos,*" Jaycen eventually broke down and spoke, still unused to the odd way they had of communicating underwater. For a while, he couldn't tell if Marcos even heard him. He continued to look straight ahead, his mouth set in determination. Jaycen's mind had already moved back to his own thoughts when Marcos finally responded.

"*You losing your nerve, Landy boy?*" Marcos asked.

"*No!*" Jaycen shot back. "*I'm just being realistic. We were both up all day and all through the night. I don't want to make any mistakes that could cost Marin her life.*"

"*Neither do I. But tell me, what choice do we have?*"

Jaycen didn't have an answer to that. The sea was getting much brighter, with shafts of sun slicing down through the water in straight iridescent beams. Multicolored fish darted around like flocks of birds, looking for something to eat. Jaycen contemplated how beautiful it was down here, how peaceful, if only they weren't headed towards their likely deaths. Dark thoughts dragged his heart down as they drew nearer to the flashing light on the tracker. They were getting close.

Marcos slowed the skimmer to a crawl. "*I don't see him yet, do you?*" Jaycen strained his eyes ahead but only the unbroken expanse of the ocean met his gaze. "*It feels like we should have been there long ago,*" Marcos said.

"*What, are you getting tired, Water-Boy?*" Jaycen prodded him, but he immediately regretted it. Marcos looked at him quizzically and burst out laughing.

"*Water-Boy? That's all you can come up with?*" The tension and quiet between them lifted slightly with his laughter.

Jaycen shrugged. "*Hey, it's been a long couple of days. I'll roast you to your satisfaction when this is all over,*" Jaycen said with a half-smile.

"*I'll believe it when I see it, Landy.*" Marcos chuckled. "*Thank you for that, I needed a good laugh.*"

"*No problem.*"

To the left of them it looked like a gorge opened up—a black zig-zag that cut through the grey-blue silty ocean bottom like a lightning bolt, growing deeper and wider the farther along it they travelled. Piles of rock were mounded here and there, as if whatever ancient calamity that caused the gorge to form had also thrust up chunks of sea floor at the same time. They drifted closer to the edge until they were almost above it, gazing down into its depths.

"*Hope he's not parked down there,*" Jaycen joked, expecting Marcos to shoot him another insult, but instead he agreed.

"*I hope not, as well. But I do not think so. He should be up ahead somewhere.*"

"*Hey, turn off the skimmer for a minute,*" Jaycen suggested. "*Let's see if we can hear anything.*"

Marcos turned off the engine. The machine started to sink and they guided it to the edge of the abyss where they stood, listening, feeling everything around them.

A very faint, almost imperceptible vibration was coming through the water from the opposite direction of where Hahn's ship was supposed to be.

"*What time do you have?*" Marcos asked, concerned.

Jaycen looked at his watch. "*It's around ten a.m.*"

"*We've been at this for nine hours?*"

"*We haven't been making very good time,*" Marcos said in a somber tone. "*I calculated this based on how fast I can go on a skimmer. I didn't take into account how much drag an extra body would be.*"

"*What are you saying? Do you think they're catching up to us?*" Jaycen asked, alarmed.

"*I suspect that's them we're hearing. I would estimate they are about fifteen minutes away.*"

"*Crap!*" Jaycen said, slamming his fist into the skimmer dashboard. "*We've got to find Hahn's ship first before they get here!*"

They started up the motor and headed toward Hahn as fast as they could.

"*Jaycen?*" Marcos asked, his voice strained.

"*Yeah?*"

"*You think she's still alive?*"

Jaycen was lost in thought for a moment. "*Man, I gotta believe she is,*" he said quietly.

"*I know what you mean.*"

"I don't want to imagine the torture she may be going through, but I can't help it. It's giving me nightmares, and then I wake up and it's even worse, because I know it could be real," Jaycen admitted. Marcos shot him a haunted look, and Jaycen knew his mind had been living in the same dark places.

Ahead of them a black shape began to take form, hovering about a hundred yards from the rim of the abyss. It was enormous. Marcos pointed.

"This is it." Marcos slowed the skimmer to a crawl as they approached it. Jaycen stared at the huge sub, suddenly feeling very hopeless and totally inadequate for the task at hand. Somehow their plan went from being workable to seeming as silly and childish as a mosquito attacking a dragon. He took a deep breath to steady himself. Marin was inside the belly of that dragon. There was only one choice he *could* make. Ice filled his veins as he considered the very real probability that going forward would likely mean the end of his life. He looked over at Marcos, reading the same feelings playing across his face.

"Marcos, we'll find her. Don't worry," he said, almost as much for his own benefit as for Marcos's.

Marcos's face hardened with determination. *"Yes. Of course we will."*

"Then we can go back to fighting about which one of us she likes more, okay?"

Marcos chuckled grimly. *"And I can go back to resenting you like normal, eh?"*

Jaycen grinned. *"And I can go back to hating your face. And hair. And basically everything about you."*

"Deal." Marcos made a move to go forward, but Jaycen held him back.

"Wait! We need to send word to the Minnow. Make sure they have Hahn's exact location. You know, in case..." Jaycen said, unwilling to finish the sentence.

Marcos nodded grimly and pulled out the transmitter. He clicked on the tracker so Minnow could find them and then sent them the exact coordinates to Hahn's ship before stowing the transmitter back in the skimmer's compartment.

"Hey, Marcos?" Jaycen asked, feeling an impulsive wave of camaraderie with the last somewhat friendly face he might see in this life.

"Yeah?"

"I don't really hate you."

Marcos punched him lightly on the shoulder. *"Come on, Landy."*

They started up the skimmer, concentrating on the objective ahead of them, fighting the demons of fear and doubt, when a dark shadow shot toward them from below. Whatever it was slammed solidly into Marcos, knocking him sideways and loosening his grip, sending the skimmer into a tailspin. Jaycen didn't even have time to register what happened before the ocean was spinning in a blur. He held onto the skimmer for dear life, his pulse pounding in his ears and his stomach churning. Marcos lost his grip and dropped out of sight. Once Marcos's hand released the accelerator, the skimmer lost power and its violent rotations slowed. Jaycen let go and watched it spiral into a mound of rocks with a crunch.

Dizzy, but nerves on fire with adrenalin, he doubled back to find Marcos, but came face to face with the open jaws of a grey skinned shark the size of a small car. He jerked out of the way just as the beast flew past him, giving Jaycen a too-close view of the rest of the thing's huge, mutated body. It had the prominent dorsal fin of a great white, but bony spinal growths came out of its back and on the tips of its tail and fins were knobbly appendages that looked like fingers and toes. Jaycen's heart burned with dread. It was one of Hahn's monsters.

Jaycen tried to force his fear-frozen mind to work, but he couldn't stop staring at the creature, as if not accepting that it was real would make it vanish. Instead, it swung its huge tail, turning around for another run at him. Jaycen frantically dug through the dive pack at his waist for something to defend himself with, but he couldn't keep his trembling fingers from fumbling. The knife he was searching for slipped out and drifted to the ocean floor. The shark thing was getting closer. Jaycen dove for the knife, scrambling with one hand in his pack for a backup. The shark followed him, increasing its speed to close the distance between itself and Jaycen. Jaycen didn't have to look back to see how close it was, he could feel it in the water immediately behind him and the knife lay another ten feet below him. His right hand closed around a handle and he jerked out the meat fork, spinning to face the monster just as it overtook him. He threw one arm up to shield his face and the shark bit down on it, rows of razor-sharp teeth sinking into his flesh.

214

"AAAGGHH!" Jaycen's scream echoed through the water. He brought his other hand up in a desperate swing, stabbing the fork through whatever he could reach on the monster, and sank it into the shark's gills. The shark shook its head, jerking Jaycen around by his arm, as if trying to escape the pain it was in. Jaycen grit his teeth, trying to ignore the fire racing up his shoulder and the feeling that at any moment his arm was going to snap. He wrapped his legs around the body of the shark and pulled the fork out with all his might. The beast convulsed violently, almost forcing Jaycen to drop the gory weapon, but he caught it, tightening his fingers around it and stabbing it all the way up to the handle into the glassy eye of the monster. The shark creature screamed, a horrifyingly human scream that made Jaycen's soul cringe, even as its grip on his arm loosened. He tried to pull his shredded arm from the monster's mouth.

"Help…me," the monster gurgled as it began to lose its battle with its wounds. Blood poured out over both of them as the shark drifted downwards. Its mouth opened and Jaycen fell free, his heart and head both pounding in shock. The shark twitched a few more times, sending it in a different direction before it stopped face first in the sandy water and lay still. Jaycen hit the bottom of the sea with a bump and lay there for a few moments, stunned, staring at the corpse of the once human beast. This was just *one* of Hahn's creatures and it could have easily destroyed him. How many more would Hahn have guarding his sub? And now he was wounded, and Marcos was gone and may very well be dead. He didn't want to give in to despair, but it was hard to think straight, lying alone on the ocean floor with an arm looking like raw hamburger and bleeding like a faucet. He closed his eyes, and he lay in the sand feeling cold, sick, and hopeless.

"Jaycen! Are you all right? Wake up! Jaycen!" Marcos was suddenly above him, shaking him and slapping his face repeatedly.

"Hey, quit it!" Jaycen murmured irritably, trying to sit up. Marcos smiled with relief and helped him to a sitting position. He inspected Jaycen's wounded arm, his face growing dark with concern. He slowly shook his head.

"Your arm is in very bad shape."

"Yeah, today kinda sucks so far."

Marcos shrugged in agreement and took out his knife, cutting some of Jaycen's mangled wetsuit away from his arm and used it to crudely bind the worst of Jaycen's wounds. Jaycen winced as Marcos tightened a couple of bands.

"It seems I am always the one to bandage you up, Landy boy. You need to quit getting hurt," Marcos chuckled.

"Well, next time it can be your turn, okay?" The faint sound of a motor startled them both *"Dude, we don't have time for this,"* Jaycen struggled to his feet. The pain in his arm was excruciating, but he didn't have time to feel it right now. *"We've got to get to Marin!"*

"Jaycen, you have to stay here. When the Minnow gets here, you need to get on board and get this taken care of. You're not going to be much help messed up like this."

Jaycen shook him off. *"I'll be alright. It's not as bad as it looks,"* he said, noting Marcos's doubtful look. *"I'm a fast healer."* Marcos crossed his arms. *"Seriously, this is our only shot and you will need me, no matter what shape I'm in. So, let's get going."*

"The skimmer is toast. And the Minnow has got to be near. Can you even swim?"

"Yeah, I'll figure it out," Jaycen said. His hand still shook from the shock of the attack.

"Neither one of us are going to like this, but hang onto my shoulder with your good arm. And keep an eye out for any more of those monsters!" Jaycen made a face but grabbed Marcos's shoulder and they kicked off toward Hahn once more, only this time much more slowly. Jaycen could hear the hum of Hahn's sub more clearly once they started moving, but behind them, the sound of Minnow was getting louder by the second. He pushed himself to try to kick faster to help Marcos, but they were running out of time. He knew he was holding Marcos back. He hazarded a glance over his shoulder and caught sight of the Minnow gaining on them and his heart sank. *They* couldn't make it to Hahn's in time, but Marcos could.

"Marcos, they're here. We'll never make it like this. It's all on you, man."

Marcos nodded. *"I've got this. Stall them if you can,"* he replied.

"Good luck!" Jaycen said, letting go and drifting behind.

CHAPTER 42

PAUL

PAUL OPENED HIS eyes a few hours later feeling mildly less fatigued. He rubbed his face, wondering what woke him, when he realized the sub had slowed. He hopped off the bunk and headed to the cockpit to see what was happening.

Frank was driving, with Dawes in the copilot's seat and Riggs crouching between them. Frank's jaw was clenched and Paul could feel the enmity rising like smoke between him and the two men.

"All I'm saying is I need to speak with General Holt. He's been my liaison with the President and I want to make sure he is aware of the situation," Frank said tightly.

"What situation?" Paul asked, leaning into the room over Riggs.

"We think we've picked up the boys on radar," Frank said. They aren't too far ahead and are stopped for the moment. It looks like we have a shot of catching up with them before we get to Hahn's last position."

Paul let out a huge sigh. "That's good, right?"

"Not necessarily," Riggs said. "They are still ahead of us and still have a chance of compromising our mission."

"Our mission is to rescue Marin. They have as much chance at succeeding as any of us do," Paul replied angrily.

"They have cut off communication and gone rogue!" Dawes snapped.

"Most likely because they feared you would prevent a rescue mission, something I am worried about myself," Paul shot back.

Dawes's eyes flashed menacingly. "Is this your doing? Did you send them out there on purpose to sabotage this mission?"

"This *IS* the mission, you thick-headed idiot," Frank snarled, losing his cool.

"And your boys out there are jeopardizing it!" Dawes shouted back. Something beeped on the monitor and Frank looked down anxiously.

"What is it?" Dawes demanded.

"The boys have just made contact," he said quietly. "They are just ahead to the right."

"Did they send in Hahn's coordinates?" Dawes asked impatiently.

Frank glanced at Paul and back at the display. "Not yet." Paul could see from his angle that a string of numbers had been sent along with the message. He groaned inwardly, hoping Riggs didn't notice.

"We've got to catch up to them, get moving!" Dawes ordered. He reached for the radio and picked up the headset, putting it on.

"This is as fast as this ship goes, Dawes," Frank muttered.

Paul strained his eyes out the viewport at the open sea, alternating that with watching the radar apprehensively as they followed the tiny blips representing the boys. At the edge of the screen, a larger dot suddenly appeared. Hahn. Dawes flipped on the transmitter.

"Dawes here, patch me through to the President," he said into the headset. The radio crackled and a few minutes later Paul heard a voice pick up on the other end and he strained to hear what was being said.

"Mr. President, we have located the rogue agents. We are in pursuit."

The dot on the monitor grew closer. Riggs shifted around in his uncomfortable position and finally stood up. Paul held his breath, praying he wouldn't notice the numbers displayed on the communicator screen. Frank looked over his shoulder at Paul, locking eyes with him. Sweat was beading down his face.

"I need to speak to General Holt," Frank said loudly.

Dawes scoffed at him.

"Holt has no authority here. We are acting under the President's direct orders."

Suddenly Riggs bent down over Frank and looked closely at the communicator. His eyes widened, then immediately narrowed as he glared at Frank, thrusting a finger toward the screen. "He lied to us! They *do* have Hahn's coordinates."

Dawes' jaw clenched angrily as he clicked the button on the communicator again. "Mr. President, we have acquired Hahn's exact location. I'm sending the coordinates now," he said, typing the numbers into the radio keyboard.

Sweat began pouring down Paul's face as well. This was getting out of control. "Dawes, we need to go over the plans for the rescue mission. We'll be there soon," Paul said, fighting down the sick feeling growing in his stomach.

Dawes turned to him icily. "Don't be stupid! There was never going to be a rescue mission. There is too much at risk."

"NO!" shouted Frank. "Let me talk to the President!" He reached for the headset, but Riggs blocked him.

"We have an affirmative on Operation Serpent Strike," Dawes said. Paul's heart clenched.

"NO! You can't do this!" Paul shouted.

"Yes, sir, order them to fire at will," Dawes said, leaning away from Frank's reach. Paul's breath was knocked out of him.

"No!" Paul shrieked, diving across Riggs to get to Dawes.

"No! You can't! You can't!" Frank cried, reaching around the burly form of Riggs to grab the headset out of Dawes's head. "Mr. President, please, no! My daughter is on board! You have to wait! You gave your word!"

Paul struggled with Riggs to get into the cockpit, but suddenly a loud *crack!* boomed through the radio. "What was that?" he whispered with dread. Numbly, he dropped his hands as another object entered the radar screen, moving rapidly towards Hahn's sub.

"No! Mr. President, please! Call off the attack! My daughter is still in there! You gave your word!" Frank croaked in desperation. No response came from the other end. The object fell swiftly, and for a moment nobody spoke. Paul watched the dots move closer and closer together. Within seconds the two dots merged. Paul dropped to his knees.

"Marin," he whispered, his heart tearing in two. "No, no, no, not Marin!"

A blinding light lit the cockpit with the power of the sun, and a moment later the ocean trembled, rattling the sub like an empty tin can. The shaking intensified and a second later the sub was thrust backwards through the water. Paul was launched into the hallway, banging violently against the wall and rolling across the ceiling, objects flying everywhere, hitting him and bouncing around the sub. He closed his eyes, bracing for the implosion that was sure to come, but the movement of the sub slowed. He grabbed the edges of a door to try to stabilize himself, wincing at the sounds of groans and whines coming from the seams as the sub rotated and then slowly righted itself.

Something wet and salty filled his right eye, which he assumed was sweat, but when he wiped it out with the heel of his hand, it was covered with blood. Gingerly, he inched his way towards the cockpit and looked inside. Frank and Dawes had been strapped in and seemed shook up, but otherwise fine. Riggs had been banged around in the doorway and was nursing his shoulder and had several cuts along his forearm and on his face. Paul angrily wished both of their heads had been busted for the terrible injustice they had just done.

"Frank," Paul said softly. "You okay?"

Frank took off his seatbelt and stood up, his face looking as hard as marble. "We need to go outside and find the boys," he said quietly, striding past the two men. Paul followed him down the hallway. Emily ran towards them, a slight limp in her step. Paul wondered if she'd been wounded, but remembered her legs had trouble anyway.

"What happened?" she asked, searching his face worriedly.

"They…" Frank tried to make his voice work, chewing the insides of his cheek to keep his composure. "They launched a missile and destroyed Hahn's sub," he said flatly. Emily's eyes flew open wide and her face blanched.

"No!" She cried, sinking to the ground. Frank knelt beside her, holding her. Paul leaned against the wall, his soul bleeding. Marin was gone. His sweet little girl, the one he'd spent his life raising and protecting, who had finally overcome so much, was gone. The depths of his heartache couldn't be measured.

Frank took a deep breath and looked up at Emily. "We have to go find the boys. They could be injured," he said shakily.

Emily nodded. "I'll...I'll come with you." Paul watched them go to the lockbox and close the door, hearing the quiet hum of the valves letting in water. He couldn't bring himself to move, let alone join them. What did it matter? The world had stopped. His little girl was gone. The wall was the only thing keeping him standing. Finally gravity overcame him and he sagged down, sinking to a sitting position, and dropped his head into his hands.

CHAPTER 43

JAYCEN

BEFORE MARCOS COULD make it twenty yards away from Jaycen, movement in the distance above them caught Jaycen's eye. A large silver cylinder, like an oversized bullet, shot down at a steep angle, leaving a trail of blue-white bubbles in its wake. The object was headed straight toward Hahn's sub! In the millisecond it took him to register what it was, the object impacted with the sub in a billowing black cloud with a fiery orange explosion at its heart.

Jaycen shot out his hands as if he could stop it from happening, a scream of horrified agony being ripped from his throat. *"Marin! Nooooooo!"* The sub expanded outward and then crumpled inward almost instantly with a massive ballooning of air bubbles. An expanding shock wave rippled rapidly outward, hitting Marcos and then Jaycen, with the force of a truck that sent them spinning through the water like rags. The power of it knocked the breath out of Jaycen, bursting his eardrums and tossing his body like a stick in a whirlwind. It was all he could do to stay conscious as the water shoved him backwards, the entire ocean a blur. He couldn't think, couldn't grieve, couldn't react.

As suddenly as the shock wave hit him, it was gone, leaving him bobbing in the choppy wake it left behind. He slowly opened his eyes and tried to take in a breath of water. Every millimeter of him hurt, especially his wounded arm. He was drifting somewhere over the abyss. Hahn's sub was sparking and groaning as it sank to the edge of the canyon, a massive hole blasted through its center. He held his injured arm to his body and watched numbly as the sub hit the bottom and shuddered, crumpling in on itself, just like his heart. Marin. No one could have survived that blast. He stared in shock at the wreckage, watching his hopes and dreams die in front of him. His heart was an empty hole, black and jagged, pierced and destroyed by the torpedo that sank Hahn's ship.

Reluctantly, he looked around to get his bearings and found Marcos lying inert on the ocean floor several yards from him. He headed over to him, more out of reflex than concern, for he was far too numb to feel anything. Marcos had a small cut along his forehead and tiny pink strands of blood drifted out of it. Other than the fact that his eyes were closed, he looked fairly uninjured.

"Marcos," Jaycen said, shaking him. He put his fingers on his carotid artery and felt for a pulse. There it was. He was alive. Jaycen took his good arm and tried to heft Marcos to a sitting position. Marcos took a deep breath and started to stir.

"Hey, you okay?" Jaycen asked. Marcos stared at him blankly and shook his head. He glanced at the remains of Hahn's sub and leaned forward, his head in his hands. Jaycen looked down at his wounded arm and noticed distractedly that beneath what was left of the makeshift bandages, the worst of his wounds were already healing up. Some part of his brain thought of the serum derived from Marin's blood; that miracle injection that had turned him into an Arydian and gave him the ability to heal so quickly... it was a part of her that made him who he was. He caught his breath in anguish.

The Minnow drifted into view near the ruined skimmer and stopped. A few moments later, two people emerged, circled the broken skimmer and turned toward Jaycen and Marcos. As they got closer, Jaycen recognized Frank and his wife, Emily. The way they moved divulged the weight of loss they were feeling as well. Everything was slower, harder. Even breathing in and out was laborious. To Jaycen, it seemed like it took them forever to cross the distance between them, and it didn't matter. The world had stopped for them all. Nothing, not even time, had meaning anymore.

Frank and Emily swam up to the two young men wordlessly. Marcos stood up to face them, his face a mask of stone. No one could speak. There was nothing to say. The fresh knife wound in all their hearts was visible on every one of their faces. Frank and Emily put their arms around Marcos and Jaycen and pulled them close. The tender gesture broke Jaycen and he fell apart, the agony of his loss coming out in helpless sobs. He could feel the cries of everyone in the group, their shoulders shaking, their tight grips on each other's shoulders. Mourning the life they had all struggled so hard to save.

Frank was the first to step back, giving Jaycen's shoulder a final bracing squeeze. Marcos looked pale, his eyes red. Emily looked more frail than Jaycen would have thought possible and she clung to her husband for strength.

"It was our fault, wasn't it?" Jaycen choked out. *"They didn't trust us to get Marin and they didn't want to risk losing Hahn."*

Frank looked at them tenderly. *"Don't think like that. It wasn't your fault. This is the fault of Hahn, and Hahn alone."*

Marcos looked up angrily. *"Hahn didn't pull the trigger that just murdered Marin. That was us! Our people! The ones that were supposed to HELP us!"* He cried. *"And we led them directly to her!"* Marcos shouted bitterly.

Frank put a hand on Marcos's shoulder. *"This wasn't your fault. And as much as I want to hate and blame our people, they had some rough decisions to make as well. In hindsight, I fear this was their plan all along; I was just too blinded by hope to see it. They had to think about the safety of everyone, not just Marin. It was too dangerous to risk an extraction."*

"It's not fair! After all she must have gone through, just to..." Jaycen stammered. *"We tried so hard to get to her in time. If we'd just left earlier, or gone faster..."*

"Then you would have been killed, too," Emily said softly. *"That wouldn't have helped save her."*

Frank reluctantly inclined his head toward the Minnow. *"C'mon, boys. Let's get back to the ship."* He and Emily started back, and Marcos and Jaycen trailed slowly after them, each lost in sorrow.

CHAPTER 44

MARIN

WATER FILLED THE remaining space in the lockbox of Hahn's sub, and Marin took a deep breath of the cold seawater, filling her lungs and losing her buoyancy. She sank eye level with the window and with Hahn, almost unrecognizable in his mask of roaring fury, as he beat the window with a metal bar that pinged with each stroke. She sank away from his violent attack and tried the hatch once again. This time, it opened almost without effort and some part of her brain remembered learning that a pressurized hatch will only allow one door to open at a time. Meaning, now Hahn had to wait until the hatch was closed again and the water was able to drain and the room repressurized, before he could open the compartment to come after her. Then he would have to wait for it to fill with water before he could get out! And…if she left the hatch open, maybe he couldn't get into the compartment at all, if there wasn't another way out.

Miraculously, she had a head start! She dived straight down through the hatch and swam into open water, fear of Hahn propelling her faster than she ever imagined she could swim. The wide ocean stretched out forever on all sides of her. She had no idea where she was, but she knew she was free and planned to stay that way, streaking away from the sub, not caring which direction she was going. The sub was hovering over a massive canyon with huge pillars of rock lining it. She swam deep, looking for somewhere she could hide in case Hahn came after her.

Just as she reached the rim of the canyon, she felt something move in the water behind her. She twisted to find the massive stingray that brought her here. She scrambled backwards just as it swooped towards her. The huge fins of the man brushed her feet, but his oddly-shaped, grasping hands barely missed her. He struggled to turn, giving her just a few seconds before he came in for another swipe. She didn't wait for him, diving rapidly into the abyss, aiming for the rock formations below her. The ray beat his fins hard, breaking the distance between them quickly. She knew he could swim faster than her, but it looked like he had trouble maneuvering as well as she could.

She made it to a crack in the wall and pushed herself back into it as far as she could. She could feel him close behind but doubted he could get in there. She was wrong. The man turned himself sideways and slid into the crack with ease, his thin body filling the only escape. His face was to the wall, but his hands, embedded in the edge of the fins, grasped the rock face and helped him scramble blindly into the crevasse. She pushed herself into the fissure as hard as she could, scraping her skin as she inched away from him, but he reached out a clawed, gnarly hand, grasping at her.

He caught her, stabbing into her ankle with a long nail, his hand closing around her foot like a bony pincer. She screamed, kicking against him, but he pulled her out inch by inch, as she strained to keep her grip on the rock wall. She continued to kick him with her free foot, but it was like kicking a wet mattress and it didn't seem to have much effect. His soft, rubbery body undulated with the water, sucking her slowly out of the ravine. Blood rose from the wound in her ankle, and for a moment she had a fleeting hope that her blood would change him, as it had Dave so long ago, but it was nowhere near his face and didn't seem to affect him. She had to try something else.

Abruptly, she let go and let him pull her out into the canyon, dangling by her trapped foot. He reached for her with his other mutilated hand, but when he got close, she turned towards him with a vicious snarl and a sharp rock in her hand. She raised it as if she were going to stab him with it, but instead brought it down into the palm of her hand with a shout of pain. It cut deeply into her palm and blood poured out darkly into the water. She shoved her hand into the pleated gills near his face, forcing him to breathe in her blood.

His mutated face showed surprise, then confusion. Then he began to change. The eerie, blanket-like shape of his body contorted and shrank. He jerked his hand free of her foot and he wrapped his bat-like arms around himself. A spine emerged along a line in his back, and a head of grey hair evolved behind the toothy face. Legs split from the body, and the hands were now attached to arms. The thing shrieked in an inhuman voice, kicking and arching in circles as he transformed back into a man. Marin held her wounded hand to her chest, backing away from the horrible sight, but unable to look away.

The transformation ended. A completely naked old man floated in the water in front of her, as his gills, the last vestiges of the manta ray, disappeared from his neck. He looked surprised as he drowned, choking on the water that filled lungs designed for air. After a few short convulsions, he stopped moving and sank into the depths below her. She watched him, completely horrified, sobbing with fear tainted with regret. Her hand had stopped bleeding, but she kept it close to her anyway, like it was a loaded weapon she was afraid of using.

Part of her brain kept screaming at her, telling her to keep moving, to hide, or flee, but she couldn't tear her eyes away from the white, wispy hair sinking below her. Suddenly, she had that prickly feeling that she was being watched. She snapped her face up and saw it- pair of eyes staring intently at her from across the gorge, maybe twenty feet away. It had a long, lithe body, bulbous head, and stringy arms and hands. It drifted in and out of shadows; its ribbon-like body waving gently in the current. It had the face of a human, but with a wide, freakishly disproportionate mouth sporting long, saber-like teeth. It floated a careful distance away from her, watching every move she made. She grimaced inwardly. Of course Hahn had more of his monsters out here patrolling the ocean. How many, she had no idea. This one looked like some form of a moray eel. They stared at each other, weighing their options. It seemed the creature had seen the death of the other man and was calculating how to capture her without suffering the same fate.

She grimaced, knowing Hahn was not going to stop pursuing her. Her head start was running out. She glanced to the left, up the channel of the vast gorge, wondering if she could outrun it. As if sensing her thoughts, it moved closer to her, its huge, snake like body twisting, its fringes rippling, almost gracefully.

Obviously this thing would have no trouble outmaneuvering her, and it likely possessed speed equal or greater to hers. She glanced over her shoulder and up toward Hahn's sub. There was movement at the bottom of it, as if there were divers coming out. She didn't know if Hahn still had the ability to breathe underwater, but it didn't matter. Anyone coming from that ship was an enemy. The thing moved closer again, positioning itself to block her escape and keep her between it and Hahn's sub. It opened its overlarge mouth in a menacing hiss. It seemed like it was trying to either hold her or herd her closer without having to actually touch her.

She lunged toward it, testing her hunch. The creature retreated a few feet, as if surprised, but then coiled up and faced her again. She spun and dove, kicking as hard as she could to the nearest reasonable retreat, the gorge. Maybe, just maybe, she could lose the thing in the walls. She pumped her legs and arms as fast as she could, adrenaline giving her extra energy. She didn't pause to see if the eel was following her, but dashed into the towering walls, twisting and turning around tall columns of stacked rock lining the canyon, moving as far away from the sub and the creature as she could.

Suddenly, she was jerked to a stop. The thing seized her leg with its long tail and was pulling her backwards. It passed a rock column and wrapped its upper body around it, holding her in place. She turned, using her hands to pry herself out of the anaconda-like grip of the thing, but it didn't help. She looked at her hand, but it was no longer bleeding, and she had no way to try to cut herself again. Besides, the thing's head was well out of her reach and now Hahn's people were getting closer.

"Give it up, my pet. There's no place for you to go down here. I rule the ocean now."

Hahn. Marin's soul shivered at his words. What had her blood done to him? Was he like her now? An Arydian plus whatever else she could do? She hated to think he had the same powers she had. Still, it had taken her time to figure them out. That gave her an advantage.

She filled her heart with rage, pulling power from wherever it was she was generating it from. The creature shifted his grip on her nervously. Her hands tingled with blue fire. When she felt it was strong enough, she laid her hands on the creature's sinewy body and released it with a blast. The thing's muscles contracted uncontrollably, tightening its powerful grip on her leg so hard she worried it might break, but then the thing's entire body went slack. She felt, rather than heard, Hahn's curse. She yanked her leg out of its grasp and raced away from Hahn as fast as she could, reaching out her senses in every direction to feel for any more of his monsters out in this mountainous underwater maze.

Rounding a corner, she looked back and saw that they were using some version of skimmers and were gaining on her. She passed a very narrow crevice partially hidden behind a pillar. She ducked into it, scooting as far back into it as she could force herself and held her breath, trying not to move. Her face was pressed painfully against the rocks, but she didn't dare adjust herself.

A couple of moments later, three men on skimmers made the turn and then slowed, hovering above the canyon mere yards from her hiding place. She could see Hahn's black hair slicked back from his face as he glided by, his dark eyes scanning everything around him. The two others wore odd helmets on their heads that seemed to be filled with liquid. She willed her heart to quit beating so loudly in her chest as his gaze brushed past the crack she was wedged in. She closed her eyes, hoping he wouldn't feel her looking at him, but couldn't bear the suspense for long. When she opened her eyes, they had drifted further from her hiding spot.

"I know you are near, my dear. I can feel you nearby. Don't worry, we will find you soon enough. Then you will feel the pain of my revenge!"

They moved lower into the canyon and spread out, each going a different direction. She could no longer see them, but she could hear the hum of their machines. It wouldn't be long before they found her, but for now they were looking in the wrong direction. She inched out a little so she could move her head more freely and looked up. The opening she was hiding in went straight up about twenty feet to the top of the canyon. She could see lighter blue high above her.   If they continued looking for her *inside* the canyon, she might just be able to get away out of the top of it and gain some time. Feeling around above her head, she caught hold of a rock and started to pull herself up, hand over hand, moving as quickly as she could without making any sudden movements. The crack tightened as she crawled around an outcropping, forcing her out towards the canyon to get around it, but then she pulled herself back in, reaching like a rock climber scaling a wall.

She heard the sound of a skimmer coming close, and she scrabbled up the last few feet, pulling herself up over the lip just as the sound of a skimmer went past below. She held still, willing herself to be one with the ocean floor until the humming went by. She raised her head and saw a mound of white crabs watching her with beady stalk eyes. They moved away from her cautiously. She kicked her feet, trying not to raise any sand into the water and swam from the canyon as fast as she could, keeping Hahn's sub behind her.

Once she was far enough away, she put on a burst of speed, kicking her feet and pulling with her arms until she thought her heart might explode, but she refused to slow down. Ahead, she heard the hum of another vehicle, large, but not as big as Hahn's sub. She turned parallel to the canyon and continued to swim, keeping the sound on one side of her, the canyon on the other, Hahn's sub falling further behind her. She didn't dare slow, but her body began choosing for her at this point. Her legs felt weak and rubbery, her arms were shaking with fatigue.

She made her way to a pile of rocks as big as a house and hid within them, gulping in great gasps of water to catch her breath. She could barely make out Hahn's sub from here, but the sound of whatever craft was coming toward her was getting louder. Probably reinforcements for Hahn, she thought dismally, since nobody had subs that could go this deep as far as she knew, except the Arydians, but how would they know where she was?

Still, she had escaped. She was alive, and as long as she could hide from Hahn, eventually she would be free. She took a deep, satisfying breath and let herself relax for a few minutes, slowing her heart rate and lessening the pounding of her pulse in her ears.

Strangely, she could hear more engines further away, probably on the surface, since the sounds came from above. She could barely make out the shadowy forms high above her.

Marin watched cautiously as the small sub approached, praying it wasn't more of Hahn's people. She could feel her strength lagging after her difficult escape, and honestly didn't know how much more she could take. Hiding seemed her best option. She watched as something smaller caught her eye, like a large animal, or maybe a skimmer with a person or two driving it. It was moving in the water ahead of the small sub, but she couldn't see it well enough to know what it was, and the fear of facing another mutant monster kept her from venturing out of the rocky mound. It seemed her best chance of survival.

Suddenly the object moving toward Hahn's sub started moving erratically. Some part broke off and fell and the rest of it spun away. A few seconds later, she heard a scream that rattled her to the bone.

"AAAGGHH!"

Startled, she readjusted her position, straining to see what was happening. There seemed to be a struggle going on, but then everything moved behind a hill and she couldn't see anything anymore. It sounded like who or whatever it was needed help. She almost darted from her hideout to see, but stopped herself. She needed help, too, and without knowing who or what was over there, she didn't dare risk leaving.

With a resigned sigh, she sank back behind the rocks and waited, listening carefully to the new sub coming closer. Then it stopped. She didn't dare hope it was the Arydians, but she wished it with all her heart. It had to be something going on with Hahn's creatures, perhaps fighting amongst themselves. But just in case…she crept forward out of her hiding place, quietly trying to get a better look, but couldn't see much. If it was the Arydians—she took a deep breath and eased out into the open.

"There she is!" Hahn called, rising up from the edge of the abyss, his two cronies in tow. Marin cursed herself for her stupidity. It was too late to hide, she had to run. She took off toward the smaller sub, not knowing if she

was headed into the arms of friends or the clutches of enemies, swimming as fast as her exhausted body would let her. Hahn and his men on their machines were closing in fast. Suddenly the ocean trembled and a bright light flashed out of the corner of her eye. She glanced over her shoulder just in time to see Hahn's sub implode on itself. Hahn and his men stopped dead in their tracks. She slowed in awe to watch the incredible sight. She looked at her pursuers triumphantly.

"*Yes!*" she crowed to Hahn, pumping her fist in the air.

A tortured scream echoed through the area, startling her.

"*Marin! Nooooooo!*"

She took in a deep, sobbing breath of unbelief. She *could not* believe her eyes or her ears. It couldn't be true!

It *was* Jaycen! Her heart jumped with joy! They *were* here to rescue her!!

Hahn's face hardened into a mask of hate but then his mouth curled up in a sneer. He took one finger and tapped the wrist of his opposite hand.

"*The clock is ticking my dear. You might win the battle, but the war is mine.*"

The ocean around them rumbled and an invisible ripple hit Hahn and his men, cracking the helmets of his two henchmen and throwing them all like toys. Marin barely had time to brace herself before the wave hit her, sending her flying through the water like a rocket.

She held onto her head, tumbling end over end until the force of the wave stopped. Gingerly, she straightened out, grateful to be in one piece. She'd been blown to the other side of the abyss. Hahn's men were either injured or killed; they drifted below her in the dark expanse. She scanned the depths for Hahn and finally saw him, floating by the cliff wall. She prayed he'd had his head bashed in by the blast, but she wasn't going to go near him to check, just in case.

She forced her aching muscles to pull her across the expanse toward the Arydians, making no noise in case Hahn had more creatures lurking around. The small sub had been tossed by the explosion, but appeared to still be working. It stopped and people came out. She raced towards them, straining so see who they were, afraid to believe they were actually Arydians and not Hahn's people. It *had* to have been Jaycen's voice she heard! She was so fatigued and stressed, she didn't know what to trust. She pushed herself to swim faster, but before she could make out their faces, they turned and started back to the sub.

"*NO!*" was all she could think to scream, hoping they would turn around, hoping beyond hope they were her friends. They turned as one and paused. She dredged up the last of her adrenaline reserves to bridge the gap between them. One pulled closer, swimming faster than the others. Her heart cried with relief when she recognized Marcos! He jetted toward her, joyfully shouting her name again and again. Moments later she was in his arms, safe, protected. She clung to him, sobbing with relief. Seconds behind Marcos, Jaycen appeared, throwing his arms around both of them, joined by Frank and another woman, wrapping her in a cocoon of love and protection. She was weak with gratitude, holding on to them all, soaking up their strength and support. She pulled away just a tiny bit to get a breath and Frank took her hand.

The look on his face was like nothing she had ever seen. There was a light of joy shining in his eyes that defied description. He turned her to face the strangely familiar woman.

"*Marin, I'd like you to meet your mother.*" The woman bit her lip, smiling nervously while Marin tried to comprehend what her father was saying.

"*But…I thought,*" she stumbled, looking at her father. "*You said…*"

"*I was wrong!*" Frank beamed, slipping his arm around the woman. "*I was wrong! Never have I been so glad to be wrong!*" Marin studied the woman, her tear-filled eyes so familiar it was like Marin was looking in the mirror. She reached out a hand and touched her cheek, seeing pieces of herself in this beautiful woman. Emily wrapped her fingers around Marin's hand and pressed it to her face, kissing her palm. She reached out to Marin and embraced her once again, holding her tightly. Marin melted into her mother's arms, years of wishing for a mother replaced with the indescribable joy of finding her. The tears of happiness flowed with the water as they made their way as one back to the sub.

CHAPTER 45

MARIN

OPENING THE AIRLOCK door, Paul let out a choked cry of disbelief, sweeping Marin into his arms. "Oh, my baby girl!" he sobbed into her hair. "I thought I'd lost you!" he said, his voice husky. Marin clung to him, not wanting to let go, afraid they would all disappear and she'd be back in Hahn's clutches.

"Is this real? Please, tell me this is real. I'm not dreaming, right?" she sobbed. She felt a warm hand close over hers and she looked up over Paul's shoulder to see Jaycen wiping tears from his smiling face and finally knew. She had never seen Jaycen cry, and doubted she would dream it. His blue eyes sparkled with tears of joy. She grasped his fingers and squeezed them tightly, gratefully. Everyone was slapping each other on the back and laughing triumphantly, celebrating the miracle of her rescue.

They moved their rejoicing into the galley and Emily threw a rough, green blanket over Marin's shoulders while Paul started hot water boiling. Her emotions felt scrubbed raw from the extremes of torture and jubilation she'd experienced. Paul and Frank were more weepy than Marin had ever thought possible, and everyone wanted to touch her, hold her, have a hand on her, as if they never wanted to let go. She welcomed every touch, everything that made this seem more real for her, too, as she soaked in every detail of every face, still; struggling to believe her ordeal was over.

Suddenly, a burly stranger butted in on the reunion and asked gruffly, "Was Hahn on the sub when it was destroyed?"

Marin looked at the stranger uncertainly. "Who are you?"

"Chief Petty Officer Ed Dawes, special liaison to the President," he said sharply.

Something about him bothered Marin, but she couldn't put her finger on it. "I honestly don't know where Hahn is," Marin said, not even sure why she was being evasive.

"I didn't ask where he was. I want to know if he was on the sub when it was destroyed," the man said, not about to be deterred.

Marin dropped her eyes. "No. He and a couple other guys were coming after me when the torpedo hit."

The man's mouth puckered up in a pinched circle. "We are going to have to mount a search for him," he said. "We can't let him escape."

"No, we don't have time for that!" Marin said suddenly. "We have to warn everybody! Hahn set up an automatic timer. We have only 36 hours until all three warheads ignite!"

Frank's eyebrows shot up. "36 hours! Are you sure?"

"Yes! And I know where they are and how to turn them off, if we get to them before he can change the password."

"Wow, I'm impressed," Frank said, blinking in surprise at his daughter.

Dawes leaned his head toward another man that had joined him and they spoke quietly together. With a scowl, Dawes cleared his throat, as if making an announcement. "We are required to conduct a search for Hahn if he is still alive."

"Are you kidding me?" Paul shouted. "We don't have time to worry about Hahn right now! Lives are at stake! We have 36 hours! Aren't you listening?"

Riggs joined Dawes, standing and blocking the door. "We are going to mount a search. We can send the information on, but our orders are to secure Hahn. And we will be using this sub to do it."

Marin's jaw dropped. "You don't understand! These warheads are too far down. The only chance you have to reach them is if *we* help!"

Riggs looked uncertainly at Dawes, but Dawes stood his ground. "Until we hear otherwise, we will search for Hahn."

Frank stood and tried to shoulder past the men, but they shoved him backwards into the table.

"Hey!" Paul shouted. Malcolm, Marcos, Jaycen and Paul stood up in unison, ready for a fight. Dawes snarled and pulled a knife from his waistband, pointing it at Frank. Everyone stepped back.

Marin's heart was pounding in her chest. Whoever these men were, they didn't feel like they were on the same side as her friends and family. Paul helped Frank back to his feet, glaring at the men the whole time. Marin let her fear and anger build inside her until she felt now-familiar prickle rise along the back of her neck.

Frank stepped towards Dawes fearlessly. "You think you can intimidate us? After you pulled the trigger to have Marin killed? Now you think you can use us to clean up your mess?" The man stared down Frank, not even flinching. "You can't kill all of us," Frank said, moving even closer.

"Dad, don't!" Marin said, stepping between him and the men.

"Marin, get out of the way!" Frank demanded.

"You should listen to your daddy," Dawes sneered, shoving her away with one hand. The moment he touched her, she let go of a bolt of electricity that dropped him like a rock. Riggs stumbled into the hall in shock, and everyone looked from Dawes's inert form, to Marin, with dropped jaws.

"Marin, how did..." Emily asked in amazement, but before she could finish her question, Frank snatched the knife from Dawes' twitching hand and pointed it at Riggs.

"I know you have a gun on you somewhere. Give it to me!" Frank demanded. "Slowly."

Riggs held up his hands. "You can't attack us, we have authority from the President himself! We were just following orders."

"He said, give us your gun," Paul growled menacingly. "And the knife and any other weapon you brought on board."

Riggs glared at him but pulled his gun out of his waistband and handed it to him, handle first. He reached slowly into his right pants pocket and pulled out a menacing looking knife.

"There. That's everything," Riggs said.

"Frank, cover me while I frisk him." Paul patted down Riggs and produced another folded knife and a multi tool with a hidden razor blade. He put them on the table and frisked the unconscious body of Dawes, adding his weapons to the pile on the table.

"Wow, looks like you forgot a few things," Jaycen added dryly. Marcos laughed.

"Jaycen, grab me some zip ties from the cupboard over there, will you?" Paul asked, nodding to the corner of the galley. Jaycen tossed them to him and he trussed up Riggs as well as Dawes. "Any ideas where to store these two?" Frank asked.

"Lock them to the bunks," Malcolm suggested. They dragged the men to the back of the sub, zip tying them hand and foot to the steel bunk rails. Frank handed the gun to Malcolm. "Keep them under guard, will you, while we contact the government?"

"With pleasure," Malcolm agreed, taking a seat on an empty bunk.

"Marin, Jaycen, meet me up front," Frank instructed, heading to the cockpit. "I have a friend to contact."

CHAPTER 46

JAYCEN

MARIN AND JAYCEN followed Frank, but as soon as they passed the bathroom, Jaycen stepped inside, pulling Marin in after him and closing the door. She looked at him quizzically, but smiled, which made his heart flutter. He half reached out his arms to her, but seeing how Marcos had been looking at her, he didn't know if she would be interested in a hug. She surprised him by following through with his gesture and putting her arms around him and squeezing him tightly. All his anger about Marcos and her melted at her touch. He rested his head on her hair.

"Jaycen, I'm so glad you're safe. Thank you for coming to rescue me," she whispered into his shoulder. She stepped back so she could look at his face, keeping her hands on his waist. His skin tingled everywhere her hands touched him. "Did you find your mother?" she asked, concern sparkling in her beautiful eyes. Jaycen found it hard to answer, but as she waited expectantly, he refocused his mind on her question.

"No. No, I didn't," he said. "I made it to her house, and her crutches and meds were there, but I couldn't find any sign of her." Her eyes darkened with compassion, and she leaned back against the wall.

"I'm so sorry, Jaycen," she said softly.

Jaycen nodded and gave her a half smile. "It's been a tough few weeks for all of us, not just me," he pointed out.

"You're right," she agreed.

"I never thought I would see you again," he said quietly, running a finger across her cheek. "It almost destroyed me inside to leave you. And I've regretted leaving ever since,"

"I know. I felt the same."

"Felt?" he asked, hoping that didn't mean what he feared.

"You're back. It's in the past now," she said simply. Jaycen relaxed a bit and gave her an encouraging smile.

"So what now?"

"I...don't know," she said almost guiltily. Jaycen's hopes sank. "I think the most important thing is to find a way to stop the mutagen. If we live past that, then I guess we'll have to figure the rest out."

"The rest?" he asked heavily. So, she did love Marcos. *Of course*, he moaned inwardly. Still, she cared about him, too. She had to! And if she felt even a fraction for him that he felt for her, he wasn't going to let go that easily. Marcos would have to fight to keep her. He took a finger and tilted her chin up to meet his gaze. "I just want you to know I thought about you every day, Marin. You were the only thing that kept me going. I never stopped loving you, not for a minute. I would have searched the world's oceans to find you, I hope you know that."

Marin looked at him with such a tender expression that he could almost imagine everything would work out between them, but then the look changed. "Oh, Jaycen..." she began, then dropped her gaze. "I honestly don't know what to feel about us. I'm sorry, I know it isn't fair, but I have a lot going on in my head and heart right now." He dropped his hand from hers, his heart growing painful ice crystals inside of it.

"You mean, Marcos? Marcos is what's going on in your heart?" he demanded bitterly.

"Jaycen, don't," she begged.

"I'm sorry," he said with a resigned sigh. "You've been through a lot. I don't mean to pressure you. It's just...you told me before I left that you loved me. I've spent every moment since then believing you. I know you spent a lot of time with Marcos, and I could see how you could care for him. I just need to know if you...do you...still love me?"

Marin met his gaze and he could see the conflict in them, but he held firm, needing an answer, some solid ground to stand on as everything else he clung to was washed away. He didn't know what he would do if he lost her, his one anchor in the storm they were all living through.

"I…" She looked for a second like she really would deny she loved him, and his heart constricted around the ice crystals excruciatingly, but she dropped her eyes and let out a soft, hiccupping cry. "I do," she said, tears now trickling down her cheeks. "I *do* love you, Jaycen. I've spent all this time wishing I didn't, hating that I couldn't turn it off after you left, but you've stayed in my heart every day." Jaycen lifted his eyes, feeling hope rise once again, but her eyes still looked pained. "But I don't want to lie to you either. Marcos means a lot to me. I honestly don't know how this will end!" She sniffed back tears, but her face suddenly hardened. "And what does it matter anyway? Who cares what I feel? Or what you feel, or Marcos, or anyone? It doesn't change anything. We could all be dead before this is over. We probably will be!"

Jaycen lifted hand above her shoulder, wanting to comfort her, but paused, wrestling with his own feelings of jealousy. He kicked himself and touched her anyway, placing his hand gently at the back of her neck. She leaned into him, sending a mixture of hope and confusion pulsing through his heart. "It's okay, Marin. Take the time you need. I'll be here for you when you decide," he said, trying to sound more kind and confident than he felt.

Marin turned her face to him, smiling gratefully. Her tears made her eyes sparkle and for a moment all he wanted to do was kiss here, here and now. He cradled her face hesitantly with one hand, bringing her face closer to his, feeling his heart pounding beneath his shirt loud enough she could surely hear it, but she let him move nearer. He bent down, feeling her breath on his face, longing to touch his lips to hers.

The door to the bathroom opened, startling them. Frank looked at the two of them quizzically. Jaycen's face turned scarlet and he hastily backed away from Marin.

"I'd wondered where you two disappeared to! You were right behind me and suddenly you vanished. You coming?"

"Sorry, yes," Marin mumbled. Frank gave Jaycen a raised eyebrow but seemed to know better than to ask what was going on. Marin turned her face to the side, shooting Jaycen a guilty grin before snatching a tissue and following her father out the door. Jaycen trailed behind them to the cockpit, beaming.

CHAPTER 47

FRANK

THE SPEAKER CRACKLED to life as Frank flipped the radio on, clearing his throat. "U.S.S. Carl Vinson, this is Dr. Franklin Gilbert on board the Minnow. I need you to patch me through to General Holt in Washington D.C."

"Minnow, this is Chief Communications Officer Ben White of the U.S.S. Carl Vinson. Hold please and we will try to connect." They waited several anxious minutes before the response came in. "I'm sorry, Doctor Gilbert, General Holt is unavailable. President Thompson is on the line and wants an update. Please report your status."

"I'm sure you know Hahn's sub was destroyed. That missile you detonated hit pretty close to us. We've had some damage and injuries, including your two guys, but we are alive at least. Since Holt is unavailable, could you patch us through to…" Frank glanced at Jaycen, "Sergent Major Peter Bale," he finished.

Jaycen reeled back in surprise. "My stepdad? Why would you want to talk to *him*? I wouldn't trust him with anything! He's the one that put me in prison. Can't you talk to someone else?"

Frank clicked the microphone to mute. "Your *stepdad*? He told me he was a friend of the family!"

"Well, yeah, guess he's pretty friendly with my mom," Jaycen said sarcastically, "but not me!"

Frank considered for a moment. "Do you think he's in league with Leviathan? He's one of the only two people I know with access to decisions in the White House. I have a bad feeling about the President right now. I don't know if I have a choice but to turn to your stepdad."

Jaycen shrugged. "I really don't know, I'm sorry."

"Sergeant Major Peter Bale," Frank repeated into the microphone. "Can you please get him on the line once you report to the President?"

"Yes, sir, I will try," the man on the other end said.

A few moments later the line clicked. "Sergeant Major Bale on the line, Doctor," the communications officer said.

"Gilbert, what's going on?" Jaycen seemed to bristle at the sound of his stepfather's voice.

"The President ordered a strike and took out Hahn's sub," Frank snapped.

A heavy sigh came in from the other end of the line. "I'm just now hearing about that," Bale confirmed. "Was the rescue a success?" he asked, sounding like he already knew the answer would be no.

"The President gave his word he wouldn't launch until we tried to extract my daughter and Hahn. He lied," Frank said flatly.

"I know. I am truly sorry. It was not something either I or General Holt were in favor of. President Thompson made the call." Frank waited silently on the line, fuming.

"I want you to know I deeply regret the loss of your daughter, Dr. Gilbert. But know that her death means that millions of others may live."

"Perhaps you think your condolences would make up for the death of my only child," Frank spat acidly, "But that would never be the case, even if what you suppose is true. What your President did has made things infinitely worse, not to mention the fact that the guys he sent to 'help' us pulled a knife on me, forcing us to lock them up."

There was no response, so Frank continued. "At this point, I don't know if I can trust the President or anyone near him, but I don't have much of a choice. My daughter escaped from Hahn moments before the explosion." A huge sigh of relief came from the other end.

"I understand your feelings of distrust, Doctor. It is becoming increasingly difficult to recognize a friend from an enemy, but I swear, I am on your side. It may not mean much to you, but I am truly glad she escaped." He sounded sincere, but Frank grumbled anyway under his breath before he continued.

"Hahn was outside the sub looking for her and was not killed, either. My daughter has critical, time-sensitive information we need to act upon immediately. Hahn's sub had a failsafe locked into it in case something happened to him. When you people blew up Hahn's sub, it started a thirty six hour countdown to detonation of three submerged warheads near the coast of highly populated continents. If any of these three warheads are destroyed, the other two will automatically detonate. We have information that can stop this, but I need to talk to someone I can trust, and honestly I don't know who that could be other than General Holt and I can't get ahold of him."

The line was quiet for a moment. "Get to the surface. The Carl Vinson will pick you and your party up as soon as you can make the rendezvous point. I'll meet you in San Francisco in two hours. Tell no one what you've told me."

"Two hours? We're in the middle of the Pacific over two thousand miles from the U.S. mainland!"

Frank could hear the smile on the other line. "Doctor, I think we can get you there in plenty of time. Leave that part up to us."

Frank nodded to himself. "Okay, but bring General Holt or no deal."

"He'll be there. Over and out."

CHAPTER 48

MARIN

MARIN STOOD WITH her family and Jaycen on the open deck of the U.S.S. Carl Vinson breathing the sea air in gratefully. It felt like years since she'd been above the water, and it felt wonderful. She remembered Marcos saying one time that he missed being dry. Even though she had been inside this whole time, she understood what he meant. Just seeing the wide open sky was enough to bring tears to her eyes. She rubbed a hand up and down her arm subconsciously, as if trying to erase the memory of Hahn's knife now that she was free of him.

"This is taking too long!" Frank grumbled and Emily put her hand on his back lovingly. It was odd to go from having only her sweet adopted Uncle Paul in her life, to having Paul, plus a father, and now a mother. She was happy for Frank, and had gotten more used to the idea that he really was her father, but having Emily in the picture complicated things more. She'd known Frank for years, but this woman was basically a stranger whom she was expected to automatically love. She wanted to, but how could she love someone she didn't know? Plus it took part of Frank away from her, which made her feel oddly jealous. She shook her head. On top of sorting out her feelings for Marcos and Jaycen, her weird family dynamics were like the icing on the world's most confusing cake.

Paul moved closer and put an arm around her shoulders, giving her a quick squeeze, as if reading her mind. She threw him a grateful smile. He always knew exactly what to do to make her feel better. Sweet, steady Paul. Jaycen moved near, too, his arms crossed, his face brooding, his blonde hair tossed by the breeze. She wondered what Jaycen was thinking as he watched the helicopter hovering over the Minnow to pick up Marcos, the last crew member to come on board. As awkward as it was to have the two rivals for her love in such close proximity to each other, she was secretly glad they were both here. Everyone in the world she cared about was within her arms reach, safe and secure.

Despite her joy, Marin could feel every minute slide through the hourglass, ticking away the seconds until the detonation that would end the lives of millions of innocent people. It seemed like time was in high speed, but everything *they* were doing seemed to be moving in slow motion and she could do nothing to speed things up. Thankfully, the weather was milder than it had been in the morning, and the eight members of the crew had been moved to the floating warship fairly quickly. Two crewmen from the carrier were sent over to pilot the Minnow and escort Dawes and Riggs to be questioned back in California. Finally, the helicopter lifted with Marcos in tow, dangling above the ocean until they reeled him up through the open chopper door.

"Doctor?" a man in a flight suit addressed Frank.

"Yes?"

"I'm Commander Steven Davenport. I'll be in charge of your transportation to the mainland. If you would all follow me," he said, turning.

"Wait! We've got one more person coming," Marin called out, pointing to the helicopter bringing Marcos to the ship. "What about him?"

The commander stopped and looked at her. "Don't worry, we won't leave until he lands," he smiled reassuringly. Jaycen frowned.

"Oh, that makes sense," she said, sheepishly. The helicopter landed and Marcos jogged across the flight deck to them, smiling excitedly.

"First ride in a helicopter! That was incredible!" he said, punching Jaycen in the shoulder companionably. Jaycen smiled slightly.

The commander led the way to the flight deck where seven other men stood waiting.

"Wait, we're being taken in F-15's?" Jaycen asked incredulously.

"F-15 *Eagles*," the commander said with a smile. "We travel at about eighteen hundred miles an hour, getting you to Edwards Air Force Base in a little over an hour and a half."

"YES!" Jaycen crowed. He turned to a beaming Marcos and they gave each other a high five. Marin shook her head in disbelief.

"Boys are so weird," she muttered to herself. The commander escorted each of them to a fighter jet and helped them strap in before leading Frank to the last one and getting inside himself.

"Are you okay back there?" her pilot asked through the intercom in her helmet.

"I think so," she said.

"It's a pretty intense rush, flying in one of these. If you start to feel sick, grab the bag near your right," he said. "But do us both a favor and don't get sick. I'll keep it on an even keel, all you need to do is keep your head pressed against the headrest and you'll be fine."

"Ok," she said, feeling more nervous than before he started talking. The plane's engines roared to life, and they maneuvered onto the tarmac and lined up for takeoff. They were first in line. Her hands began to sweat as she clutched the sides of her seat.

"Here we go," the pilot said. Instantly, Marin was crushed back into her seat as the incredible speed of the launch grabbed hold of her. They rushed forward and dipped slightly as they hit the end of the short runway, then swung out over the open sea. The jet banked to the left and for a moment she could see the massive U.S.S. Carl Vinson shrinking in the distance, the Minnow off the port bow looking like a tiny speck in the water before the fighter was engulfed in clouds. The pilot switched something on the comm link letting her hear the other jets as they took off. Jaycen was unmistakable with his whoop of exhilaration as his fighter took to the sky. Marcos shouted in excitement as well. Marin chuckled to herself at their boyish delight. Frank shouted out a "Yee Haw!" as he joined their ranks, and her mother, Emily, laughed out loud in glee. Paul, the last in line, kept saying, "Oh no, oh no, oh no," louder and louder until he was almost screaming in the microphone, and then he yelled, "Oh my word, this is AMAZING!"

Suddenly they tore through the clouds to a stunning panorama of unbroken fields of clouds stretching as far as the eye could see, the afternoon sun almost blinding on the snow-white landscape.

"Wow," she breathed in appreciation.

"Yeah, it never gets old," the pilot responded. "No matter how dismal and dreary it is on the world beneath us, the sun is always shining above the clouds."

"That's incredibly profound," she said appreciatively.

"Well, you get a lot of time to think when you're flying."

***

The ride was exhilarating, but by the time they landed, Marin was more than ready to get out. Her legs felt like rubber as she climbed down the ladder to the ground. The moment the rest of their group landed, they were escorted into an armed military shuttle.

Frank was seated next to Emily and Marin squeezed in beside them and next to Paul. Marcos and Jaycen sat facing them. Frank held his wife's hand, looking happier than Marin had seen him before, despite the tense situation.

She tried to slow her mind, to stop thinking, but as much as she wanted to close her eyes and sleep, her nerves were so worked up it was almost impossible. She opened her eyes slightly. Jaycen's head was leaning back against the headrest, his long lashes closed, his sandy hair tousled, so handsome in his California-boy style that it made her heart pound in her chest to think that he actually loved her. He was thinner and tanner than she had seen him last, making him look older and more mature, and so much more handsome in person than in her memory. The memory of the almost-kiss in the bathroom made her pulse flutter and she wondered what it would have been like if Frank hadn't come in and interrupted them. She let out a slow breath, remembering their last kiss, knowing he had to say goodbye, possibly forever. It had broken her heart, and she knew it had broken his, too, but there was no way to avoid it. Part of her loved him all the more because of his devotion to his family and his sense of duty. And after all the heartache, he still hadn't been able to find and help his mom. Maybe things would have been different if he hadn't left.

But he *had* left. She had tried to put him out of her mind, resigning herself to the fact that he would never find them again, never return to her...even if he wanted to. And Marcos was there, doing his best to make her want to forget. It was easier that way. Jaycen was gone with no hope of returning, leaving her free to explore her feelings for Marcos. And she had, learning to communicate with him on levels she didn't know were possible. Learning to rely on him, to trust him...and... to love him.

Now suddenly, Jaycen was back, alive and well, inches away from her, and making her heart ache with confusion. She glanced at Marcos, awake and looking down at his hands, as if deep in thought. Guiltily, she wondered what happened to Marcos during his captivity and how he managed to escape. She hadn't thought to ask him until now. When he felt her gaze upon him, his eyes snapped up and met hers, sending a jolt of emotion through her. She could see how much he yearned to talk with her, but with everyone around, it was impossible. The shuttle jostled and he used the opportunity to stretch his leg out next to hers letting it lean against it, looking at her expectantly. It was an invitation. Her ability to connect to people's thoughts through touch was getting better and she reached out. She felt him almost instantly. Marcos grinned with delight.

"Hey," she thought, her mouth curving up in a small smile.

"Hey, back. I've missed you! Are you okay?" he asked anxiously. His concern and love for her warmed her heart. Connecting with him on this level felt like a warm breeze on a cold day. Oh, how she'd longed for this comfort and closeness during her time in captivity. She could feel he felt the same way.

"I'm all right. Are you?"

"I am now," he said earnestly.

She concentrated on sending direct words to him. She wished she could just give him access to her thoughts and feelings like she did underwater, but she didn't want her feelings about Jaycen to come through and hurt him. Plus, she didn't know how much of her time with Hahn she wanted to share. It was too horrible for *her* to remember, let alone make *him* live even a small part of it through her memories. She bit the inside of her cheek, wrestling with indecision. She felt a nudge from him, an acceptance almost.

249

"It's okay if you want to talk about it. Or not. I just want to be here for you," he said.

"I do, but it's awful. Too awful."

"I don't care. If it will help you to share with me, I am willing."

She took a deep breath, drawing back some of the barriers, letting the memory of what she had gone through since her capture pour out faster than words. She could feel Marcos's heart begin to pound as his rage at what Hahn had done to her became so intense, she almost broke the connection, but she held on accepting his feelings as he accepted hers.

"If I ever get my hands on Hahn, he is a dead man," Marcos thought, his words laced with fury.

"Get in line," Marin added. When she got to the part where they found her, they both relived the joyous reunion and relief that the nightmare was over, but she put up barriers to her thoughts about Jaycen, hoping Marcos wouldn't notice. Marcos sent her waves of empathy and comfort, a healing balm to the horrors etched in her mind.

"Your turn. What happened to you after Isla Cedros?" she asked. He let her rummage through his memories, living with him in his imprisonment at Leviathan, the loneliness, the uncertainty. She saw Zar and his casual disregard for his life; felt her own indignation at the pain and humiliation Greg and Dr. Curtis had inflicted on Marcos. She re-lived his elation at being rescued, his anger at Jaycen, worry as Jaycen was wounded and they escaped through the pipes. Then came the desperate attempt to rescue her, and the absolute devastation he felt, watching the sub he thought she was on destroyed by a missile strike. She was surprised and touched that both he and Jaycen had worked together to try to save her.

They hit a speed bump a little too fast and Jaycen woke up, snapping his head up and looking around, disoriented for a moment. His gaze landed on Marin and he gave her an encouraging smile. Then he noticed her leg leaning against Marcos's and his face fell into such a hurt look that Marin drew her leg back beneath her. Marcos's expression soured and Marin sighed in frustration. Her feelings were too complicated to deal with right now. The buildings still looked a few minutes away, so she closed her eyes and tried to relax her exhausted and over-stressed mind and body.

The second she fell asleep, she was instantly assaulted by nightmares that broke through her defenses, taking her breath away. She was tied up and Hahn was coming for her, moving closer and closer as she struggled to free herself. He smiled at her with his perfect teeth and his perfectly manicured hair, but his eyes were dark swirls of smoke.

"You can't run, my dear. I am coming for you." He moved closer, reaching out a clawed hand to her face. She jerked back, screaming.

"Marin!" Paul said, shaking her awake. The vision of Hahn was replaced by concerned faces turned toward her. Even Jaycen and Marcos were leaning in, trying to comfort her.

"What? Are we there?" she stammered, confused. She looked out the window and saw they were pulling up to a large grey building with darkly tinted windows.

"You were having a nightmare," Jaycen said, touching her hand across the aisle.

"And sharing it with the rest of us," Paul added in amazement. "We could see every detail." Nods of agreement met her from everyone. Jaycen's eyes were wide with shock as he stared at her.

"Oh, no!" she said, covering her face with her hands, her cheeks aflame with embarrassment.

Emily stroked her hair comfortingly. "It's okay, Marin. You couldn't help it. You've been through a lot, it's completely understandable."

"It's not okay!" she shot back. "Would any of you like your dreams broadcast to everyone?" They all looked uncomfortably back at her. She looked down at her trembling hands, her eyes filling with frustrated tears. "There are things, abilities I've been discovering. They seem to be getting more powerful. I don't know what to do! And this? This has never happened before!" She turned and looked at her mother. "What is happening to me?" she whispered. Nobody had an answer for her.

As the shuttle came to a stop, the driver got out and opened the doors for them. Two men in uniform and several armed guards flanked the sidewalk and crowded in behind them as they made their way into the building.

CHAPTER 49

PRESIDENT THOMPSON

THE PRESIDENT READ the executive order for the third time. It was so hard to keep the facts straight. He rubbed his tired eyes, trying to get the fog to lift from his brain so that he could understand what his Chief of Staff was having him sign. She stood at his shoulder, clicking her tongue impatiently—a habit he had always detested. All it did was add to his distraction.

"This is a simple page, John!" she grumbled. "I've already explained it to you! Can you please just sign it?"

The President scowled at her and started reading from the beginning again. The cup of coffee she'd brought him sat untouched on his desk. She'd pushed so much coffee down him lately he didn't think he'd be able to sleep for a month.

"Your coffee is getting cold," she said in an irritatingly motherly voice.

"I'm sick of coffee, Judy. I'm swearing it off for good. I don't like the way it makes me feel."

Her face contorted in a mixture of fear and anger, which surprised him, but she quickly replaced it with a kindly smile. She leaned closer to him, her voice dripping with honey. "Just have a little bit. I went through all that trouble to get it for you. I made it just the way you like it!"

Some part of his brain longed to obey her every word. He even reached out his hand and touched the handle, and her expression changed to delight. That was good, he needed to make her happy. He picked it up, but the door swung open unexpectedly and an aide rushed in. The President jumped, startled, and the cup slipped from his fingers, falling to the edge of his desk and shattering. Judy quickly snatched the page from his desk and put it in a folder in her briefcase before the aide could get closer, then produced a wad of tissues to clean up the mess.

"Mr. President!" the aide stammered, clearly out of breath and rattled himself.

"Yes?" he asked, concerned. He rubbed his eyes, wishing the fog of his mind would clear.

"It's Dr. Boscolo. He's dead!"

The President took in a sharp breath and stood up, leaning across the desk, a jolt of emotion and shock clearing the fog in his brain almost instantly. "Dead? How? When?"

"In his cell this morning! He gave the secret service a full confession but wouldn't reveal his affiliations. When they left the room, he sliced his throat with a shard of a coffee mug."

The President shook his head in disbelief staring at the coffee dripping from his desk, shards of mug littering the floor. Judy kept puttering around him, picking up pieces of his cup, mopping up that blasted coffee from his shoes and making that annoying sound with her tongue. And looking strangely unfazed by the news. He bent down and picked up a sharp fragment of his cup, turning it absently in his fingers, searching to hear the voice screaming silently in the back of his head. It was important, he knew it, but he just couldn't reach it. The aide kept talking but he couldn't keep his attention on what he was saying. Judy was sopping, clicking, cleaning, and driving him crazy. He felt his temper rise and though he tried his best to control it, every second she was down there fussing about nothing when someone they had both worked with had just died; it got harder and harder for him. Then she lifted up the hem of his slacks to clean his sock and something broke inside him and he lost it.

"Judy! OUT! Get out of here! I've had enough of you and your constant...everything! I don't want to see you for at least a week." The anger poured out of him, fueling him. He felt strong and powerful for the first time in months. Maybe he couldn't control everything going on around him in the country. Maybe he couldn't control the horrible things that happen to people or save them from the choices they made. And maybe he *was* a terrible President, just waiting out the last months of his time in office like the lame duck he was, but there were things he *could* control, and by heaven, it felt good to do it for once.

She stood up, her hair disheveled, her mouth open like a fish, her hands clutching the damp brown tissues and shaking like she was about to fall apart. How did he not see how abhorrent she was, not just in her appearance, but her demeanor, her attitude, her very soul? How had he put up with her for so long?

"John, you can't mean that. We have so much work to do!"

He took a step back from her. "I want you to understand something, Judy. *I* have work to do. *You* do not. I'm not kidding; I want you out of here, out of my sight, out of my office and out of my White House. I don't want to see your face until I ask for it. Do you understand?"

The aide looked at the President, nodding his agreement with everything he said. Apparently the staff wasn't crazy about Judy, either. Judy glanced between the aide and the President, angry and frightened.

"You can't mean that, John. You're just upset about Sergio. I understand, I am, too. Let me just get you a cup of coffee and you'll be fine."

"ENOUGH WITH YOUR INFERNAL COFFEE!" he shouted, not caring who heard. Several men in black suits came in through the open door, hands on their weapons.

"Sir," the aide said quietly. "She brought a cup of coffee to Dr. Boscolo shortly before his death."

The President stared at him, letting the ramifications of his words fall into place. Judy's shaking became worse and her face went white. The President sank back into his chair as if all his bones were gone. The warnings of Frank Gilbert began to push through his memory, echoing in his mind.

"Judy," he whispered, looking in her eyes. Everything he needed to know was there. She didn't look surprised; she looked guilty. "What have you done?"

What have I done? He asked himself, mortified that these criminals, these terrorists had controlled him all this time. His mind quailed at what these people might have gotten him to do in the past months while he was in some sort of drugged stupor. Every decision he'd made, every conversation he'd had was suspect now, would need to be analyzed and repaired. The sheer enormity of it all threatened to crush him. He turned the piece of his cup around in his cold fingers. Sergio.

He felt the eyes of everyone in the room pressing down on him, waiting for him to act. All he wanted was to curl into a ball and scream until the walls fell down around him. But that was not an option. He would do what he had to, despite the consequences. He would work the problem until a resolution was found. He would right the wrongs with whatever time he had left. And he would tell the world what had been done to him. He set his mouth in a determined line and rose to his feet, pointing a finger at Judy.

"Arrest this woman and interrogate her! Find out who else she is working with using whatever means are at your disposal. Search her room and find out what she's been drugging everyone with and I want you to get me a list of everyone she has spent more than five minutes with in the last two months, especially anyone who's been given anything to eat or drink by her. Be aware, there might be more of them among us. I want a full guard on her twenty-four hours a day, and no one, I mean *no one* is allowed to see her unless you get direct verbal approval from me. Is that clear? This is treason at the highest level." He snapped his gaze to her.

Judy fell against the desk, melting into a crying mess. The men marched forward to grab her, but her hand curled around a monogrammed letter. She jerked away from their outstretched hands and positioned herself behind the President, wrapping one arm around his chest, and holding the letter opener against his throat. The men stepped back, drawing their guns in unison.

"Tell them to stand down," she hissed in his ear.

John Thompson shook his head sadly. "Judy, these guys are not going to let you out of here," he said meeting the eyes of the closest man meaningfully.

The man gave an imperceptible nod.

"They have to if they want you to live," she retorted, pulling him backwards and trying to angle him between herself and the Secret Service men.

"I'd be more concerned about yourself at this point, Judy," he said. Looking at the closest agent he added, "I don't want her dead. I need to know who she's working with." Again the man nodded.

"Drop your weapons or I put this through his artery!" she demanded, backing toward the door. He felt the tip of the metal piercing the skin of his neck and his heart skipped a beat.

The President nodded, keeping eye contact with the man in front, hoping the man knew what he was doing. Everyone slowly lowered their weapons. When the barrel of the nearest agent's gun was pointing down, he pulled the trigger, shooting Judy in the thigh. She jerked back with the impact, clutching the President for support, screaming out in pain. All the security agents swarmed them, prying her hands off his neck, but she drew her arm back and thrust the letter opener into the President's back with all her might before she crumpled to the ground under the weight of the men. The President stumbled forward into the arms of an agent, confused at the pain shooting through his body.

"She…she stabbed me!" he wheezed out incredulously. Blood pounded in his ears as his heart tried to compensate for the sudden injury. His breath came in short bursts; it hurt too badly to take in a full breath. He slowly sank to his knees. Voices shouted orders all around him, people rushed in from everywhere. Judy was screaming like a madwoman, dragged out through the doorway by half a dozen armed men. People turned him face down and lifted him, carrying him fireman style out of the room as his heart struggled to keep beating. A puddle of thick red blood spread out below him on the beautiful white carpet of the oval office, and he frowned at the stain, saying a silent prayer that he would live long enough to right the wrongs forced upon him.

CHAPTER 50

MARIN

GENERAL HOLT, HAVE you even slept since I saw you last?" Frank asked. Marin noticed dark circles around the older gentleman's eyes.

"Have *you?*"

Frank shook his head. "No, not really,"

"Yeah, neither have I," the man chuckled grimly and held open the door to a dimly lit conference room, greeting everyone by name as they came in and found a seat at the already crowded table.

"This must be your brave daughter and lovely wife," he said as she walked in, followed by her mother. They paused and he took each by the hand.

Frank beamed. "Yes, sir, this is…" his voice grew husky. "I'm sorry, you just don't know how long I've gone thinking I'd never have a chance to say these words. This is my family." Marin was suddenly hit with a wave of tender fondness for both of her parents as she and Emily put arms around Frank encouragingly. He squeezed them close to him, his face radiating joy. "This is my *family*."

The General clapped Frank on the shoulder and gave it an encouraging squeeze. "I'm so happy to meet you all, and I'm glad you were able to get to her in time. I can't tell you how distressed we were when the order came for the missile strike."

Frank's face clouded over. "Where, exactly, did that order come from?" he demanded.

The General pursed his lips and gestured for them to take their seats. "I'll address that in a moment," he said stiffly.

Most of the people in the conference room were strangers to her, but Frank inclined his head toward a few of them, so she assumed he probably knew them from his last meeting in Washington D.C. She took a seat across from Jaycen and flashed him a smile, which he returned, but then he stiffened as his eyes fell on a heavily decorated man near the head of the table. He nodded awkwardly toward Jaycen. Marin wondered who the man might be, then realized that this might be Jaycen's stepdad Frank had been talking to.

Jaycen dropped his eyes to the table, but the man watched him carefully, as if evaluating him. *Odd*, she thought to herself. Something about him reminded her of Jaycen, like the way he held his pen on his second finger to write, and how his hair swung up on the left front side. She shrugged and turned her attention to the General, sitting down now at the end of the table. He cleared his throat and the room grew still.

"Normally, we would begin these proceedings with introductions, but quite honestly, we don't have time. Suffice it to say that my team is staffed with people I know I can trust, and the rest of these people are my guests from the Arydian Nation." Marin was surprised to hear their people recognized as a separate nation. "They have information critical to stopping the terrorist threat that is putting the world in peril." He looked down at his hands and Marin was surprised to see they were shaking slightly. Frank's eyebrows constricted in concern.

"What I share with you now is beyond classified, and I need to have your utmost assurance that the information revealed here will not leave this room." He glanced at his team quickly, as if they knew the drill, but his eyes lingered on each Arydian, as if to bore into them the importance of secrecy. Holt paused, waiting, until every Arydian gave a verbal commitment before he continued. "President Thompson has been under the influence of hostile forces for over a month, maybe longer." He paused as a buzz of shock circulated the room. "We are certain there are more operatives involved in this and are working to get to the bottom of it, however, in the meantime," he said, looking around the group meaningfully, "we are on our own for the time being. Once the coup was discovered, the traitor attacked the President, gravely wounding him. He was rushed to the hospital and is in critical condition as we speak."

Several people around the table gasped and Frank raised his hand to his forehead. "This is a tough blow indeed. General, this couldn't come at a worse time," he said heavily.

"I'm aware of that. If we ever need the leadership of our President, now is the time. I fear this will cast a cloud over everything he's done and destroy all his credibility in the future, assuming he's even able to recover. Between the attacks on California and Lanai, and now this....it is truly the darkest hour our country may have ever faced." The man's eyes looked hopeless, and Marin felt a pang of sympathy for him.

"However, it is about to get much worse if we don't move quickly. This young woman, Marin Donnegan, was recently held captive by the man responsible for this and thankfully escaped with information that could help us avert a calamity the likes of which the world has never known. Miss Donnegan, could you please tell us your story."

Marin's heart began to pound in her throat and her mouth went instantly dry as these powerful men and women turned their gazes to her.

"Um. Yes. Hahn kidnapped me from the island of Lanai the day of the attack. I saw the attack happen." Whispers circled the room and one woman with extremely short hair interjected.

"Why would he want to kidnap you, specifically?"

Marin paused and looked over at Frank, who nodded to her reassuringly.

"Well, he has the ability to breathe underwater, like we...our people... do, but his version was less effective. I'm not sure what the problem with his was, but people couldn't live on land again without a certain serum, which Hahn had to take daily and was very painful. He wanted me because he thought if he had some of my blood, it would help him." She swallowed hard, uncertain how to handle this. There was no way she wanted to tell these people she had the ability to heal others. Her father must have felt her hesitation and he shook his head no almost imperceptibly. Good, he didn't want people to know either.

259

"He thought having some blood from an Arydian would help him be able to stay out of water longer," she finished. The woman nodded.

"And did it work?" she asked.

Marin shrugged, hoping the lie wasn't all over her face. "I didn't really see. He just kept taking my blood and running experiments on me." Marin shuddered at the memory. "Please, this isn't an important part of the story, and I really don't want to relive it in front of you all."

The General straightened in his chair. "Of course, please go ahead."

"Okay, the important part was that he got comfortable enough talking to me that he explained his plan. He used the monsters he's created to plant warheads off the coasts of three major land masses. One is in the English Channel, one is in the Arabian Sea, and the last is in the Hudson Channel near New York." The room was silent in shock. She took a sip of water from a bottle in front of her and went on nervously. "He told me there was a failsafe built into the submarine that would cause a thirty-six-hour count-down to detonation if something happened to himself or his ship. And he has the warheads tied together in some way so if one is destroyed, the others immediately deploy." The room erupted into exclamations of alarm.

"We are six and a half hours into that countdown," Frank interrupted loudly, quieting the room.

"Plus, Hahn was not in the sub when it went down," Marin said quietly. "I saw him outside after it blew up."

"What is in these warheads?" Jaycen's step dad asked. "The same stuff he used in Lanai?"

"Yes," she said.

"Do you know what it does?" he pressed.

She glanced around and Frank stepped in. "It is likely in the form of a hyper-compressed gas. The goal is to launch the warheads into the air and the jet stream spread it across highly populated areas. It changes the lungs to breathe water, but they can't breathe regular air, rather like a fish. They suffocate surrounded by air they can't breathe. The effects last about three hours, so it works quickly, but dies out quickly." explained Frank.

"So, we just tell everyone to put their heads in the bath for three hours?" a man at the end of the table said incredulously. "This is insanity!"

"No, that's not a good option, we all have to agree," the General said. "Especially if we take into account how many people would actually *get* those instructions and reduce that by how many would actually *believe* them, not to mention people who couldn't follow them, like the elderly or small children or those hospitalized or injured. The human losses would still be catastrophic."

"So we need to conduct a coordinated attack. Drop a bomb on them all at the same time," the short-haired woman declared as if it was an open and shut case.

Jaycen's stepdad shook his head. "I'm afraid it's not that easy. We only have a vague idea of the whereabouts of these things. If we just start dropping bombs on the ocean floor, we run the risk of destroying one and triggering the detonation of the rest."

The woman scowled at him. "Then we scan the areas with radar and sonar and once we find them, we target them and take them out with a missile strike."

"Let me explain how this works, Vanessa. Our missile systems are designed to take out other submarines at a maximum depth of two thousand feet and to launch waterborne missiles into the air, not the other way around. I'm certain Hahn knows this and that is why these warheads of his were planted at a depth well below anything we've had to deal with before, meaning we have no idea what kind of accuracy or effectiveness our missiles might have, or if they would function at all at that depth." General Holt growled. "Our hands are tied and he knows it."

"Then we shoot them out of the air as soon as they launch!" another man interjected, leaning forward passionately. He had a heavy moustache and a chest so full of ribbons and medals that Marin was surprised he could sit up straight.

"Which would release the gas, exactly like Hahn wants," Frank said in exasperation. The man sat back in his chair.

"Then what are we supposed to do?" Jaycen asked in frustration.

Marin paused before continuing. "The warheads have to be found, and then we need to enter a password. Hahn said it was the only way to disarm them."

"And how are we supposed to know this password?" Vanessa demanded. "I don't suppose Hahn gave it to you?" She snorted derisively.

"I *do* have the password," Marin said quietly.

"Pray, tell. Why would he have given it to you, a prisoner?" Vanessa asked suspiciously.

Marin looked to Frank for help, but he just shrugged. "I escaped and… wounded him. He thought I was going to kill him, so he told me the password." That was true. Mostly. She wished this grumpy woman would get on board and quit fighting her on every point.

"So, we are to assume that he told you the truth, and that he didn't immediately change the password, or is changing it as we speak."

"He was badly wounded. Almost delirious. I can only hope he doesn't know or remember what he told me."

"The safety of the world, millions of lives, depends on the instructions of a delirious enemy?" Vanessa exclaimed, her voice rising in pitch. "You have *got* to be kidding!"

"I agree with Vanessa, this whole scenario is ludicrous. If I didn't know this was a secure room, I would be waiting for the hidden cameras to appear!" The man with the medals said, throwing up his hands in disbelief.

"Jim, I assure you, this is anything but a joke. And this is the only intel we have to go off of. I know it's hard to believe, but we are truly in uncharted waters here, not just metaphorically. And I swear to you all, the threat is real and the clock is ticking."

"I don't know what you want us to do, then. It sounds like Hahn has got us over a barrel. If we can't get to the warheads, and we can't shoot them down, the last option is to surrender or mitigate the damage after the attack," Jim summarized.

The General leaned back in his chair and rubbed his chin thoughtfully. "What are your thoughts, Dr. Gilbert?" he asked. The look he gave Frank made Marin uneasy, as if they had already discussed this. She had a bad feeling about where this conversation was headed.

Frank crossed his arms and let out a long, deep breath, looking almost guiltily at the exhausted faces of his friends and family. Marin couldn't tell if he had an idea, or if he felt just as helpless as the rest of them did.

"You are all correct. There is not much *you* can do to stop this, but *we* can. I think we, the Arydians, need to divide into three teams and go after the warheads as soon as possible."

"Dad!" Marin choked out. The last thing she wanted after finally getting reunited was to split up again. "We've done our part! We got the information to them! It's *their* job now. They are the ones with all the ships and armies and…" He heart shook with fear of losing everyone, or anyone.

"Sweetheart, I know it's not fair. But we have to do everything we can to help stop this. Everything," Frank said softly. He put a reassuring hand over hers and squeezed gently, but it didn't do much to calm her pounding heart. She looked up accusingly at the General and noticed he looked relieved, not surprised.

"I don't know how much help we can give you," the General said, confirming her suspicion that he'd already sketched this out in his mind. "There is a lot of tension across the world right now. We can certainly give you full support for the Hudson, but there's no way we can get any serious coverage in the Arabian Sea. We have a couple of units in the area, but nothing near enough to get there in time. And it's iffy on the Celtic as well, though we hope to have more success with the governments of Great Britain and France."

Frank pulled a crumpled bit of paper out of his pocket and smoothed it out on the table. "Look, I've gone over this a million times in the past few hours. I would love for us to all be able to work together, but there is just no physical way to get this done otherwise. So this is what I've come up with: Malcolm and Paul will take the one in the Arabian Sea, Emily and I will take the one in the Celtic, and Marin, Marcos and Jaycen can take the one closest to home in the Hudson."

"You're leaving us here?" Jaycen scoffed.

"Jaycen, what choice do we have? I want you three closest to home in friendly waters, where you can have the best chance for success and protection. And I'll bet everyone at this table feel the same," he said. Malcolm, Paul, and Emily all nodded in agreement. Jaycen and Marcos fumed but remained silent.

Jaycen's stepdad uncapped his pen, ready to write. "Tell us what you need."

"We want seriously detailed maps of the areas mentioned, and immediate transportation. Plus any support you can get the other governments to lend would be helpful. If you can get access to subs to take us down and provide cover for us, we would appreciate it. Also, we'll need some sort of skimmers to travel quickly once we locate them."

"Skimmers?" the General asked.

"Diver propulsion vehicles. DPVs. We call them skimmers. I know they may not work at that depth, but every second counts, so we'll use them as long as they last. We need a way to communicate with each other. We'll also want sonars and anything else you can send our way."

Bale was writing notes furiously but looked up to ask a question. "I don't suppose any of you have passports or identification?"

"I do," Paul, Frank, Marin and Jaycen said.

"My passport expired long ago," Malcolm said, speaking up for the first time. "And everything I once had was destroyed by Hahn and Leviathan. Surely you can work around such things," he said, his deep bass voice carrying around the room.

"It might be hard to get you into foreign waters without a passport," Bale frowned. "It would be much easier if you were under the umbrella of the United States."

"As citizens of the Arydian Nation, we should be immune to such ridiculousness, aside from the fact that we don't have time for it!" Emily said imperiously, using her English accent to add to the effect. Marin watched her mother, impressed. She hoped she would get the chance to get to know this woman better. She seemed extremely smart, very tough and increasingly cool.

The general tapped a finger to the table for a few seconds, thinking. "That may be true, but for the purposes at hand, would you all please submit to having a photograph taken so we can issue emergency passports and visas to you? It would actually help us speed up the process and save us time we do not want to waste."

Emily and Frank exchanged wordless glances and then agreed.

"Wait a minute," Vanessa interrupted. "The girl hasn't told anyone the password! If something happens to her, we are all dead."

The General inclined his head towards Frank. "Gilbert?"

Frank slid the paper over to Marin and Jaycen's stepdad rolled her a pen. She wrote the words down and handed the paper to Frank.

"We will share this with those disarming the warheads, no others. It wouldn't do them any good, anyway," he said, before Vanessa could object.

General Holt rubbed his hands together. "Okay let's get the ball rolling. Dr. Gilbert, if we are able to pull this off and stop this attack, the world will be in your debt."

"Thank you. I'm sure we'll all appreciate that when the time comes," Frank said.

"Good, let's get to work!"

CHAPTER 51

JAYCEN

JAYCEN SAT IN a 1970's style reception area complete with wood paneled walls and burnt orange and mustard yellow vinyl chairs, anxiously waiting for the rest of the group to arrive. He knew he should be wiped out, but he was so full of adrenaline that he didn't really feel tired. The arrangements had all been made, and now they were just waiting for the passports and their transportation to arrive, but since he already had a passport, and all they had to do was reprint it from files, he was the first one done. He assumed Frank and Malcolm were still talking with all the government dudes, so he got sent ahead to the waiting area. He took a seat on one of the outdated chairs and rested his elbows on his knees.

The door opened and Pete, his stepfather, walked in purposefully and sat down next to him. Pete clasped and unclasped his hands together uncomfortably as if he wanted to say something, but couldn't figure out how to get around to it. Jaycen tightened his lips, bracing himself for whatever it was Pete wanted. Basically, nothing Pete could say would matter to him, unless he knew where to find his mom. But up until now, Pete seemed more clueless than Jaycen about her whereabouts. At least Jaycen had gone to his mother's house trying to find her. All Pete did was lie about everything. Jaycen simmered in anger and frustration as he watched Pete sit there fidgeting.

He was surprised to notice Pete wore a weathered wedding band on his ring finger. He tried to remember if he'd had it on before, when he was locked up in Pete's army base, but he hadn't really paid attention.

Jaycen couldn't stand the silence much longer. He sucked in a breath, not daring to look Pete in the face.

"Pete, tell me the truth. Do you have any idea where my mom is?"

Pete let out a slow, unsteady breath. Jaycen watched him through the corner of his eye. Pete was leaning forward on his elbows, in much the same pose as Jaycen, his head hanging down.

"Yes. I know where she is."

Jaycen's heart surged with hope and he lifted his head. "You do? Where is she?" Pete's posture didn't change, and the hope Jaycen felt sank to the bottom of his stomach and dissolved into despair.

"She…" Pete cleared his throat, his lips twitching to the side. "She didn't make it, son. I'm sorry."

Jaycen felt like he'd been doused in ice water. His hands started shaking and his voice almost failed him, but he had to ask the horrible questions. "How? Why?"

Pete rubbed his face and let out a long sigh. "She was having one of her good days," he said. "I was called in to work. I didn't want to leave her, but she said she was going to spend the day working in that blasted garden in the back that she loved so much," he said angrily. "That blasted garden," he repeated, pausing for a moment, lost in faraway thoughts, then he shook his head and resumed. "Then the earthquake…"

Jaycen's heart stopped when he remembered the backyard of his mother's small home. The neighbor's brick chimney had fallen down, breaking down the fence and burying the backyard in rubble.

"No!" he whispered. He couldn't bear the thought of what Pete was implying. How could his mom be gone? She was his rock, his biggest cheerleader. His eyes stung. He'd never gotten the chance to introduce her to Marin. And all he'd gone through trying to find her, all he'd sacrificed leaving Marin to be with Marcos…it was all for nothing! The vision of that pile of rubble in his backyard burned like lava into him. He scrubbed his eyes with the heels of his hands, trying to erase that memory from his brain. She'd been there the whole time. How long had it taken? Did she lie there, crushed and bleeding and alone, until her body finally gave out? *Oh, please, no!* his heart cried. It had to have been quick. It had to have been. He couldn't bear to think about it otherwise.

"No!" He glared at Pete, feeling his hurt morph into anger, fueling accusations. "How would you even know? I know you lied to me about going to the house. Her house. The door was locked…you never kicked in the door!" He felt like he was babbling, but he didn't care.

Pete met his accusation with a defiant stare. "I did go, but not inside. As soon as the earthquake hit, I raced home. It took too long, getting through the rubble and the broken streets. Mrs. Moyer, from the house behind, saw the whole thing and told me what happened. I got there as fast as I could, but she was long gone before I ever made it back home. We didn't have the equipment or the manpower…and we were needed elsewhere. We just had to leave her there…like that." Pete looked close to tears and Jaycen suddenly erupted. Who was this guy pretending to care about his mother? It made his insides boil and he fed that feeling, needing the anger to quell the agony ripping apart his soul.

"What kind of game were you playing with her, Pete?" he spat. "You just messed with her heart so you could get to me? So you could spy on Gilbert and COAST? There were a million ways to do that without getting her involved. Why did you bring my mother into this?" The fury felt good, it gave his soul something to hang onto, something with purpose.

"I wasn't playing a game, Jaycen!" Pete shot back. "From where I stood, your Arydian friends destroyed California and killed thousands of people, including the woman I've loved my whole life. And you weren't even sorry! When I learned you were one of them, I went crazy! Everything that came out of your mouth was a lie, and I was so blinded by anger and grief, I wanted to tear your heart out."

"Don't pretend you cared about my mom. You make me sick," Jaycen snarled. "You're so broken up about my mom that you won't even tell her son that she's dead! All for what, Pete? I don't get it! Why did you ever come into our lives?"

Pete looked like he was going to shout something back, but instead, he dropped his shoulders, looking defeated.

"Jaycen, I'm sorry, truly sorry for the things I've said and the things I've done. I've made some terrible mistakes in my life, but I wanted to change that. Cheryl gave me that chance, even though I didn't deserve it." He hung his head again, looking completely unlike himself. The hard-core military sheen was gone, and a broken man was left in its place. Jaycen knit his brows together, confused.

"Come off it, Pete. You were seeing my mom for a couple of months, tops. You were married for what, a couple weeks?" he scoffed.

Pete sat back, stunned. "What are you talking about, Jaycen? Cheryl and I got married right out of high school! We were married for six years before..." his face contorted with regret, "I...made a mistake. I lost my way. I broke her heart and destroyed our marriage months before you were born. She never wanted anything to do with me again, not even a dime to help either of you. She hated me for what I'd done to her. When you were born, she didn't even put me down on the birth certificate. She went back to her maiden name and passed it on to you. And I didn't blame her."

Jaycen's eyes narrowed skeptically. What Pete said was impossible. There was no way it was true. He didn't respond, so Pete kept on talking. "I've kept an eye on you, son, watched you grow, hoping you would reach out to me. And then, out of the blue, she called me. She told me about her diagnosis, not because she wanted my pity or money, but because she was afraid she didn't have much time left and she didn't want you to be alone." He looked up at Jaycen, the expression in his eyes unreadable. "We've been talking to each other for over a year, but it was just recently she gave me the only thing I've ever wanted. A second chance." He cleared his throat again, his voice rough. "She didn't give you my name, but I thought she would have at least told you who I was."

Jaycen sat back in his seat, squeaking against the vinyl, shaking his head. "No. There's no way. You're making this up."

Pete took Jaycen's hand and pulled it over next to his. "Look at our hands, Jaycen. We have the same hands. Your pinky finger is double jointed just like mine. And the way your hair curls around on the left side of your forehead? That's been in my family for generations. That's why I always keep my hair cut short." He flashed a wistful smile at his son.

"You. My dad." Jaycen said flatly. "I…can't. I don't believe it. I don't even want to believe it." Jaycen shook his head. "I don't know what to do with this, Pete," he said quietly. "I don't know what to believe." Everything he had ever known was being tossed like a hurricane inside him. His mom was gone. Buried under a ton of bricks. He forced that part out of his brain before it drove him crazy. He would have to figure out how to deal with that later. He took a deep, shuddering breath and sucked in the inside of his cheeks, refusing to cry in front of this *maybe* father of his. There would be time to mourn later.

Pete opened his wallet and pulled out a worn photograph, yellowed with age, and handed it to Jaycen. Two people smiling like idiots standing in front of that same cheesy 'Chapel o' Love' where Pete and his Mother had gotten married…no, *re*-married not long ago. He recognized the younger version of his mother immediately, and the man next to her did resemble a thinner, less severe version of Pete. He was wearing his military uniform, with a lot less decorations and medals on it, and she was wearing a light blue and white dress with her hair down, loose over one shoulder. Jaycen ran a finger over his mother's face. It had been years since she cut her hair short. He'd almost forgotten what she looked like before. Pete put a heavy hand on Jaycen's knee.

"You hang on to that, son, for as long as you need," Pete whispered. Jaycen nodded mutely. "I'll leave you alone if you want. I understand. But I'll be here if ever you want to know more. And I'm sorry, son. For everything. Maybe when this is all over we can…" Pete stopped talking as if he ran out of words. His mouth worked to figure out what to say, and finally he whispered gruffly, "…we can give your mom a proper burial." Pete shook his head, got to his feet and walked heavily out the door.

Jaycen watched him go, holding his breath until the door closed behind him, then letting it out in one long gush. A few moments later, Malcolm entered the room.

"They are ready for us outside. I was sent to get you," he said. Jaycen nodded and followed him out of the room.

CHAPTER 52

MARCOS

SEVERAL HOURS AND a ride in a posh military Gulfstream 550 later, everyone touched down at Stewart International Airport in New York. As the plane taxied into a hangar, Marcos his legs and yawned. This was the first bit of sleep he'd had for days, on the luxury airliner usually reserved for the highest-ranking government officials in America. The seats were comfortable, reclined almost completely horizontal, and they were all so tired that they had conked out almost immediately. Marcos hoped to be near enough to Marin to talk with her some more, but she was sitting with her family. It was only natural, he supposed. They were all facing some incredible challenges ahead, with no guarantee of success or survival. Marcos suppressed an involuntary shudder at the morbid thought.

Guiltily, he glanced over at his own father, Malcolm, and wondered why he hadn't made an effort to sit near him. It really hadn't occurred to him until just now, if he were being honest. Still, he rationalized, things had been this way for years. He and Malcolm worked together, did what they had to, but in a detached way. No emotion involved. Except for the hug Malcolm had given him when he'd been rescued, they rarely talked and never touched. Because of Katerina, he was sure. And because of his mother.

His father blamed Marcos, and rightly so. They were both broken because of it. Talking would never bring them back, so what was the point?

He stood up and followed everyone down the steps into the hangar. A light mist clung to the air, making everything feel damp and dreary. Three vehicles waited to take them to their separate destinations. His father and Paul to India; Frank and Emily to London; and the rest of them to a port near the Hudson canal. Marin huddled with Paul and her parents, hugging them and saying tearful goodbyes. Jaycen stood behind them, near General Holt and Sergeant Major Bale, watching them, apparently lost in his own thoughts. Jaycen seemed…off. Something happened to him back at the base, he was sure of it, but didn't know what it could have been. Just then, Malcolm moved close to Marcos and put his hand on his shoulder, surprising him.

"I know it hasn't been easy, Marcos," he said quietly. "I was not the father I could have been. It is hard to go on when your heart has been removed."

Marcos looked at his normally stoic father in surprise, but his eyes were on Marin and her family in their tight group.

"We could have been like that, had your mother…had things been different. But I could have been better to you. I should have…." he said, leaving the rest hanging unsaid in the air. Marcos felt his throat tighten as he saw this oddly vulnerable side of his father. He missed the man his father used to be. The proud papa, who was his son's hero. Marcos had ruined that, ruined his father, ruined his mother, lost his sister. The guilt that hung around his neck and only surfaced in his nightmares threatened to show its ugly face here and now. Instinct begged him to tamp it back down, to avoid the pain like he normally did. Hide it in the wall of unsaid words built between himself and his father. But what if something happened on this dangerous mission? Was this what was prompting Malcolm to talk of these things they never spoke of?

Suddenly, impulsively, he turned to him and asked, using a title he hadn't used since he was a boy, "Papa, do you think we are all going to die?" He wanted him to say no, to comfort him as he did when he was a child, long before all this began. He wanted, needed his father to tell him it would be all right and not to fear.

Malcolm's face tightened and he shook his head slowly. "I do not know, my son. I have a heaviness in my heart that speaks of bad things ahead of us."

Marcos felt disappointed and a sudden surge of anger. "Why do you have to say that?"

Malcolm looked up, surprised. "Because it is the truth. Hahn would not have left these warheads unguarded. Though we captured many of his creatures, I fear he has more. And we are ridiculously underprepared, though how you could prepare for something like this is beyond me." He tilted his head to one side. "What do you want me to say? That we will be fine?" He scoffed. "You want me to lie to you?"

"No, I want you to be kind! Treat me like your son, not just another person. Can't you for once try to care about how I feel? Comfort me instead of pushing me away? You've spent years punishing me for what happened," he said, his voice rising. "I know it was my fault. I should never have told Christos about your project. It's my fault they died. But can't you move past that even for one day?"

Malcolm turned and faced Marcos, both their chocolate brown eyes meeting. "Marcos, hear me. I have *never* blamed you for that!"

Marcos blinked in shock. "Of course you have! We haven't talked for years because of it. It's why you turned into the ogre of a father you have been ever since."

Malcolm stepped back as if struck. "No! No, that was never the case at all!" He placed both hands on Marcos's shoulders and squeezed them tightly. "My son, you were just a little boy! I knew how dangerous that information was. People had already died for it. What business did I have sharing it with children? It was my own weakness that lost us your sister and your mother. It was my fault. I knew better, and I can never forgive myself for bringing you into it. Every time I looked into your face, I saw the pain I put there. And so I withdrew, hoping you would find better people to take my place."

Marcos stared at the naked openness of his father's face as if seeing him for the first time. "I...I thought you hated me," Marcos whispered, his voice shaking.

Malcolm drew his son into a tearful embrace. "And I thought you hated me. But never, my son, never did I blame you for my terrible judgement. I only hope you can forgive me for my mistakes."

Marcos held his father close, his heart aching at the love they had lost because of their guilt and assumptions.

"I'm sorry to disturb you all, but we are quickly running out of time," General Holt said gently to the group.

Malcolm pulled back and looked his son over. "When this is over, things will be different between us, yes? Perhaps I will not be so much of an 'ogre', eh?"

Marcos gave him a watery smile. "Yes, Papa. Things will be better." Malcolm squeezed his shoulders once again and Marcos put one hand over his fathers'. "I love you, Papa. I always have."

"And I, you, Marcos. God go with you!"

"Until we meet again, Papa." Marcos watched his Father get into a car with General Holt. Paul gave Marin a last, lingering hug and followed. Frank, Emily and Marin held each other one last time and they, too, got into the back seat of the vehicle, leaving Marcos, Marin and Jaycen behind with Sergeant Major Bale. Tears coursed down Marin's face as she watched her family disappear around the hangar, piercing Marcos's heart. He drifted over and put his arm around Marin's shoulder. She leaned into him, and he tightened his arms around her comfortingly, leaning his cheek against her head, lending her his strength. He hoped she would reach out to him and talk through their touch like she had before, but to his disappointment, this time she stayed silent. Jaycen glanced over, but he didn't say anything. Inwardly, Marcos smiled. Another victory over Jaycen.

***

After a short car ride they were dropped off at the New York Coast Guard Station and ushered into a waiting submarine. Marin seemed hesitant to board the vessel, and Marcos completely understood why, after her imprisonment on Hahn's sub. Marcos stayed close to Marin, touching her hand or shoulder when he could, to let her know he was there if she needed him. Each time he did, Jaycen would react in subtle ways, with a wince or a sucked in breath. Either Marin didn't care, or she was too distracted to

274

notice, and Marcos used it to his advantage, hopefully widening the gap between Jaycen and Marin.

A short man in a captain's uniform stuck his hand out to them when they reached the bridge. "Welcome aboard the U.S.S Rhode Island. I'm Captain Edward Woods. And you must be the fish people we're expecting?" He gave a dubious laugh.

The Sergeant Major glared at him. "Captain, surely you've been briefed on the sensitive nature of this mission?"

The Captain looked abashed. "Yes, yes, of course. The mission. But the part about fish people? That's what I found amusing," he chuckled.

Nobody smiled and the Captain stopped laughing. Sergeant Major Bale spoke in a dangerously low voice, forcing the Captain to lean in closer to hear him.

"This isn't a joke. Get your head around it and keep it off the record. We need to get moving. We are running out of time."

The Captain drew his eyebrows together and looked over his passengers again, this time much more carefully, before turning and shouting orders to his crew. The sub moved forward with a lurch, causing them all to stumble back a step. The Captain turned to his next in command, a blonde man with a serious expression on his young face.

"Jones, please show these people to the galley and make them comfortable. Get Blake to rustle them up something to eat or drink." Jones nodded curtly. Marcos's stomach grumbled in anticipation of food. He couldn't remember the last time he'd eaten.

The Captain turned back to his guests. "My apologies for anything I might have said or done to offend," he said with a slight bow. "Please, make yourselves at home. It will be a half hour or so before we make it out to open water, and then who knows how long until we find anything. We'll do a thorough scan of the Hudson Canyon and let you know what we come up with. With any luck, we'll get this located and neutralized and be back in time for lunch!"

***

They sat in the galley, rocking with the gentle movement of the submarine and drinking hot chocolate. The cook, Blake, brought them each a plate of scrambled eggs, toast, and gravy with a carafe of orange juice to share.

"I'm sorry; they told me you just got in from California. You're probably more in the mood for dinner, rather than breakfast. I'd offer you some of the prime rib we had last night, but they cleaned me out."

"You know, you could have just given this to us and we would've been happy," Jaycen grumbled. "Now we feel robbed of prime rib!" The Sergeant Major chuckled as the cook shrugged and left them alone.

"Sergeant Major?" Marin asked, but he held up his hand.

"Please, call me Pete. I don't have the energy for all the Sergeant Major stuff."

"Okay...Pete," she said. "Maybe you and Jaycen have talked about this, but I was wondering if you learned anything about Jaycen's mother?"

Jaycen and Pete exchanged a dark glance, and Pete didn't answer her question, instead directing his attention to his plate. Marcos shrugged and went back to work on the eggs, dipping the toast in the gravy, not really paying attention to the awkward stop to all conversation. He was chewing his last bite when he finally noticed nobody else was eating, and Jaycen was just pushing his food around with a fork.

"Still mad about the prime rib?" Marcos jabbed at him gently. Jaycen didn't take the bait and instead just shook his head.

"I'm not hungry."

"How can you not be hungry? We haven't eaten in forever!" Marcos said incredulously. Marin reached out and took Jaycen's hand, shooting Marcos a nasty look. Marcos felt his insides shrivel up at the gesture.

"Jaycen, what's the matter? What happened back at the base?" she asked softly.

Marcos watched him struggle with his emotions before he tried to answer, and suddenly Marcos realized why Jaycen had seemed so off. He had to have heard bad news about his mom. He swallowed the last bit of food in his now dry mouth, feeling awful for not noticing. No wonder Marin had glared at him.

Jaycen glanced up and met eyes with her, let out a heavy sigh, and shook his head. Marin carefully prodded further.

"It's your mom, isn't it?"

Jaycen nodded imperceptibly.

"Oh, Jaycen! Is she hurt? Or…."

Jaycen nodded his head. "She's gone," he whispered. Marin scooted closer to him and put her arm through his.

Marin leaned her head against Jaycen's shoulder. "I'm so, so sorry, Jaycen. And Pete. I'm sorry for both of you," she said. Pete shrugged and Jaycen kept pushing his food around. Marcos kicked himself for being so clueless when everybody else obviously knew something bad had happened. And, despite all the other feelings he had about him, he felt awful for Jaycen.

"Hey, I am sorry, Jaycen. I know what it's like to lose your mother. It is a hole in your heart nothing can fill," Marcos said softly. Jaycen gave him a half smile.

Suddenly the room jerked sideways, sending their food flying across the table. Lights flickered and came back on accompanied by a red flashing light and the wail of an alarm.

"What on earth was that?" Pete shouted, grasping the edge of the table for support. The sub turned sharply, almost as if in the grip of a giant hand. Marin and Marcos blanched.

"Aaron," they said in unison.

They sprinted through crowded passages back to the bridge, fighting through throngs of sailors scurrying to their posts. The Captain was shouting orders to everyone in sight when they burst into the room.

"Out!" he screamed at them, pointing them back the way they came.

"We know what hit you," Marin said in a rush. "Maybe we can help!"

"I already know what hit us," he shouted, gesturing to the monitor in front of him. A thick tentacle the size of a full-grown anaconda slithered past the view screen. "Off! Get off the bridge!" He pushed a button and shouted into a microphone, "Full reverse! Get back into the bay! Contact base and get us some backup!"

They stood in the corner helplessly and he turned his attention back to them. "If I need you, I'll send for you. Get them out of here!" He grabbed the nearest man by his sleeve and pointed him their direction. The man ushered them out the door and told them to go back to the galley as the lights sputtered off, then came back on at half power.

They retraced their steps as the sub shook, revving into reverse. "Something is wrong with their props I bet," Jaycen commented.

"Or their engines," Marcos added. The sub was hit again, flickering the lights and throwing them against one wall. Marin crashed into Marcos's shoulder and stumbled. He took her hand and helped her up, feeling a warm rush at their touch as she flashed him a thankful smile. He hoped that meant she'd forgiven him for his earlier cluelessness. By the time they made it back to the dining room, the lights stuttered back on.

"We can't have gone too far from the harbor," Pete said, taking a seat at one of the galley tables. "Is it attacking everything coming out of New York?"

"Probably everything that's headed straight towards the Hudson Canyon, but who knows?" Marin slid into a seat across from Jaycen and next to Marcos. It was hard to keep himself from reaching out and touching her, just to feel that connection again. It was intoxicating, even with the world falling apart around them. Maybe *because* of the world falling apart around them. One of the few things he was certain of was how much she meant to him. Whether or not she felt the same remained to be seen. He let out a long, frustrated sigh, chiding himself. It was stupid to worry about his love for her until they knew what the next hours would bring.

They waited, hoping they had moved out of Aaron's protection zone and were no longer a threat. Nothing happened for several minutes, and they started to relax when the sub was hit again, hard, and again and again. At one point the lights went completely out, leaving them cringing in anticipation in the blood red emergency lighting.

Pete cleared his throat uncomfortably. "So...you can all breathe water, right?" They nodded. "That means if we sink, at least you'll still be ok?"

"I'm sure we won't sink," Marin said hastily. "We'll *all* be fine."

"We're not going to sink, Pete," Jaycen said dully.

Pete looked hard at Jaycen, who was staring intently at his clasped, white-knuckled fists on the table.

"Sure, we'll be fine. But I feel better knowing you can survive," he said. It seemed he was talking only to Jaycen and Marcos wondered why he was zooming in on him alone. "You know, to carry on the name and all."

Jaycen's eyes snapped up to meet Pete's. "I don't even have your name, Pete. Mom never told me about you. From my point of view, you're just some military guy that married my mom a few weeks ago. A stranger." Marcos and Marin exchanged confused looks.

"I know that, son. I just…if something was to happen, I want you to know how much I wanted you in my life. It wasn't my choice, it was your mom's." He reached out his hand as if to grasp Jaycen's, but Jaycen drew them back under the table.

"Wait, Pete's your dad?" Marin asked incredulously. Pete nodded, but Jaycen looked sullen.

"You made the choice that tore our family apart. It's the consequences you didn't like," Jaycen snarled. The sub rocked, metal moaning as if in pain. "Look, can we not talk about this right now?" Jaycen snapped. Somewhere in the distance, they could hear water hissing.

"There might not be a later," Pete pointed out. An enormous bang echoed through the sub, rattling them to their teeth. They felt a moment of weightlessness before they hit something hard, throwing them against the wall. The room felt like it was sliding and rolling to the right. They scrambled on their hands and knees, falling, rolling, trying to keep up with the movement of the sub as items banged and crashed around them. Finally, the sub came to a grinding stop and slowly righted itself, mostly. The four of them lay in a tangled heap between two bolted down tables.

A ghastly, metallic shriek shuddered through the sub and Marcos's heart sank. That could not be a good sound. Even the emergency lights went out this time, leaving them entombed in darkness. Marcos reached out a hand, not caring whose it was this time, just to know he wasn't alone. He caught Marin's cold fingertips and squeezed them. Someone held tightly to his arm. Time stretched out unnaturally long, with only darkness and the ominous sounds of the wounded sub to keep them company as they waited for certain death. But it didn't come. The emergency lights blinked on, bringing them a wave of relief. They shakily got to their feet and Marin let go of Marcos's hand, but he kept his close to hers. Moments later, a young woman in a rumpled officer's uniform ran into the kitchen, startling them.

"Captain needs you on deck!" she said breathlessly. They rose and followed her to the bridge. A wispy haze of smoke hung in the air, smelling of ozone. The shouting and rushing from earlier was gone, and the bridge was eerily silent. Marcos couldn't help but notice the ashen faces of every man and woman at every console.

"That thing just took out what was left of our props. We're dead in the water," the Captain said matter-of-factly. "There are two subs in route, the U.S.S. Cheyenne and the U.S.S. Jackson, but with that thing out there, I don't know how they will get to us."

"We need to get out there and try to stop this," Marin said. "Just let us out and we'll go on our own from here. It can't be too far."

The Captain shook his head slowly. "You don't understand. The props are gone, we are teetering on the edge of the canyon at a depth of one thousand feet, and that thing pinched off the end of this sub like the cap off a cigar. Including the airlock. We are all trapped in here."

CHAPTER 53

PAUL

PAUL HATED FLYING, being much more comfortable in water rather than the sky. He could almost feel every minute of the long, arduous, crowded journey ticking away their last twenty-eight hours until detonation. They had changed planes in France and were headed toward their final destination of India, but Paul's sense of time was so messed up that he had no idea what time it was supposed to be. All he knew was he was tired; there were two more hours until they landed; and Malcolm was snoring nosily. Paul knew he needed more sleep, but the snoring was loud and difficult to ignore. He scrubbed at his tired eyes. It wasn't really Malcolm's fault. Paul felt on edge, his emotions sharp and his brain alert, a familiar feeling he always had back in the service before a big operation. They were going into battle soon, of some form or another. There was little information about what was going to be waiting for them, but it would be stupid to assume the warheads would be left unguarded. Two things would be certain, Hahn would have planted them deep and he would have them protected.

A tone sounded overhead and the pilot turned on the PA system. The message was given in two languages, causing the people around them to murmur in what looked like protest. People were waking up, nudging one another and gesturing to the cabin. Finally it was repeated in English.

Malcolm awoke with a snort.

"Did we arrive?" he asked sleepily.

"Shh!" Paul hissed at him. "Something's up."

"Ladies and gentlemen, we are so sorry for the inconvenience, but our plane has been diverted to Pakistan. We will be landing in Karachi to deboard two passengers, and then we are cleared to refuel and carry on to Ahmedabad. We apologize for any inconvenience this may cause you. Thank you for flying with us, and we will get you to your destination as soon as possible." Everyone was looking at each other with a mix of apprehension and curiosity.

Paul and Malcom exchanged worried glances. "You think this is for us?" Paul whispered. Malcolm shrugged slightly.

"I suppose we shall soon see." The next hour and a half passed agonizingly slow, with everyone talking in hushed whispers and looking suspiciously at each other. The plane dipped down with a stomach-sinking bump, and then rolled to a stop in front of a modern airport terminal and stopped.

They waited.

And waited.

"Something has *got* to be up," Paul said quietly. Malcolm agreed. Finally, the doors to the plane opened and six armed Pakistani soldiers entered and spoke to the steward, showing them a photograph. The woman looked shaken and immediately pointed to Paul and Malcolm. The entire plane turned to stare at them and Paul's mouth went dry. "This doesn't look good."

"No, it does not."

The soldiers stopped at their row and the one that looked in charge spoke in a heavy accent. "Please, sirs, you come with us."

"Why?" Malcolm demanded. "We haven't done anything wrong!"

"Please, sirs, you come with us," he repeated. "Now, please."

"We need to get to Gujarat immediately!" Paul said loudly. "We are on an urgent mission for the United States of America," he said, producing his passport. The soldier looked it over and motioned to the two soldiers behind him. They drew their weapons amid the gasps of the other passengers.

"Please, sirs, you now come with us."

"What, are you going to shoot us? We are trying to save the lives of everyone on this continent!" Malcolm rose from his seat.

"Sirs, you must come."

Malcolm looked down at Paul, who began to pick up his belongings. "I don't know that we have much choice, Malcolm," he said with a shrug.

"Isn't Pakistan an American ally?" Malcolm pressed the soldier. "Why are we being taken prisoner?"

The soldier didn't answer, but gestured for them to move, and then backed down the aisle, followed by Malcolm and Paul. People clicked photos of them as they passed, whispering to each other in a variety of languages. Once they were off the plane, they were escorted at gunpoint through the crowded terminal and out into the hot Pakistan afternoon. Paul put his hand in his pocket and tried to text a message to Marin without looking. He pushed send, hoping he'd gotten the number right and the message made sense, before one of the soldiers jabbed him and told him to keep his hands in the open. Two sandy-colored Humvees waited for them with open doors.

"Can you please tell us what this is about?" Malcolm asked.

"You don't understand how urgent this is. Please, call the U.S. Embassy! Call the President for crying out loud!" Paul turned toward their captors, begging.

"Sirs will get in, please," the man said. They took off through the bustling streets, tearing around corners until they got to a highway where they increased their speed.

"Can you at least tell us where we are going?" Malcolm snapped.

"Sirs will speak to commander soon," was all the man said. Paul tried to watch out of the extremely dark windows to see where they were headed, but having never been there before, he had no idea what landmarks to look for. Every spy movie he'd ever seen played out in his mind, complete with visions of being taken to a quiet place to be shot and forgotten. He looked down at his watch. Twenty-six hours until detonation. He vowed to make a break for it once they got out of the vehicle, and hoped Malcolm was thinking the same thing. There was too much at stake for this nonsense!

The vehicle slowed down and they were waved through a guard post into a military facility overlooking a deceptively serene ocean bay. They stopped and the door opened. For a split second, Paul poised to run, Malcolm behind him, but the guard pointed with his gun, gesturing for them to walk around the building where a modest dock ran out into the sapphire water. *Well, at least it's a pretty place to be shot,* Paul thought grimly. An older gentleman in a khaki uniform, with peppered black hair and eyes so dark they almost looked black, walked toward them from the end of the pier.

"Welcome to Pakistan, gentlemen!" The man extended hand. "I am sure you are surprised to be here."

Malcolm shook his hand, followed by Paul. "Yes, you could say that," Paul said warily.

"Please excuse our method of extracting you, but as you are well aware, time is critical," he said apologetically. "I am Commander Barqi."

"Why on earth have we been waylaid here?" Paul interrupted.

"I was just getting to that point. Two days ago, our military radar discovered an object at extreme depths that match your government's description of the warheads this man, Hahn, is threatening us with. We have been in contact with your government and between us, feel the fastest route to get you to it is through Pakistan, rather than the much longer journey through India," the man said simply.

"So you are here to help us?" Paul asked.

The man smiled, his teeth exceptionally white. "Yes." Malcolm and Paul visibly relaxed.

"And you've already found the warhead?"

"We believe so. There are ships scanning the entire Arabian Sea, but this is the closest we have found. We have what you need and are ready to set sail if you will come with me."

"That's what I'm talking about!" Paul grinned at Malcolm. "This is going to be easy!"

Malcolm shot him a dubious look, "Please, do not jinx us. I will not breathe easy until all of our missions are complete."

"True, true," Paul said, following Commander Barqi to the end of the pier, where a sleek black submarine waited for them. "But this beats the way I thought this was going to end, hands down!"

CHAPTER 54

EMILY

FRANK AND EMILY touched down in London without much difficulty. A man in a tuxedo and a flat hat was waiting for them in the airport lobby. He led them out into the pouring rain and into a gorgeous cream-colored Rolls Royce.

"Wow, I could get used to a car like this," Frank said, settling into the back. The driver sat behind a Plexiglas window that was cracked open slightly.

"Mmm. This is the way to travel," Emily agreed. "I feel like the Queen of England in this car."

"Actually, mum, this car does indeed belong to Her Royal Majesty," the driver said over his shoulder. "She sends her regards and wishes you the best of luck on your mission." Emily blushed, realizing the driver could hear her, but was delighted that the Queen herself was aware of them. "She also sent along a little something to help you pass the time until we get to the Royal Shipyards. It's in the cupboard to your right."

Emily grinned like fangirl and opened up a wood grained door in the wall. A small china plate sat in the nook holding two ribbon wrapped packages of oatmeal cookies, several nougats of chocolate and two cold bottles of chocolate milk.

"Hobnobs!" Emily exclaimed with delight, examining the cookies. "I haven't had these since I was a girl."

The driver smiled at her in the rearview mirror. "Forgive me, Mum, but you sound like you're from around here yourself."

"Yes, I was born and raised in Blackheath. Then I ran off and married this Yank," she laughed, tipping her head toward Frank, who gave her a playful pout.

"Well, whatever you are up against, I'll feel better knowing a lovely Brit is at the helm," the man joked, winking into the mirror. "No offense, sir," he said with a roguish smile.

They nibbled at the treats, taking extra care to not spill in the car and leaned back in the luxurious seats. Frank took Emily's hand.

"This could almost be a second honeymoon, if the circumstances were better," he murmured.

"If only." Emily drew her hand away from his and used it to brush her hair away from her face, then set it down on her lap instead of taking Frank's hand again. She knew she had to talk to him, but didn't dare bring it up right now, especially with what they were facing, no matter how much she longed to confide in him. In the meantime, guilt weighed her down. Nothing happened between herself and Nathan Greer when he helped her escape, but the fact that she started to fall for him during that time ate at her. She felt unworthy of the love of her husband, presumed dead all these years. And the added guilt that he had died as a reward for saving her life was like a festering knife wound.

"Worried, Em?" Frank probed, taking back her hand. She flinched inside, hating herself for the feelings she had to hide from him.

"It's...a lot to deal with, yes," she said evasively.

"Is that everything that's bothering you?" he pressed gently. "You've seemed distant..." he trailed off. Emily bit her lip, dying a little bit inside. In a matter of hours, they would be underwater, facing whatever Hahn had in store for them, perhaps dying. Maybe this would be her only chance to tell him, to ask his forgiveness. She paused, teetering on the edge of indecision, when the words came out on their own.

"There was a man, Douglas. I have to tell you about him. He worked for Hahn. He rescued me from him," she began in a rush. The story poured out of her, like poison from a wound, and she told him how Greer took her across the country and protected her. She recounted the death of the ranger at Blue Hole, the murder of their old friend Mac Pachello, and Mac's revelation that Frank was alive. Frank's blue eyes looked hollow by the time she told him about their plane ride to Isla Cedros to find Marin, and she stopped, hating herself for opening her mouth, for hurting him, for betraying him if only in her heart.

"You're telling me this because you love him. This man that rescued you," Frank said flatly, but she could hear the devastation in his voice, the damage she had done to his heart.

"I...had begun to. Yes," she admitted, hanging her head. "But nothing happened between us. And I thought you were dead! I had no hope to even hang on to!" she pleaded. "Surely in all this time you thought about moving on?"

"I *had* a girl in my life. Our daughter. Keeping her safe and concealed has been my only concern," he said harshly. Emily shrank inside, feeling awful for almost hoping he'd had some outside feelings to justify hers. They sat in a hard silence for several blocks before Frank spoke again, this time softly.

"And would you rather be with this man, than me? Than with our daughter?" He asked, looking into her eyes in disbelief. He reached out a finger and ran it down the side of her face.

"No! No, I couldn't! As soon as Mac told me he thought you were still alive, everything changed. I did all I could do to get to you as fast as possible."

Frank looked past her out the window. "Where is this man now?"

Emily pushed past the lump in her throat, the one that formed every time the gruesome scene played across her memory, of kind, sweet Nathan screaming out for her to run as they slit his throat, scarlet blood bursting out onto the sandy beach. His last thought was for her, to try to save her. He'd done nothing selfish in all the time she knew him, other than to covet her love.

"He's dead. They killed him for helping me and slit his throat on Isla Cedros."

Frank was silent for a while. Emily wiped a tear that escaped from her eye and looked ahead, not able to bear the pain she knew she would see if she looked at her husband.

"I'm not sure what you want me to do with this, Em. I don't know what I should feel," he said honestly.

"I want you to forgive me for caring about someone else, Douglas," she burst out. "And I want to forgive myself for getting an innocent man killed for his kindness," she added in a choked sob.

Frank hesitated, then put his arm around his wife, embracing her. Emily broke down in tears into his shoulder, crying out all the pain she'd bottled up since she escaped. The car rocked slowly side to side as they traversed through the countryside.

When she couldn't cry anymore, she whispered, "Douglas, I just want you to love me. And I want to spend the rest of my life showing just how much I love you, if you'll give me the chance. If you'll forgive me."

"Nothing you could do would make me stop loving you, Emily. It hurts, but I understand." He hugged her, resting his chin on the top of her head as she soaked in his love. "And it sounds like I am deeply indebted to him for saving your life." He let out a long, slow breath, ruffling her hair. "We'll be okay, Em. We can figure this out, weather this storm. We'll be okay."

Emily wrapped her arms around him and held him close. She glanced up at the rearview mirror just as the driver wiped a sympathetic tear off his cheek and quickly looked away.

CHAPTER 55

MARCOS

MARCOS SHIVERED AS he walked into the dining room, which had become their temporary home while stuck on the derelict sub. Sixteen miserable hours had passed and the only good news was that there hadn't been any more attacks. Two compartments had been flooded and seven crew members were dead or unaccounted for. The U.S.S. Cheyenne had come within a hundred feet of the sub ten hours ago, but fell under attack and was forced to retreat, leaving them with few options left. Since both he and Jaycen had experience working on subs, they had been taking shifts with the other crew members to try to repair what they could. Jaycen had come to relieve him just moments ago, and now Marcos was looking forward to finding something warm to curl up in and a bit of sleep. Pete was lying on some pushed together bench seats in the corner, snoring. Marin sat at a table with her back to him, wrapped in a blanket. Her head was laying on her folded arms. He touched her gently on her shoulder and she startled, but once she saw his face, she relaxed.

"I'm sorry if I frightened you," he whispered in her ear so as not to wake Pete.

"You're freezing!" she whispered back. "Here, take my blanket," she said, wrapping it around his shoulders.

"You're cold, too," he reminded her. "Perhaps we could share?" She nodded and he pulled her into the warmth of the blanket. "Thank you!" he said, his teeth chattering. "I've been in one of the partially flooded areas trying to patch a pipe." Pete moved in his sleep and they got quieter. She grabbed Marcos's hand and reached into his thoughts. The warmth that flowed from her exceeded anything the blanket was doing for him. Having her in his mind was like coming home.

"I thought this might be an easier way to talk," she said to him. *"We won't wake anyone up this way."* She smiled, clearly excited to share some news with him. *"I heard from the first mate, Jones. He said they got word from Paul and your father! They've found their warhead already!"*

The hope they both felt that one of their group might succeed soaked into his stressed soul. *"Have they heard from Frank and Emily?"* he asked, feeling her anxiety for their safety.

"They are having trouble finding it," she said. *"Marcos, what happens if this warhead detonates with us above it?"* He thought for a moment, weighing the possibilities he'd not really wanted to consider.

"The best-case scenario would be it goes by us and pushes us farther from the ridge. Worst case, it goes through us, I suppose. Though that would be one way to stop it," he said ironically.

"If that doesn't happen?" she asked.

"If there is anyone left above after it detonates, then I guess they come rescue us. Or we eventually cut our way through the hull on our own and escape. But I fear that would kill everyone else on board. At that point, it may not make much difference though."

"That would be horrible for poor Jaycen! He just lost his mother, then his dad," Marin said sadly. Marcos stiffened, but she rested her head on his shoulder and he relaxed.

"And then what will happen to us?" Marcos asked. Marin didn't answer, but he could feel sorrow clouding her thoughts. Marcos tried unsuccessfully to hide his sadness that the choice was so difficult for her. Why couldn't he be the clear winner? They were so close, they could communicate almost soul to soul. And he had known about Marin, and loved her, long before Jaycen even knew her. He didn't want to make her sad, but didn't he deserve

to know where he stood? Wasn't his heart on the line as much as hers? He felt her stumbling through his feelings; the things he usually tried to shield her from, but he didn't close them off this time. He wanted her to know the depth of his love for her, to know the anguish caused by her and her feelings for Jaycen, even though it was tearing her up inside.

"Oh, Marcos!" She cried, laying her head back down in her arms. He wrapped both arms around her, wanting to comfort her, but needing comfort himself.

"I'm sorry, Marin. I told you once that it would break your heart to see the depth of my love for you. Because it breaks mine. And now you know."

He held her for a long time, neither one knowing what to say. Words wouldn't change anything, anyway. Finally, she broke the silence, moving away from one impossible subject to another. This time she used her voice, speaking softly.

"Marcos, how long can these people last down here? Pete, Jones, all the rest?"

Marcos didn't want to answer, but she could probably guess his response anyway. "Not long with the heat going out. It's going to get bad."

"We have to find a way to get off the ship and stop Aaron. I don't think we can wait any longer."

"I know," Marcos said. "I just kept hoping…"

Pete stretched and sat up, blinking in the dim light. He looked down at his watch and let out a deep sigh.

"I'm sorry to wake you, Pete," Marin apologized. "But Paul and Malcolm's team located one of the weapons," she said, trying to sound upbeat.

"Good, good." He stood and walked over to the table they were sitting at and sat down. "Listen, kids. I could hear you talking and you're right. It's time to face the facts. We have to get you out of here. You know that. You've done your best to help us, you're going to have to move on to the next part of the plan and leave us behind."

Neither Marcos nor Marin could reply. It seemed too hard and too horrible, but there was no other way forward. Pete stood up, taking charge. "Marcos, go get Jaycen. We need to have a talk with the Captain."

***

Pete leaned across the table with the sub's schematics laid out between himself and the Captain. Marin, Jaycen and Marcos surrounded them. The Captain, his lips pale with the cold, seemed dubious and concerned.

"Cut through the hull?" The Captain repeated with a slow blink.

Marcos nodded. "We have to get out there and disarm the warhead. We can't wait any longer." Marcos knew how crazy it must sound to someone not familiar with the Arydians.

"Do you know what the pressure alone would do to you people?" The time had long since passed of trying to keep their identity a secret on the sub. Marcos had certainly spent plenty of time underwater trying to help them patch holes in the seams.

"We've explained this already. Our bodies can handle it. We are not... human like you," Marin interjected. Marcos recoiled at that comment. He'd never thought of himself as not human.

"And what about the creature out there?" the Captain added. Marcos didn't have a good answer for that one, but Marin interjected.

"We can deal with him. But only once we get out there. That creature was once one of us," Marin said. "We need to contact him and try to communicate, but we can't from inside here."

The Captain was silent and solemnly cast his eyes around his crew. "If you breech the hull at this pressure, this whole ship may implode. Have you considered what a hull breech would do to the rest of us?" he asked quietly.

Marcos nodded. They had all discussed this thoroughly before coming to the Captain, and still had not been able to come up with better options. Pete put a hand on Jaycen's shoulder. For once, Jaycen didn't flinch at his touch.

"We understand the risks, Captain. I'm not Arydian like these three, and I will share the same fate as you. But as a member of the military, I have sworn to lay down my life to protect the lives of others, just like you and all your crew. If this is the way I have been called to do it, then so be it."

"We can use one of the partially flooded compartments." Jaycen added. "If we seal it off, there's a chance it will hold. Once we get the creature out of the way, they can launch a rescue from the surface. It's the best chance any of us have, Captain. And we're running out of time."

Marcos looked at the faces surrounding the room: men and women, most barely older than him, people who had lives and families, who were somebody's sisters, brothers, parents, children. They were asking them to risk everything on this one chance. He swallowed past the lump of pride and humility in his throat for these noble humans, as one by one they all nodded their agreement.

The Captain took a deep breath. "Okay. Let's rock and roll."

CHAPTER 56

PAUL

MALCOLM AND PAUL stood on the bridge of the submarine as they moved closer to the target, entering a canyon in the deep waters a hundred miles off the coast of Pakistan. Another warship circled above them, and an American sub was en route from the Persian Gulf to offer backup.

"Take us down as low as you can go and hold position above the target," Commander Barqi ordered the navigator, who nodded in compliance. The sub creaked and groaned as the pressure around it increased. Paul stifled a yawn as they scanned the area.

"Normally, civilians would be nervous diving this deep, yet you seem almost bored," the commander observed. "It is more pleasant to travel with seasoned sailors than panicking civilians. Can I offer you a drink? Coffee or tea?"

"Tea would be nice," Malcolm said. "Thank you."

"You don't happen to have a Dr. Pepper, do you?" Paul asked with a joking grin.

The commander said something to a nearby ensign and turned back to Paul with a strange look. "You and I share the same taste, Mr. Donnegan. I do have a small stash of Dr. Pepper in my personal stores that I am willing to share with you."

Paul's grin widened. "Thanks!"

They continued to dive at a steep angle, and Paul stretched his jaw back and forth as the heady feeling of the sub's air pressure made his ears crackle. The commander was handed a note, which he read, his dark eyes turning serious. "It's an update from your government. The London group arrived safely and is in search of the device. So far they have had no luck. Odd, since the water is fairly shallow in that area," he commented. His mouth constricted into a frown. "The Hudson group has run into trouble," he said. "Something about a creature. There is a picture." He gasped audibly as he read it, then handed it to Paul, who snatched it from his hands so he and Malcolm could read it together.

"Oh, no," Paul whispered, rereading the missive. He caught Malcolm's eye, knowing Malcolm was experiencing the same panic for their kids.

"I have travelled the seas for many years," Barqi exclaimed, "but never have I encountered a creature such as this. Do you know what it is?"

"It has to be Aaron," Malcolm said, taking the photo from the commander. "Guarding the Hudson warhead."

Paul nodded numbly and handed the pages back to Barqi.

"A boy?" Barqi said in confusion.

"Thank you," Paul said quickly. "Please let us know if you hear anything more about them. Our children are in that group."

"I will, and my condolences," Commander Barqi said solemnly. "But I must insist, what kind of monster is this and are we going to encounter those as well? For the safety of all of us, I need to know."

Paul looked hesitant, but Malcolm spoke. "They have a right to know, my friend. We may all face these challenges soon." He turned to Commander Barqi. "Hahn has access to genetically mutated creatures. Monsters, if you will," Malcolm said. The Commander looked at him in disbelief. "This one is the largest we know of."

"You called it Aaron," he pressed. He looked like he was waiting for the punchline of a joke.

"Yes, it's a long story. But this is extremely serious. This creature is capable of taking instruction and inflicting extreme damage."

Barqi's face quickly turned into concern. "And will these be guarding every warhead?"

Paul and Malcolm shrugged. "Perhaps not him, but creatures like him. Hopefully not as huge," Paul said.

The commander shook his head. "If this is so, how do you plan to fight them?"

"Any way we can," Paul said quietly.

"Commander, we have located the target and reached depth. It's directly below us," a man to their left said, just as the ensign returned with a cup of tea and a cold can of soda.

"Time to go," Malcolm said. Paul nodded.

"Keep that cold for me, will ya?" Paul asked the ensign.

***

They quickly changed into wetsuits and were shown into the airlock, where two water scooters waited. Commander Barqi followed them into the room alone, handing them each what looked like a rifle.

"These are APS underwater assault rifles. They have supercavitating bullets that can travel more than thirty meters underwater. Made in Russia. This should protect you from anything that gets in your way," Barqi said, pausing at the end as if he had more to say, but was unsure whether or not to go on. His face became more resolved and he took a deep breath.

"There are several things about this mission that have been kept from me, gentlemen," he said sharply. "I have remained silent because of the importance of the goals, but it seems ridiculous to allow you to leave at this depth, let alone try to travel to this warhead. We are at two thousand feet, and the object is another thousand feet below us. You should be crushed as you leave this ship, yet you seem determined to go."

Both men nodded warily. "What are you getting at?" Paul asked.

"You obviously have technology you are keeping from our government. Technology well beyond anything we have dreamed of. I cannot keep silent on this. My superiors will have to know what America is doing."

Malcolm's face hardened. "This has nothing to do with American secrets, commander. The tech we have was just as much a surprise for them, I assure you. They've had about four days longer than you to try to figure it out. And, for the record, I am not American, neither is this terrorist threatening your world. There are things going on beyond the scope of borders, if

296

you can't tell. So, please get out of our way. We have a job to do and we are running out of time to do it."

The commander looked like he was about to protest, but backed out of the airlock. Malcolm and Paul strapped on weights to their ankles to help them sink, placed dive knives within easy reach, and slung the weapons over their shoulders. Paul reached over and sealed the airlock. The commander watched them through the thick glass window. His eyes flew wide when the water came up to their shoulders and he seemed to realize they didn't have any oxygen tanks. He shouted at them through the window, but Paul smiled and gave him a thumbs up, sinking under the water and taking a deep breath, still slightly amazed at his relatively new ability to breathe water. It sure made things easier not to have to mess with tanks and pressures and all the other constraints divers had to work around. Malcolm joined him, sinking down beside him. The commander's jaw hung open in the last of his protests as he watched them, awestruck.

Water filled the top of the airlock and the two men twisted open the bottom hatch, sliding out with their weapons and the two water scooters that had been left for them, moving out into the open water, and leaving the commander and his questions behind. Malcolm fastened a length of cable to a rung on the outside of the sub and let it fall. Holding the cable loosely in one hand, they both let the weight carry them straight down to their destination.

The greenish black water pressed in on them, lowering their visibility. Both men clicked on the lights of their scooters, following the signals on their dive watches. At twenty-five hundred feet, Paul's dive watch cracked.

"I've lost my watch," he lamented.

"I hope that's all we lose on this adventure," Malcolm said wryly.

"But now I can't tell how long we have until detonation," he protested quietly. *"Besides, I liked that watch."* He couldn't see Malcolm's face, but he could tell he was probably laughing at him.

"We have about fifty feet left to go. Keep alert!" Suddenly, Malcolm's hand tightened on the cable, stopping his descent. Paul followed suit.

"What's up?" Paul asked.

"Something is directly below us," Malcolm said in a hushed whisper.

Paul strained his eyes but couldn't make much out. He could feel something in the water, though, something big. His pulse began to pound in his ears, kicking him into battle mode. He slid the rifle off his shoulder and made sure it was loaded, then aimed it at the shape below him, waiting.

"It's heading toward us. Can you see it?" Malcolm hissed urgently. Paul felt something pulse in the water behind him and turned in time to see a lithe ghostly shape lunge forward. He ducked, but the thing swiped at Malcolm as it passed, stabbing into Malcolm's shoulder with a barb protruding from its head.

"Agh!" Malcolm shouted, letting go of the cable and grabbing his shoulder. His rifle fell into the darkness below him. The long tail of the creature whipped out of sight.

"Malcolm! Are you okay?" Paul asked, grabbing his arm before he could fall too far. He threw his own gun around his shoulder and grasped the cable, stopping their descent.

"It...stabbed me!" he said, gasping in pain. *"It feels..."* He cut off again as he let out another gasp of pain. *"It stabbed me with something. It burns!"*

Paul held onto the cable and Malcolm, his brain racing, trying to figure out what to do. He looked below. The shape was coming around again, moving closer by the second. His heart pounded in his brain, making it hard to concentrate on his options.

"Malcolm, can you hold onto the cable? One of us has to get to the warhead. Just hold on and I'll be back in a few. Can you hold on?" he repeated. Malcolm nodded. Paul aimed the rifle downward and loosed a couple of rounds into the water below him, then handed the rifle to Malcolm.

"Don't let anything get near you, okay?" Paul wrapped the strap of the rifle around Malcolm's good shoulder.

"You take it. You may need it," Malcolm groaned.

"I'll be fine. You cover me, okay?" He didn't wait for Malcolm to answer, but started his dive again, this time faster. The shape that had been below him was gone. He hoped he'd hit it with at least one of the bullets he'd fired, but he had no way of knowing for sure. The cable ran out about twenty feet before the bottom of the gorge, and he paused, dangling from the end. Below him in the murky depths, Paul could see the dim outline of the cone

of a warhead surrounded by a simple support scaffolding. He glanced up at Malcolm and let go of the cable end, dropping the rest of the way to the canyon floor.

The warhead was a lot bigger than he imagined. The gorge sloped down and away from him into blackness, and he couldn't help but worry that the creature that attacked Malcolm, and probably others, were lurking down there, watching him. The canyon walls were several meters away from him on both sides, filled with piles of rock and smaller canyons breaking off in all directions. He grasped the hilt of his dive knife hard and trudged through the deep silt around the object in search of the control panel.

The base of the missile was a thick metal pad and once he'd circled it, he took off the dive weights and swam the perimeter, not seeing any access panel or any way to get into the missile. The metal scaffolding surrounding it made it difficult to get in close, but it looked like he was going to have to figure out how to squeeze in there if he wanted to get anywhere close to the thing. He grumbled to himself, remembering Jaycen's jabs about him being too beefy and wondering if maybe he'd had a point.

He rose up the length of the cone, looking for anything that would get him inside the casing, his hopes sinking as he rose. *Oh, man. This is going to be harder than I thought.*

There was nothing, no features, no marking, just a long pencil-like cylinder. He sank, circling it slower this time, shining his beam across every surface. Movement vibrated the water and he cast his light downward. Paul jerked backward, almost losing his light as it played across the swollen, mutated features of a hammerhead shark prowling the water below him. A wide head, eyes bulging from each end of it swung back and forth like a dog sniffing for its prey. It was huge, at least twelve feet long with a barrel shaped body and bat-like fins sprouting out of its flank with fists emerging at the end, clenching and unclenching as if aching for a fight. This was the first time Paul had seen one of Hahn's monsters, and his stomach constricted with a mixture of revulsion, pity, and fear. Mostly fear.

The knife in his hand felt woefully inadequate to defend himself against this beast. He didn't know what the thing was waiting for, but he wasn't going to waste any time finding out. Paul pushed his legs through the scaffolding and was trying to squeeze his top half in, when the creature turned upwards with a sudden burst of speed, headed directly for him. Paul got his head and shoulders into the scaffolding, but his wetsuit caught on a rivet at his hip and he stopped, everything inside the cage but his backside. He grabbed onto the metal and heaved with all his might, dropping his knife as the shark opened its jagged jaws below him. He heaved, adrenaline giving him the strength he needed and the wetsuit ripped, flooding his lower half with icy water. He flew inside just as the monster snapped its jaws as it glided past. Paul twisted around, trapped, his back to the missile, panting, searching the water for the shark.

It swung around and faced him, fixing its bulbous eyes on him, its freakish hands clenching and unclenching. Paul maneuvered to a different position, more protected from the predator as it hit the scaffolding with its head, shaking the entire structure, then swinging away for another pass.

"Hahn won't be happy if you knock this warhead down," Paul said to the beast, mostly to keep himself from freaking out. To his surprise, the thing turned and looked at him, its expression unreadable behind the mask of its grotesque features. It slowed its pace, coming up to the scaffolding and turning sideways. The left hand reached between the rails, grasping for Paul, who shrank back, moving lower and away from the creature. The thing reached further, pushing itself against the bars and for a moment it caught the fabric of his ripped wetsuit and pulled Paul toward itself. Paul hung onto the bars, straining as hard as he could away from the thing. It banged its head in frustration as Paul slipped from its grasp, but wiggled its head inside the bars and snapped its teeth at him threateningly.

Paul squirmed further away from the monster, trying to assess the situation. He was unarmed and pinned down. The only thing he had going for him was that he was close to the missile, and if he couldn't figure out where the access panel was, his only choice was to try to outmaneuver the shark until he made a mistake and became shark food, or until the missile launched with him practically attached to it, whichever came first.

CHAPTER 57

EMILY

A GRAND SHIP, THE H.M.S. Duncan, waited in the harbor for Emily and Frank. Hand in hand they walked up the gangplank and onto the deck. The ship was ready to sail and had a small submarine suspended by two large cranes on deck. The Captain introduced himself as Grayson Butler and showed them to their stateroom as soon as they left the shipyard.

"Please, make yourselves comfortable," he said, gesturing them into the tiny room furnished with a built-in bunk bed, two chairs and a wooden table. "We shan't be more than an hour away from the deepest part of the English Channel, but you may wait here until we get closer," he said in a sharp British accent.

"Thank you," Emily said, taking a seat. "Have you heard anything from the other groups? Our daughter is with Group Charlie." The Captain pursed his lips together in a frown.

"We have been in touch with your American government, and you should know the Alpha Group has been diverted to Pakistan and should arrive in approximately eight hours. They will be the tightest on time, though we've heard they may have already found their warhead." He waited, looking uncomfortable.

"And our daughter's group?" Frank asked anxiously.

"They have run into a spot of trouble," he said, causing Emily to rise back to her feet.

"Trouble? What kind of trouble?" she asked.

"This may seem...rather incredible...but a creature of some sort attacked them as they got close to the Hudson Canyon. The sub is disabled and taking on water. The U.S. is trying to get help routed to them. I'm so sorry to bear such ill news," he said apologetically. "And I know it seems fantastic. Creatures and such." He shook his head in disbelief. "Anyway, I will be on the bridge if you need me," he said briskly. "I will let you know of any changes." He stepped out, closing the door behind him. They both sank down into the bed, digesting the news.

"I bet Hahn left Aaron to guard the Hudson warhead," Frank said to Emily. "Man, I hope Marin and those boys are all right. That kid is a mess and he is absolutely huge!" A thoughtful look crossed Frank's face. "Unless... do you think it's possible that Hahn made more monsters like Aaron?"

Emily scooted closer and put her head on his shoulder. "I don't know. According to Nathan, the man I mentioned earlier, Aaron was kind of a prototype, but he'd been working on controlling him for years through a woman at Leviathan. I don't know if he would have had time to create more. But I've given up on thinking things fit into my understanding of possible." She frowned and Frank leaned over and kissed her forehead, then her cheek, then her lips.

***

Forty-five minutes later, they were brought up to the bridge.

"Have you located the warhead?" Frank asked hopefully. Emily could tell the answer by the look on the Captain's frazzled face.

"No sign of it. We have four ships scouring the Channel, plus this one, and three on the west side and four more in the Celtic Sea. Are you certain of your information source?" he asked skeptically.

"As certain as I am about everything concerning this," Frank answered. "May I look at your maps?" The Captain gestured to a counter near him with a satellite image of the area, marked in various colors with the routes that had been run by them and the other ships. Emily looked over the Captain's shoulder.

"I don't get it," she remarked.

"Get what?"

She panned out of the immediate area and moved over to the Arabian Sea and zoomed in closer. "See, in the other two locations the warheads were hidden deep, so no one could get to them." She moved the map to look at the Hudson Canyon and pointed to that one as well, then brought it back to the English Channel. "But the water here is relatively shallow. Why would Hahn put something here that anyone could get to?"

Frank's forehead wrinkled. "That's a good point. Do you think we're looking in the wrong place?" Emily searched the map and shook her head.

"I don't think so. If we are assuming he wanted to affect the highest number of people, he would most likely target London and let the jet stream carry it through France, Germany and Belgium. I mean, that makes the most sense to me, anyway," she said.

"Yes, that was our thought, too, but then here we are, coming up with nothing," the Captain said from across the counter.

"Captain Butler, if you were going to plant a device like this with those parameters, where would you put it?" Emily asked.

The Captain leaned forward, examining the map. "Here," he said, putting a finger down on Lundy Isle on the west side of England. "It's isolated and remote and he could hit most of the lower half of England."

"And a lot of ocean," Frank pointed out. "The fallout would be much less impactful. I don't think that's our target." The Captain shrugged.

"I'd put it here," Emily said, pointing to a tiny spit of land. "St. Anne Isle," she said firmly. "If it exploded there, it would sweep east and hit a huge swath of Europe."

"But we've just passed that and have seen nothing; just like the other six times we've scanned the area. How on earth could we miss it?" The Captain frowned. Frank's eyes lit up and Emily nodded at him knowingly at the same time.

"The same way we hid Portus," Frank exclaimed. "He hid it right under our noses! There's got to be an overhang, a crevice or something that's shielding it from our radar."

"We need to be looking for any sort of rocky formations. Tell all the ships. And maybe send some divers in the water around Lundy in case we are wrong, but I feel like we need to get to St. Anne's immediately," Emily said. The Captain gave the orders and the ship swung around. Soon, the ship was next to the tiny island and weighing anchor.

Emily and Frank were sent to suit up with the rest of the divers, Emily grumbling to herself that they had to be cumbered down with diving gear they didn't need, but knowing it was necessary to keep their abilities unknown. Ten other divers were preparing to go with them armed with sonar equipment and radars.

"Where are the weapons?" Emily asked them as she pulled on her dive hood. The others laughed at her.

"Whot, ye think ye'll be eaten by a dolphin, miss? We're still in the Channel! There's nuffin out there!" a young man guffawed. Frank stepped forward as the Captain walked in.

"I can guarantee you there is something out there guarding this missile. We are not going down there unarmed," Frank said.

"What kind of armaments do you need, Doctor?" the Captain asked.

"I would take an amphibious rifle, if you have any," Frank said, but the Captain shook his head. "Then a spear gun and diving knives for everyone."

The other divers rolled their eyes at him, but the Captain looked at them sternly and they filed out, returning with a meager supply of spear guns and knives. Frank and Emily took one of each and followed the rest to the deck. The evening sun set the sea on fire, but scarlet clouds to the west threatened rain. They got into two smaller boats that were lowered by pulleys into the water.

"Head to the shore. There's more chance of overhangs there," Frank directed. The motorboats buzzed to life, taking them to the tip of the island. Half of the divers, including Frank and Emily, tipped backwards into the ocean and flipped on their lights. The surf was rough so they pushed down to the seafloor and spread out.

"*Can you hear me, Douglas?*" Emily asked, sending her thoughts his way. Frank nodded. This side of the island was peppered with boulders and the surf pushed them around angrily. The divers worked their way around the rocky point and back toward the sandy bay, but came up with nothing.

"*They have to find something!*" Emily said with mounting frustration. They took the island foot by foot, looking under every rock and outcropping, only finding startled fish and bits of discarded trash for their efforts. After two hours of searching, the divers came back to their starting point and the leader signaled them to surface only to be met with a lashing rain once they got to the top.

The commanding officer shook his head and shouted at Frank, "This is looking like a bust. We should head back."

"We can't," Emily pleaded. "I know it's out here! It *has* to be!"

"We've turned every stone on this isle, mum. There's nothing there, and this storm is getting worse. We're going to lose men if this continues!"

"Sir, we will lose many more men, and women and children, too, if we don't find it," Frank retorted. The officer hesitated, weighing the possibilities, before coming to a decision.

"I'm sorry, but we still have some time, and I won't risk my people when we can wait and try again in an hour or two." A flash of lightning lit up the sky, emphasizing his point. Reluctantly, they let themselves be hauled back into the boats.

"What's that over there?" Frank shouted over the rising wind. He pointed to a heap of rocks sticking up out of the water forming a small, rugged island. Ocean spray was hitting it and throwing foam high into the sky.

"That's just a rocky shoal. Nothing there," the officer shouted.

"We need to check it out!" Emily demanded.

The commander signaled the other boat to head back to the ship. "We'll take a quick look, but nobody is going into the water."

Emily nodded, relieved. They made it out to the island, fighting growing waves with each gust of wind. The storm was getting worse. A slam of the ocean against the rocks blasted upwards and covered them all with icy seawater. The commander wiped droplets from his sonar and shook his head.

"There's nothing down there but rocks," he yelled.

"That's the point," Frank replied, exasperated. "You wouldn't see anything if it was under a rock shelf!"

"I repeat, I don't want to risk my men in this weather. It's going to be dicey getting back on board as it is," he shouted back. "We're headed in!" He pointed at the driver, signaling him to head to the ship. He revved the motor just as Frank and Emily nodded to each other. As the boat took off, they each leaned backwards and fell into the water, swimming hard to get below the propellers. The boat circled back but they headed for the rocks as fast as they could.

"I hope you're right about this, Em. We're gonna have some mad divers to deal with otherwise."

She didn't answer, but dove down lower, following the tumble of boulders to the bottom of the channel. She heard splashes above her and knew at least two divers had followed them down. It wouldn't be safe for the boat to try to anchor in the rough water, so the boat circled overhead impatiently. Frank outpaced her as they got closer to the bottom and started circling the rocky jumble. She couldn't help but wonder what geological calamity dumped this pile of rocks out here so far from the mainland.

Up ahead, Frank dipped around a massive stone and disappeared. She doubled her speed to catch up to him, grabbing the rock and making the turn only to find herself looking into a dark cavity in the rock. A cave! Something raced out like a streak of lightning toward her and abruptly she was face to face with the largest eel she had ever seen. Before she could react, the creature lunged at her, snapping onto her mask and ripping it painfully off her face, one of its razor sharp fangs tearing a line in her cheek. She recoiled, grasping her face as she took in a cold breath of seawater. The eel struggled with her mask in its mouth, whipping its huge head back and forth to loosen it from its jaws and hitting it on the tip of the rock. In the dark recesses of the cave, she could see Frank struggling with a similar creature. She reached for something to defend herself, but realized, cursing her stupidity, they'd left their harpoon guns on the boat.

The creature struck again; this time aiming for her neck. She put her arms up defensively as the creature opened his razor-sharp mouth wide and bit down on both her arms and shook her, tearing at her flesh with fury. She screamed, helplessly kicking at it, but she only made contact with one feeble kick. All she could see in front of her was blood and teeth as the world was spun around her.

Suddenly, the creature jerked its mouth open and flew to the left. She pulled her arms close in, shielding them from further attack. The monster writhed in circles in front of her, spinning up the dark silt around it. She caught sight of a harpoon sticking out of its side. Arms caught her, dragging her to the surface. She protested, screaming for her husband, but the divers only held more firmly to her. Her body began to feel numb from shock, her breaths ragged. She was shoved painfully over the side of the boat into the equally wet weather, coughing out water and sucking in air.

"Douglas is down there! You have to help him!" she screamed as hands tried to staunch the bleeding in her arms.

"Calm down, we're sending more people down. We need to get you to a doctor immediately!"

"No, no don't worry about me. Get Douglas! That thing will kill him," she ranted. "He won't heal like me, he'll die!"

The commander held her down. She felt the engine of the boat rev faster, taking her away from the rock island and toward the ship.

"Please," she sobbed. "Let me go back and help him!" They passed the other boat heading out to the island and the commander issued some quick instructions as they passed, then the boat sped off into the rain.

"Help is headed his way. Try to relax," the man said gently.

Instead, she cried angry tears as they held her down in the bloody, water-filled bottom of the boat.

CHAPTER 58

MALCOLM

MALCOLM HELPLESSLY WATCHED Paul sinking below him, unarmed, into the darkness. His chest where the creature had punctured him was on fire, and his left arm was numb and practically useless. He cursed himself for not being more vigilant, as Paul fell out of view. Suddenly, the line went slack. Paul had let go. Malcolm strained his eyes to see if he needed help, but it was too hard to see. If something came at Paul from below, he couldn't offer any cover without endangering Paul with a stray shot. Regardless of what happened to them, they were this continent's only hope of survival. He decided to take action.

He grimaced, winding the cable once around his waist, tucking it under his wounded arm, and squeezing it against his body to control his descent. He slid downward, keeping the rifle in his good hand, finger poised on the trigger. A few minutes later, an object came into view, rising from the ocean floor. The warhead. He stopped, panning his light slowly around the missile below him. Suddenly, the scaffolding around the site swung hard as if it had been hit.

"Hahn won't be happy if you knock this thing down!" he heard Paul say aloud. Abruptly, a white shape materialized in front of Malcolm. Sinuous and deadly, with a nasty barb protruding from its bulbous head, and teeth

like knife blades, the ghostly creature came toward him like a lightning strike. Malcolm swung the rifle toward it, shooting as he did, but the water impeded his movements and he missed, though the rifle itself caught the creature in its flank as it lunged, deflecting the dangerous barb before it could pierce him again. The thing slid past his ear so closely, he could feel its slick body touch his cheek. He released his hold on the cable, trying to get away from it, feeling the cable fly around his body, unwinding. Abruptly, the cable ended and he was freefalling through the water, arms and legs in a jumble. Above, he caught a glimpse of the thing swimming into the darkness before he hit the warhead, knocking the breath out of him. He swung backwards, caught by the strap of his rifle, banging into the scaffolding surrounding the missile, the rifle almost strangling him as it bit into his neck.

His feet scrambled for a foothold and finally his heel caught and he was able to pull himself upright. The scaffolding shuddered again with an impact, but he held on until it steadied. Paul had to be close. He worked his feet out of the weights and began to creep over the top.

"Paul, I am on the nose cone. What do you need?"

"There's a huge hammerhead thing down here, be careful!" he said. *"If you can get inside the scaffolding, you might be better protected."*

"I think I am safer out in the open. I won't be able to use the gun if I am stuck in there. Besides, that ghost fish is around here somewhere and it is small enough to get through the bars. I will take my chances out here." Malcolm winced as he put too much stress on his wounded shoulder. The pain was creeping across his chest, but he tried to ignore it, as well as the dread about whatever toxins the fish had injected into him. Strangely, the poisonous barb was the least of his problems right now. *"Have you found the access panel yet?"* he asked.

"No luck. Watch out, it's headed your way!"

Malcolm looked over the side and saw a hammerhead swimming straight up the scaffolding toward him. It wasn't nearly as fast as the ghost fish was, but its size was terrifying. Malcolm straddled the nose cone and took aim with the rifle, squeezing the trigger. The first shot went wide, but the second caught the thing in the right eye and it exploded, sending the shark careening off to the side, hurling its shrieks of pain echoing through the water.

"We have to find that access panel!" Malcolm exclaimed in frustration.

"You think?" Paul shot back. *"We're not doing so hot so far. By the way, I think these creatures might be able to understand us."*

Malcolm felt the scaffolding sway and glanced down to see Paul squeezing himself through the bars. He put his hand down on the nose cone to steady himself and quickly removed it when he felt an indentation under his fingers. Turning his light downward, he found a ridge about six inches below the tip of the warhead.

"I may have found it!" Malcolm shouted.

He felt the water move behind him only seconds before the ghost fish raked over him, slicing his wounded shoulder with its razor teeth. He lost his balance, tipping sideways, but caught himself before he fell.

"Get up here, the other one is back!" Malcolm commanded, reaching up with his good hand to inspect the damage on his shoulder. He instantly regretted it, feeling the shredded suit and flesh. At least his shoulder was numb enough it didn't hurt much. Paul reached the top and he handed him the rifle before turning back to the task at hand. He felt along the ridge until he snagged the indentation again, pressing his finger into the socket. A six by six-inch panel swung open and lit up, revealing a display screen and a keyboard under a thick, rubbery, protective cover.

A slash of white raced between them, all teeth and barbs, hitting Paul and sending him tumbling over the side. He felt Paul hit the side and held on as the scaffolding shook once more. The fish spun around to take on Malcolm, its pale flesh almost iridescent in the dim light. He glanced down and tried to punch in the phrase every one of them had so carefully memorized before leaving the United States. *W...a...t...a...* Malcolm barely had time to think as it twisted toward him. He tried to get all the letters typed in, but he didn't have time. The thing opened its jaws, aiming for Malcom. The blood pounding in his neck seemed to be daring the creature to sever his arteries. He slid his dive knife out of its sheath, slashing blindly at the beast as it swam by. Its teeth razed Malcolm's good hand, sending a puff of blood into the water. Malcolm jerked his hand back as he heard a shot ricochet off the scaffolding near him. It didn't get anywhere near the creature circling above but it made the thing hesitate. He took a chance and looked down at the screen, typing, *S...H...I...W..A...*

The thing dove at him again. Paul's head came up over the side of the scaffolding and he shot again, missing, but staving off the attack. The ghost fish sped back into the darkness once more. Malcolm didn't dare hope the thing would stay away, and who knew if the shark was still around here somewhere, wounded, but most likely alive.

Quickly, he typed in the last few letters, *K...A...M...I. Watashi wa kami.* He held his breath, waiting, praying it would work. The screen went blank and Malcolm looked up as Paul crested the top of the scaffolding.

"Is that what it is supposed to do?" Malcolm asked.

"Beats me," Paul replied. The screen flashed brightly for a few seconds and the word 'disabled' appeared. The warhead trembled underneath them, and a hatch opened up about eight feet lower than their perch. The whole structure shuddered as a huge, cylindrical capsule, filled with yellow liquid, was expelled from the body and dropped to the ground with a *thunk.*

"Well, it seems like we turned it off. What are we supposed to do with this?" Paul huffed, throwing his leg over the top rung of the scaffolding. *"Hey, isn't it supposed to be a gas?"* Paul asked, looking concerned.

"When you pressurize gas enough, it becomes a liquid," Malcolm said. He shrugged with his one good shoulder, instantly regretting it, as it hurt too. But then his eyes flew open wide. Behind Paul's head the ghost fish appeared, moving slowly.

"Watch out!" Malcolm shouted. Paul spun around, gun drawn. The creature stared at them with unblinking eyes and moved slowly closer.

"What's it doing?" Paul asked, confused. The creature inched in, winding its overlong tail back and forth. Paul hesitated, lowering the weapon slightly. The fish reared back, baring its fangs in a vicious hiss and lunged toward them. Paul raised the rifle and loosed a shot that went straight through the creature's head. The force of the shot sent it drifting backward and down, trailing gore as it fell to the sea floor.

"What was that thing?" Paul asked in disgust.

"Chimaera, I believe. Or Hahn's version of one."

311

Paul shuddered. *"So what now?"*

Malcolm let out a deep sigh. *"If this contains the mutagen, I don't want to deliver it to anybody. It needs to die down here, agreed? Then the men up top can drop a bomb on the rest of this and bury it for good."*

Paul seemed to consider it for a moment before he nodded his approval. He looked at the rifle.

"We have a couple of shots left in this. How about we do some target practice?"

Malcolm forced his face into a grin. Paul brought the rifle up to his eye and aimed at the pod of swirling yellow mutagen.

"Ready?" Malcolm asked.

"Ready." Paul pulled the trigger and sent a bullet speeding into the pressurized casing. The entire canister imploded instantly into a yellow cloud.

"That was disappointing. I was really hoping after all we went through, that it would explode or something," Paul muttered. Malcolm laughed aloud.

CHAPTER 59

FRANK

FRANK SAW THE cave and his heart did a leap of triumph. They'd found it! He slid past the boulder and into the mouth, pushed by the pulsing tide until he was inside a rounded cavern that must have extended most of the way through the rock island. Steel beams had been installed to reinforce the structure around a deep hole. Well below the surface, the nose of a missile could be seen. He didn't know what he was expecting, but this huge thing wasn't it. The hole went down beyond his sight in the dim light.

His feet lightly touched the ground as he leaned over the hole to get a better look at the warhead. Suddenly he was slammed up against the roof of the cavern. He gasped, trying to catch the breath that was knocked out of him. Something heavy wrapped around his waist and threw him against another wall, sending a shower of debris onto his head. He glanced out the entrance and saw Emily struck by a huge, serpentine creature.

"*No!*" he shouted, launching himself toward her. He was jerked back by one leg and thrown against the wall again, this time hitting his head hard enough to see stars. He curled up out of reflex and saw an enormous eel-like monster, identical to the one attacking his wife, come at him with fangs bared. He dived as the beast rushed him, quickly snatching his dive knife strapped to his thigh. The creature had to turn to avoid the wall, and Frank slashed at the beast as it flew by. He barely caught it, slicing a small gash along its flank, and not accomplishing much more than making it angrier. He heard Emily scream in pain and he turned again to help her, giving the creature the opening it needed. It struck Frank, its bottom teeth catching his lower back, but its top teeth pierced his oxygen tank. It shot out a flurry of bubbles, jetting into the creature's open mouth. It backed up, shaking its head and jerking its teeth loose, retreating into the shadows. Frank pushed his back to the wall, keeping one eye on the creature, the other on his wife. A dart flew through the water and struck the eel attacking his wife, and he almost cried out in relief. The divers made it to her! She looked injured, but he could hear her yelling at them, so he knew she was alive. Freed from that worry, he turned his attention back to the problem he was facing inside the cave.

His oxygen tank burped out its last bubbles, so he yanked off his mask and dropped the extra weight, not caring any longer about divers seeing him. Now, without the needless bulky equipment, he could maneuver. The pain in his back was bad, but he knew it would heal. The real problem was keeping that thing at bay until he disarmed the warhead.

The light was fading fast and he'd lost his flashlight. Frank couldn't be sure if the storm was getting worse, if the sun had gone down, or a mixture of both. Either way, he was grateful when two divers appeared at the entrance to the cave, switching on their lights. He reached out a hand to take one, but the diver jerked back in shock at the sight of him without a mask or an oxygen tank. Frank rolled his eyes. He didn't have time for this. He flashed them the okay sign and put his hand out for the light. The seaman hesitantly handed it over. Frank flashed it into the recesses of the cave where he'd last seen the eel, but it was no longer there.

He motioned them over to the void and pointed his light down, show-ing them the warhead. He could tell they were talking in their intercoms excitedly, but not knowing what they were saying, he tried his best to ges-ture to them. *You, cover us,* he thought, pointing to one of them. *You, come with me.* They nodded as if they understood, and the first man brought his harpoon to bear, facing the hole. Frank and the other man descended, sweeping the area with their flashlights, senses on high alert, trying to find the monster guarding the warhead. *Or monsters,* Frank thought glumly. The diver next to Frank paused, touching his ear. He was getting something, some instructions. The man nodded and gestured to the top of the nose cone, jumping over the gap to land on the warhead. Frank swept the light below them, searching quickly for any unwanted creatures and then followed the man up to the top.

The man gestured to an indentation in the metal and then pushed it with his gloved hand. A door slid open, revealing a small keyboard. The man smiled at Frank, who beamed and gave him a double thumbs up. They'd found it!

Frank kept the flashlight trained on the keyboard and the man reached out a hand to type. As the man touched the keyboard, a swish in the water next to Frank startled them. The eel jetted out of a crevice in the rock, mouth wide open, fangs bared, and took the whole hand of the man into its mouth, biting down hard. The man tried to jerk away, releasing a flurry of bubbles from his mask, but the thing clamped down even harder, yanking hard to the right and tearing the hand completely off. The man let out a muffled scream, backing away from the monster as fast as he could and almost falling down the abyss. The diver above shot a harpoon that narrowly missed hitting Frank. The monster swallowed hard, a lump moving down its thick neck. Frank gagged, scrambling for his knife as the monster finished his bite and turned to take aim at Frank.

Frank took a quick look at the display, but there was no way to get the code typed in time. He glanced up at the diver that was supposed to be covering him, but he was busy trying to get to the wounded man. He braced himself, holding his knife out to ward off the attack as the wounded diver was pulled dragged up and over the rim, leaving Frank alone.

The thing snaked through the water, its pale eyes staring, mouth opening and closing in sync with its breaths. It swiped by Frank and he struck out, missing it completely. The thing's tail flew by, and it spiraled around, coming at him from the back, but Frank twisted, positioning his knife between himself and the beast. It hovered, calculating, darting forward, then quickly back, testing Frank's defenses. It came at him again and he swiped at its face, this time connecting. The beast recoiled with a silent hiss, a slice across the side of its pale face. Frank kept his back to the closest wall so the creature could only attack him from the front or sides, but that wasn't going to accomplish anything long term. He had to think of something else.

Frank felt his way to the tip of the warhead, not daring to take his eyes off the predator facing him. He reached down blindly, feeling around until he found the keypad. The eel backed up as if ready to strike. Frank glanced down and typed the first letters into the keyboard. *Watashi.* The eel struck again, and Frank dodged, kicking sideways off the warhead and slamming into the cavern wall. The eel flew past him and Frank slashed, catching it in the middle and cutting deep. The thing pulled away leaving a trail of red in its wake. Frank raced back to the warhead. *W…a…* he typed in.

The eel was back, swimming awkwardly, but still fast and deadly. It snapped at Frank and withdrew, but as Frank moved toward the keypad for the final word, the thing shot back at him from below, catching his forearm in its razor teeth.

No! Frank screamed, pulling his arm toward him and reaching up with his other hand, sinking his dive knife into the belly of the beast up to its hilt. The eel let go, reeling back, pulling away from the wound, leaving the gory knife in Frank's hand. The eel seemed confused, writhing away down the side of the warhead. Frank ignored his wound, reaching out with his left hand to type in the final word. *Kami.* The screen read 'disarmed' as a whirring below him vibrated up through the warhead. He shot his light down below and saw a huge canister of Mutagen sliding out of a compartment in the side. The shape of the eel sank beside it, twitching as it died. He took in a huge breath of water and swam up to the mouth of the cave.

CHAPTER 60

ZAR

ZAR STOOD OVERLOOKING the deck of an American warship, watching anxiously as a small submarine, with the word "Minnow" painted along the side, was hoisted from the ocean by a heavy steel crane. The crane swung the sub over the deck and settled it into a net cradle. He spoke a few words to the Captain standing next to him, who gestured to soldiers below. They drew their weapons and one man from among them stepped tentatively forward and rapped on the wall of the craft. Zar listened to the creak of the hatch as it swung open and Hahn walked out, clothes wet, hair plastered to his forehead, shielding his eyes from the bright sun, followed by Riggs, Dawes, and two other men. The armed guards surrounded Hahn and prodded him up the stairs to Zar.

"Leave us," Zar said to the Captain and his men. They retreated immediately without question. Zar looked Hahn over appraisingly.

"Hahn, you look surprisingly healthy. Especially for a man who has been adrift under the ocean for over twenty-four hours. The last time I saw you, you looked sickly and pale," he said, trying to keep the disbelief out of his voice. Hahn's bulbous, frog-like eyes were gone; his thin, wispy hair was replaced with a lustrous, full head of black hair. He almost couldn't reconcile the memory of Hahn with the strong, youthful man in front of him, wet and haggard as he might be.

"You searched for me, yet you seem surprised to see me," Hahn said. "Or was the search merely a precaution to make sure you killed me when you destroyed my sub?"

"If I wanted to kill you, you wouldn't be standing here," Zar pointed out. "I sent everything after you, pulled every string to find you. It was the rest of the organization that wants you dead."

"What do *you* want?" Hahn demanded. Zar bristled. Didn't the little creep in front of him realize he wasn't in charge of anything anymore?

"How about instead I'll tell you what I *don't* want. I don't want to rule a dead world! I want the world bowing to me, not choking to death at my feet. What were you thinking, you fool?"

Hahn's face moved into a steely grin. "Threat without reality is useless. Besides, it wasn't my plan to detonate ALL the warheads; just the ones where I didn't receive compliance. Unless I was dead, and in that case, I wanted the entire world to burn behind me."

"Hence your ridiculous countdown."

"Exactly." Hahn sounded smug.

"Well, it doesn't seem to be working out for you. The countdown has begun and soon the world will be dying. Who are you planning to rule then?"

"I can stop them."

"How?"

"Get me to them. I have enough time."

"You're too late," Zar said. For a moment, Hahn looked panicked, and Zar enjoyed the moment before Hahn forced his face back into its confident mask.

"Get to the point," Hahn said sharply.

"The Arydians are working to disarm your warheads."

"Impossible," Hahn scoffed. "Let them try."

"It seems they have a way," Zar said, crossing his arms across his chest. "As a matter of fact, they have already taken down two of them."

Hahn's eyes popped. "Impossible!" he shrieked.

"You keep saying that. Clearly it's possible." Zar was enjoying this immensely. Hahn seemed to pride himself on being one step ahead of everyone. Now who was one step behind? Zar almost wished he could kill Hahn now and get it over with, but he needed him for one last thing.

Hahn's eyes narrowed to slits. "Again, I ask, what do you want?"

Zar rubbed his hands together. Now he was finally catching on. "I want you to make sure the last one, the one aimed at Washington D.C., detonates. Clearly, the Arydians have found a way to disarm them. I need you to stop them. The American government is too full of themselves to submit to outside rule. Take out the east coast and the rest of your mutagen will drift harmlessly out to sea, leaving the rest of the country leaderless and intact, as you well know. As sole surviving member of the Presidential Cabinet, I'll step into the void and become the new leader. With me as President, and the continued threat of the warheads, our plan of creating a one-world government will be easy to achieve."

"What do I get out of this?" Hahn asked.

"Power. Equal to mine. I'll do the politics, you do the science. Each one to their forte. And together we will have the world at our feet, as a team."

"I need to get to New York immediately then," Hahn said curtly.

Zar smiled, his white teeth bright in the darkness. "Transportation has already been arranged." He waved through the window for the Captain to come back in. He and two guards walked through the door.

"Get Hahn to New York," he said. The Captain moved next to Zar and Hahn smiled menacingly, like a cat who'd just caught a mouse. Zar pulled his eyebrows together, feeling nervous for the first time. Why did Hahn keep smiling like that, like he was waiting for Zar to catch up to the punchline of a joke? Zar took an uncertain step away from Hahn, his breath quickening, his eyes widening. He'd been around enough criminals to recognize that look.

Before he could even think to react, Hahn lifted his hand to the Captain and gave him a quick signal. The Captain pulled a knife blade out of his pocket and shoved it into Zar's rib cage. Zar's eyes opened wide with shock and he slid to his knees.

"You...can't!" Zar gasped, his breath dying on his lips as his collapsing lung filled with fluid.

"Power 'equal to yours'? I don't think so. Nobody will be my equal.

You always thought you had more power than me, Zarobi. Look where your ambition got you." Zar reached out his hands to grasp Hahn, wanting nothing more than to wrap them around that scrawny neck and strangle the worthless life out of him, but his body refused to cooperate. He fell further, catching himself with one hand. Hahn stepped back distastefully. "I am only on this ship because I chose to be, it has nothing to do with you."

Zar gurgled, trying to speak. Foamy red blood poured out his mouth. Rushing sounds filled his ears, and darkness closed in on his vision. Still, he reached out with his one remaining hand, straining to hurt Hahn one last time.

"I have people everywhere, Zar. You are nothing but a bad memory." Zar fell to the ground, gasping. Hahn kicked him out of the way and turned to the Captain.

"Well," he said, gesturing to Zar, "you heard the man's dying wish. Get me to New York immediately. And get me a computer. I need to change my codes."

"Yes, sir," the Captain said. Zarobi Akuna panted, trying to save his last seconds of breath, straining against the bonds that death was shackling to him. He felt himself lifted by his hands and feet and carried down the steps. Suddenly, there was a moment of falling, wind rushing around him, red spittle flying up from his face, and then the agonizing slam as he hit the water, pushing the last ounces of precious air from his lungs as he sank to his death.

CHAPTER 61

JAYCEN

JAYCEN RUBBED HIS palms against his thighs nervously as the Captain of the dying U.S. S. Rhode Island embraced the three Arydians at the top of the steps to the flooded engine room. The water level had remained steady but would be chest-high once they descended the stairs. Time had run out and their options hadn't changed, and the last effort at a rescue had ended miserably. There was only an hour and a half left until detonation.

"God bless you all, and may He protect you on this mission," the Captain said solemnly, almost as a benediction. Pete also gave each of them a hug, lingering on Jaycen, unwilling to let him go, so Jaycen patted his back awkwardly. Jaycen still didn't know how he was supposed to feel about this man, but he had grown to respect him over the last few days. He was strong and stoic and cared more about others than himself. He supposed, as far as fathers went, he could have had much worse.

"Pete, how about we go golfing when this is all over?" Jaycen said impulsively into the man's shoulder. Pete stepped back and smiled.

"You like to golf?" he asked in surprise.

"Dunno. Never been."

"I'd like that. Very much, son." Tears glistened in Pete's eyes, and his mouth twitched with the effort of controlling them. Jaycen clapped him one last time on the back and took a few steps down into the black water. Pete and the Captain stepped back and sealed the bulkhead doorway, locking them in, watching them through the thick glass portal. Jaycen turned and took one last look at Pete, hoping they would both live through the day.

Marcos led them down to the bottom of the steps, swimming to the bulkhead wall, and slipping on dark goggles. "Look away, this will be bright." Marin moved back with Jaycen and the equipment, and they closed their eyes while Marcos lit up the welder. Jaycen turned his back to Marcos and opened his eyes slightly. Bright rainbows of light flickered on Marin's face and closed eyes. His heart caught in his throat as he wondered what kind of future, if any, he had with her.

She'd been so kind to him as he dealt with the family bombshells he'd been dealing with, he couldn't help but dream of a future with her. But he knew if she truly loved Marcos, she should be with him. He could accept that, if it weren't for the way she looked at him sometimes. He wondered if she thought about the almost-kiss as much as he did. He'd given up on hating Marcos. He was a decent guy. A good guy. Perfect in every way, except one...his love for Marin. But he couldn't even blame him for that, just resent it.

The flashing stopped and Marin opened her eyes to see Jaycen staring at her. There, there was that look again. His heart started pounding and impulsively he grasped her hand, squeezing it.

"Marin, in case...you know..."

"Inner hull is breached. Jaycen can you help me move it out of the way?" Marcos called, sounding irritated, as if he could hear him. He didn't finish his sentence, but he hoped she could see it in his eyes. Marin squeezed his hand back, and he released it reluctantly before he turned to help Marcos. The metal weighed a ton, and it took precious time and all of their strength to maneuver it out of the hole Marcos had cut. Finally, it fell to the side with a heavy thump.

"This next one will be more dangerous. It's already bulging inward. Hold on to something," Marcos said.

Jaycen went back to the stair rail and held on with Marin near the pile of underwater scooters and weapons the crew had assembled for them.

Marcos lit the welder and made his first cut. Water gushed in, throwing Marcos back against the stairs and extinguishing the welder.

"This is it..." Marcos said nervously. Jaycen cast a glance up the steps, hoping to see Pete one last time, but he was gone, hopefully far away from the breach they were making. The ship rumbled, trying valiantly to withstand the pressure when suddenly the wall tore open, sending a torrent of water blasting through the room. Jaycen felt as if he were in a washing machine, ripped from the stair railing and thrown hard against the wall. He covered his head with his arms to protect himself from anything hitting him.

"Aaaagh!" he shouted as something bashed into his back and he stiffened, waiting for the end to come. This was it; the ship was going to implode and crush them all and they were going to die! Sparks flew and were immediately extinguished as equipment shorted. All the lights blacked out and they were left in total darkness except the blue light coming through the ripped hull. Water filled the room, racing into every last crevice, and when it had nowhere left to go, spun slower and slower, until it finally stilled, leaving the room filled with ghostly bits of floating debris and sand.

Jaycen uncurled, wincing at the pain in his back. *Crap!* he muttered to himself. Just what he needed, a broken rib or two! It hurt whenever he took a deep breath. He shrugged it off, resolving to just not breathe deeply. He flipped on his headlamp, searching the room for his companions. Marin was splayed out on the stairway as if she had been pushed against the railing through the whole ordeal. He rushed over to her.

"Are you hurt?"

She seemed dazed but shook her head no. *"Where's Marcos?"* she asked. They searched the flooded compartment for him, picking up pieces of equipment that had been scattered along the way. They found him pinned beneath the piece of metal he had cut away, near the gaping wound in the hull.

"Need a hand, there?" Jaycen asked lightly. Marcos grimaced. The three of them pushed the chunk off him and Jaycen helped him get upright. A gash ran across his chest through his wetsuit, but otherwise he seemed unharmed. Marin swam up the stairs to the doorway and looked in. It seemed the door held.

323

"It worked!" she called down to them.

"Great, let's go! We have…" he glanced at his dive watch, *"just forty-five minutes until detonation,"* Jaycen said, turning on his scooter. Thankfully, it still worked, despite the beating it had just received. It looked like they lost one of the harpoon guns. Marin's scooter had a shard of metal sticking out of it and it wouldn't start. Jaycen tinkered with it and finally gave up.

"You'll have to share with one of us," he said, taking her hand and leading her out the jagged hole and into the open water, but frowned as she cast Marcos an apologetic look over her shoulder. It was daylight and the water was bright. From outside, they could see the extent of the sub's damage better. Three-fourths of the craft rested on the crest of the canyon, with the nose hanging perilously over the edge.

They motored down the canyon walls into the darkness.

"I'm starting to see a pattern here," Marin said.

"Huh?" Jaycen answered.

"The last time I escaped a sub, I hid out in a canyon. Seems like de ja vu."

"Hahn must like hanging around canyons," Marcos said simply. *"Deeper, safer for him. He can go anywhere as long as he's deeper than anybody else."*

"Like a snake hiding out where nobody can get him. Makes sense," Jaycen said.

"But the sub he kept me on seemed like a normal sub. How come he could go deeper than the military?" Marin asked.

"I think we can assume he has better tech than the military at this point. I mean, we do. Our skimmers are much faster than these things. Landys just don't know how to design stuff for deep water."

"Watch it, water boy," Jaycen laughed at him. Marin shot him a confused look.

"How are we supposed to find this thing?" Jaycen asked after several hundred feet of diving. The canyon walls rose around them like giant monoliths, casting them into shadow. High above them they could still see the nose of the stranded sub peeking over the edge like a curious dog.

"I can find it," Marin remarked. *"I saw it in Hahn's mind."* This time it was Jaycen's turn to give her a confused look, but she stared straight ahead, so he looked over to Marcos, who shrugged. The bottom of the canyon got

closer, and Jaycen started noticing cracks in the chasm walls twisting into darkness.

"*Aaron could be hiding in any one of these offshoots, guys,*" Jaycen said, the hair on the back of his neck beginning to raise.

"*I see it!*" Marin shouted, pointing. Near the base of the canyon wall, a cylinder appeared, pointing toward the surface. Jaycen felt his pulse begin to race. If Aaron was going to come for them, it would be soon.

"*Promise me one thing,*" Marin said quietly into their minds. "*We are almost out of time. The goal is the warhead. We are secondary. If one of us gets hurt or caught, the others will still go forward and disarm the warhead. Agreed?*" Reluctantly, Jaycen agreed, followed by Marcos, though secretly he wondered if he could keep going if the one that got hurt or caught was Marin.

CHAPTER 62

MARCOS

MARCOS KEPT ALL his senses alert, pulling ahead of Jaycen and Marin. He had lived in the ocean for years and suspected he had a better grasp than the other two of how to tell if there were predators near. Plus, Aaron was his friend, and he hoped that if they ran into him, that part of Aaron would override any desire Hahn placed in his mind to kill them. The warhead loomed up closer and he could tell there was some form of metal skeleton around it, supporting it. The light was even dimmer here in the abyss, but directly behind the warhead was a circular blackness he couldn't quite make out. His pulse quickened as he realized what it was.

"*Cave!*" he shouted, pointing ahead. The ocean trembled. Something big was moving. His heart sank and he tensed, waiting for his friend, the monster, to appear. A rounded head and a dozen tentacles jetted out of the blackness toward them. Marcos quailed at the sight. The harpoon gun in his hand looked like a toy.

The creature bridged the distance to them in seconds, reaching grasping tentacles out to them.

"*Aaron!*" Marcos cried out in desperation. "*Aaron, stop! It's me! Marcos!*" Aaron slowed, letting his momentum carry him toward them.

A rumbling, surprised voice met him. *"Marcos?"* Hope swelled in Marcos's heart.

"Yes, yes it's me, your buddy Marcos!"

"Why…why are you here?" Aaron shook his head, as if stung. *"You can't be here."*

"I came to see you, buddy. I want to…" he trailed off, looking for an excuse to be here that didn't draw attention to their mission. Marin and Jaycen slowly inched to either side of the massive creature, closer to the warhead. *"I…want to help you."* Go, go, go, he thought to the other two. They were almost beneath him now.

"You can't be here Marcos. Nobody can." Aaron's voice sounded so flat, so depressed, it broke Marcos's heart. How could Hahn have been so cruel to him? Marin and Jaycen split up to go around Aaron's huge form.

"Not even your friend?" Marcos pushed, trying to distract him.

"I can't. You have to leave. Now!" Aaron said, his huge, misshapen face contorting as if in pain.

"I want to help you," Marcos repeated.

Aaron shrieked, the sound deafening, echoing off the canyon walls and making rocks tumble around them. *"You can't help me. If you stay, he'll make me kill you!"* Marin was behind him now with Jaycen close behind. If they could just make it to the warhead…

"You don't want to kill me, I'm your friend! I want to help you!" Marcos exclaimed. Just then, Marin's scooter made an odd popping sound and stopped. Aaron spun, surprisingly fast for his size, and wrapped a tentacle around Marin's waist. She screamed.

"YOU!" he roared, shaking her. Jaycen paused and Marcos could see indecision fighting across his face.

"Stop! You're hurting her!" Marcos commanded. Aaron twisted to face him.

"You care more about her than you ever cared about me," Aaron snarled, shaking Marin in front of him. Her eyes were wide with panic.

"AARON! Please! I'll do anything you want. Just please, don't hurt her!"

Aaron stopped, considering. *"Go, Jaycen, hurry!"* Marcos thought.

Jaycen started moving toward the warhead again. A thin tentacle appeared and flicked him sideways, knocking him into the wall of the canyon. Jaycen hit with a small avalanche of rocks. Another tentacle dug him out and brought him forward.

"Who is this guy?" Aaron demanded, his voice low and threatening. *"You're not here to help me. You're here to hurt me!"*

"Stop, Aaron! He's...he's my friend, too. His name is Jaycen," Marcos murmured.

"A Landy?" Aaron said like a curse. *"He smells like a Landy."* Marin looked like she was having trouble breathing in Aaron's crushing grip.

"Please, Aaron, you're hurting her!"

Aaron's eyes narrowed to slits. *"You'll do anything, Marcos?"*

"Anything. Please, please don't hurt them." A wicked smile spread across Aaron's wide mouth. He shoved Jaycen and Marin out in front of Marcos like two toy dolls.

"Choose."

"Wha...." Marcos stammered, searching his brain for some way out of this. *"What do you mean, choose?"*

"You say the Landy is your friend?" Marcos nodded apprehensively. *"And we know how you feel about this one,"* Aaron said, wagging Marin back and forth. *"Let me see what you really think of your...friend. Choose which one I should kill. Then maybe I'll let you go."*

Marcos searched the faces of his friends, desperate to find a way out of this horrific situation. Marin shook her head no, and Jaycen's face hardened with determination. He knew which one Jaycen wanted him to pick.

"Either way, I lose, Aaron. I don't want anyone to die."

Aaron's expression hardened. *"The last time you chose, someone DID die! My mother, torn in half by someone who loved her. Did you care about that?"* He roared. *"You could have gone to help them, our people, my mother. But you chose her!"* he shrieked, lifting Marin high above him as if he meant to dash her to the ground.

"NOOOOOO!" Marcos screamed, throwing his arms out as if that could stop him. Marin splayed her hands out on the rubbery surface around her, the water whipping her hair crazily and she began to glow with a bluish

aura. Just as Aaron started his downward thrust, an electric pulse jerked him, blue lightning crackling around his skin.

"*Agh!*" He wailed, dropping Marin and bringing all his tentacle to his face. Jaycen wriggled out of the loosened arm and swam toward Marin who seemed to be struggling to swim.

Marcos kicked his scooter into high gear and sped over to them. Marin was gasping for breath. Jaycen supported her with one arm.

"*I'll be fine! We need to get to the warhead, now! We've only got a few minutes left!*" Marin gasped.

"*You two go, I'll try to keep him distracted,*" Marcos offered, but Marin shook her head.

"*Let me try,*" Marin insisted. "*I think I can help him.*"

"*I'll stay with her, you go,*" Marcos said. Jaycen nodded uncertainly, but he took off toward the rocket.

Aaron flexed and unflexed his tentacle, grumbling to himself.

"*Aaron,*" she said gently. Marcos felt waves of comfort emanating from her, like a warm breeze. "*Aaron, let me see your hurt arm,*" she said. Aaron held it close to himself for a moment, then, surprisingly unrolled it toward her. Was she actually manipulating his feelings? Marcos stared at her in awe. They had joked about the idea before, but he hadn't thought it was real. And the electricity, whatever she used on Aaron….that was *definitely* real. It was hard to believe, but he had seen it with his own eyes, and he could feel it, pulsing around her, this feeling of calm, of comfort.

"*Does it still hurt?*" she asked, her voice soft and soothing. Aaron nodded his massive head.

"*NO!*" She heard Jaycen shouting in anger. "*The code doesn't work! He's changed it!*"

Suddenly, Aaron snapped his arm away from her and spun to attack Jaycen.

"*Jaycen, move!*" Marcos shouted. Jaycen kicked away from the warhead just as Aaron approached it, tentacles shooting out to him. He ducked into a crevice, swimming as fast as he could. Aaron slammed against the wall, sending a shower of rocks down around him.

"*Jaycen!*" Marin screamed.

Aaron kept digging into the wall, trying to reach Jaycen. Marin ventured forward.

"*Aaron?*" she asked, sending out waves to him that Marcos couldn't help but feel. "*Aaron, don't you want to help us? We have to destroy the warhead, Aaron or many people will die.*"

Aaron spun toward her, his face in a snarl. "*The bomb? Nobody can destroy it! I have to protect it!*"

"*But why, Aaron? Why can't you help us? I know you don't want people to die,*" she said. Aaron came close to her with his face.

"*Don't you get it, cousin?*" he spat. "*I HAVE to protect it. I have no choice!*" he picked up a boulder as if to throw it at the warhead, but before he even got it over his head, he shook as if shot with a thousand volts of electricity. "*AAAAAGGGHHH!*" he screamed, his massive body shaking. Rocks crumbled around them. Jaycen pushed through a tumble of dirt and emerged from his hiding place, and Marcos sighed in relief. Jaycen was okay. For now. When the shaking stopped, Aaron looked at them in anguish.

"*He knows! He knows when I even think about disobeying him. And he punishes me! You can't imagine the pain I feel!*"

"*Aaron, what if I could break the thing that hurts you?*" Marin asked. Aaron pulsed closer to her, looking hard at her as if he didn't believe her.

"*How?*"

"*With electricity…I could touch you with it and try to short out the circuit…*"

"*NO!*" he roared. "*It would HURT!*"

"*But maybe it would stop it from hurting again! Forever! Isn't it worth a try?*"

Aaron nodded and Marin swam close to his head. Marcos stared in awe as Marin began to glow once more, her hands sparkling with power. Aaron closed his eyes and leaned away, but she touched him, jolting him with power.

Aaron screeched, his tentacles flailing, and Marin swam as fast as she could towards Marcos.

"*NOOOO! It hurts! You hurt me!*" he yelled, shaking the water with his voice.

"*Did it work, Aaron? Can you see if it worked?*" Marin said gently, sending out her waves of comfort. Aaron opened his eyes and tried to hit the warhead. He hit an invisible wall and screamed in pain.

"It didn't work!" he cried in despair. He sounded so lost and broken that Marcos almost couldn't stand it. But they *had* to find a way to stop the warhead. Time was running out.

Aaron turned his eyes to Marcos. *"Is there a way to change me back, Marcos? I'm sorry I hurt you, Marcos. I'm sorry, I didn't want to hurt anyone. He makes me do it. But I don't want to be like this anymore. I want to go home!"*

Marcos moved closer to Marin, shaking his head. Jaycen whispered to the both of them, *"The timer said there was only eighteen minutes left until detonation."*

"What are we going to do?" Marin asked in dismay.

"Can you get him to break it, or block it or something?" Jaycen asked. Marin turned back to Aaron.

"Aaron, if you could break it, would you?" Aaron nodded and was hit with another blast, leaving him gasping in great breaths of water when it stopped. Marin looked at him in pity.

"Aaron, can you…can you even touch the warhead?" she asked.

Aaron looked at her, puzzled for a moment, then reached out a tentacle, touching the smooth metal surface. *"Yes, I can touch it,"* he said.

"Can you…push it?" she asked. Aaron put pressure on it and started convulsing in pain, his tentacles constricting as the waves pulsed through him.

"Stop hurting me!" he roared at her. Jaycen looked at his dive watch.

"Fifteen minutes," he said. Marcos searched his brain for any options, panic pounding in his ears. Suddenly, a horrible thought hit him.

"Aaron, can you…hold it?" Marcos asked, his voice cold and shaky. Part of him prayed the answer was no.

Aaron blinked his large eyes at him. He wrapped his body around the warhead and then let go. Marcos caught Marin's eye, willing her to read his mind. She blanched as she realized what he wanted Aaron to do. Jaycen's jaw dropped in shock. Marcos tried to ignore them. He tried to ignore everything except the only option they had.

"Help me…please?" he begged Marin, hating himself for what he was asking. Her face contorted in anguish, but she poured all her emotions into Aaron.

"*Aaron, I…I want you to hold it. Can you hold it, tight, for a few minutes?*"

"*Why?*" he asked, eyeing her skeptically.

"*Aaron, I need you to help us. Can you help us?*" she begged. Marcos could tell it was taking every ounce of energy she had to impose her feelings on him.

"*I…want to help. But what if the bomb goes off?*"

Marcos touched her hand and suddenly he could feel Marin trying to control her racing heart, to send out calm feelings, to let him know it would be okay, but her own knowledge kept breaking in. Aaron's face grew somber.

"*If I hold it and it explodes, I'll die. You…you are asking me to die? You… want…me to die?*" Aaron asked in disbelief.

Marin almost lost her nerve. "*No, Marcos, there has to be another way!*" Marcos squeezed Marin's hand, living everything along with her.

"*Ten minutes,*" Jaycen said quietly.

"*Hurry,*" Marcos whispered to her, trying to send strength he didn't have.

Marin resumed her thoughts. "*Aaron, I want to help you. If you do this, the pain will be over, I promise. You'll never hear the voices again.*" Marcos choked back the guilt, the anguish of what they were asking this poor kid to do.

"*It won't hurt anymore?*" he asked. That was something she could guarantee with certainty, so she poured all her feelings into that one hope. "*I promise, there won't be pain anymore. Hahn will never bother you again. He made you do terrible things, he made you destroy your home, kill people, wound your friends, even people you've never met. Now he wants you to hurt the world. If you don't do this, he will keep on hurting you and making you hurt others for as long as you live.*"

Aaron stared at them.

"*I… don't want to die! I just want to go home. I want my mom, my hands, my arms, my body back! I want to go back to Portus before you ever came there.*" His plaintive cry stung them all to the soul. He could feel Marin's heart ache, knowing she could probably heal him, give him what he was begging for…his life, his body back, but knowing he *had* to stay like this to stop the warhead.

"I'm sorry, Aaron. We don't want you to die either. But you can't go home. Your mom is gone. Your body is gone. Portus is gone. There is no way back. And Hahn will never, never stop the pain. I promise you that. I'm so sorry, Aaron. It's not fair. It's not right. I wish I could think of another way, but we are running out of time. I'm asking you to be braver than you should have to be. But this is one way you punish Hahn for everything he has done to you and keep him from destroying the rest of the world." Marin concentrated, and Marcos could feel her trying to sending him feelings of resolve, bravery, anything the poor boy could use to make this horrible decision. Finally he nodded.

"Do you...do you think I'll see my mom again?" he asked softly.

"I really do, Aaron. I think she'll be waiting for you, as proud as a mom can be." Aaron nodded slowly and moved toward the warhead. *"You guys should get out of here,"* he said sadly. They paused, and then started to swim upwards when Aaron stopped, panic written all over his face. Marcos held his breath, willing him the courage to go on, but he could feel him wavering.

"I...I can't do this! I'm scared! I don't want to die alone!"

For a moment they all stared at each other, each of their veins turning to ice. Marcos saw fear taking shape in both Jaycen's blue eyes and Marin's green ones, but she acted before either of them could speak.

"It's okay, Aaron. I'll stay with you," she said, pulling away from the others.

"No Marin, you can't!" Jaycen protested, Marcos echoing his objections, but Aaron interrupted them.

"I don't want you," he said. *"I... I want him."* Aaron pointed a tentacle at Marcos. Marin's pale face blanched even more, and she fell apart.

Aaron waited expectantly. *"He was my best friend before you came and ruined it all. He chose you last time; this time I want him to choose me."*

"No, you can't take him!" she cried. Aaron's face began to falter. It was falling apart.

Marcos felt like his limbs were frozen, but he moved close to Marin, enveloping her in his arms. *"It has to be this or nothing,"* he whispered for her alone to hear. *"We don't have time for another solution. We don't...have... time."* His words caught in his chest. *He* didn't have time. This was it. This was the end of his life. Could he really do this, give everything away, his hopes, his dreams, his breath, his body, for people he never even met? Yet

333

weren't they asking the same of Aaron, a kid, used by people his whole life: manipulated by Leviathan, stabbed in the back by them, twisted and tortured. If they were asking Aaron to die, he *had* to do it. The choice was made.

He held Marin close, not able to force his arms from around her. He bent down his head and kissed her, feeling that rush of oneness one last time, seeing glimpses of her life, sharing all that he had, all that he was with her. Pouring his heart and memories into hers like a life raft, hoping for some form of safety.

"Give us strength, please?" he begged. *"And…remember me,"* he whispered to her, finally finding the strength to let go. She held on, eyes wide with fear.

"No, Marcos, no. Please, no!" she cried, fingers digging into his arms. Marcos almost wavered for a moment, but he looked at Jaycen.

"Get her out of here!" he said, ripping her hands off him and shoving her toward him. *"And take care of her…for me."* Jaycen closed his eyes tightly and opened them again, nodding. He wrapped his arms around her waist and swam as fast as he could, dragging her screaming away from the canyon. Marcos swam toward Aaron and laid a hand on him. Aaron wrapped himself around the warhead, almost obscuring it with his bulk and dug his tentacles into the canyon wall, anchoring himself.

"Come on, buddy. Let's go see our moms."

CHAPTER 63

MARIN

THIS WASN'T HOW it was supposed to end! It wasn't fair! She couldn't move, couldn't think. Marin was almost delirious with shock and grief as Jaycen pulled her away from Marcos. She fought to keep the connection with Marcos, sending him comfort and hope she couldn't feel herself, trying to hang on to the seconds they had left. Jaycen checked his watch and turned them down into one of the many canyons branching off from the main channel. She didn't know how long they had left. Each second felt like an eternity as she concentrated as hard as she could, curled almost into fetal position with her effort.

"Hold on, Aaron, hold on. It's going to be okay soon," she cried over and over.

Jaycen just kept swimming, dragging her, probably trying to find a safe place to hide from the blast. He stopped in a crevice with sturdy looking walls.

Marin was sobbing helplessly. Jaycen wrapped his arms around her and wedged them into the gap, but she could barely feel him, or the rocks scraping against them. She didn't resist. Maybe the rocks would bury them all and end this pain. She clung to Jaycen, waiting, trying to block out the awfulness of two innocent people freely giving their lives away when she heard Marcos speak one last time.

"I love you, Marin. It's going to be okay."

Suddenly the ocean shook. Marin screamed Marcos's name as he was ripped away from her mind, her heart feeling like it was being torn out of her chest. The connection with Marcos was gone. She felt him die. He was gone and nothing mattered anymore. Jaycen held her even closer, as if bracing for the shock wave that came almost immediately. The water blasted around them, shaking the canyon walls in a massive earthquake. The water tore at them, slamming them into the walls and knocking the breath out of both of them.

Marin caught a glimpse of the ocean bulging above them in a yellow concussive wave that rained silt and debris all over them. Then, as soon as it started, it stopped, leaving them floating in a choppy aftermath. Marin drifted limply, completely empty of emotion.

"Marin!" Jaycen cried in concern. She shook her head but couldn't speak. He wrapped her arm around his shoulders, towing her upward like she was injured. She let herself be dragged, unable to help. It was like she had completely shut down.

Jaycen swam up the steep canyon wall, pumping his legs hard for the both of them.

"I can't see the submarine. Hope it survived the blast," he murmured.

Marin barely noticed the ocean open up as they reached the top of the abyss, but suddenly, a bullet ripped through Jaycen's side. He dropped Marin in surprise, contracting around the wound. She floated away from Jaycen, her mind struggling to comprehend what just happened. A man was speeding toward them, some kind of rifle in his hand. Jaycen held one hand over his wound, reaching out to Marin. She lifted her hand to his, but froze in terror as the man stopped in front of them, leveling the gun at Jaycen's head. It couldn't be him! Marin glanced upward and saw a large boat floating above them on the surface, waiting.

Hahn had found them. Jaycen tried to straighten up, but the bullet wound kept him tight and helpless. Hahn killed Marcos, and now he was seconds away from killing Jaycen. She sucked in a deep, strengthening breath, her tortured soul turning to stone.

"I don't know how you destroyed my warhead, but it won't matter, at least

to you," Hahn said bitterly. He cocked the rifle, but before he could pull the trigger, Marin dove between them.

"You've killed enough innocent people today, Hahn. It's me you want, isn't it?" she said.

Hahn looked surprised by her. *"Aren't you the brave one now?"* he asked, as if strangely proud of her transformation. *"As I said before, I don't really need you anymore. But I will admit, you made a lovely pet.* He smiled at her, making her want to kick his face in.

"Leave him alone! I'll go with you," she shouted bitterly.

"No, Marin, don't!" Jaycen groaned.

"Oh, I don't think you are in a position to give me demands, my pet. One twitch from my finger, and he's dead anyway. And I still have you."

"But wouldn't it be easier if I just came with you peacefully?" she asked, lacing her words with trust, but Hahn didn't seem fazed.

"Oh, my dear, that is so…intoxicating about you. I love the emotions you force upon me. Truthfully, I crave them. They are all so intense, like flavors from a master chef. But don't be foolish enough to think I don't see them for what they are…a mere distraction." He lowered the gun and shot her through the thigh. She screamed, pressing her hands to the wound. Jaycen yelled, trying to get closer to her, but Hahn pointed the gun at his head once more.

"I can just wound you enough that you can't fight back and still take you with me. You'll heal in plenty of time for me to wound you again. And again. And again!" His eyes flashed with insane hunger. *"Until I grow tired of your screams. You think you've destroyed me? You think you've saved anything? I have resources the world over. I can make a new Aaron. I can create this mutagen again. I will reign on this earth and there is nothing you can do to stop me!"*

Jaycen straightened slightly, and Marin glanced at him, but quickly turned back to Hahn, hoping to keep his attention off Jaycen and the gun aimed at his forehead.

Marin's blood was pooling around her leg but she ignored the pain, knowing it would heal, and glared at Hahn with all the hatred in her soul. Her fingers glowed blue and little strings of electricity wormed into the water from her hands.

"No you don't. Or your sweetheart here dies." He gestured to Jaycen. Her

337

gaze dropped and the aura dissipated. *"Interesting. I may have to bring him along. You may tolerate your own pain, but I wonder how well you'd like to see your friend here suffer. That would indeed add a new depth to our sessions."*

Marin was running out of options. Empathy wasn't doing anything. Electricity wasn't going to work. She let her shoulders fall in defeat, drifting ever so slightly closer to Hahn. The gun trained on Jaycen was in his right hand, but his left hand was free. She lunged toward his free hand, grabbing it with both her hands, not knowing if it would work. She felt his surprise as she forced her way into his waking mind, pushing through and rummaging around like a looter until she found what she was looking for, like a dark wall. His subconscious. She felt fear building behind the wall and took purposeful strides toward it. The ground around her feet pushed backward against her, his mind trying to expel her from within it.

"Sleep," she said, shutting down his conscious mind like flipping off a light. She felt his resistance fade, but a new energy was building behind the wall. He could remember now, how he experienced this before, and he was preparing to fight back. Good, she thought. She felt up to a fight. In fact she wanted one. She got to the wall and pushed through it like a thick, black spider web. Beyond the wall stood the same ragged little boy that was in his last dream. He stared at her, his arms crossed, defiant. The jungle was quiet and empty this time.

"You can't hurt me here," small Hahn said in his freakish man's voice. "This is *my* mind! Get out!" She felt a force pushing against her, like an invisible wind. The grass beneath her feet moved backward, sliding her back toward the wall.

Marin took in a deep, angry breath, gathering her strength. She was raw, wounded inside, and she fed it, taking it all and forging it into a massive ball of fury. She was done being afraid of this piece of garbage.

"I can do anything I want to here, Hahn. This is *my* domain, not yours. And this time, no one is here to save you." She saw fear flash in the kid's eyes. He knew she spoke the truth, but that didn't mean he wouldn't fight back. The kid threw out his hands at her, and rocks flew out from his fingers, pelting her and pounding divots in the tall grass. She flinched, throwing up an invisible barrier.

When the barrage stopped, the kid was gone. She followed, racing after him inhumanly fast, deeper into the dark forest of his mind. The kid flitted among the shadows, hiding now. Marin formed a shield around herself, walking confidently through the trees like a panther stalking her prey. She could feel him around here, but he was concealed, out of sight, watching her. She bent and picked up a stick, throwing it to the ground. It moved, growing bigger, transforming into a huge serpent with a thick, sinuous body. The snake lifted its head off the ground, tongue flicking in and out, tasting the air, then it struck, wrapping itself around a tree and pinning the boy to it.

"You can't kill me, an innocent boy," Hahn cried, contorting his face into a pathetic grimace.

"Don't you ever get tired of underestimating me, Hahn? There are no books written for this new world we've created. I'm a whole new species. And you are no innocent!" she pointed a finger at him and he melted into the man version of Hahn.

"A truly innocent boy gave his life today, and someone I love with him. And it's for them and all the innocent people who have suffered at your hands that I do this, Hahn." She flung her hands up, making the trees quake with her power, wind whipping her hair, fire burning in her eyes. Hahn squirmed against the pressure of the snake holding him to the tree, but it was no use. Marin reached into the air and a branch flew into the palm of her hand. She caught it without looking, stretching it, growing it, extending the point to a razor-sharp barb.

"I felt him die, Hahn! I stayed with him, connected to him until the very end. I felt him ripped from my mind, my heart and my life. Do you know what that's like?

"No! Please! Have mercy!" Hahn screamed, his eyes wide.

Marin's eyes grew dark, blue lightning crackling from the tips of her hair and fingers. "Mercy is for the merciful," she spat. With both hands she hefted the spear above her head and plunged it into Hahn's heart, burying it in the trunk of the tree. The world flew into a maelstrom, darkness filling the sky, as if the world itself was dying and in the throes of agony. Marin forced herself to let go of the spear, and instantly, she was back in the water, letting go of Hahn's arm. He twitched, convulsed and finally relaxed, drifting down into the water. Jaycen caught the gun as it fell from his limp hand and trained it on him, looking like all he wanted was an excuse to use it. He looked at Marin questioningly, oblivious to what had just happened, but she couldn't answer. She just watched his inert body sink into the abyss and disappear. It was only then she remembered Jaycen had been hurt.

"Are you okay?" she asked, hurrying over to look at him. The wound was knitting itself back together as she watched.

"I'll be fine. Are you?" he asked, his eyes full of concern. She shook her head, wishing she could forget everything that had just happened, wishing, like poor Aaron, that she could go back to the before. The time when all she had to worry about was passing her dive test and whether or not Jaycen had a crush on her. She just wanted to go home, sit and watch a movie with Uncle Paul on a Saturday night, eating popcorn and drinking root beer like before she ever went to COAST, before everything changed.

"Let's get out of here," Marin said finally. *"I'm sick of the water."*

CHAPTER 64

MARIN

J AYCEN AND MARIN paused to check on the sub, which was pushed several feet away from the rim of the abyss and was lying on its side. Jaycen beat on the hull with a rock and waited breathlessly until they heard a quiet hammering in response. Someone was alive in there. They raced to the surface of the water to get them help.

Late morning light made the waves glitter like silver, even though a crisp breeze carried the coolness of fall in its embrace. Marin wondered how the world could keep on revolving as if nothing had even happened. She felt as if part of her soul had been destroyed and she was going to have to keep on moving without it, like an amputee who suddenly lost a leg. The trauma was so fresh, she felt numb and disjointed.

Red and blue lights flashed from a ring of police boats in a perimeter around them, blocking off all ocean access to New York and New Jersey. Jaycen threw his hands in the air, yelling until he caught the attention of one of the patrolling boats. They tread water until the boats got close enough to haul them on board. Marin was grateful for the help, as it took all her energy to keep breathing in and out and moving her legs to walk.

A police officer put a blanket around both of them and someone placed a cup of something warm in Marin's hands. She didn't drink it, just held it in her shaking hands, looking out over the bay while the boat bumped over the waves, carrying them to shore. She let Jaycen take care of the details: getting clearance to talk to the military, getting routed to the right person, and finally being picked up by a car to take them to a secure building at Fort Hamilton. She didn't care where they were going. It didn't matter now. The fight was over and her fight was gone.

They were placed in the corner of a room with large windows and a bunch of important-looking people bustling around them, trying to figure out how to raise the sub from the rim of Hudson Canyon. They could see and hear everything going on, but everyone either looked at them distrustfully or ignored them completely. She couldn't help but wonder how many of them even knew who or what they were, or why they were here.

Unbidden, one of her first memories of Marcos came to mind, of him telling her he was a farmer, growing plants on the seafloor to support the colony. Althos Beta. She smiled, remembering the time he fed her a strange berry that changed the way she tasted food when they were on Isla Cedros. She let out a short hiccup of a laugh that caught in her throat and turned into wracking sobs. Tears ran down her face uncontrollably, bleeding her pain down as if it would never end. Jaycen put his arm around her, pulling her close enough that she could lean her head on his shoulder. People stared out of the corner of their eyes as they passed by, but she didn't care. Jaycen didn't say anything; there was nothing *to* say. But he lent her his quiet strength and for that she was grateful. Her thoughts spun around the last few hours, no matter how hard she tried to suppress them, and with every memory a fresh wave of tears assaulted her.

Aaron was gone, a kid who never had a chance in life, who gave his life to save people he'd never met. And Marcos, the kindest, saddest person she had ever known, was gone for the sake of friendship. The worst part was, she honestly didn't know if anyone would ever know what they sacrificed to save these people, to save the world. If the Arydians were supposed to be kept a secret, she doubted anyone would know the truth about what happened. Somehow that made the loss even worse.

An older man in a uniform stopped and handed her a box of Kleenexes and a sympathetic smile before rushing off on whatever errand he was on. Marin cried until her tears were spent and she felt like she didn't have another ounce of water in her body. At some point she closed her eyes, leaning into Jaycen's sturdy frame, and fell asleep.

A few hours later, she awoke to excited exclamations coming from everyone in the command center. The emotions in the room were palpable, as the latest attempt to bring up the U.S.S. Rhode Island was initiated. Two other subs arrived while she slept and they had been able to harness the Rhode Island between the two vehicles. They were slowly moving toward the surface. Jaycen leaned forward, watching a large screen showing the viewpoints of both subs, as everyone in the room tensed with each passing minute. After about a half hour of breathless waiting, the subs breached the surface of the bay. The entire room erupted into triumphant shouts. Jaycen's shoulders relaxed visibly, and he flashed her a smile that she tried her best to return.

"He'll be okay. Bet you'll get to have that golf game after all," she said.

"Guess so. It's weird, you know. I still don't know what to think about Pete." Marin thought about her own father, Frank, who had been in the wings most of her life while she was being raised by Paul, without her knowing who he was.

"I totally get it," she nodded.

News came trickling in after the sub was brought into port, and people started to get off into the waiting arms of paramedics and emergency crews. Apparently, two more people had died from injuries sustained in the attack, but the rest of the grateful crew rejoiced in setting foot on dry land again. They caught a quick glimpse of Captain Woods and a tired, unshaven Pete walking along the makeshift gangplank to the sidewalk.

A young woman approached Marin and Jaycen and smiled.

"I have a message from the President of the United States," she said, looking both excited and nervous. "He called here directly!" she said breathlessly, waiting for a reaction, but they were both too tired to really care.

"Um, I'm sorry," she said, putting on a more serious tone. "He would like me to tell you that both of the other parties are on their way back here. He has arranged for you to stay in a hotel and get some rest. You have a flight to Washington D.C. tomorrow morning to meet with them, and to give him the details of your assignments. Please follow me."

They moved out of the building, and Marin was surprised at how late it felt. It was dark as she got into the waiting vehicle and buckled her seatbelt. It felt nice to be dry, she thought, then tears filled her eyes once more, as she remembered Marcos saying something similar to that shortly after she met him. She leaned her forehead against the cold glass, letting the tears drop to her lap, as she watched the lights of the passing vehicles outside her window from a distance, not even feeling like she was really there. They were shown inside a luxurious hotel with bright golden lights overhead, and overly shiny surfaces everywhere.

"May we take your bags?" a man in a stylishly casual uniform asked. Marin blinked at him, too tired to even answer.

"We don't have any," Jaycen replied for her.

"I see. Well, President Thompson has asked us to take care of everything while you are with us. Is there anything you need?"

Jaycen cleared his throat. He sounded so tired, but he took charge, which Marin appreciated. "A couple of changes of clothing would be nice. Water, food...um..." he said, rubbing the blondish stubble of his face, "something to shave with, a comb and a brush...basically anything you would need for a few days. We...lost our luggage."

"A toothbrush," Marin interjected. The man nodded knowingly. "Very well, please follow me."

They were shown into an attractive suite with two bedrooms and wide windows looking out over the city.

A plush sofa with fluffy pillows looked out over the view and Marin sank into it, ignoring Jaycen and the man talking until she heard the door close. Jaycen sat down next to her, putting an arm around her comfortingly. He pulled a velvety footstool close so they could both put their legs up on it and recline. She curled up against him and drifted into oblivion.

CHAPTER 65

JAYCEN

A KNOCK ON THE door woke Jaycen. Sometime during the night, Marin had moved into the bed and was fast asleep. He had just fallen over and slept on the couch, too tired to move. The knock on the door came again, and he stood, stretched, and went over to open it.

"Breakfast and all the items you requested, plus some we thought of, compliments of the hotel. Please enjoy," a uniformed man said, wheeling a cart into the room and then leaving quietly. Marin sat up in the bed, groggy looking, but still beautiful. Jaycen rolled the cart next to her and sat down. The top held covered plates filled with fruit, sausage, bacon, French toast, juice, milk and ice water with frozen raspberries floating in it. They both scooted close to the edge of the bed and wolfed down breakfast.

"Do you even remember the last time we ate?" Jaycen wondered before taking a long drink of apple juice. Marin shook her head no. Once they slowed down, they started picking through the bags stacked on the lower shelves. Expensive clothing, toiletries, even shoes for each of them in carefully wrapped packages.

Marin unwrapped everything and laid it out on the bed, fingering a soft shirt thoughtfully.

"You okay?" Jaycen asked tentatively.

"No," she said simply. "Are you?"

Jaycen shook his head no. "I don't know if it's possible to be okay after all this."

"We're going to have to tell Malcolm." Her breath caught in her throat.

"I know," Jaycen said sadly. The idea of retelling what had happened seemed too horrible to face, let alone to Marcos's father, who had already lost everyone else in his life he loved.

"I can't believe Marcos is just…gone. It's so unfair." Her eyes sparkled with a new set of tears. Jaycen felt a slight pang, but at the same time, he understood her completely. Weeks ago, he would have been jealous, but he couldn't think about Marcos like that ever again. All the times he'd wished Marcos wasn't in the way of him and Marin weighed on him. He never wanted it to end like this.

"No, it's not fair." He grew silent, but the fear and guilt that was hanging around his heart pushed out through his voice. She would have been happier if it were Marcos with her now, and *he* was the memory left behind on the ocean floor.

"It should have been me," he whispered. His eyes prickled and his voice caught in his throat.

Marin's eyes shot up to meet his. "What?" she asked incredulously.

"It should have been me. He loved you, you loved him. It should have been me."

Her eyes flashed with anger. "It shouldn't have been *anyone!* Not you, not me, not Marcos, not Aaron! *Nobody* should have had to go through what we've gone through; nobody should have died. This was Hahn's fault!." She took his hand with both of hers. "It shouldn't have been anyone."

Jaycen nodded and squeezed her hands back, holding on to her like a lifeline, then gathered her into his arms like he would never let her go. The ache in his heart was almost too much to handle, the guilt unbearable. Marcos loved her and let her go so that they could live and breathe and love and have everything he would never get to experience again. And the worst part was, Jaycen didn't know if he could have done the same…if he could have been brave enough to do what Marcos did. It scared him to wonder that about himself. But it made him *want* to be better, to try to live up to the memory of someone much braver than himself. Marcos was never going to go away. He knew that now. He would always be there in the shadows of both of their lives, a memory, a friend, a what-could-have-been, a martyr, a hero. But somehow, that was okay. He didn't blame her for falling apart, for grieving Marcos. They both would, in their own way. And as long as she would let him, he would be here to protect her, watch over her, and to love her. For him and for Marcos.

He let her go, leaning back a little so he could see her face. He gave her a soft, sad smile and brushed a tear from her cheek.

"Let's get ready. We have a plane to catch."

CHAPTER 66

JAYCEN

THE HOSPITAL CHAPEL was set aside for the group to wait in. Malcolm was the only one there when Marin and Jaycen walked in together. Jaycen put a hand on her shoulder and gave it a squeeze.

"Are you sure you want to be the one to do it?" he said quietly. She nodded and walked over to Malcolm and sat down. Jaycen sat down near the back and watched the older man's shoulders slump when she told him what Marcos had done. Malcolm hung his head, his long, graying hair hanging around his face. Marin put her hand on his, talking low. Jaycen couldn't hear what they said, but he didn't need to. He was living it all over in his mind just as she was, the jarring reality of it all still shocking him. He jumped when he felt someone touch his shoulder.

"What's up?" Paul whispered, nodding to Marin and Malcolm huddled together. One look at Jaycen's face must have told the story, because he sank to a chair next to Jaycen. "Oh, no. Not Marcos?"

Jaycen nodded, not trusting his voice to speak.

"I'm so sorry, kid. So, so sorry."

Jaycen lifted one shoulder in a halfhearted shrug. Paul patted him on the back as Frank and Emily came in and sat down with them, their faces white with concern. He took a shaky breath and started to relay the unbearable events between choking sobs. Marin and Malcolm moved over to him and he looked up at Marcos's father, unable to continue. They made room for them to sit down, turning their chairs to one another in a circle.

"Here," Marin said, taking Malcom's hand and offering it to her mother at her side. "Join hands," she directed them. They pulled each other close as if it could shield them from the truth, but all of them, especially Malcolm, needing to know. Her memories flowed through them all as if they were there, all of them reliving the horrific scene through her mind. Tears of grief ran freely, their arms around each other, pulling the circle tighter and tighter, their hearts and minds knit as one, watching the sacrifice of a hopeless boy and the heroism of his friend.

Jaycen couldn't help but wonder if it was cruel or kind to make them actually live through it, but somehow reliving it with the others by his side gave him strength and courage. He could feel such love and concern flooding through their connection, and suddenly nobody was alone in their heartache. They all understood. The sacrifices were shared, and most importantly, Malcolm was there for the final chapter of his brave son's life. He could feel the agony of his soul, but also overwhelming gratitude, and pride for what his son had done. None of them moved, none of them wanted to break the connection.

"I'm so sorry to disturb you," a nurse said quietly, "but the President is awake and will see you now. Follow me, please." One by one, they stood, trailing behind her. She led them through a labyrinth of hallways, to a glassed-in intensive care unit surrounded by bodyguards and secret servicemen. The President was covered in wires and had an oxygen tube under his nose. He did not look good, but he waved them inside.

"I…" he coughed a few times. "I want to thank you for the service you've rendered for this country and for the world. We are forever in your debt." He laid back, his chest heaving with effort.

"Thank you, Mr. President," Frank said, speaking for the group.

"I want to express my sincere condolences for your loss, and assure you, Mr. Minas, that your son will not be forgotten." Malcolm twitched his lip and nodded appreciatively. The President waited, breathing deeply before he continued.

"I also want to apologize for my actions that were taken while influenced by the conspirators that infiltrated my staff. I wish with all my heart that I could have a chance to..." he coughed some more, wincing as if in pain. "to undo the damage I have done." His face grew paler and Jaycen wondered if the man would live much longer. He lay back on his pillows, holding a napkin to his mouth as he coughed once again.

Frank touched his wife and Marin, who nodded, as if they were silently communicating with each other. They moved close to the President as if they were trying to hear what he said, but at the same time Frank was quietly unhooking one of the bags of fluid being pumped into the President and handed the end to Emily. She sliced off the end and attached a long, flexible needle to it, deftly inserting it into Marin's arm. Jaycen heard her suck in a quick breath.

Paul and Jaycen moved closer, obscuring the view of the President to anyone around them. He looked up at them in confusion, but Frank spoke to him in quiet tones.

"This is a gift from our people to you. Make sure you use it well," he whispered. After a few minutes, Emily removed the needle and forced it back into the hanging bag, disposing of the tubing and passing Marin a gauze pad as if nothing had happened. The President closed his eyes, his breathing slower, calmer. Jaycen began to wonder if he had fallen asleep, until he began to speak.

"I need to warn you, the Pakistani government is aware of you. They are pressuring us for your secrets. I'm sorry, I know I told you I would try to protect your identities, but it has turned out to be impossible. I can't think of anything I can do to stop this fire from spreading." The President's voice was growing stronger, color returning to his pallid face. He looked at them in amazement. "I'm...I feel...how did you do that?" he whispered to Marin. She shrugged, giving him a knowing smile.

His mouth opened in awe and he reached out his hand and took hers. "Thank you."

It was Emily's turn to speak. "Mr. President, we had thought about the ramifications of getting involved before we agreed to it. And this is our solution. I have just released a copy of the drug, Arydia, on the internet. Everyone on earth will have the composition to it soon."

The President's eyes widened. "You…you can't have!"

"I have. This was meant to be something to help better mankind, to give us access to the oceans and lakes of the world, so we can better understand them and live with them. We never intended it to be a weapon to use against others. This is the only way to ensure it is used for the purposes we envisioned."

"But…you've just redrawn our borders, perhaps upset international economies, maybe turned the world upside down!" he said, gaining strength and sitting up. "Do you have any idea what you may have done?"

"And we have a good man at the helm to help define those borders and right the world," Frank replied.

"Trust me, Mr. President. This is going to be for the best. You'll see," Emily said with a smile.

CHAPTER 67

SEVEN YEARS LATER

JAYCEN PUT THE car in park and opened the door for a little boy with dark hair and blue eyes, who had just unbuckled himself and was waiting to jump out of the car.

"Don't forget your backpack," his mother said, as she unbuckled a rosy cheeked little girl. Her blond curls hung around her face, framing a toothy grin and green eyes like her mother. The boy reached in and pulled out a bag, throwing it over his shoulder and racing for the school doors.

"Slow down, Marc! We have to get you registered first!" his mother said, heading over to a table set up under the shade of a canopy near the school doors. Jaycen herded his son away from the playground to the table.

"Hope he always stays this happy to go to school," Jaycen chuckled, putting his hands on his son's shoulders to keep him from running off. Marin laughed and turned to the desk, placing the toddler on one hip.

"Grade?" the woman at the desk said without looking up. Marin started fanning herself. The summer heat was hanging on long into August.

"Kindergarten," Marin replied. Her daughter popped her thumb into her mouth and started sucking loudly.

"Age?"

"Tell her how old you are, champ," Jaycen said.

"Five anna half!" the boy said proudly.

"My, you two don't look nearly old enough to have a five-year-old," the woman exclaimed in surprise. Jaycen and Marin pretended not to hear her so she went back to her forms. "Well, let's get on with it, shall we?" She paused and smiled at the boy, then put a hand out to Marin. "Immunization records?"

Marin reached into her bag and produced a piece of paper. The baby squirmed, complaining about the heat and wanting to get down.

"Just a minute, sweetheart. We'll be done soon. Then we'll go swimming." The girl clapped her hands and wiggled in excitement.

The woman looked over the sheet, ticking off squares on her registration until she got to one box and stopped.

"Wait a minute...this boy hasn't had his drowning vaccine," she said with a disapproving frown.

"He doesn't need one. He's immune," Jaycen said, fishing out his wallet. He produced a metallic card and set it on the table. The woman looked at it closely and handed it back to him.

"An Arydian!" She whispered reverently. "Oh my, I never thought I would actually meet one of you! And we'll have one in our school? That's wonderful!" She bubbled excitedly. She scribbled down some notes on the paper and set her pencil down.

"Oh, and we forgot the most important part. What's your name, little boy?" she asked, leaning forward.

"Marcos Gilbert Webb!" the boy recited with a grin.

"Well, Marcos," she said, extending her hand over the table to shake his. "What a wonderful name you have! Did you know this school has your same first name?" she said smiling broadly. "Marcos Minas Elementary. He was an Arydian, too!" She turned her attention to Jaycen and Marin. "You must have named him after our school," the woman joked.

Marin and Jaycen shared a sad smile and Marin quietly replied, "Yeah, something like that."

Acknowledgements

The whole trilogy is finally finished! I had no idea when I started writing down a cool dream in a journal years ago that it would turn into a book and then into a trilogy! I'm relieved it's done, but also sad for it to end. I've grown to love my characters as I've gotten to know them, and closing the cover on ABYSS and saying so long was hard!

As I said in AQUA, just as it takes a village to raise a child, it takes a ton of people to write a book. It's a result of a million interactions with people, inspirations, places and ideas. I'd like to take a moment and thank a few of the many people that have been part of my journey through life and in particular, this journey through writing these books.

Thank you to my amazing husband, Kelly, who has always loved to hear my stories. Jaymes, for perfecting the logo designs, and Liz, who puts me up when I'm in Utah for book stops; Mckay and Haley for being super encouraging and loving; Matthew for reading the first draft and editing it so well; Michael for his enthusiasm and digitizing my logo; and Daniel for his love of adventures and designing the new logo.

Thank you to my big beautiful family of brothers and sisters, cousins and nieces and nephews, in laws and aunts and uncles.

I'm grateful for my beta readers, Jenn Meldrum, Crystal Fisher, Jill Bowcutt, Courtney Johnson, Tressa Fischer, Elizabeth Hardwick and Dianna Mannewitz for their comments and thoughts on my manuscript. Your insight and encouragement was so incredibly helpful!

I'm super grateful for my beta editors, Karen Gruszkiewicz and Geri Anne Larimer that tore my manuscript apart (that's a good thing) to help me find all the ugly bits and fix them, and Heather Godfrey, my final editor, who has been with me and encouraged me through all three books. You guys rock!!

And thank you to Kirk Edwards from Scene Company for believing in the Arydian series and publishing it. It's such a dream come true.

Thank you to my awesome illustrator, Shannon DeJong! Her wizardry with all three of my covers and promo material is astounding. I love her work!! Thank you so much!

And I promised a shout out to Jon Schoeneck at Integrated Aquasystem, Inc. for answering all my weird aquarium plumbing research questions so patiently! Thank you!

I'd especially like to thank everyone who has read this series and enjoyed my books. If writing were like playing an instrument, not having readers would be like practicing all your life only to end up performing to an empty concert hall. I'm so grateful to those who have taken time to journey into a world of my creation and be part of it with me! Can't wait to share some new worlds with you!

ABOUT THE AUTHOR

KATHERINE ARMSTRONG WALTERS has been making up stories since she was old enough to talk. She was born and raised in Salt Lake City, Utah, but moved to Texas where she and her husband, Kelly, have enjoyed living in the country and raising their five fabulous sons, two cats, one snake and a small herd of chickens. When she's not writing she loves sketching, editing, painting, reading, being outdoors, remodeling, and travelling with her family. Her favorite hobbies include boating and Star Wars.

If you loved THE ARYDIAN CHRONICLES

CHECK OUT MORE EXCITING BOOKS FROM SCENE CO.

At Scene Co. our mission is to elevate family entertainment. As the industry moves ever more toward content that is not appropriate for children (or selective adults for that matter), we strive to create stories that will inspire andentertain, without being overly "preachy" or low quality, two traits unfortunately synonymous with family media. Our media is free from profanity, sex, popularizing drug use and gratuitous violence.

We also publish good informational titles for families, such as healthy eating, emergency preparedness, and self-confidence for young women.

If you see the need for this kind of entertainment in the world, please join us at: *TheSceneCo.com*

CPSIA information can be obtained
at www.ICGtesting.com
Printed in the USA
FSHW021902270521
81888FS